RECEIVED

OCT - 6 2005

By _____

the tin box

the tin box

holly kennedy

A TOM DOHERTY ASSOCIATES BOOK   FORGE   NEW YORK

THE TIN BOX

A Forge Book
Published by Tom Doherty Associates, LLC
175 Fifth Avenue
New York, NY 10010

www.tor.com

Forge® is a registered trademark of Tom Doherty Associates, LLC.

ISBN 0-765-31244-1
EAN 978-0-765-31244-0

First Edition: October 2005

Printed in the United States of America

0 9 8 7 6 5 4 3 2 1

For my husband, Rick,
who encouraged me to chase this dream.
This first one is for you.

a c k n o w l e d g m e n t s

The Tin Box began as a short story that eventually grew into the book that you have now. It is my first novel, and without the encouragement and support of many others, it could have easily become a discarded dream. For this, I will be forever grateful to the following people:

In memory of Sean Henderson, a courageous and unforgettable young man.

Liza Dawson, my agent: Thank you for believing in this story and for taking me under your wing as you helped launch my writing career. Every writer should be so lucky. Claire Eddy, my editor: Thank you for giving such thoughtful and intuitive suggestions as I fine-tuned the manuscript. It's a better book because of it.

Chandler Crawford, who promoted foreign rights with unwavering enthusiasm, as well as Todd Siegal, who recommended the book to my German publisher, and Mary Anne Thompson, who recommended it to publishers in Greece and France. Author Linda Holeman, for encouraging me from the beginning in a tiny classroom at the University of Winnipeg, and Charlie Newton (from one writer to another), for pushing me to finish during the worst of my second-guessing.

Francis Ford Coppola's Zoetrope Writers' Workshop in Belize (including Melissa Bank and Chris Spain). Denise Miller, fellow writer and Belize roommate. Maui Writers Retreat and Conference (especially Susan Wiggs and Jillian Manus).

Bob Turner and Teresa Cuda, for answering medical questions unrelated to Proteus Syndrome, and Lindsey Henderson, my wonderful Proteus Syndrome resource. Any inaccuracies are mine.

My mom, for her unshakable faith in me. My dad, for moving our family to Athabasca all those years ago. Jim Kennedy, who wanted to see this book published in English almost as much as I did, and Thelma Kennedy, because I know you're watching.

Others who played a part whether they realize it or not: My brother, Eric, for helping me build a tree house on paper. Andrea and Russell, because being your stepmom for so many years has added great material to my storytelling. My brother, Ian, for lending me a laptop when mine blew up. Damian and Ted at DCF, for making copies of the manuscript whenever I needed them. The Manitoba Writers' Guild Emerging Mentorship Program; David Elias; Ed Stackler; Deb Gray; Steve and Sally Weingartner; Keith Davidson; as well as family cheerleaders Ron and Marilyn; Randy and Karen; Bob and Gail; Melissa; Jennifer; Sydney; Al; and Marilyn "2."

And finally my children, Thomas and Marcus. Oh, what you do to my heart . . .

the tin box

prologue

Every great mistake has a halfway moment,
a split second when it can be recalled
and perhaps remedied.

—PEARL S. BUCK

HOW CAN I TELL MY HUSBAND I'VE BEEN LYING TO HIM for years? Kenly closed her eyes and pinched the bridge of her nose. Just thinking about it made her sick. The words had been there for fifteen years. She'd thought them often; she'd just never said them out loud. So now she leaned against the deck railing, cleared her throat, and whispered them into the still morning air. Softly, but with enough force to feel their weight against her tongue. Loud enough that when she heard them she dropped her eyes and shifted from one hip to the other, then back again. The shame came then, washing over her hard, and when her shoulders fell, the coward inside inched forward to state the obvious: *You don't have to do this.* Resting her elbows on the deck railing, she set her chin in her hands and whispered, "Yes, I do."

Most mornings she stood there and waited for it—that split second when night and day collided across the lake and then moved off in opposite directions. It was her favorite time of day—the morning mist curling its way along the water's edge as the moon faded and the sun rose, spilling light through the trees into their yard. But today she wasn't paying attention. Instead, she was thinking about how her confession would change them, how it might even kill their marriage.

Kenly rubbed her forehead with the heel of her hand. There was an ache behind her eyes from crying the night before that wouldn't go away. Two hours from the airport home, weighing the same pros and cons she had for years, until she finally accepted how much courage this would take. She and Ross were alone this morning, so that was good. Their son, Connor, had left early to catch the team bus for an out-of-town soccer tournament, and even their dog, Motley, was cooperating by not demanding his usual morning jog along the lake. Instead, he was barking at an old tomcat curled on the roof of their shed.

A cupboard door slammed inside and she pulled herself up straight, bracing for what was ahead. A jelly glass filled with daisies sat on the patio table—daisies Ross had bought to cheer her up, now limp and beaten down from rain the night before. A squirrel nattered at Motley from the safety of an oak tree and she could hear the sticky swish of tires passing by on the wet pavement out front. Connor's Rollerblades were propped against a deck chair, his favorite sweatshirt tossed in a forgotten heap next to them. She stood silently, taking all of this in, but everything that was familiar and normal suddenly left her weak.

She adjusted the belt on her bathrobe, slid the patio doors open, and stepped inside. Crushing her hands deep into her pockets, she bit her lower lip. Ross was at the kitchen table, coffee in hand and brow furrowed as he flipped through the *Chicago Tribune*. He glanced up and smiled. "Morning."

Her throat was dry and there definitely wasn't enough air in the room. Not trusting her voice, she gave his shoulder a squeeze and crossed the kitchen. The tin box was on the counter next to his laptop, exactly where she'd left it the night before. Part of her hoped he'd see it and ask what it was, but he didn't. Instead, he took a bite of toast and went back to reading the paper. She picked it up and turned around, keeping her eyes on the floor, on Motley's water bowl, on the recycling bin Connor had forgotten to take out. Then she slid into the chair across from him, deciding to get straight to the point. Resting the box on her knees under the table, she inched forward and opened her mouth, then closed it again when Ross stood, folded the paper, and swallowed the last of his coffee.

Kenly fingered the lid as she chewed on her bottom lip. She knew she should open it and show him, talk to him about what was inside and explain how it had happened—starting years ago, at the very beginning. Instead, she watched him pull a file from his briefcase and flip through it, looking distracted. "See you tonight." He leaned down, cupped her chin, and drew her face up for a kiss.

Her voice wasn't working properly, and as he stepped away, all she could think about was how much she wanted to know him when he was old—even now, after all these years of marriage and with everything they'd been through. Part of her wanted to raise a hand to get his attention but it, too, failed her, lying useless in her lap, unwilling to cooperate as she wrestled with how to do this. The thought of telling him made her stomach hitch. Kenly wasn't confrontational by nature. Instead, she was a master at mollifying those who were, a trait acquired from years of living with her father, trying to smooth off the edges and keep their lives as normal as possible.

Leave it alone, the coward inside warned.

Ross's cell phone rang and he took the call, slapping at his pockets on his way across the kitchen. *I know you so well,* she thought, pointing to where his keys were lying on the counter. He grinned, snatched them up, and mouthed, "I love you," on his way out the door. Moments later, the garage door rumbled shut, and she listened to his car back down the driveway, then silence.

Kenly put the tin box on the table, nudged it away, and laid her head on her arms. Years ago, the biggest lie of her life had been uttered with an ease that now sickened her, and the glum knowledge—the near certainty—that it had the ability to destroy everything that mattered to her made her stomach do a quick, agonized flip.

Straightening, she exhaled toward the ceiling. More than anything, she wished Ross would come back, take her by the hand, and lead her to their bedroom. Take control and undress her in that sexy, confident way he had when she was the only thing on his mind. She wanted to feel him nuzzle the back of her neck as he slid his arms around her and turned her into the best kind of mess. But even more than that, she wanted to hear him tell her that he loved her and that they were going to survive this.

On her way home the night before she'd stopped to pick up milk and was wrestling with her seat belt when she saw a man and woman walking into the grocery store. The man had his hand on the small of the woman's back and when he leaned down to whisper something, she flushed and gave him a playful swat. Snaking an arm around her waist, he hugged her and grinned as they disappeared into the store together. Thinking of them now, Kenly swallowed hard, knowing that was what she'd miss most—the intimacy that comes from sharing daily, mundane tasks like getting groceries, walking the dog, arguing over whose turn it is to do dishes. All those tiresome, day-to-day things that mesh you together as a couple and so often get taken for granted. Things most people never consider intimate at all—until they lose them.

Kenly ran a hand over the tin box, then opened it, and played with her full bottom lip, staring at what was inside. Her secret stared back like a bed of nails she had to lie on whether she wanted to or not—all that she'd never dared tell anyone. Mortified it had come to this, she dropped her shoulders and tears welled in her eyes. Motley sprinted through the open patio doors and nudged her with his nose, yanking her back from worries about how this would end. She glanced down and gave his ears a rub. "Five more minutes, Mot, then we'll go for our run, okay?"

Drawing her feet up under her on the chair, she closed her eyes and twisted her neck back and forth, thinking it through. When he got home tonight, she would hand the tin box to Ross and tell him, talking so fast her voice shook as she tried to get the words out, trying hard not to cry as she did. Pinning her hair back away from her face, she shifted on her chair. Then, for the second time that morning, she cleared her throat and said the words out loud, even though her voice went up at the end, wavering with indecision. "Ross, there's something I should have told you years ago that I never did. . . ."

chapter 1

KENLY ALISTER WAS FIFTEEN YEARS OLD AND IN THE middle of year-end exams in Kalispell, Montana, when her life started falling apart all over again. She and her dad had been living there eight months and four days—something she tracked religiously on her bedroom calendar. It wasn't a record, but it was a good sign that maybe this time they would stay put until she graduated from high school.

She was lying on the couch studying, surrounded by the cracked, gunmetal-gray walls of their living room, when she heard her dad's heavy footsteps come up the walk an hour earlier than usual. Frowning, she looked at her watch. They had a routine, and this wasn't part of it. Every morning, he drove nine blocks to school, parked, and disappeared into the teacher's lounge half an hour before she even rolled out of bed. Then, at the end of each day, she got home at least an hour before he did. Pushing aside a twinge of worry, she told herself everything was fine. When he pulled the screen door open and dropped his briefcase on the floor, she tried to convince herself it was just her imagination that the air in the room had changed or that he seemed to be avoiding her eyes. Muttering under his breath, he yanked the door shut and gave it the extra tug it always needed, prompting her cat, Java, to come skidding around the corner, where she disappeared underneath the couch.

"Stupid bloody cat," he said, shedding his jacket on his way into the kitchen.

Kenly chewed on the ice from her drink and gave his back a heavy stare. She'd found Java a year earlier under the front steps of the house they were renting, and had had to tear a few old boards off with a crowbar and wriggle underneath through the dead grass just to catch her. Emaciated, starving, and with the jittery personality of someone who's sucked back a pound of espresso, the cat seemed to fit the name "Java" perfectly. She followed Kenly everywhere, but she turned into a nervous wreck whenever she saw Kenly's dad.

Clearing her throat, Kenly held her spot in the textbook with a finger and called out, "My day wasn't bad, thanks. How about yours?"

Her dad taught tenth and eleventh grade remedial math for students who either were struggling with the basics or were behaviorally challenged—neither easy to work with. He muttered something unintelligible, then came back around the corner with a drink in one hand and the tense, uneasy look of someone who's just been pulled over for speeding. The cuffs of his shirt were rolled back and his tie had slipped out of the knot he'd put it in that morning.

"What's wrong?" she asked. "Have trouble in one of your classes today?"

He raised his eyebrows and grabbed the remote control. "Something like that." He flipped through the channels, then set his drink down and made a big production of rubbing his shoulder, slowly kneading it with the heel of his hand as if she was supposed to believe he was having a drink because it ached after a hard day of teaching and not because of the drinking problem they both knew he had. Disgusted, she lowered her gaze back to her textbook.

"Math exam?" he asked.

She nodded but didn't lift her head.

He turned off the TV and went down the hall to his bedroom; then she heard the telltale squeak of his closet door and knew he was looking for the bottle of vodka he kept hidden on the top shelf behind his suitcase—the one he thought she didn't know about. She swallowed hard, rubbed her temples, and went back to studying, dangling the fingers of one hand to entice Java back out.

It was five o'clock when she glanced up and saw a leggy redhead striding up their front steps. They almost never got company, and rarely anyone as crisp and all-business as this woman. Sensing something was wrong, Kenly frowned and slid off the couch, but her dad came down the hallway and pushed past her on unsteady legs. When he pulled the door open, Kenly saw the determined look on the redhead's face and guessed that these two weren't going to mix.

"Well, *hel-lo.*" He let his eyes slide over the woman as if he had the right, then made a box with his fingers and peered through it with a lopsided grin. "Now isn't *that* a picture."

Kenly's stomach rolled and she tried to grab his arm, but he shook her off. Staggering back against the door, he motioned their visitor in with a dramatic sweep of one arm.

The woman didn't move. "Mr. Alister?"

He pulled a pack of cigarettes from his shirt pocket, lit the last one, and tossed the empty pack on the floor. "Call me Steve."

She handed him an envelope. "Okay, *Steve,* this is for you."

His face darkened for a split second, and then he grinned with one side of his mouth, pulled hard on his cigarette, and blew smoke in a stream over her head. Kenly waited a half beat, slipped past him, and took the envelope from the woman, nodding politely to her before closing the door. He had a tendency to push things too far, but when he was drinking they spiraled out of control even faster than usual.

Her hand was shaking when she gave him the envelope. "What's going on?"

He didn't answer, just tore it open and read the letter from top to bottom as she inspected one of her fingers, half-guessing at what he would say next. Finally he murmured, "It was time to move anyway."

"You can't be serious."

"Sometimes change is good."

But she saw his hands shaking and knew it wasn't true, knew he hated moving as much as she did, and saw the flicker of worry that told her he'd been fired again. A familiar feeling of panic rose up and circled her chest, looking for a spot to land. This would be their sixth move in less than three years. "I don't want to move."

"You're just nervous."

She leaned forward, trying again. "But it's hard making new friends."

"You do fine."

"Dad, you're not listening."

His eyes met hers and held them until she looked away. "I'm listening, Kenly, but it doesn't change the fact that we're moving."

Looking around the kitchen, her eyes settled on a stack of boxes she'd left by the back door weeks ago. Boxes she'd asked him to take out to the shed, filled with things they never used. One crammed with photo albums, another stuffed with camping gear, and the last one taped shut, her mom's broken studio stand wrapped up inside next to a bag of oil paints. Now the boxes would all be moved somewhere else, where no one knew Kenly and her dad, and where they'd get another new phone number and another fresh start.

As reality hit her in the face, Kenly's hopes evaporated and she left the room, rounding the corner into the hallway, where she stopped and pressed her back against the wall. Moving meant starting over again, and that thought sent a wave of nausea through her. She wanted to go back and ask him why. Why he kept getting fired, why he drank so much, and why he didn't seem to care about anything anymore. Grandma Alister often said he used to love the challenge of teaching, but that was years ago, before her mother died. Now he was the kind of teacher who didn't last in the good schools and couldn't even hold on to the jobs he found in small towns.

"He never got over losing your mother," Grandma would often say, defending him.

Kenly sighed, knowing that she'd seen the signs, but had ignored them. After all, he'd called in sick twice last week, and then Grandma had phoned when he didn't show up to drive her to Missoula. That alone should have set off alarm bells. A friend of Grandma's had won two tickets to a George Strait concert, and even though she was seventy-eight, Grandma couldn't wait to go. She thought George was the sexiest country singer alive, and going to his concert was all that she'd talked about for months.

Kenly's dad had been passed out on the couch while Grandma cried at the other end of the line—wilting sobs that made Kenly feel so sick she'd flopped into a chair, pinched her eyes shut, and lied. "He feels just sick about it, Gran. That stupid car of ours broke down again and . . ." It was one of her better performances, and when she finally hung up, she flicked off the lights and went to bed, hoping that he'd sleep through the night and leave her alone. Often when he drank, he'd shake her awake in the middle of the night in one of his the-world-has-shit-on-me moods that made her so crazy. Then he'd sit on the edge of her bed and give her the same speech every time, the one he always offered to justify why he was who he was today.

"I met your mom the year I graduated from college, and do you know that the first time she smiled at me, I knew? The way you know when you've been looking for years, dating lots of different women, waiting, and watching—absolutely certain of what it is that you're looking for. Then she shows up, isn't *anything* like you'd imagined, and you go stupid when she smiles at you."

He would slump forward with his elbows on his knees, like a man defeated by something he hadn't seen coming, then say, "Tell me, how are you supposed to keep going when you lose a woman like that?" Kenly never answered, just sat with her legs pulled against her chest, staring at his high bald forehead or scraping at the polish on her fingernails, listening until he ran out of steam.

Biting the inside of her cheek, she poked her head around the corner and watched him, bent at the waist and back humping convulsively as he dry-heaved into the kitchen sink. When he straightened, he opened the fridge freezer, dropped a handful of ice into a glass, and filled it with vodka from an almost-empty bottle he'd hidden in the pantry. She knew tomorrow he'd look for another job and then go through a week of predictable just-you-watch-me speeches when he found one, puffed up and full of bluster with a clean slate in front of him.

Heading for the back door, Java bolted between Kenly's legs into the kitchen, and her dad stumbled backward, almost tripping over her. "Neurotic bloody cat!" Pushing the screen door open, he kicked her outside, guzzled his drink, and threw the empty vodka bottle at the garbage can, but he missed and it shattered against the wall.

Kenly shrank back around the corner and crept downstairs to count how many boxes they had, how many they needed, and how long it would take to pack everything up again. When Java didn't come home later that night, Kenly spent an hour prowling the neighborhood, calling out for her. It was after midnight when she finally gave up, left the front door propped open with a soup can, and fell asleep on the couch, waiting for Java.

The next morning, she woke up when the screen door bounced shut against its frame. Sitting up, she leaned over the back of the couch and rubbed her eyes. Then they widened and she went absolutely still. Rain streaked sideways across the window, blown by the wind, but she could see her dad in the street using the toe of one foot to poke at Java's motionless body. Her heart started to pound until it filled her ears. *Not Java!*

Her dad bent over, slowly shaking his head.

Oh, God, please not Java!

He scooped her up with one hand and walked back to the house, the cat's limp body flopping back and forth in time with each step that he took. As Kenly watched, a rush of tenderness flowed through her, a hot sweetness she could almost taste as she clenched her fists against her knees. Java, as endearing as she was neurotic, twining herself around her ankles or trailing after her in the wet grass, shaking one foot and then the other before climbing into Kenly's lap and falling asleep curled nose to tail.

She slammed both palms against the window, startling her dad, and when he looked up, he gave her a brisk shake of his head that told her Java was dead. Unable to pull her eyes away, Kenly watched as he laid the cat in a cardboard box on the front steps and then disappeared with it around the corner of the house.

Chest heaving, she pressed her hands against her mouth to muffle what would fly out if she didn't hold it in. Then a burst of anger bubbled up inside, and she pushed off the couch and ran into the kitchen. Slipping on her shoes, she pushed the back door open and hurried down the steps. Her dad was next to the fence, shovel in hand as he stood over two yellow circles of dead grass where their garbage cans usually sat—the same garbage cans where he usually stashed all his empty vodka bottles, thinking she wouldn't see them.

Java was lying in the box on the ground next to him.

Kenly's legs felt like sacks of cement as she made her way across the yard, icy wind tunneling up her sleeves and pant legs. Java had been hers. Hers to feed and take care of, and hers to babble to at the end of each day, in a world where she'd learned to make a game of each move that she and her dad made. How close would their new phone number be to their last? Would their new neighbors be married or single, old or young, have kids, grandkids, or pet parrots? (One of their neighbors the year before had had two.) Would their new house number be odd or even? Or would they live in a house at all? Maybe this time it'd be a trailer, or an apartment, or a drafty basement suite. She would jot down all her guesses, seal them in an envelope, and open it after they'd moved, writing in the correct answers next to each one.

She was crying when she came up to him, hands clenched before her. "L-let me d-do it."

He turned and raised his eyebrows. "Kenly."

Not allowing herself to look at Java, she motioned for him to give her the shovel. He gave her a worried look, but handed it to her, and at that moment, Kenly had no idea where she would bury Java, except, of course, not here. Not underneath two circles of dead grass where someone else's garbage would rot on top of her grave long after Kenly and her dad were gone.

Lightning zigzagged across the sky in the distance; then thunder boomed overhead. Holding the shovel in one hand, she picked up the box and cradled it under her arm, then walked out of their yard and down the alley to a path she knew would take her to a grassy hill—a quiet spot where she'd often brought Java when she did her homework.

And it was here that she buried her in the pouring rain.

Here that she struck her fists against her knees and hovered over Java's grave, crying in silence.

With each move, the loneliness had gotten worse, and Kenly became even more distanced from anyone she'd been close to before. When letters sent to old friends went unanswered, she'd stopped sending them, recognizing that her friends were busy and had moved on to other friends. No one visited Kenly and her dad anymore except a relative now and then or Grandma Alister, who didn't travel much, although eventually she always showed up, no matter where they moved. Grandma never said much. She just walked in, gave a big smile, and took over. She would wander around the house, bony hands on her narrow hips, then set about organizing.

"Let's get you fed," she'd say, steering Kenly into the kitchen.

Kenly often wondered what it would have been like to have a mother like her. With arms that hugged tight and left you weak when they pulled away; arms you wanted to crawl straight into after you'd had a bad day. Grandma had a way of leaning forward when she listened that made Kenly feel like she mattered. She would perch on the edge of a chair and prop her chin in her hands, weighing every word Kenly said before offering any comments. And no matter what, she always found a sliver of good in everything.

The only time Kenly ever saw Grandma cry was the day that Kenly's mom died. The morning before that, Kenly had waved to her parents as they drove off for what was supposed to be just an overnight trip to a friend's wedding north of Chicago. Grandma was taking care of her and they spent that afternoon and evening rooting through old boxes in the attic.

The next morning, Grandma was pale when she slid into bed next to Kenly and told her that there had been an accident. Her mom was in the hospital and her dad wouldn't be home for a few days. Even though Kenly was only seven, she would never forget how scared she was when she came downstairs later that afternoon. Grandma was at the kitchen table with the phone beside her, receiver dangling to the floor, her hair falling out of its combs. Her face was in her arms and she was crying so hard that her back shook. Grandma crying like she wasn't Grandma anymore, and then the sound of her dad's voice at the other end of the phone when Kenly picked up the receiver and held it to her ear.

"Jesus, Mom, she's dead," he wailed. "Lara is dead. . . ."

Kenly had stood there frozen with the phone against her ear until a warm stream of pee trickled down her legs and she, too, started to cry.

After that, things were never the same. Her dad sat alone in the living room for days after the funeral, never saying a word, even when Kenly curled up in the chair across from him. Then, when he was "let go" from his job six months later, it took him almost a year to find another one. She was nearly nine when they moved away from the only home she'd ever known in Chicago, and that's when the roller-coaster ride of moving from town to town had started, increasing in speed and intensity over the last few years.

There were things Kenly couldn't remember about her mom anymore, but there were some she knew she'd never forget, like how she could make Kenly's dad laugh the way no one else could or the way she used to whisper against Kenly's ear each night at bedtime, "I'm loving you, sweetie, and I'm always here if you need me." She had a habit of running her finger around the top of her teacup when she told stories in that hold-your-breath voice of hers Kenly loved so much, and she used to hunch forward and squint whenever she worked on one of her sculptures.

Although her mom had her teaching degree and taught at the same school Kenly's dad did, she loved to sculpt. The year Kenly turned four, her mother bought herself a studio stand and set it up in the basement, where she would often disappear for hours at a time. Kenly wasn't allowed to play with her kickwheel or any of her chisels or rasps, but she watched her use them as she lay stretched out on the floor at her feet. Her mom would tie on a canvas apron, hunch over, and work with the wet clay until her face and arms were covered with gray flecks of it. Now and then she'd stop and pull Kenly into her lap. She would adjust the seat, drop a lump of wet clay onto the flywheel, and make certain it was centered before she took Kenly by the elbows and gently shook out her arms to "get rid of the cobwebs" before they started.

"How do I do it?" Kenly would ask.

"Just close your eyes," her mom would say with a smile. "And let your hands tell you."

So Kenly would close her eyes and roll her thumbs in slow circles, dipping and curling them against the slick wet clay until something began to take shape and her heart started to pound with an eerie excitement.

"You'll know when it's right," her mom would whisper, pushing the hair off Kenly's face. "You'll feel it deep inside of you and then your hands just . . . take over."

After she died, her dad often found Kenly outside, crying softly as she crouched next to a puddle of mud, fingers pressed deep into the slick muck underneath, staying close to her mother the only way she knew how. Shaking his head, he would scoop her up and carry her inside to wash her off without ever saying a word.

His drinking got worse after he lost the first job, and that's when the anger started to take over. Days after she turned nine, Kenly spent an hour one night huddled in a corner of the living room with her knees pulled to her chest, watching in horror as he stormed through the house methodically smashing every sculpture her mom had ever made. He was raging at a demon she couldn't see, eyes filled with anger and tears and something else she couldn't understand. Shards of ironstone and tiny pieces of gray boneware flew everywhere, landing on the furniture and all over the floor. There were even tiny pieces of it that stuck in her hair and came to rest against the bare skin of her feet.

When he was done, he made his way into the spare bedroom where they kept her mother's things and Kenly crept after him. Through the crack of the doorway, she watched him rise up on the balls of his feet and bring a hammer down against her mom's treasured studio stand again and again until it lay in broken pieces on the floor. Then he dropped to his knees and buried his face in his hands, sobbing, either unaware or unable to care that his daughter was watching.

Kenly crawled back into the living room, reached up to the shelf behind her mother's rocking chair, and snatched the one piece he'd missed. It was her favorite: three hands curled together and shooting up out of a clay base. A man's thick, callused fingers engulfed a slender woman's hand, and the pudgy fingers of a child's curled into a tiny fist between them. Beneath it, on a small brass plate, was one word: family.

She sank back into the corner, instinctively knowing that if he saw it, he'd smash it, too. She curled the bottom of her nightshirt over it and pushed it deep into her lap, sitting small and still until she could sneak upstairs and hide it. The next morning, she went looking for her mom's leather sculpting pouch with her chisels and rasps rolled up inside and the rocket-red scarf she used to wear around her neck. She found the pouch in an old canvas jacket and the scarf inside a box of clothes marked for giveaway, and over the years, whenever they moved, these were the first things she packed to take with her.

FRIDAY AFTERNOON, KENLY SLIPPED THROUGH THE FRONT DOOR, sniffed the air, and managed a small smile. The aroma of fresh baked bread was everywhere, and that meant Grandma Alister was here. She dropped her jacket on the couch and then froze when she heard Grandma's voice.

"Damn it, Steven, it's time to get a hold of your life!"

"I'm doing the best I can." His voice was flinty, like it got whenever anyone told him what to do.

"What kind of life is this for Kenly?"

"It'll have to do."

"It's pathetic and you know it."

He sighed. "Look, you know damned well Lara begged me to have a kid for years so I finally agreed, but raising her on my own was never part of the plan. All things considered, I think we do just fine."

Kenly felt like she was in a badly written movie and not the hallway of their dilapidated town house. The air suddenly got thick and there wasn't enough of it as she pressed her hands together to stop them from trembling.

"What the hell *happened* to you?" Grandma asked, the devotion to her only child overshadowed by a disgust Kenly had never heard before. "I'd like to think it's the booze talking when you say garbage like that, but sometimes I worry that it goes deeper and then I wonder what kind of son I managed to raise."

Her dad's silence was a punishment of sorts, and Kenly knew he was probably standing there with his jaw tight and his arms crossed. There was a long silence, and Grandma finally sighed. "Well, it's a little late to change things now, isn't it? Kenly's your daughter, and I think it's time you put her first for a change."

Her dad sat down hard, the feet of his chair scraping against the kitchen floor. "Do you know that after she was born, every time I tried to hold that kid, she cried? Christ, I felt like I'd grown a third eyeball or something. But not Lara. She could cuddle her, make dinner, and have the phone tucked under her chin, all at once, and Kenly would grin like an angel just because her mom was holding her."

Kenly covered her ears and shook her head to clear the image that came to mind. The one where she had a mother who bounced her against one hip while she made dinner, folding her into her life the way someone does with a child she loves—the way her dad never had. Taking slow breaths, she tried to imagine what Grandma was wearing to get her mind on something else. She knew her long gray hair would be pulled up in that wispy way she had, where a few strands always fell out of their combs and caressed the back of her neck.

"Steven, how often have you tried spending time with her since

Lara died?" Grandma asked. "And I don't mean time spent breathing or eating or doing laundry together. I mean moments or hours or days when you're just *with* her because you want to be."

Kenly closed her eyes. *She'll have a dress on, like she always does, and her narrow feet will be pressed into her favorite slippers.*

Her dad didn't answer. Instead he carried on with his own thoughts, murmuring in a low voice. "Sometimes when I look at her, she's so much like Lara it stuns me. . . ."

And her shoes will be at the back door where she always leaves them; next to that tattered canvas bag she carries, filled with all her knitting things.

". . . and it takes me right back to the day she died—"

Grandma's voice cut in, interrupting him. "I don't want to hear this!"

"Well, maybe you should."

Kenly grabbed her knapsack and slipped outside, tears threatening to spill as she hurried along the side of the house, across the yard, and into the back lane. The gate shut behind her and she traipsed back and forth along the fence where she couldn't be seen, crossing and un-crossing her arms. *Where do you go when you feel like you don't belong anywhere?* she wondered for the hundredth time. She couldn't stay with Grandma, who lived in a seniors' complex in Kalispell with forty other old people. She knew she could visit (the management had, on occasion, moved a cot into Grandma's room so Kenly could stay the night), but moving in wasn't an option. And she did have an uncle in San Francisco, but even though he was her mom's brother and had been polite to her the few times she'd met him, he didn't seem like the type who'd throw his arms wide if she showed up on his doorstep asking to move in.

As she leaned against the fence, a tiny flash of movement caught her eye. Turning, she saw a spiderweb built into one corner near the gate, with dozens of intricate, silklike strands glistening in the sun. Caught in the middle was a fly with one of his wings stuck and the other flapping as he tried to free himself. Kenly unzipped her knapsack, grabbed a pencil, and carefully broke the strands that trapped him, then lowered him onto the grass, where he sputtered up into the air and back down again a few times. A sad smile worked its way across her face as she watched and she found herself thinking, *Well, there you go. At least now you have options.*

A WEEK LATER, SHE WAS READING IN HER BEDROOM WHEN HER dad called her into the kitchen to break the news that he'd taken a teaching job in Canada.

"Where?"

"In northern Alberta. You'll love it."

She stood so fast that her chair fell over. "Are you trying to be funny?"

He closed his eyes.

"Because this *really* isn't funny."

"Athabasca is the name of the town," he said, talking slower now and with exaggerated patience, "and there are only four hundred kids in the entire high school."

She dug her hands into her hair and groaned. "This just keeps getting worse, doesn't it? I mean, two years ago we moved from Billings to Rapid City, where you told me I'd love living in the hills and visiting Mount Rushmore whenever I wanted. We were there six months, Dad, and I never even saw Rushmore. Then it was off to Idaho, where you spent three days a week teaching part-time in Boise and the other four drinking. . . ."

"I don't need this crap from you." His voice was cold and detached, like he didn't care what she thought.

She ignored him, pacing back and forth across the kitchen. "After Boise, it was Grandma who got you this job, wasn't it? Someone she knew who knew someone else in Kalispell with just enough pull to get you a teaching job here, where it would be a lot harder to come up with reasons to avoid seeing her more than twice a year."

"Don't be a smart-ass with me," he said, raising a finger and jabbing it into the air between them.

Kenly stared at his finger, then picked up the chair, and stood it back at the table. She wanted to ask him what made him hate himself so much. What was it that life had dished out to him that was any worse than what it gave everyone else? She curled her hands around the back of the chair, opened her mouth, and hesitated. *Here we go again,* she thought, and as she stood there she was saddened beyond explanation. She'd let her guard down months ago and had even considered painting her bedroom, then allowed herself the luxury of imagining what kind of graduation dress she'd wear when she finished twelfth grade here in Montana. But now those daydreams wilted like a flower and evaporated completely when her dad lifted his eyebrows and gave her a look that told her whatever she had to say would be a waste of time.

"I'm not packing your things this time," she said, her voice catching.

She turned and left the room with her shoulders squared and tears in her eyes, then closed her bedroom door and lay across her unmade bed. Minutes later she heard him leave, and when the sound of his car faded into the distance, she got up and dug an old pair of running shoes out of her closet. They didn't fit anymore. The last time she'd worn them she was nine, but they had a row of notches carved into the outside of each rubber sole: one for every move they'd made since her mom had died. Taking out the pocketknife her dad had given her for Christmas, Kenly sat on the edge of her bed and carefully cut one more notch into each sole, not bothering to count how many there were.

chapter 2

FALLING BACK ON OLD HABITS, KENLY SAT DOWN
cross-legged on her bed the next morning with a pad of
paper, a pen, and her usual list of questions. Then she pulled the
phone into her lap and called directory assistance for the province of
Alberta in Canada. The phone call she made took less than five minutes and gave her all the information she needed.

The town of Athabasca had a population of nineteen hundred and
there was no mall, movie theater, bowling alley, or any kind of fast-
food monster chain. Main Street started at the top of a long hill that
came into town from the south and ended a few hundred yards before
the hill ran into the Athabasca River at the bottom of a valley. There
was only one traffic light in town, at the bottom of that hill, and you
had the choice of turning either right or left when you came to it.
Turning right took you up out of the valley through the east side of
town, although halfway up you could cross a bridge over the river
if you were going north. Turning left pulled you up another hill that followed the river west toward Baptiste and Island Lake. The town itself

was built into the hills surrounding the river basin. Most of the business core could be found in the valley, and you had to parallel park on all four of the downtown streets, although no one did it well here—a testament to their refusal to embrace change easily, and something the woman at the other end of the line actually seemed proud of.

"All in all," she told Kenly in a perky voice, "Athabasca survives off farming and the oil and gas industries."

There was a long pause at Kenly's end of the line.

"Was there anything else?" the woman asked.

Kenly stared at the ceiling, thinking. The TV in her dad's bedroom was turned up so loud that she could hear it through her door. Her bottom lip trembled as she folded her arms over her stomach and cradled the phone against her chin. "How far do you have to go to get somewhere real?" she asked.

"Pardon me?"

She put her feet against the headboard of her bed and tried to keep her voice from shaking as she spoke. "You know, a city. Where you can order takeout or catch a good movie. Where they deliver mail to your house and not to some post office on Main Street, and where you have a half-decent shot at finding a Dairy Queen if you want a banana split. I mean, how far do you have to drive to get somewhere *else?*"

The woman cleared her throat. "It's really a nice town," she said loyally.

"I'm sure it is," Kenly said, doing her best to be polite. "Thanks anyhow."

After she hung up, she puttered around her room, rearranging things and rummaging through her dresser. Finally, she flopped onto her bed, pulled her hair back into an elastic band, and lit the only cigarette she could find. When she was done, she crushed it out into the pickle jar she kept under her bed and resigned herself to the fact that it looked like Athabasca was going to be one more wasted stop before her life really began and she could put all of this behind her.

Grabbing a pen, she scratched out a few calculations on a piece of

paper. Counting this month, she had 742 days before she would graduate from high school. Which meant only two more Thanksgiving weekends where she and her dad would make a lame attempt at polite
conversation while they ate an undercooked or badly burned chicken.
("Why waste good money on a turkey when there're only two of us?" he
usually said.) Just two more Christmas mornings where she would open
her gifts in front of their barely decorated tree while he slept in, and two
more Easter Sundays where there would be no chocolate bunnies or
colored eggs to make up for all the years when there should have been.
Kenly lay there thinking about everything she would do when she was
free, staring up at the hairline cracks in the ceiling until the light faded
outside and it got too dark to see them.

IN A FLURRY OF RENEWED OPTIMISM, HER DAD TOOK CARE OF
getting a work visa so he could teach in Canada as well as the docu-
mentation needed for Kenly to attend school there. Suspicious, she
read the paperwork twice before agreeing to sign it.

"What's the problem?" he asked, standing over her.

She tapped her pen against the table. "I'm just making sure I don't
have to give up my U.S. citizenship to go live in nowhereville, Canada."

He crossed his arms. "The name of the town is Athabasca, and no,
you aren't giving up your U.S. citizenship to go there. This allows you
to attend school there, that's all. It doesn't make you a Canadian citizen, and we have to renew it each year."

Satisfied that he wasn't trying to trick her into staying in Canada if
she didn't want to, Kenly signed her name on the last page and handed
everything back to him.

SIX DAYS LATER, HER BARE LEGS WERE STUCK TO THE FRONT
seat of their car in a film of sweat when she and her dad finally drove
down into a lush valley where the Athabasca River snaked along the
bottom and the heart of the town took shape. She shifted for what

felt like the hundredth time, glad to have the grueling nine-hour drive over with.

They pulled into a Texaco station halfway down the hill into town and she listened with disinterest when her dad got out to ask the attendant for directions as they gassed up. When they were finished, the attendant leaned over, nodded to Kenly, and said, "Welcome to Athabasca." She managed a pinched smile and fought the urge to give him the finger as they pulled away. After all, the fact that they were here wasn't his fault.

Her dad handed her the gas receipt. "In a few more minutes we'll be sitting in our new castle," he said with a laugh. Kenly didn't answer, just crumpled the receipt into a tight wad, tossed it in the air between them, and punted it into the backseat. She hated it when he tried too hard, but she hated it even more when he tried to be funny.

When they pulled up in front of their new home, he slammed the car into park and leaned back, pointing out how the sidewalk out front stopped at the end of their street, where a well-worn path carried on, up a hill through the bush and to another sidewalk that led to the high school. "It'll only take us a few minutes to get to school each morning," he said.

Kenly didn't answer.

"The house is small," he said. "Not quite a thousand square feet, but it's forty years old and has tons of character."

Kenly didn't look at him, just nodded as she stared at the house in front of them. It had puke green siding, a porch that looked level only if you tilted your head to the left, and a warped picket fence someone had tied to a spruce tree out front so it wouldn't fall over. Separating their yard from the neighbors on one side was an unruly, six-foot-high caragana hedge that had taken claim to part of the fence, smothering it until it no longer looked like it was even there. Someone had torn the fence down on the other side, replacing it with a lush row of golden elders that looked in desperate need of a good trim.

She rolled her window down but didn't say anything.

Her dad pointed to the peak of a small window jutting out from the roof and told her this was her bedroom. "The landlord told me it's the biggest room in the house," he said, bouncing the palms of his hands against the steering wheel.

Kenly was almost in tears and having trouble hiding it, thanks to a quivering bottom lip. Reaching into the backseat, she grabbed the cracked laundry basket she'd filled with her things and pulled it into her lap. Then she slid out of the car, hoisted the basket onto her hip, and made her way up the sidewalk to the front steps, where she sat down with her elbows on her knees. Her dad followed, sitting next to her. Neither of them said anything, but then they didn't have to. They'd both been here before; same spot, different town.

When he rose to unlock the front door, she clenched her teeth and followed. He pushed it wide and they made their way in and out of each tiny room, then up the stairs to a dusty atticlike loft he said was all hers. She followed him back down to the kitchen and when she saw the ancient gas stove and refrigerator, she almost groaned, certain that neither actually worked and they'd be stuck cooking on her dad's old camp stove under an open kitchen window like they had when they'd lived in that old trailer outside of Rapid City two years ago. After he lugged a cooler of food in from the car, Kenly busied herself making sandwiches and then they leaned against the kitchen counter and picked at their food, knowing it was only a prop, a way to avoid discussing what was really on their minds.

The moving truck Grandma Alister had paid for wouldn't arrive until the next day, so for the next hour they emptied the trunk of the car and made a weak effort at unpacking what they had with them. Neither bothered to say anything; their silence was raw, and Kenly was relieved when they were done and she could go upstairs. Tossing her knapsack on the dusty floor of her new room, she shut the door and stood with her hands on her hips, trying to decide where she would put her bed when it got there the next day.

AFTER THE MOVING TRUCK ARRIVED THE NEXT AFTERNOON, Kenly propped open the front door and sidestepped movers for an hour as they tramped in and out of the living room, piling box after box in a heap on the floor. The painters came next, ten minutes apart and each taking his turn at what she now considered the doorbell from hell. When she finally dropped into a chair, she glared at her dad, stretched on the couch snoring, with the remote control in one hand and a half-empty glass of vodka in the other. Someone had obviously tattooed the word "servant" on her forehead without telling her.

As she reread the first page of *Flowers for Algernon* for the third time, the doorbell rang again. Tossing her book on the floor in frustration, she climbed over a box to pull the door open. Standing on the porch with his back to her was a young guy. Taller than she was, long arms, nice build, and thin blond hair. But when he turned around his face jumped out at her like something from a horror movie. His right cheek was pushed out like a hardened balloon and a thick cauliflower-like growth extended down the right side of his neck and disappeared into his shirt.

Kenly instinctively stepped back.

"It's okay. I don't bite," he said, raising his hands.

One of his eyes looked smaller than the other from the pressure of extra skin and bone that didn't belong, and his forehead protruded at an unnatural angle, bulging with what looked like swollen lumps, piled one on top of the other.

Kenly swallowed, her voice shooting high. "C-can I help you?"

He nodded, shifting from one foot to the other. "My name's Tommy Naylor. I live next door but I got locked out."

She tried to remember what the movers were talking about earlier. *What was it they'd said? Something about the kid next door. That it looked like he had some kind of* condition.

"Could I use your phone?" he asked, then waited as she stared, obviously used to getting this kind of reaction.

She finally pointed to the kitchen. "Uh, sure. It's . . . in there."

As he maneuvered his way across their living room, she slid back into her chair and peeked at him from around the corner of her book, wondering what was wrong with him. Then she shot a glance at her dad, worried about how he'd react if he woke up right now. In Kalispell, one of their neighbors had been a seventy-year-old woman who'd meditated nude in her backyard each afternoon, and every day when he got home from teaching he would stand at their open kitchen window and complain loud enough for half the neighborhood to hear, "Jee-zuss, who needs to look at this shit?"

One of the painters was working on a ladder in the kitchen. Distracted, he glanced down at Tommy, did a double take, and froze with his paint roller in midair, dripping yellow paint all over the floor.

Tommy grabbed the phone and dialed. "Hi, Andrew. Is Mom around?"

The second painter came into the kitchen with an armful of wet drop cloths and Kenly watched him squat to put them on the floor.

"Hi, Mom," Tommy said, shifting from one foot to the other. "I forgot my key but I'll wait outside 'til you get home. . . . Look, it's no big deal. I just didn't want you to get worried if I didn't answer the phone."

When the painter straightened, he saw Tommy, narrowed his eyes, and squinted like maybe he was seeing things. Then he cringed like a cut worm and whispered up to his buddy, "What the hell happened to him?"

Tommy covered the phone, gestured to his face, and whispered back, "They don't know what it is, but they think it might have something to do with the paint fumes I sniffed as a kid."

The guy on the ladder dropped his paint roller and Kenly bit back a laugh as it bounced off their oak kitchen table and splattered against the fridge.

"No, Mom, it's nothing. I'm just next door, using the new neighbor's phone. I'll see you in an hour, okay?" He hung up, nodded politely to the painters, and slipped past Kenly in the living room on his way to the front door. "Thanks a lot." And then he was gone.

As soon as the screen door bounced shut, she was out of her chair and straining to watch him from the front hallway. He stopped halfway down the sidewalk, glanced back, and grinned. "See you around," he called out.

Kenly flattened herself against the wall, then heard another voice outside. Leaning forward again, she peered out and saw an older man standing beside Tommy at the gate. He was bald with a thick, white mustache and beard, both trimmed short and kept impeccable. He laughed at something Tommy said, then waved good-bye on his way up the front walk.

Kenly met him at the door before he could use the doorbell. He lifted his eyebrows in surprise. "Hello, young lady. I'm your landlord, Max Varda."

"Hi, Max Varda," she said, pulling the door wide. "I'm Kenly."

Even if she'd wanted to, it would have been impossible not to like Max. He had the kind of panache that made her want to inch closer just in case some rubbed off. He wasn't a big man, but he seemed big to her, probably because he walked with his shoulders back and his head up. Confident, sure of himself, and brimming with energy for a man who looked like he had to be at least sixty. His clear blue eyes looked straight through Kenly and when he laughed, his cheeks lifted into half-moons that made his eyes almost disappear, even though he wasn't a heavy man.

"I own this house," he told her. "Lived in it for thirty years with my wife, Sophie, but when she died, it bothered me so much I couldn't stay here anymore. So, when the house two doors down went up for sale, I bought it and moved three hundred feet away. Sophie would get a kick out of that," he said with a wink. "I'm not a big risk taker, you see, and she was always pushing me to make changes."

They were in the kitchen and he was showing her how to light the pilot light on the stove. "It can be a little tricky sometimes."

He was there for half an hour, showing her how to get into the attic, where the key was for the shed out back, and who to call if the roof started to leak again. "I'm having it reshingled next month, so it's just a short-term problem."

Kenly jotted the number down.

Max glanced over to where her dad lay on the couch, snoring. "Did you want to wake him up to go over this with us?"

"No, it's okay." When he frowned, she tucked her hands into the back pockets of her jeans and added, "He was up late last night unpacking."

"I see," he said, taking a long look around at all of the boxes stacked in their living room.

Kenly made a halfhearted effort at distracting him. "I was wondering, do you allow pets?"

"Sure do," he said. "You got one?"

"Not right now, but I was thinking about getting a cat."

Max smiled and his eyes lit up. "Hey, why don't you come with me and I'll introduce you to a dog you'll never forget."

Kenly brightened, happy to leave the painters and her dad behind. "Sounds great."

As Max headed out the front door, she lagged behind and snatched a cigarette from her dad's pack on the coffee table. Tucking it into her jacket, she slipped out the front door and followed Max down the sidewalk to his house, two doors away.

"Come in," he said, opening the front door. "I'll go get Oscar."

She stepped inside and glanced around a huge country kitchen. Lined up on the windowsill, behind an oak kitchen table, were four pots of African violets, an English ivy, and a lipstick plant in full bloom. On the counter was a coffeemaker, a small television, and a stack of old books. A stone fireplace took up the far corner of the room and in front of it sat two well-worn easy chairs with matching crocheted armrests. The floor was hardwood and the walls were pale yellow with a strawberry-red border that ran along the top, next to a cove ceiling.

Then Kenly noticed something else.

About a foot up from the floor was a wide, black smudge line that ran along all four kitchen walls and then continued out into the hallway. She crouched to take a closer look, heard Max coming, and straightened again.

When he came around the corner he was carrying a dog in his arms. "This is Oscar," he said, squatting to set him on a small throw rug that was pushed up against one wall. He picked up a bowl and darted around the corner, calling out over his shoulder, "Be right back."

Kenly frowned, wondering why he'd had to carry Oscar into the room.

Oscar was keeping eye contact with her as if his life depended on it. He had long, coal-black hair like a retriever, but looked like he weighed no more than thirty pounds. He whimpered a little and shivered a lot, but otherwise he didn't move from where he sat leaning against the kitchen wall.

She crouched down and held out her hand as she smiled. "Come here, boy." At the sound of Kenly's voice, Oscar's body shook with excitement from head to tail, but he still wouldn't move. "It's okay," she said, cooing now. "C-o-m-e on, come here . . ."

Stretching his neck to the ceiling, he let loose with a long howl that made her push back on her heels, and it was then that she suddenly noticed how everything in Max's kitchen was pushed a foot away from the walls. Swiveling around, she watched Oscar take off and run around them at lightning speed. He raced behind the china cabinet, under the legs of the telephone stand, around the back of the fridge, and up to the edge of the doorway on the other side of the room, where he skidded to a stop, leaning against the wall as he pawed at the air between them.

Kenly's eyes went wide and a smile spread across her face. "A little unstable, isn't he?" she asked Max when he came back with a bowl of dog food.

He grabbed a metal slicker brush and knelt on the floor next to Oscar, talking as he brushed. "Sophie found him at the dump when he was just a puppy a few years ago. Someone drowned a whole litter, and then pitched them all out in a cardboard box. When we drove up, there he was, sitting on top all them dead puppies, whimpering like a baby."

As Max brushed, Oscar's eyes drooped shut and his mouth went slack. "He started leaning against the walls a few weeks after we got him home. It almost drove us both crazy at first. The vet says he's got tunnel vision. He won't go anywhere unless someone's holding him or he can lean against something. He pees outside every morning and again at night, but it takes him ten minutes to find the courage to even do that. He spends a lot of time with Tommy next door and now and then I take him for a drive in my car."

He sounded matter-of-fact, like it was no big deal to have a dog like this.

Kenly's throat tightened, because even though Oscar was obviously high maintenance and an odd duck of a dog, Max loved him anyhow. *Nice town,* she thought, biting back a smile. *A neighbor kid who looks like he just crawled out of a car wreck, a landlord who moves two houses away after thirty years, and a dog that needs therapy more than Dad and I do.*

Max's voice followed her down the sidewalk when she left. "Look, if you and your dad need anything at all, you just give me a call. Athabasca's a good town. Trust me, once you get settled here, you won't wanna leave."

Kenly smiled but didn't answer. He seemed like a nice man and she didn't have the heart to tell him that they'd probably be gone long before they had the chance to get "settled." And yet, as she made her way back down the sidewalk, she caught herself humming and thought, *I must be getting better at this, 'cause suddenly living in nowhereville, Canada, for a few months doesn't seem so bad after all.*

chapter 3

KENLY WAS STRETCHED OUT IN HER HAMMOCK ON the back porch the next morning when Tommy rounded the corner of the house pushing an old lawn mower. He was wearing jeans and a T-shirt with an Edmonton Oilers hockey logo on it. He had a portable radio strapped to his belt and he was singing, loud—hoofing along to the beat of Billy Joel's "Only the Good Die Young," voice off-key and hands drumming against the handle of the lawn mower.

She rolled over onto her stomach, propped her chin in one hand, and took a drag off her cigarette. *This guy needs help,* she thought, watching him thump one hip against the lawn mower, throw his arms wide, and lift his face to the sun as the song came to an end.

She sat up and adjusted her long legs.

Tommy saw her and flushed. "Oh, hi . . . Max pays me to cut your grass every week."

Kenly stubbed out her cigarette and pushed her hair behind her ears but didn't say anything.

"I usually do it Mondays," he said, shifting from one foot to the other. "Can you ask your parents if that's okay?"

She lifted a hand to shade her eyes from the sun. "Mondays are fine."

Shrugging, he pushed the mower across the yard to a shed at the edge of the property.

"It's just me and my dad," Kenly called out. "Trust me, he won't care."

He glanced back over his shoulder. "Great."

She dropped her legs off the hammock onto the porch and followed him, cringing as dozens of grasshoppers billowed up in front of her, leaping in every direction. "Are they *always* like this?"

"Nah, this is the worst we've seen them in years. Everyone's talking about it."

Fighting the urge to run back to her hammock, she bit the inside of her cheek and tried to act like it didn't bother her, even as she wondered if there was anything about this place that was normal. Trying to make conversation, she pointed to the beat-up lawn mower. "Does this thing actually work?"

He disappeared into the shed, rummaged around, and came back with a gas can. "Yup. It's Max's. He oils it, cleans it, and keeps it purring like a kitten." He filled the tank, pulled the starter, and it settled into a lazy pattern that defied reason when you looked at the machine itself. "Voilà," he yelled over the motor.

She put the palms of her hands against her ears. "By the way . . . *my name is Kenly.*"

"I thought so," he yelled, pointing to the T-shirt she was wearing with her name embossed in bold black letters across the front. He let out the choke on the mower, tugged his T-shirt over his head, and tossed it on the grass. Kenly swallowed. He was wearing a muscle shirt underneath, but one of his shoulders and the opposite arm were covered with discolored splotches of raised skin, like someone had tossed black coffee all over him.

Tommy caught her staring and smiled. "You'll get used to it," he

said over the mower. "Everyone says after a while you don't even notice."

She flushed, then pointed to his head. "No, your hair's sticking up."

He smoothed it flat and grinned. "At least that's what they tell me."
Then he turned the radio up and started across the grass with his head
bobbing in time to the music.

Pinning her hair back away from her face, Kenly went back to the
safety of her hammock. Her hair was a mass of loose curls, the color
of walnuts and streaked with amber from where the sun had taken
its turn, but it was forever in her face, so she usually pulled it back
into a thick ponytail and stuffed it into a baseball cap.

"You've got your mama's hair," Grandma Alister often said with a
sigh. "But you've got your grandpa's eyes." At fifteen, Kenly stood
five seven barefoot, with curves women envy and husbands day-
dream about, but it was her eyes that everyone noticed first. They
were so blue that strangers usually looked twice when they met her,
startled by the color. Even so, she flushed hard when men stared at
her or fell over themselves to get her attention; she was surprised
when she looked in the mirror and didn't see the insecurities that
floated around inside staring back. Those invisible stutterings that
pushed against her chest, took the air from her lungs, and left her
nauseous whenever she met new people. The same ones that made
her sneak away to her room when her dad had friends over, the way
he used to before his descent into liquor and depression made him
more reclusive.

The panic she sometimes felt that made it hard for her to breathe
would slow to a crawl only after a few drags on a cigarette, something
she'd learned when she started sneaking them from her dad two years
ago. And even though she felt bad doing it, now and then she snuck
an English Old from her grandma, too, but she always saved those for
special occasions, when she could really enjoy them.

A few days after they moved to Athabasca, Kenly's dad asked her
about Tommy. "Have you met the kid next door yet?"

Kenly felt her stomach tighten. "His name is Tommy."

"And . . . ?"

"And what?"

"What's wrong with him?"

She shrugged. "I didn't ask."

He dropped his glasses, rubbing the bridge of his nose. "Just keep in mind that taking on his problems isn't something you need right now, okay?"

Her eyes narrowed. "What do you mean?"

He leaned forward with his elbows on the table. "Look, Kenly, we both know you've got this thing for picking up lame ducks. You know, people who aren't strong. People who end up leaning on you all the time. It worries me, that's all."

"People like you?" she shot back.

He folded his hands together and stared at her.

"Ever wondered *why* lame ducks are drawn to me, Dad? In the past six years we haven't lived in the same place for more than—what?— nine months? By the time anyone figures out who I am, we're gone. So you know what? If a few loners are nice enough to make me feel welcome, why should you care?"

She was yelling now, bent at the waist and ready to battle. He stood, clenching and unclenching his fists before leaving the room without meeting her eyes. Grabbing her jacket, she snatched a cigarette from his pack on the table and ran out the front door, letting it slam behind her. She lit up with shaking fingers and pulled hard, letting the useless frustration she felt take over as she marched off down the street.

When she returned half an hour later, he was sitting in his recliner with a glass in one hand and a bottle of vodka on the table next to him. "These idiots don't even know how to play football," he said, pointing to the TV.

Kenly leaned against the door frame. "What's in the glass?"

"A couple drinks never hurt anyone."

"Maybe," she whispered, "but it's killing you."

He chuckled. "Nah, us lame ducks are tougher than we look."

She crossed her arms and stared at him, willing him to look her in the eye so he could see that she knew better. When he didn't, she turned and left the room, locking the back door and taking bread out for breakfast, turning off the kitchen light and putting clean towels out in the bathroom for morning. *You're not tough,* she thought, climbing into bed. *And you need me in your life more than you realize or will ever admit.*

chapter 4

KENLY WAS HOME ALONE TWO NIGHTS LATER WHEN she looked out the kitchen window and saw flames licking at the sky beyond the golden elder bushes in their yard. Almost tripping over a stool, she stumbled to the phone and dialed 911.

"Emergency. How can I help?"

"Fire! There's a fire. . . ."

"Okay. Calm down and give me your address."

Slapping one palm against her forehead, she closed her eyes, trying to remember. *What is it again? Oh, right.* "We're on Forty-ninth Street, just down from the high school."

The woman at the other end blew her nose. "Is the fire inside your house?"

"What?" Kenly was on tiptoe, peering out the window. "No, not *in* our house. *Outside.*"

The flames were getting bigger now, dancing even higher than before.

"Outside?"

Kenly pushed some stray hair behind one ear and gripped the phone, her eyes wide. *How could this woman be so calm?*

"Yes, there's a fire. I'm looking at it through the window right now. Outside. Just a few houses away, down the hill behind the high school."

Silence.

"Hello?"

"Did you just move in two doors down from Max Varda?"

Kenly pulled the phone away from her ear and shook her head. "What?"

"Because the fire's most likely coming from Max's fire pit," the woman explained. "You see, he has that thing going almost every night. My name's Myrna Simonchuk, by the way. I'm the local dispatcher here in Athabasca. Anyhow, Max keeps a hose close by, so it shouldn't be a problem even if he does pump it up higher than usual. No point in going off half-cocked, sounding a false alarm, and getting our volunteers all worked up for nothing now."

Myrna paused to blow her nose again. "Could you head over there and take a look for me, though? If I don't hear back from you, I'll know everything's okay."

The phone went dead and Kenly stared at it in disbelief before hanging up. *This place is getting nuttier by the day,* she thought, standing on tiptoe to look outside again. The flames were smaller now but still there, sparks spitting into the black sky above.

Slipping on her sandals, she hurried across the backyard. The shrubs between their house and the Naylors' were thick, but as she got closer she could make out a fire pit in the middle of Max's backyard a few hundred feet away. Max was there, sitting with his back to her and with both feet braced against the bricks of a circular fire pit. Across from him was Tommy, squatting to drop wood on the fire, and next to him sat a woman Kenly assumed must be his mother.

Oscar, who, apparently, had been curled on Max's lap, stood with his hair raised and a shaky growl growing inside him. Max swiveled and squinted into the darkness.

"It's just me, Mr. Varda. I wasn't sure about the fire. . . ." Kenly's voice trailed off.

He grinned and patted the empty seat next to him. "Come on over and join us."

She hesitated for a split second, then decided she might as well. Her dad wasn't home and with no cable and only two TV channels, she was sick of watching reruns of *M*A*S*H* and *Three's Company*.

Tommy stood up from the fire and called out, "Hi."

She slid into the chair next to Max. "Hi."

The pit was full of birch firewood that crackled and spit while it burned. Kenly breathed in the smell of it, holding her hands out to the warm fire. Max handed her a Coke without asking if she wanted one, then turned to the woman across from them.

"Jean, this is Kenly Alister. She's our new neighbor."

"Nice to meet you. I'm Jean Naylor, Tommy's mother."

"Hello." Kenly could see she was tall even though she was sitting. Her hair was silvery gray, but it hung to her shoulders in long layers that framed her face, making her look younger than she must have been. She wore eyeglasses that dangled from a chain around her neck, and in the glow from the flames, Kenly was sure she saw freckles across the bridge of her nose.

"Help yourself," she said, passing Kenly a plate of cookies. "If you don't take one now, these two will eat them all."

Max rolled his eyes. "Jean thinks her baking is irresistible."

"It is," Tommy said from where he was finishing stacking firewood.

Max rubbed Oscar's back. "By the way, Tommy, let's head down to your tree house this week so I can caulk that window. Last thing you need is to have it start leaking when it rains."

Kenly's eyes lifted from the fire. "You've got a tree house?"

"You'd have to see it to believe it," Max said with a chuckle. "Trust me. This isn't your average tree house. Ask Tommy to show you sometime."

Tommy shrugged and dropped into an empty chair. "Sure. If she wants to."

Kenly put her palms up to the fire again, curious, but too shy to ask if she could see it.

Although she hadn't planned to, she stayed for almost an hour listening to an animated conversation among the three of them about what the local newspaper was and wasn't lacking, something they all had an opinion about.

Max explained that he owned *The Athabasca Press* and that Jean was his editor. It was a weekly paper with one full-time photographer and a staff writer, but because every taxpayer in the county of Athabasca received a free copy, more than four thousand copies were printed each week. He and Jean spent Thursdays finalizing it; then they drove into Edmonton on Friday mornings to have it printed for delivery the following Monday.

Kenly glanced over at Tommy a few times, doing her best not to stare. The way he looked took some getting used to, but he seemed like a nice enough guy. As she ate one of Jean's cookies, she wondered what was wrong with him. It was hard not to feel sorry for him, even though she somehow sensed that he wasn't the kind of person who would want anyone's sympathy.

Tommy leaned forward as he talked. "But Max, if the paper doesn't cover more school events, how do you expect to interest readers my age?"

"And you honestly think covering a baseball tournament is going to do that?" Max said, sounding skeptical.

"Not on its own," Tommy shot back. "But I think it would if you had a column dedicated to school events. It could cover hockey, soccer, basketball, cheerleading tryouts, even academic events like chess. You could interview some of the players, their parents . . ."

"We already have a weekly column for town events," Max argued.

Tommy sat back, laughing. "That's true. And what did it cover last week again? I can't remember. Wasn't it the local geriatrics subcommittee meeting on whether the county office needs to invest in chairs that have lumbar support?"

Max crossed his arms.

Kenly stared at Tommy. His voice was strong and he sounded sure of himself, the way she rarely felt when she was around adults other than her dad. She dropped her eyes to the fire, thinking how great it was that he had opinions and wasn't afraid to say them.

"No. Wait," Tommy said, snapping his fingers. "I think I remember. Didn't last week's column cover how Louie Johnson won the annual lottery up at the old folks' home where he guessed correctly—as he does every year—exactly how long this year's July first fireworks would last from start to finish?"

That does sound pretty boring, Kenly thought, biting back a smile.

Max glared at him, but didn't answer.

"It *was* eight minutes, wasn't it?" Tommy pressed.

"Okay. Enough," Jean said, stepping in to referee. "Kenly's never going to come back if you two keep this up."

Max turned and winked at Kenly, confirming what she'd begun to suspect. That he enjoyed arguing with Tommy like this and had probably even baited him to get him going so it would kill off any nervousness she might have about joining them at the fire.

A few minutes later, she thanked Jean for the cookies and said good night, and when she came through the shrubs into their yard, she saw that her dad still wasn't home. The house was quiet and dark and uninviting. As she opened the screen door, she stopped and looked back at the faint glow from Max's fire, and suddenly, inexplicably, she envied Tommy.

MAX HAD A FIRE ALMOST EVERY NIGHT THAT SUMMER. SIX cedar Adirondack chairs circled the pit and during the day they sat empty, but when he started the fire each night, it wasn't unusual to see all of them taken plus people sitting on lawn chairs, squeezing in wherever they could fit. Weeknights were quieter, but on weekends people came and went at a steady pace, dropping in for a drink and a chance to visit. Voices rose and fell in tune with the conversations that went on. There were good-natured arguments, serious discussions, and, at times, even crazy laughter that infected all of them when someone got off on a tangent with a well-told story.

Kenly felt invisible when she was at the fire pit and she liked it like that. No one ever asked her to join in on the conversation and no one expected anything from her. And as she sat there and listened, often with her chin in her hand, a peacefulness that she hadn't felt in a long time came over her.

Gradually, she got to know Tommy, too. He was a year older than she was and he didn't go to school. Instead, he was homeschooled, and his day went from nine until two during the week—the equivalent of correspondence classes. He also worked three afternoons a week at the paper, helping proof articles and do odd jobs.

The fire pit had a few regulars who came every night. Two were sisters who shared a house three blocks away: Florence and Becky Harris. Becky was in her sixties and Florence was just a few years younger. Neither had ever married. Florence was tall, thin as a rail, and rarely spoke. She arrived each night wrapped in the same navy sweater and carrying a wool blanket she used to cover her knees when she sat down. She would sit in the same chair every time, rub her hands in front of the fire, then dig out her cigarettes and settle in to listen to everyone else.

Becky was stocky and full of bluster, and you usually heard her long before you ever saw her. She was almost always ranting and raving when she came across the grass, both arms flying to stress a point. There was always something. Gas prices were a conspiracy; the county office was overrun with fools who had no vision; the bank was screwing her out of interest she had coming; the neighbor's cat was pissing in her flower beds. Kenly loved listening to Becky, but Florence just shook her head and sighed, like she knew there was no use debating with her and understood if everyone else decided to bow out of the conversation, too.

The first time Walter Dunning joined them at the fire pit, he was wearing work coveralls with rubber boots. Walter was six feet tall with a barrel chest, a big belly, and a mop of thick gray hair that screamed "cut me" every time he pushed it off his face. He had a lumbering walk that made Kenly think of someone in slow motion, and he was forever chewing on a toothpick, rolling it from one side of his mouth to the other. A young girl trailed along behind him. Her red hair was cut short in a funky style Kenly never would have had the courage to try, and she had a pissed-off attitude that clearly said "leave me alone."

Kenly could tell from looking at her that this girl didn't follow trends; she set them. She exuded a kick-the-door-down confidence that seemed meant to intimidate as she walked past them with her head high, dropped onto the grass twenty feet away, and showed zero interest in their conversation.

Kenly leaned over to ask Tommy who they were.

"Her name's Lexie," he whispered. "And Walter is her uncle. Last winter her mom ran off to live with some guy in Toronto and dropped her off to live with Walter. Far as I know, no one's heard from her since."

Lexie was sitting on the grass cross-legged, holding a flashlight and a dog-eared book. She looked older than Kenly, but it was hard to tell. She wore a big sweatshirt, skintight jeans, and a pair of sandals. A few times, Kenly caught her looking at them. Finally she tilted her head and whispered to Tommy, "Why doesn't she just come over and sit with us?"

He shrugged. "She's mad that Walter makes her come along with him. He's pretty strict and won't let her get away with much. I've asked her to join us a few times, but she says she's not interested in what a bunch of old people have to say and doesn't need anyone in town thinking we're friends."

Kenly was glad it was dark and he couldn't see her face. "That's awful."

He shrugged like it was no big deal. "I don't blame her. Think about it. She moves here to live with her uncle and everyone in town's talking about it. Then she has to fit into a school that's pretty cliquey and she also has to sit here a few nights each week all summer long. I know what other kids in town say about me, too, so I can see why she keeps her distance."

Kenly thought about this, then smiled. "What about me?"

"Huh?"

"I live next door to you and I sit around this fire pit almost every night, so my chances at social climbing in September must be getting a lot slimmer."

Tommy looked at her with a slightly raised eyebrow. "I was wondering how long it'd take you to figure that out."

She caught a flash of mischief in his eyes reflected from the fire, almost a dare that said he didn't care. Did she? Pulling a loose string off her sweatshirt, Kenly tossed it into the fire, smiling. "No loss. I've never been all that social anyway."

Max was midway through telling Becky and Florence what he thought they should do about the slugs in their garden when Walter interrupted. "You should just plow your garden under," he said, hitching up his coveralls. "It's had slugs for as long as I can remember and every year you two sit here and complain about it, but you never find a solution to the problem."

Becky's eyes narrowed, but Florence put a hand on her arm and said, "Walter, if we want your opinion you can be sure we'll ask for it."

Becky smirked with approval and Kenly raised her eyebrows, biting back a smile. For the last week Florence had said barely ten words, so this was something new. Walter deflated and sat quiet for the rest of the night, but when Florence and Becky left an hour later, he did, too, pulling his head at Lexie for her to follow. His hands were in his pockets as he walked backward in front of them across the grass, bobbing his head in agreement to whatever Florence was saying.

Jean patted Kenly's leg. "Flamboyant, isn't he?"

"I think he likes Florence, too."

"They were engaged years ago, so I'm sure there's still some feeling there."

"They were *engaged*?"

Jean stood, brushing ashes from her jeans. "They were."

"I never would've guessed."

"Yes. Well, we all have our secrets, don't we?"

Kenly nodded and looked at the fire, thinking about a few of hers. Like the time her dad passed out and she drove his car two miles to the swimming pool in Boise so she wouldn't miss her lessons. She had been only fourteen and didn't have her learner's permit yet, but no one caught her. Or how she always wore her mom's red scarf pinned to the inside of her coat when she started at a new school. And when they did move somewhere new, how she'd wait a month and then mail a letter to the principal, telling him how much she liked the new math teacher they'd hired, going on to praise her dad's teaching techniques, and signing it *Anonymous.*

Transfixed by the glow of the fire, she thought she now understood why some secrets came about in the first place. How something that was private or intimate or special to you might look altogether different if it were held up to the light for everyone else to look at and judge—and how the telling of it would change everything.

chapter 5

LEXIE ARRIVED AT THE FIRE PIT TWO NIGHTS LATER wearing chunky black boots, torn jeans, and a tie-dyed T-shirt. She flopped into the same spot as last time and within minutes had a book in her lap, a flashlight balanced under her chin, and to Kenly's surprise, a cigarette dangling from the corner of her mouth. Although Walter glared at her disapprovingly, no one else seemed to notice.

Max, Jean, and Becky were having a heated discussion about whether the town bridge needed to be replaced when Kenly lifted her eyes from the fire and squinted into the darkness. Tommy stepped into the light with his jean jacket buttoned shut and Oscar's head bobbing out the top. She watched as he lowered himself into a chair, undid the buttons, and let Oscar slide out onto his lap.

Oscar's eyes darted around the fire, taking in each face before he curled up into a ball, looking content. Kenly bit into the apple she'd been palming and smiled. *Cute dog,* she thought. *Kind of a misfit, but aren't we all.* Then she stopped chewing and looked slowly around the fire the way Oscar just had, realizing for the first time that every person there was as imperfect as she was, in a way that made her feel safe and warm and welcome—in a way that filled her with happiness.

The wind shifted and the smoke from the fire came straight at her. Flapping a hand in front of her face, she moved over next to Tommy on the other side of the fire. The others were now arguing good-naturedly about who they thought had broken into the liquor store the week before, and the discussion was heating up.

Becky scratched her hip and tried to interrupt Walter while Florence sat on the edge of her chair, poised to play referee. Walter raised his voice, karate-chopping the air between them to make his point. Becky glared at him, then reached down and pulled a jar of peanut butter out of her canvas bag. Setting it in her lap, she crossed her arms and grinned. Walter flushed deep red and sat back in his chair.

Florence clenched her fists. "That's enough. Both of you!"

"He's allergic to peanut butter," Tommy whispered to Kenly.

"I was just trying to get a word in edgewise," Becky said.

Walter tossed back the last of his beer. "No problem. The floor's all yours." He nodded to everyone else and stalked off into the dark.

An uncomfortable silence followed as Florence folded her arms and Becky lowered her head, chewing on her bottom lip. Max asked if anyone wanted a beer and Jean passed around a plate of cinnamon buns. The awkwardness faded a few minutes later when two neighbors from down the street arrived swinging a flashlight and dragging their lawn chairs.

Tommy leaned close to Kenly and lowered his voice. "When Walter and Florence were engaged years ago, he canceled dinner with her one night and said he was sick with the flu, but Becky saw him up at the bar later that night watching strippers with some friends, and she had Florence believing he'd made a fool out of her in front of the whole town. She even talked her into breaking off their engagement. There's been bad blood between them since."

Kenly frowned. "Why didn't Florence give him another chance? I mean, he lied to her, but he was watching strippers, not sleeping around."

Tommy shrugged. "I guess some people find it hard to forgive."

"I guess."

He leaned forward and tossed some wood on the fire. Kenly waited a half beat, then jumped in with both feet, changing the subject and asking the question she'd been wrestling with since they'd met. "Tommy, can I ask what's wrong with you?" As soon as the words left her mouth, they sounded careless and she regretted them.

He rubbed his forehead, startled by the sudden shift in their conversation.

Kenly flushed. "Sorry. It's none of my business."

"Don't worry about it. You just caught me off-guard." He stretched his legs, shifting Oscar into a new position. "No one ever comes right out and *asks*. They usually gawk at me or else they pretend there's nothing wrong."

From the corner of her eye Kenly saw Lexie lift her head a few notches. Ignoring her, Kenly tugged at the drawstring on her coat and focused on Tommy. "Does it hurt?"

He told her everything. How the tumors were recurring and had plagued him since birth. How his right leg was two inches longer than his left and that his skull had what was called a "partial gigantism," or an overgrowth of bone and tissue. "They can call it whatever they want," he said. "I just wish they could fix it. After I was born, my mom moved to Edmonton for a year so they could do tests on me. She worked part-time and took me from doctor to doctor while they tried to figure out what was wrong."

"That would've been tough."

Tommy nodded. "After a year, they still couldn't tell her what I had, so she moved back here and got her old job back. Then Max and his wife, Sophie, bought this house as an investment and rented it to us pretty cheap. We've been here ever since."

Florence and Becky interrupted to say good night, and Jean followed, waving as she crossed the backyard. Max slapped his hands against his thighs as he got up and rumpled Tommy's hair. "Make sure the fire's out when you leave."

Tommy nodded. "I'll put Oscar in the back door on my way home."

While they were talking, Lexie gathered up her things and slipped into an empty chair across from Tommy, holding her hands out to the fire. Max raised his eyebrows in surprise, then winked at Kenly. "'Night, kids."

The wood had burned down to a huge pile of embers that glowed and flickered. Kenly grabbed a piece of birch bark and tossed it in, watching a burst of flame ignite and then fizzle away. "So what about your dad? Where's he?"

Tommy sighed and shook his head like that was a story he hadn't told in a while. "He asked my mom to marry him when she got pregnant. They picked a date, booked the church, hired a band, and even sent out all the invitations. I would've been three months old the day of their wedding, but when I was born like *this*"—Tommy gestured at his face—"everything went out the window."

Kenly stared at him in disbelief and Lexie's eyes got bigger.

"The doctors said I probably wouldn't live more than a few months and even if I did, the costs would be crippling. They also said if I did live, the tumors might affect my eyesight and my brain development, but Mom told them they were wrong."

He lifted his chin, pride blazing in his eyes. "They suggested institutionalizing me and my dad told my mom he wouldn't marry her unless she agreed. She sat back and thought about it for a few seconds, then told him she'd drop to the floor right there in the hospital and scream until she turned blue if he didn't get the hell out of our lives." Tommy chuckled. "We never heard from him again."

"Have you ever tried to find him?" Kenly asked.

He paused. "Why? I'm sixteen and I'm slowly dying."

Kenly winced. "S-seriously?"

"Shit," Lexie muttered, sitting up straighter.

Tommy stroked Oscar's back, keeping his eyes on the fire. "Well . . . they don't know what I have, but there's no known cure for it, and even with all the chemotherapy I've had over the last five or six years, the tumors keep growing back. And my emphysema's getting worse all the time, so that's not helping, either."

His voice was flat, like he'd deadened his nerve endings to the reality of what he was saying. "Anyhow," he said, pulling his shoulders back, "if my dad wanted to be in my life, he blew his chance years ago. I'm happy with how things are. Athabasca is home, the people I love are here, and I know I'll probably die here. Spending time I don't have chasing down some guy who never wanted me in the first place seems stupid."

"And I thought *my* life was screwed up," Lexie murmured.

"Really," Kenly echoed, playing with the zipper on her jacket. "This makes my dad look like father of the year."

Tommy cleared his throat and smiled. "Nice to know this little feel-sorry-for-me chat cheered you two up."

Lexie looked at her hands, seemed to consider something, and then leaned forward. "At least you never had a mother who spent more time teaching you how to shoplift than she did teaching you how to read."

"Are you serious?" Tommy asked, eyes wide.

Lexie nodded. "I didn't know how to read properly until I was almost ten."

"No! I mean, did she really teach you how to *shoplift?*"

"Well, she sure gave it her best shot, but I wasn't any good at it, so she eventually gave up. At first, she had me practice with her at home, then she dragged me out to a few shopping malls to watch her in action, but when it came down to my first big heist," Lexie said, laughing, "I was so nervous that I stuffed a T-shirt down the front of my pants, walked past the register, and puked all over the floor."

Kenly shook her head in amazement as Tommy laughed.

"That's nothing," Lexie said. "Once, when I was twelve, she and her boyfriend woke me up in the middle of the night to go steal hubcaps with them."

Now Tommy's mouth was open. "No shit?"

"No shit," Lexie deadpanned. "Her boyfriend even warned me that we might get caught, but if we did, I was supposed to create a big scene, start crying hysterically, and throw myself down on the ground so it'd buy us some sympathy and give them a chance to get away."

He inched forward on his chair, looking fascinated. "Did you get caught?"

"No, but I got eight hubcaps and I learned how to take them off pretty fast, too."

Kenly and Lexie exchanged a quick look as Tommy threw his head back and laughed even louder. "That's crazy. I'm gonna have to remember to look Mom's car over tomorrow morning!"

Lexie looked like she was enjoying the sudden attention, but Kenly could also tell she was putting the kind of spin on her mother's failures that made them seem a lot funnier than they really were in an effort to lighten up the conversation and make Tommy feel better. And as she did, Kenly sat there speechless and grateful for the distraction. Tommy had just told them he was dying, as calmly as you might tell someone you're allergic to cats, and just like that tough-as-nails Lexie had changed into this sweet, compassionate person—and that was all it took for Kenly to instinctively know they were going to be good friends.

KENLY'S DAD DIDN'T WARM TO LIVING IN ATHABASCA AS WELL as she did, and he only joined them around the fire pit twice that summer. "What's the appeal?" he asked Kenly one night. "I spend a few hours listening to a bunch of people gossip; then I crawl into bed stinking of smoke and covered in ashes."

Kenly crossed her arms. "I guess it's how you look at it, isn't it? I think they're nice people, and they aren't gossiping; they're just living their lives, interested in what's going on around them. Also, I happen to love the smell of the fire. There's something magical about watching it burn down to ashes like that. And you know what, Dad? I always leave feeling better than when I came."

They were eating breakfast, and when he rolled his eyes and took a bite of toast, a determined look came over Kenly's face. She was thinking about her new friends. How she and Tommy always seemed to be on the same wavelength, the way Lexie sat at the fire now instead of by herself on the grass, how Jean and Max always made her feel welcome, and the wave of pleasure that rushed over her when Florence gave her shoulder a squeeze before she sat down each night. She liked it here and she didn't want to leave.

"By the way," she said, picking up her plate. "I was wondering if you could give me some money so I can buy a few gallons of paint."

He frowned. "Why?"

"Because I'd like to paint my bedroom," she said, taking her plate to the sink.

"Really?"

"Yes, really. And when I'm done with mine, I'm going to do yours, too."

He stared at her for a few seconds, looking perplexed, then pushed back from the table and pulled out his wallet. "Just make sure you don't make a mess," he said, giving her a handful of bills.

A WEEK LATER, SHE AND HER DAD GOT HOME LATE AFTER A trip into the city for dental appointments and the fire pit was already roaring in Max's backyard. Kenly tossed her knapsack on a kitchen chair, grabbed a Coke from the fridge, and slipped outside. She was sprinting across the Naylors' backyard when she heard the music and slowed to a stop, blinking in disbelief at what she saw.

Max was planted in his usual chair at the fire pit. Tommy was sitting next to him, feet braced against the bricks and face lit with a smile. Becky was there, too, clapping wholeheartedly in time with the music. Florence was in her usual spot and Lexie was sitting next to her, but it was Walter Dunning who had everyone's undivided attention. He was revved up and toe-dancing around the fire pit with James Taylor singing away in the background about how whenever he saw someone's smiling face it made him smile himself.

Walter stopped in front of Florence, unzipped his jeans, and kicked them off, almost falling over in the process. He never stopped moving—fast, furious, and full of moves a man his size didn't usually have, even though his face was filled with a mixture of discomfort and vulnerability.

Becky was holding her stomach now, brushing away tears with one hand as the boom box at Lexie's feet blared into the night. Someone's pretty little pout was turning James Taylor inside out as Walter danced around the fire pit like he'd been hypnotized into believing he was good at it, making Kenly wonder if all this wasn't just a big joke.

Max shook his head like he knew he was losing Walter to some sad disease, but there was no way to save the fool now. Florence's face went from stunned shock to teary amazement as Walter continued strutting around the fire, belly flopping and wearing nothing now but a pair of boxer shorts and rubber boots. Becky whistled and kept clapping; then Walter stopped in front of Florence a second time and Lexie stopped the music.

"Okay, Florence," he said. "Years ago you said the only way you'd ever see me again would be if I stripped naked in front of a bunch of strangers, remember?"

Florence nodded. She did.

"Well, these people aren't strangers, but as you can see, I'm dropping my drawers and making an ass outta myself for you. I won't strip naked, mind you. . . ."

Becky slapped a hand against her forehead like she was thanking God for small miracles. Walter stood there shaking, his putty-colored legs and beer belly exposed to everyone. His voice cracked and his shoulders dropped. "So what do you think, Florence? Think you could give us another chance?"

There was a long pause during which everyone seemed to be holding their breath. Then, being the lady that she was, Florence flushed, grabbed his jeans, and held them out with a smile. "Get dressed, Walter," she said calmly, "and we'll talk about it later."

Walter hopped into his jeans and sat down, keeping his eyes on the fire as Max handed him a beer. Kenly hesitated in the shadows, then joined them, saying hello to everyone like this was any other night.

When Florence finally rose to leave half an hour later, Walter jumped up, too. They both said good night, she slid her arm through his, and they made their way across the grass, heads held high and with Becky trailing behind.

Tommy chuckled. "Now *that* was embarrassing."

Jean shrugged into her sweater as she stood to go. "I don't think so. Sometimes life gives you second chances, but sometimes you have to make them for yourself."

Tommy rolled his eyes. "My mother, the philosopher."

Jean acted as if she hadn't heard him, giving everyone a wave on her way across the yard. A few minutes later, Max left, too, reminding Tommy to put out the fire when they were done. As soon as they were alone, Lexie lit a cigarette and grinned. "It took me weeks to teach Uncle Walter to dance like that."

Kenly laughed. "Are you serious?"

"No joke."

Tommy folded his hands behind his head. "I thought you two didn't get along."

"We do okay," Lexie said with a shrug. "He bought me a subscription to this hair-styling magazine I like, and he does make the best spaghetti sauce. . . ."

"Mom thinks he's a big teddy bear," Tommy said.

Lexie laughed. "Yeah, he can be. Funny how things work out, huh? My mom had me, but now she doesn't know what the hell to do with me, and Uncle Walter always wanted three or four kids, but he never even had one."

"I'd like to have two," Kenly said, perking up. "Being an only child sucks."

"I agree," Lexie said, "but I don't plan on having any of my own."

"Why not?" Kenly asked.

Lexie started ticking off one finger at a time. "Let me see. There's diapers, spit-up, sleepless nights, more diapers, teething . . . and before all that garbage even begins to kick in, there's giving birth, and pain alone tends to be a big deterrent for me."

Across the fire, Tommy was smirking as he drained his glass.

"Go ahead and laugh," Lexie said. "You don't have to worry about labor."

"You're right, but even so, I'll never have kids."

"How come?" As soon as she said it, Lexie flushed, and her gaze skimmed over the growths on his face and neck like she'd forgotten they were there.

Tommy ducked his head, suddenly looking uncomfortable. "No, that's not it. What I mean is that because of all the chemotherapy I've had, it'd be impossible for me to even get someone pregnant."

"Oh," Lexie said.

Trying to change the subject, Kenly pushed forward on her chair. "Back up a minute, here. You still haven't told us what made Walter decide to do a striptease around the fire for Florence, especially after all these years."

Lexie lowered her voice. "I'm not supposed to say anything, but he did it because he wants to sell the farm and take Florence on a trip to Europe."

"Wow. That's incredible."

Tommy frowned. "Maybe, but it doesn't make any sense. The farm's been in his family for years. Why would he sell now?"

Lexie grabbed a stick and drew a few circles in the dirt at her feet. "Because he just found out he's got cancer."

Tommy blinked at her, startled. "Is he going to tell Florence?"

"Yeah, but he doesn't want anyone else to know yet."

Kenly's voice wasn't working. All she could think about was this sixty-year-old farmer dancing around a fire pit in his underwear so he could get the woman he loved back into his life while he still had one. "Th-that's amazing," she finally said.

Lexie snorted. "Especially since neither of them has ever been on an airplane before."

Kenly's mouth dropped. "Really?"

"Uncle Walter said when they were teenagers, Florence was always talking about going to Denmark to see this hundred-year-old amusement park called Tivoli where her parents first met, so that's where he wants to take her." Tossing her cigarette in the fire, Lexie grinned. "Makes you hope someday we'll meet a guy just like him, huh?"

Kenly's eyes were on the fire as she rolled an empty Coke can between her hands. She was trying to imagine what it would be like to have someone love you like that. Where he listened to your dreams and loved you so much that he was willing to sacrifice anything to make your dreams part of his own.

Finally, she sighed and whispered, "Yeah, really."

Tommy was watching her from across the fire, head tucked and with most of his face buried against Oscar, who was asleep. Lexie got up and tossed her knapsack over one shoulder. "I've gotta get going. See you guys later."

"See you," Kenly said.

Lexie was halfway across the yard when Tommy woke Oscar up to tuck him back inside his jacket. Kenly's eyes were on the fire and she was smiling.

"What?" he asked.

She shrugged. "I was just thinking that, normally, the three of us wouldn't have anything in common, you know?"

Tommy nodded. "We are an odd mix, aren't we? A reluctant nomad, a Pat Benatar wanna-be, and a walking advertisement for freaks."

"I didn't say that!"

He laughed. "No, but it's dead-on, so why not say it like it is?"

It was quiet and still and dark with just the two of them sitting there as the embers from the fire glowed in a heap at their feet. The scent of fresh-cut grass drifted through the air and someone's cat yowled in the distance.

"I was thinking about heading down to my tree house tomorrow," Tommy said, fidgeting with the buttons on his jacket. "You wanna come?"

Kenly lit up inside, sensing this invitation was special, that Tommy didn't invite just anyone to his tree house. Her face softened and she slapped both palms against the arms of her chair. "Of course! I was actually wondering how long it was going to take you to ask."

chapter 6

No good thing is pleasant to possess
without someone to share it with.

—RICHARD GUMMERE

GETTING TO TOMMY'S TREE HOUSE WAS AN EVENT
all its own. The next morning, Kenly followed him along
the far side of his garage, down the steep ravine behind it, and back up
a hill on the other side. They crossed a stream, passed a beaver pond,
and were still pushing along a trail through the bush five minutes later
when she grumbled, "Ever consider a recon post with the FBI?"

Tommy laughed and ducked under a tree branch. She followed,
pulling leaves from her hair, then straightened, beaming. "Wow! Now
that's a tree house."

It was built into the branches of four black poplar trees and every
plank stood out from the care and attention he'd given it. The outside
walls were covered with cedar siding, the trusses were anchored against
both trees with lag bolts for extra strength, and even the roof was
shingled. It was built fifteen feet off the ground and had a narrow
wooden ladder strapped to the biggest tree and leading up to a trapdoor in the floor.

Hanging from the floor of the tree house outside was a cedar swing, suspended by two chains and big enough to comfortably fit two people. It faced a grassy incline that led down to a small creek below, which looked so inviting Kenly had to stop herself from crawling straight into it. Instead, she climbed the ladder behind Tommy, dropped to her knees on the floor inside, and looked around at the sanctuary he'd created for himself.

It was eight feet wide by ten feet long, with a plate-glass window stretching across one wall overlooking the creek below. The window frame was painted canary yellow and dangling in full view from the roof outside were three bird feeders, each a foot apart and painted a different shade of red. A narrow mattress was pushed up against one wall, next to a wooden crate filled with magazines, a flashlight, a handful of charcoal pencils, and a few sketchbooks. The floor was covered with a green shag rug, two throw pillows had been tossed onto the mattress, and a battery-operated lantern hung from the ceiling by a chain. Three of the walls were covered with wood paneling and a shelving unit had been built into the far corner from floor to ceiling, painted electric blue, and crammed with books.

It was then that Kenly noticed the back wall of the tree house.

Tommy had painted it white and then covered it from top to bottom with a collage of people, painstakingly sketched in charcoal and with every expression imaginable captured on their faces. In the top corner he'd sketched himself as a boy, sitting on a swing with his fingers crunched around the ropes and his head thrown back in laughter. There was one of Jean sitting in an old rocking chair holding Oscar when he was a puppy, and next to her one of Max holding a thin, dark-haired woman in his lap who had to be his wife, Sophie. Becky and Florence were there, too, laughing, and with arms wrapped around each other's waists as they stood next to a huge sunflower plant. And there was one of Walter Dunning, palming a beer can with a big grin on his face. There were a few other people Kenly didn't know, but they all had one thing in common—each person had been drawn with such attention to detail that it left you breathless when you saw them all blended together.

She stepped closer and ran her fingertips over the wall. Tommy watched, eyes darting from the collage to her and back again. "Incredible," she whispered. "Did you do this?" He nodded. She shook her head in amazement and motioned to a patch of white space. "Why haven't you finished?"

He shrugged, looking uncomfortable. "I don't know. It just doesn't feel like it's ready to be finished yet."

Kenly nodded as if this made sense.

Now that she had seen the tree house, Tommy couldn't seem to hold back. He told her how long it had taken to build it (six months), how Max had donated the window (a friend had given it to him), and how he and Max almost dropped it the day they hoisted it into the tree house on a pulley system they rigged up. "There's no way I could've built it without his help."

"Well, if it were mine," Kenly said with a grin, "I think I'd move right in."

"Actually, I do stay up here sometimes."

"Care to lend it to me now and then?"

Tommy looked pleased. "Whenever you want."

"Every night would be nice," she said. "Then I could get away from my dad."

"You two don't get along?"

"When he isn't drinking and I bite my tongue, but neither happens very often."

"Your parents divorced?"

"No, my mom died in a car accident when I was seven. She and my dad were on their way home from a wedding when some guy in a semi ran a stop sign and smashed into them."

"Man, that's awful."

Kenly rested her chin on her knees. "They rushed her to the hospital and she spent the night in intensive care, but she didn't make it. She died the next afternoon."

"I'm sorry."

Kenly pointed outside to change the subject. "Who built the bird feeders?"

"Florence and Becky," he said, rolling his eyes. "I know they're a little odd, but if I take them down it would hurt their feelings. Sometimes they pick saskatoon berries back here and when they do, Florence always goes out of her way to tell me how much she loves seeing them hanging there."

Kenly leaned back against the wall. "Max was right. This isn't your average tree house."

Tommy sat across from her and as he talked Kenly could see how lonely he was. How truly thirsty—no, hungry—for company he was. Something she easily understood. He told her how much he loved to sketch (that it relaxed him) and she confided that she wanted to learn how to sculpt one day and dreamed of having her own family and living in the same place forever.

The pinched features of his face lit up when he told her about an idea he had for an advice column in the town newspaper. It was something he seemed passionate about and when he described it to her, she couldn't help but smile. He'd already talked to Max about it and had even proposed to write it anonymously so it had a better chance of succeeding. What did she think? He wanted to call it the "WIT" column— the "What I Think" column—without ever telling anyone what WIT stood for. "That way, there'd be curiosity about it right away," he explained. He exhausted the topic, working through every possible negative and positive factor, then shook his head and laughed. "This is boring you, right?"

"Of course not," she said, stretching her arms above her head. "It sounds great."

Her eye caught something on the roof then and she squinted up at what looked like an attic opening cut into the ceiling above, only smaller. It was a foot wide by two feet long and had been framed with narrow slats of wood. "Hey, what's that for?"

Tommy didn't answer.

An elbow got his attention. "You gonna tell me or what?"

He hesitated, then dragged the wooden crate across the floor, straddled it, and pushed the board away. Slipping his arm up through the hole, he felt around the roof and pulled an old tin box down into the tree house. It was the size of a shoebox, with a hinged lid and a brass lock. He brushed off some leaves and set it on the mattress, then reached up to the shelf behind him, found a key, and unlocked it.

"What is it?" she asked.

"Max gave it to me a few years ago. I'd been in the hospital for a few weeks when he came to see me one morning and I started complaining about how shitty I felt, but he just brushed it off and said, 'Look, there are lots of people in this world with problems just as bad as yours. The way I see it, you can either handle this with your head up and enjoy the life you do have or else lie there, complain about it, and drive everyone away.'

"Of course, he was right," Tommy said. "But when you're feeling sorry for yourself the way I was, you don't always hear what people are saying to you."

Kenly motioned to the box. "So, why did he give you that?"

Tommy hunched forward and put his elbows on his knees. "After he left, I put on my robe, took my IV pole, and went for a walk to the lounge, but my timing couldn't have been worse. There were probably a dozen people sitting there and when I came in, everyone stopped talking. I tried not to let it bother me, but I could feel them watching as I got myself a drink. One woman even flinched when I brushed against her table on the way by."

Kenly looked at her hands. Her heart was pounding and she didn't know what to say.

"When you look like this," he said, motioning to his face, "strangers talk in whispers and you tend to hear every word. Sometimes they cringe and look at you like you're a monster, or else their eyes fill with pity and you see relief wash over their face—glad that it isn't them. But there are times when they look at you with such disgust, you want to tell them you didn't ask for it, that it isn't your fault.

"Anyhow, I heard a few hushed whispers as I stood there with my back to the room and I got so mad that I turned around and screamed

at them. Just threw my arms wide and let it come. Said I wasn't conta-
gious for chrissakes and did they think I was deaf and stupid on top
of all my other more obvious problems? It didn't take long for everyone to clear out, and then I sat down and waited for someone to come
and take me back to my room."

His voice was barely audible as he continued. "When Max came
back that afternoon, he wanted to know why I'd created such a scene,
and I needed him to come over to my side, to pat me on the shoulder
and say it was okay, that he understood. So I dragged him to the window and showed him two kids I'd been watching outside. They were
racing and swerving and falling all over each other in the snow as they
pitched snowballs. Then I pointed to a couple holding hands and a
man carrying his kid on his shoulders through the parking lot. And I
told him I wanted what they had, what I knew I could never have, but
he wouldn't cut me any slack. He just said, 'So what? We all want
things we can't have. You're no different than anyone else.'

"I argued and said I was different, that if he took a good look, he'd
see I didn't blend in real well in a crowd. I started to cry and made a
fool of myself. I said I felt cheated and I thought it was time that I
was up for a miracle of some kind because *everything* that was important in life was out of reach for me. I'll never forget it," Tommy said,
his voice almost a whisper. "He put a hand on my shoulder and he told
me to sit down; then he gave me a pen and a piece of paper and he
asked me to write down all the memories from my life that were so incredible I'd relive them again, if I could. He said he didn't want to hear
another word until I had at least half a dozen. When I was finished, he
looked at it and told me there wasn't another list like it on this earth.
That I'd been given moments no one else had and that if I planned
to spend the rest of my life swimming in envy of others because of
moments they had that were out of my reach, he wasn't sure he
wanted to know me anymore."

Tommy tapped the lid of the tin box. "That's when he gave me
this, and he said, 'Tommy, the things that matter most in our lives

are so small most people miss them altogether until it's too late. They are those moments that fill you up so full you can't speak, the ones you go back and visit when your heart needs a little salve or you need a reminder of what living is all about.' He told me to call him when I figured out how to fit everything that was on my list into this tin box, when I was ready to appreciate what was *really* important in life. He said the things that matter most in our lives should fit inside a tin box, and if they don't, they aren't as important as we think they are."

Tommy's voice caught and Kenly squirmed, her whole body feeling his words, a lump forming in her throat. "So now I keep everything that's important to me in here," he explained. He opened the lid, pulled out an old ticket stub, and handed it to her. "My mom took me to a Billy Joel concert in Toronto when I was thirteen. It's the only concert I've ever been to."

Kenly flipped it over and smiled.

"And this," he said, handing her an envelope, "is something Max's wife, Sophie, gave me. She told me it was rare and that it would bring me good health. So far, it hasn't been doing the job, but I like it anyhow."

Kenly opened the envelope and saw a small black pearl taped to a narrow piece of cardboard inside. Next, he handed her a blue velvet pouch, pulled tight with a drawstring. "Inside this is one of Oscar's baby teeth, an army knife that belonged to my grandfather, my birth certificate, and a few pictures of me and my mom."

Kenly dumped it all into her lap and ran a finger over a tooth that looked like it belonged to a miniature shark and not panic-stricken little Oscar.

"I kept this from my first and only visit to an ocean last year," he said, handing her a test tube full of sand with a cork glued into the top. "Mom, Max, and I drove out to Vancouver; then we took a ferry to the Queen Charlotte Islands and stayed there for a few days."

He had a faraway look on his face that made Kenly smile.

"You know what? I think I know exactly what Max is saying," she whispered, carefully putting everything back inside the tin box.

Tommy closed the lid, locked it, and looked up at her with a shy smile. "Well . . . if you ever want to keep anything of yours in here, go right ahead. I keep the key on the top shelf."

MONDAY AFTERNOON, KENLY WAS SITTING AT THEIR KITCHEN table with her stomach in knots. She was flipping through a list of first semester courses and the principal was due any minute for a meeting with her dad about his new job. "Couldn't you just meet her at the school?" she asked. He didn't answer, just gave her one of those "I can't believe you're my daughter" looks and continued wiping the kitchen counter.

She crossed her arms and glared at him. When she didn't say anything, he looked up and said with exaggerated patience, *"What?"*

"I hate it that I have to meet the principal in the summer."

He closed his eyes and sighed. "Okay, then. How about this. Don't draw any attention to yourself and I won't go out of my way to introduce you. Fair enough?"

Kenly thought about it for a few seconds, then nodded and decided to slip outside and hide in her hammock for an hour. The screen door bounced shut behind her and she saw Max in his backyard, bent over a pile of lumber and squinting as he measured something. She waved and went over to see him.

"Hey, Max. Where's Tommy?"

He glanced at his watch. "I hope on his way back from the hardware store with my nails."

There were scraps all over the ground, endpieces of wood that weren't needed, and Kenly pushed them around with the toe of one shoe, bored and looking for something to do. "Think I could use some of these?"

"Help yourself."

She did and before long she was sitting cross-legged in the grass, surrounded by a pile of wood scraps, a hammer, and a box of finishing nails. The air was hot and dry, and she squinted as her birdhouse took shape, so engrossed in what she was doing that she didn't hear the car pull into their driveway or see the tall, dark-haired woman who slid out and went inside.

An hour later, Max was almost through cleaning up the mess in his yard when Kenly pounded in the last nail and sat back to admire her work. It was then that her dad stepped onto the porch with his new boss to say good-bye, but Kenly didn't notice. Instead, her eyes locked onto a huge spruce beetle flying through the air at her. It landed in the middle of her forehead and her instinctive reaction was to hit it, so she did, but she was still holding the hammer at the time, so her dad, his new boss, Max, and Tommy all watched her wind up and knock herself out cold, right there on the grass in front of them.

When her eyes fluttered open, a doctor was checking her pupils and she pushed his hands away and rolled onto her side. It felt like something had exploded inside her head. There was a throbbing pain between her eyes unlike any other she'd ever known and she had to fight an overwhelming urge to throw up.

Nancy McKinnon, the principal, had driven them to the hospital and when it was time to go home, she drove them back. Her dad had been grateful and invited her in for coffee, but that quickly turned into lunch and they spent the rest of the afternoon chatting in the kitchen while Kenly lay half-asleep on the couch in the living room. Only later would she recognize how her run-in with a spruce beetle managed to stir up even more trouble in her life by throwing her dad and his new boss together like that.

The phone rang at ten o'clock the next morning, but she plunked into a chair and fingered the lump on her forehead, ignoring it. She could already picture hundreds of nameless faces snickering at her on the first day of school next week. *How am I going to live this down?* A few minutes later, the phone rang again, but this time it didn't stop.

Kenly frowned and snatched it from its cradle. "Hello."

"Can you meet me at the tree house at four o'clock?" Tommy asked.

"Nuh-uh . . . I'm not going anywhere like this."

"Oh. Okay. That makes sense. I walk around town every day look-ing like I do, but you can't sneak through the bush to meet me at the tree house for five minutes?"

Kenly smiled. He had a point there.

HER DAD WAS PAWING THROUGH THE KITCHEN DRAWERS WHEN she came downstairs an hour later. Throwing up his arms, he glared at her. "Where the hell is our address book?"

She didn't answer, just walked past him to the fridge, grabbed a Coke, went upstairs to her bedroom, and slammed the door. He'd been drinking again, and in an attempt to stay ahead of him, she had hidden the address book, knowing he always made a ton of phone calls when he drank. One time he'd even called Grandma at three thirty in the morning.

She propped her bedroom door open an inch and listened to him find his cousin, Rob, with the help of directory assistance. At his end, the conversation ranged from accusatory to apologetic and she could tell by the rise and fall of his voice whenever someone at the other end didn't agree with him. Half an hour later, he stumbled down the hallway past her bedroom. She heard a stool scrape against the floor, then a few thumps as he swore under his breath.

Kenly stared at the ceiling, telling herself it didn't matter that he was drunk again or that he'd forgotten her birthday for the second year in a row. Peeking into his bedroom ten minutes later, she made sure he was passed out, then carried a stool down the hallway. She set it down, crawled up on it, and pushed on the attic opening until it gave way, standing on tiptoe to peer into the space above.

Lined up in front of her were six full bottles of vodka.

"Look, Kenly, a new hiding place!" she mimicked into the empty air.

Within minutes, she'd taken down all six bottles and was dumping them into the kitchen sink—slowly at first, and then faster as she shook each bottle in anger. When she was finished, she lined them up against the fridge, where she knew he'd see them when he awoke. Then she went back to her bedroom and stretched out on her bed, saying a silent prayer that he'd be able to keep this job and give Athabasca half a chance.

IT WAS A LITTLE AFTER FOUR THAT AFTERNOON WHEN KENLY slid down the hill into the ravine, pulling her baseball cap low over her eyes. School started in six days and as her fingers grazed the lump on her forehead again, she wondered if it would be gone by then. She came around the final bend in the path, stopped, and stood absolutely still. Hanging from every branch of the biggest tree, from the bottom of every floorboard, up each rung of the ladder, along the sides of the tree house, and on the cedar swing below, were hundreds and hundreds of blue balloons.

Tommy was leaning against a tree with Oscar snapped into his jacket, and when he saw her his face lit up. "Happy birthday," he said, motioning to the balloons.

She didn't answer. Couldn't. She just blinked in disbelief. Today was her sixteenth birthday, the sun was shooting through the branches of the trees onto the ground at her feet, and for a few seconds, she was speechless.

"H-how did you know?" she finally asked as she walked around the base of the tree house, staring up in awe.

He shrugged like it was no big deal. "Max asked how old you were a few weeks ago. You said you were turning sixteen on the twenty-fourth. I remembered."

"This would've taken you forever."

Tommy grinned and started up the ladder, holding Oscar tight against his chest with one arm. "Well, I did have help. Max lent me an old foot pump, Florence and Becky blew up fifty or so, and even Mom did a few dozen. Come on. I snuck us a couple beers from the fridge."

Kenly didn't trust her voice, certain that if she tried to talk she'd break down in noisy, gulping sobs and make a fool of herself. No one had ever given her anything this incredible before. She reached for the ladder, and when her fingers brushed against one of the balloons, she knew for sure. That in all of this colorful chaos, with hundreds of balloons tied to a tree house in the middle of nowhere, she finally felt like she belonged somewhere.

chapter 7

KENLY'S LIFE IN ATHABASCA DIDN'T DIVE STRAIGHT into a ditch the first day of school. That didn't happen until the Friday of the second week in September, when she and Lexie were having lunch at the Athabasca Burger Bar. She was munching on some fries, the lump on her forehead was almost gone, she actually liked her teachers, and the other kids seemed only vaguely curious about who she even was so far.

"How embarrassing! She's all over him."

Kenly stopped chewing. "Who?"

"The principal. *Miss McKinnon.* She has the hots for your dad. Look at her! She's almost pawing his clothes off."

Kenly swiveled in her seat and stared. Her dad was standing in line at the register with Nancy McKinnon next to him. She was wearing a black skirt with a crisp red jacket and she looked quite pretty, actually, when she smiled from behind all that tangled black hair that kept falling into her face. But when she brushed an imaginary piece of lint off his jacket, leaned in closer than was necessary to whisper something, and brushed her chest against his arm, Kenly quickly lost her appetite.

Lexie dipped her fingers into a bowl of gravy and touched them to her tongue, shaking her head. "Look at all that hair," she whispered. "I'll bet you ten bucks it's not her natural color." Kenly shot her a frown and groaned. If her chances at fitting in had been slim before, this new romance would kill them for sure.

THAT NIGHT SHE BARELY MANAGED TO MAKE IT THROUGH dinner, and only halfway through doing the dishes before bringing it up to him. "So what's going on with you and Ms. McKinnon?" she finally asked, handing him a dish to dry.

He arched one eyebrow and smiled. "We're . . . getting to know each other."

"But she's your boss!"

"What's your point?"

Kenly glared at him. "Aren't you risking your job if this doesn't work?"

Her dad exhaled, then answered like he was talking to a child and not his teenage daughter who'd seen him fall flat on his face more times than she could count. "I think I can handle this without your help."

Kenly wished she could thump him on the head, but instead she threw her hands in the air to let him see how ridiculous this whole thing was, sending soap flying everywhere. Her dad held up a finger to stop her from saying anything else, then set down his dish and left the room, officially ending their conversation.

FOR THE MOST PART, KENLY DIDN'T MIND NANCY, IF SHE wasn't drinking. At first, she was polite and she even acted a little shy when she came over to the house, but that quickly changed. Nancy started to relax and as soon as she had a few drinks, she'd head straight to the stereo, turn the volume up high, and become a dancing maniac, gyrating her hips around their living room and sliding her butt up against Kenly's dad's like some kind of sex-starved idiot.

Kenly blushed at first, but when she realized that Nancy didn't seem to care if she was in the room or not, and that her dad wasn't going to do anything about it, she got up and left. She marched straight into the kitchen, snatched a fistful of cigarettes from the pack her dad had left on the table, and made her way to the tree house, swearing under her breath. After all, the last thing her dad needed was any encouragement on the drinking side of things.

A few months after they starting dating, Nancy dropped by one night to make dinner and left a handful of magnets on the fridge. They were inspirational magnets, each offering a sage little piece of advice on how to improve your life, and it seemed that every time Kenly closed the fridge, one of them would fall to the floor. She never bothered to pick them up; she just kicked them under the fridge and stalked off. When she tried to tell her dad how much this bothered her, he didn't get it.

"You don't like the magnets?"

She rolled her eyes. "Well, it's kind of pushy, don't you think?"

"To be honest, I hadn't noticed them."

"It's not the magnets, Dad. It's that she has the nerve to put them on our fridge at all. Don't you get it?"

He crossed his arms while she paced around the kitchen. "I mean, how well do you really know Nancy anyhow? She comes along, dates you for a few months, then all of a sudden she's putting magnets on our *fridge*? What's with that?"

"They're just magnets, Kenly."

She dropped her face into the palm of one hand. "Yes, but a fridge is a very personal thing, Dad."

He stared at her, looking as confused as he had five minutes ago. Frustrated, she turned to leave, then stopped and fingered a loose thread on her sweatshirt. When she didn't say anything, he sighed. "Okay . . . what the hell is this really about?"

"She drinks too much," Kenly whispered, and when he didn't answer, she bit her lip, slipped down the hallway to her bedroom, and closed the door.

THAT FIRST YEAR IN ATHABASCA, KENLY'S LIFE SPLIT NEATLY into two halves, neither impacting the other and both equally important to her. First, there was school. If having a father as a teacher made everyone cautious of her, then having him date the principal gave her leprosy. Accepting it for what it was, Kenly dug into her classes with one goal in mind: get good grades and finish high school so she could move out and start her own life without her dad. Other than Lexie, Kenly didn't have many friends, so she stayed to herself and although Lexie was a year ahead of her, they still met for lunch every day.

The time she spent at home filled the second half of her life. Lexie lived ten miles out of town and took the bus home after school, so Kenly spent most of her time with Tommy, and it didn't take long before they had a routine all their own. Kenly got home from school, grabbed something to eat, and went straight to the tree house, where Tommy would be waiting for her. She watched him sketch and did her homework on the floor, stretched out next to him. They spent hours up there talking about their dreams—his of one day becoming a journalist, hers of becoming an artist. They saw each other almost every day and before long the tree house felt more like home than anywhere else.

"A good place for dreaming," Tommy would say.

"Somewhere to run to," she reminded him.

"Our special spot."

"Just ours," she agreed.

KENLY'S DAD AND NANCY QUICKLY BECAME INSEPARABLE. Either she was at their house or he was at hers, and since there wasn't much Kenly could do about it; she was at least grateful that he was managing to hold down his job.

In the middle of December, Max took her and Tommy out one Sunday to cut down Christmas trees. Kenly was so excited the night before that she could hardly sleep. She'd never cut down a tree before. Instead, she and her dad usually bought one Christmas Eve, picking from all the trees no one else had wanted. "And remember," he'd say, preempting an argument before they even got out of the car at the lot. "I'm not paying more than twenty bucks."

For years, they'd had every kind of tree imaginable—lopsided trees, trees missing half their branches, some that barely had any needles, and a few that were so small, it should've been illegal to sell them. *But not this year,* Kenly thought, smiling as she watched the moon cut in and out of the clouds through her bedroom window.

The next afternoon, she and Tommy bundled into snowsuits that made them look like the Michelin man, crammed wool caps on their heads, and jumped into Max's truck. Max had an old snowmobile and a sleigh that hooked onto the back. He drove half an hour north and unloaded both of them at what he said was "the perfect spot." Then he hooked up the sleigh and Tommy climbed in, pulling his knees against his chest and covering his face with a wool scarf.

Kenly sat behind Max on the snowmobile, her heart soaring and stomach dropping each time they climbed the rise of a hill and then careened down the other side. Going down a few of the steeper hills, she clutched Max's parka and held on so tight that she worried it might choke him. Max puttered past some spots and drove like a madman through others, following a cut line as he looked for the best trees he could find.

They stopped more than once, crunching over snow-crusted trails with their necks craning up into the trees and their breath clouding the air. Everything was covered in a thick blanket of snow. It hung off all the tree branches, disguised rotting logs, and turned huge rocks into pillowlike mounds—a blanket of white wonder. In the end, they cut down three trees: one for Max, one for Tommy and Jean, and a third one for Kenly and her dad. They were the biggest and bushiest trees they could find, and after Max cut them down, they pulled them onto a tarp and wrapped them up using bungee cords. Then they tied the tarp to the sleigh, and slowly dragged them back to his truck.

It was dark by then and it took them half an hour to reload the snowmobile and sleigh, put the trees on top, and strap them onto the truck. While Max and Tommy finished up, Kenly knocked the snow from her boots and climbed into the truck, parking herself in the middle of the front seat.

As she unzipped her snowsuit, something outside caught her eye. When she inched forward, her eyes widened in wonder as she saw a mind-boggling display of twisting apparitions—ribbons of light that were flashing and dancing against the black sky. The sight was so unexpected, so thrilling, she just sat there and stared, mesmerized. First there was one, and then another, and another—beautiful swaths of light moving to a silent beat that no one else could hear.

When Tommy got in the truck, he glanced at her and smiled. "Aurora's sure doing a dance tonight, huh?"

Kenly frowned. "What?"

"Aurora Borealis is the official name but we call 'em northern lights," Max said as he climbed into the driver's seat.

"They're incredible," she whispered.

Max wrapped both arms around the steering wheel and as his long chiseled fingers twined together, a faraway look came over his face. "My father used to say that when the northern lights get up to dance, the gods are celebrating. You know, sort of like how a lipstick plant won't bloom unless there's harmony in your home."

Kenly looked at Tommy for help, but he just shrugged, like he had no idea. "Ever own a lipstick plant?" she whispered from one side of her mouth.

Tommy shook his head. "Nope. A money plant but never a lipstick plant."

Max laughed as he turned the truck around to head home.

Kenly looked back at the curtains of light arcing and bursting across the black sky behind them, determined to stay lost in the beauty of it for as long as she could.

They lost the first tree ten minutes later. Max hit the brakes and pulled over, but by then they had their snowsuits unzipped, the heat on high, and a Thermos of hot chocolate floating among them. Kenly groaned as she looked out the back window, then at her hands, curled around the warm Thermos in her lap. Going back out into the cold was the last thing she wanted to do, but Max and Tommy made her feel so guilty that she zipped back into her snowsuit and trudged along through the snow-filled ditch with them to rescue it.

They lost the second tree as they were rolling down the East Hill into town. Max stopped again, turned on his flashers, and they all climbed out to get it. By the time they pulled up in front of Tommy's house, they were laughing so hard, they could hardly unload the trees. Kenly was cold and tired, but thrilled with the tree they would have this year. Thinking about this, she turned around and was surprised to see her dad watching from their living-room window next door, icicles fringing the roof above where he stood and a rare smile on his face.

MAX SURPRISED EVERYONE IN JANUARY WHEN HE SAT TOMMY down and told him that he could launch his weekly "WIT" column in March. "Since you'll be finished with twelfth grade in June, let's see if you have a future in this." He grinned. "If not, at least we can say you tried." Tommy couldn't stop smiling. He spent every night for two weeks plotting and planning the best way to position the column and his enthusiasm was unshakable.

Kenly helped him create a quarter-page ad that ran in *The Athabasca Press* every week during January announcing the column's launch in March, and the response they got surprised everyone, even Max. Tommy let her read all the letters that came in and asked her to help pick out the ones she thought he should respond to. Some were touching and others narrow-minded, but a solid mix of people from around the region wrote in about their problems, and Kenly had a few favorites she pinned to one wall of the tree house.

Dear WIT,

My best friend is dating this guy I can't stand and I'm worried sick. He has a ponytail and he wears an earring. I just know he's into drugs big-time and he's so quiet it totally freaks me out. I wish she'd stop seeing him! Do you think I should tell her how I feel?

—Concerned

Dear Concerned,

Just because he has a ponytail and an earring doesn't mean he's into drugs. He could love yoga or tap dancing, but this is her boyfriend, not yours, so I think you need to keep your opinion to yourself.

—WIT

Dear WIT,

I'm the guy with the ponytail and earring someone wrote in about last week. Just for the record, I don't smoke, drink, or do drugs. Actually, I'm a vegetarian and my thing is painting. Thanks for your support.

—Future Picasso

Dear WIT,

My fiancé told me if I don't lose thirty pounds before June he'll call off our wedding. I've tried every gimmick I can find, but nothing works. Know any diets that work fast? I need to lose four pounds a week (not counting Easter or the May long week-end 'cause I can't diet when all that food is floating around under my nose).

—Starving in Athabasca

Dear Starving,

Cancel the wedding, forget the crazy diets, and ask yourself if you think you'll ever make this guy happy. My guess is probably not, so why try to skinny-down just to please him? In your shoes, I'd dump the guy, but then I think I'd take a good look at the scale and consider my health, too.

—WIT

Feedback about the "WIT" column varied, but it struck a chord and got people talking. Tommy's comments were straight to the point, filled with common sense, and not always what the reader wanted to hear. In March, the column received a dozen letters a week from the region, but by May that number had doubled.

One Friday afternoon in late May, Tommy and Kenly were heading to the tree house with the mail for that week's "WIT" column when Oscar's distant barking stopped them. "He's been alone all day," Tommy said over his shoulder. "Max and Mom are in Edmonton and they won't be back until later."

Kenly smiled. "Then let's bring him with us."

They retraced the path back to Max's house and could hear Oscar whimpering from the open kitchen window. Tommy opened the door and dropped his knapsack. "Hey, buddy, it's me." He wrestled with Oscar on the floor while Kenly went to use the bathroom.

She flipped the tap on to wash her hands, then saw a book, bent at the spine and balanced on the side of Max's bathtub. Twisting her head to one side, she read the title while she dried her hands: *Older Men, Younger Women*. She sat on the toilet seat and picked it up. Some of the pages were dog-eared and certain paragraphs were highlighted in yellow, with notes written in the margins. Smiling, she flipped through it, part of her feeling guilty, but the other side curious about who Max was interested in.

"You coming?" Tommy called through the door.

She laid the book over the edge of the tub. "Be right there."

Tommy locked the door behind them and they ran across the backyard. Kenly was about to tell him about the book when she heard voices and grabbed his elbow. They stood next to Max's garage for a few seconds; then she shook her head. *Can't be.* Tommy held up a hand, gesturing for a little more time, and Kenly froze, the conversation on the other side of the garage as plain now as if she were right there.

"Can we go for dinner sometime this week?" Max asked.

There was a pause; then Tommy's mom answered, a smile in her voice. "I'll see if I can slip away Wednesday night."

"Where do you want to go?" Max asked.

Kenly lifted both eyebrows as Tommy's face twisted into a look of astonishment.

"Doesn't matter. I never taste the food anyhow." Max's voice was upbeat and over-the-moon.

Tommy looked uncomfortable as Oscar squirmed, his back legs pumping under Tommy's jacket. Kenly chewed at her lip, knowing they were stuck here until Max and Jean went inside and they could slip along the back of the garage and down into the ravine.

They joked back and forth for a minute or two, Jean chiding him about his poor eating habits and Max teasing her about her addiction to nurturing everyone.

Tommy adjusted Oscar and turned his back to Kenly, leaning against the garage.

Finally, "See you tomorrow," Max said softly.

There was a moment of silence, maybe while he kissed her; then Jean said, "You can count on it."

After they left, Tommy and Kenly fidgeted for a few minutes; then Tommy took off, running along the side of the garage, and slip-sliding down the path into the ravine below. Kenly wasn't far behind, glancing over her shoulder to make sure they hadn't been seen, and wondering if Tommy was upset about what they'd heard.

When they got to the tree house, she was panting as she pushed her hair back behind her ears and Tommy was in front of her doing the same thing. He unbuttoned his jacket, tossed it down on the ground next to the tree, and set Oscar on it. Then he wheeled and ran for the creek, sloshing in past his knees; high-stepping until the water hit his hips. Turning, he grinned at her, arms thrown wide. "This is great!" he yelled, spinning around and splashing in the water as if he were a little kid again. "Isn't this great?"

Kenly laughed. "Yeah, it's great, but if you don't get out of that water, I'm gonna have to smack you."

"Maybe they'll get married."

She crossed her arms, thinking he looked like an advertisement for Halloween with wet hair plastered to his face and every lump on him turning purple from the cold water. Flipping a thumb in the direction of the tree house, she raised her voice and said, "Get out of the water, *now.* Tommy, it's freezing."

He laughed and lost his footing as he tried to climb out, falling onto his back in the water. Standing up, he shook himself off and tried again, this time making it. Kenly handed him his jacket, suddenly hoping this was how she would always remember him. Face bright, eyes alive, and water squishing from his sneakers as he scooped Oscar into his arms and made his way up the ladder to the tree house.

"You're crazy," she muttered, climbing up behind him and dropping to the floor.

But he seemed pleased with himself. Yanking a blanket off the mattress, he pulled it over his knees and grinned, dabbing at his face with one corner as his thin body was racked now and then with involuntary shivers.

Kenly lit a cigarette and reached for the pickle jar she used as an ashtray. "I wonder how long they've been hiding it."

Tommy shrugged and hit the play button on his boom box. "Who knows."

Supertramp blared into the air and Kenly frowned, then turned the volume down. "Does it bother you, though? I mean, why wouldn't they just tell you?"

He shrugged, huddling under the blanket. "Maybe they don't want to upset me."

"You never get upset," she reminded him.

He pried off his wet shoes, looking perplexed. "Well, it's all right, don't you think? For them to be seeing each other?"

Kenly took another drag from her cigarette. "Of course."

"Then who cares. I'm sure they'll tell me eventually."

The high drama was wearing off now. He had circles under his eyes that hadn't been there twenty minutes before, and his head and shoulders were shivering. He stretched his legs out in front of him and said, "Man, I gotta get some dry clothes on."

Kenly nodded and stubbed out her cigarette. Although she offered to carry Oscar, Tommy wanted the warmth against his chest, so he buttoned him back into his jacket and they set off down the path, taking longer than usual to get home. When they did, it was almost dark and Kenly could hear his teeth chattering as he climbed the back steps to his house. The screen door opened and Jean's voice, muffled with alarm, carried through the air as Kenly made her way across their backyard.

"Oh, my God! What happened?"

Kenly turned around and watched them, lit from the light of their back door. Jean was rubbing Tommy's shoulders in small tight circles with the heels of her hands to warm him up, but Tommy just laughed. "I fell in the creek. It's no big deal."

Jean took his face in her hands and kissed him hard on his forehead. "Everything you do is a big deal to me. You're my son." She slid her arm around him and as they eased through the door together, Kenly stood there in the dark, trying to remember how it used to feel to be smothered by her own mother's kisses.

chapter 8

A man's dying is more
the survivor's affair than his own.

—THOMAS MANN

KENLY SPRINTED ACROSS THE NAYLORS' BACKYARD,
pulling air into her lungs with eager anticipation. Max's car
was parked out front, so she knew they were home from the hospital.
It was June 20, and her first year of school in Athabasca had almost finished without Tommy. He'd started coughing a few days after he had
jumped in the creek and within days he was rushed to Edmonton. His
doctors confirmed he had pneumonia, then took a series of X rays that
showed a previously undetected tumor growing down his windpipe
and around both lungs. He was diagnosed with stage-four lymphoma
twelve hours later, which was confirmed by the head of oncology.

Jean still hadn't told Tommy this when they surgically removed the
mass and learned that the tissue was normal, shocking everyone. He
didn't have stage-four lymphoma. Apparently his thymus gland had
never stopped growing. It had traveled down his torso undetected,
and looped itself around his lungs and a few other organs. The doctors explained that they'd never seen this before and Tommy was kept
in the hospital for another ten days.

The bad news came later. After countless tests, Tommy was diagnosed with Proteus Syndrome, a rare disease first identified in 1979. It was given its name based on the Greek god Proteus (the polymorphous), because of the different manifestations found in four unrelated boys who were first identified with the syndrome.

Only a few dozen cases had been diagnosed in the world so far, but Tommy had many of the conditions common to the syndrome—overgrowth of one side of the face or body, discolored skin, and, most commonly, benign tumors that popped up throughout the body; some under the skin, some on the surface. People suffering from it often had large skulls and an overgrowth of tissue on the soles of their feet. It caused excessive growth of the skin, bones, and internal organs. Essentially, parts of the body just didn't stop growing.

Tommy's long-term prognosis wasn't good. Complications from the surgeries he would need over the years would play a large part in his shortened life span and, on top of that, his emphysema was worsening, diminishing his lung capacity further. Then they broke the news that another tumor had been found on his colon and he would now have to be scanned every month so it could be monitored. Once he recovered and was physically stronger, it, too, would have to be removed. When Tommy was finally released from the hospital, Max and Jean were waiting to bring him home.

Kenly walked into the Naylors' kitchen and saw Oscar, lying with his back against the wall and his legs twitching in sleep. Max was palming a cup of tea at the table. Smiling, he slapped his thighs and rose to hug her. "Good to see you, kiddo."

Jean was on the phone, face drawn and looking thinner than a week ago. She smiled, cocked her head toward the stairs, and mouthed, "He's waiting for you."

"How is he?" Kenly asked Max.

"Glad to be home. He asked about you and Oscar the minute we got here. I carried Oscar over so he could see him and they were all over each other."

Kenly managed a dry swallow and fought the impulse to run up the stairs instead of walk, but her excitement was quickly overshadowed by reality when she stepped into his bedroom. Tommy's face was the color of putty, purplish half-moons sagged under his eyes, and his hair was plastered against his head from what looked like a weak attempt at fixing it. Muffled voices floated up from the kitchen as she stood in the doorway.

"Hey, how are you?"

He opened his eyes. "Between us, this is just my way of getting attention," he answered in a raspy voice.

Kenly nodded as if she thought so, then tilted her head to his chest. "Does it hurt?"

"No." But he said it with a forced casualness that told her it did.

For a panicky moment she thought she was going to cry. No matter how many ways she'd played this out in her mind over the last few weeks, this wasn't how it was supposed to go. He could be sick. She could do sick. He could even be terminally ill if he really had to be. She could find a way to deal with that, too. But he couldn't die. That was something she knew she couldn't handle.

Tommy swung a slack arm at her leg. "Hey, lighten up."

She kept her eyes on the floor, wanting to tell him that she was scared. Instead, she knelt beside him and laid her head on his arm. He closed his eyes and neither of them talked. After a few minutes, he fell back asleep and she squeezed his hand and tucked the blanket around him. Since the first time she'd met him, he'd never looked this frail. His breathing came in fits and spurts, more random than in any kind of pattern, and his chest rattled like something was loose inside. Everything about him looked more fragile than it had before. Even the puckered flesh on his face was paler than usual, paper-thin from weeks spent in a hospital bed.

She puttered around his room looking at the posters he'd pinned to his walls and on the ceiling. Billy Joel's face was plastered everywhere, and Tommy's jean jacket—the same one he always carried Oscar in— lay tossed on the back of a chair. There were dozens of newspapers stacked in three separate piles against one wall, with colored markers sticking out here and there to track various columns he'd read. On his desk were a few textbooks on journalism and a carefully organized stack of audiotapes. A yellow piece of paper caught her eye, tucked into the mirror over his desk. Leaning closer, Kenly read it, recognizing his handwriting: *Self-pity is a waste of time.*

Her eyes filled with tears and she chewed on her bottom lip. If anyone asked her if she'd like to parachute from a plane, she'd sputter with indecision and then probably say no, but if they asked Tommy, she knew he'd be the first in line. She shook her head, smiling with admiration. "You do everything with such optimism," she whispered, leaning down to kiss him on the cheek. Straightening, she thought of the one magnet on their fridge at home that hadn't fallen to the floor yet. It was the only one that had ever made sense to her and it applied to a few people in her life right now: *The worst kind of pain is watching someone you love in pain.*

EVEN THOUGH TOMMY WAS SICK, KENLY STILL HAD SCHOOL TO finish, so she threw herself into exams with as much focus as she could manage. Although Lexie would graduate this year and Tommy would be getting his twelfth-grade equivalency degree through correspondence school, she still had another year left. She'd also been preparing for a year-end meeting with the student council to propose the formation of a movie club. It would bring in popular movies, promote them around town, then offer them at the school's auditorium on weekends. She and Tommy had researched the costs involved, believing Athabasca's lack of a movie theater gave the school an opportunity that couldn't miss. She was excited about bringing the idea to life and on her way home from the meeting in June, she couldn't wait to tell Tommy it had been accepted for start-up in September.

When she ran down the hill, Nancy and her dad were arguing on the sidewalk in front of the house, voices rising and falling together as they tried to outdo each other. They stopped as Kenly got closer and her dad tapped his fingers against the roof of Nancy's car, something he usually did when he was upset. He reached out to hug Nancy, but she grabbed his arms and lowered them to his sides. His mouth pinched into a thin line and he nodded like he got the point, then kissed her on the cheek before she climbed into her car and drove away.

"Everything okay?" Kenly asked.

Her dad met her eyes briefly, then looked away. "Who knows," he said, tossing one hand in the air before heading inside the house.

Kenly trudged along behind him, licking a finger and holding it up in the air. "Well, it sure doesn't look like the wind's blowing your way," she said.

That night her dad was so testy, she decided to tune him out and focus on her last big exam. She was in her room when he knocked on the door an hour later.

"Kenly? I need to talk to you."

"Okay." She flipped over and propped herself on an elbow.

The door popped open and he stood there, eyes bulging as he laid down the law about her stealing his cigarettes. "And if you think I'm stupid, think again," he said. "I know when you take them and I want you to damned well stop!"

Fighting the natural impulse to argue with him, Kenly nodded. "You're right. I shouldn't be taking them and I'm sorry. It won't happen again."

He blinked at her, managed a brisk nod, and then closed the door on his way out.

LEXIE GRADUATED FROM HIGH SCHOOL IN JUNE AND STUNNED everyone when she announced that she was moving to Toronto to live with her mom. Kenly tried to reason with her one night at the fire pit after everyone else had gone home.

"But Lex, you haven't heard from her in ages. Then she phones you out of the blue and you decide to ditch your plans for college here so you can go live with her in Toronto?"

Lexie shrugged like it was no big deal. "I can go to college next year."

"You're crazy and this doesn't make sense," Kenly said, tossing her arms in the air. "How many stories have you told me about waking up as a kid and finding your mom passed out naked on the couch with some strange guy? And what about that time she took off and left you alone for three days when you were only ten? Why would you want to go live with her now?"

Lexie made a fist and coughed into it, refusing to answer.

Kenly kept pressing. "Come on, Lexie. She was caught shoplifting *twice* when you were with her and you told me she was even too drunk to take you to school when you started first grade, remember?"

"She's my mom."

"And that means she has the right to ruin your life, too?"

"No," Lexie whispered. "It just means that maybe she deserves a second chance."

Kenly slumped back into her chair, surprised at her anger. "Why don't you go work in Toronto for the summer and then come back to Edmonton in September and go to NAIT like you planned?"

Lexie lifted her chin a notch. "Uncle Walter said if I go to Toronto, even for the summer, he won't pay for my tuition at NAIT this fall, so that's not an option."

Kenly stared at her hard. "Lex, you're just starting your life and you're already settling for less. Don't you want more?"

Lexie gave her a condescending smirk. "And what about you? Think you've got it all planned out, Kenly? What are you gonna do a year from now? Head out into the world and make it as a famous artist? I don't think so."

Kenly gave her a long stare, but didn't answer. She knew Lexie didn't mean what she was saying, but it made her mad anyhow. She pushed out of the chair and was halfway across the Naylors' backyard when Lexie's voice stopped her.

"Wait . . . Kenly, come back. I'm sorry."

Kenly turned and went back, but she didn't sit down. Instead, she leaned both elbows against the back of an Adirondack chair and stared into the fire.

"She told me she loves me," Lexie said with childlike vulnerability.

"So do I," Kenly said softly. "You're the closest thing I've ever had to a sister."

Lexie nodded, looking everywhere but at Kenly; then she flicked an ant off her jeans. "You know, I read somewhere that sisters have to be there for each other, no matter what. That they have to support each other through all of life's ups and downs, even when one of them tanks or makes a really bad decision."

Tears sprang to Kenly's eyes.

Lexie snuck a look at her. "Sounds like a good rule, doesn't it?"

"Sounds like it should be a law," Kenly whispered.

SCHOOL FINISHED WITH A WHIMPER FOR KENLY THAT YEAR, and even though it meant saying good-bye to Lexie, she was glad to have summer arrive. With Lexie gone and Tommy recuperating in bed, she was bored, so when Max asked if she could help with the "WIT" column until Tommy was feeling better, she gladly accepted.

Her dad spent July focused on drinking and when weeks went by with no word from Nancy, Kenly guessed that they had split up; another reason for him to be as miserable as he was. Tommy made a few trips to the tree house that summer, but he'd lost weight and was weaker than he'd been before, so he didn't feel up to it often. Kenly rigged up her hammock inside the tree house and started sleeping there. At least way up there she could get away from her dad and the misery he was drowning in.

The big news of the summer was that Walter and Florence were getting married a year to the day that he'd stripped and danced around the fire pit for her. Max was there and Becky was maid of honor. Kenly and her dad were invited. Jean baked the cake and Walter surprised everyone when he flew Lexie home from Toronto to join them. Even Tommy felt well enough to attend the service and dinner. Sixty

Athabascans gathered to watch Florence smile nonstop while Walter strutted around like a rooster. Kenly had never seen him in anything other than coveralls or jeans, but that day he was wearing a crisp navy suit and had even gotten his hair cut. He should have been wearing a sign that said LOOK AT MY BEAUTIFUL WIFE because he glowed every time he smiled at Florence.

A malignant tumor had been removed from Walter's bladder six months earlier and he'd been given a cautious clean bill of health just weeks before the wedding. The farm had sold earlier that year and he and Lexie had moved in with Florence and Becky, surprising everyone. Two days after the wedding, he and Florence flew to Denmark for the honeymoon they'd always dreamed of, and their favorite part of the trip was the time they spent at the Tivoli amusement park.

Kenly didn't learn that her dad had been fired again until the middle of August, when she overheard Becky ask Max about it in hushed whispers at the fire pit. As soon as she did, she pushed herself out of her chair and ran home with her heart racing. Her dad was slouched deep into the couch with his feet propped on the coffee table when she stormed into the living room.

"When were you going to tell me?" she asked.

He shrugged and his face took on a look of weary concern, like maybe he'd expected eye rolling and irritation from her but not this.

"I'm not leaving," she said, even though in the back of her mind she knew she couldn't stay in Canada unless he did.

He stared at her for a few seconds. "Well, there you are."

He'd always raised her like he wasn't interested or wished he could give her back so Kenly wondered now if he'd try to talk her out of it, but he didn't. Fighting back tears, she left the room, and he followed, leaning against the bathroom door as she filled the bathtub and tossed in a handful of bath beads. Neither of them spoke and when the tub was finally full, she turned off both taps and sat there waiting for him to say something.

"I'm going on a canoe trip tomorrow," he said. "Think you'll be okay for a few days?"

"Who you going with?"

"A couple of friends."

He said it like it was no big deal. Like he went on canoe trips all the time and she was supposed to believe he had friends who did, too. Kenly turned away. It had been years since he'd gone canoeing and even more since he'd gone with anyone other than her. She tossed her hair over one shoulder, pushing aside a gnawing feeling of fear she couldn't put her finger on.

He suddenly went pale and blinked at her like he was seeing her for the first time. "Jesus, you look like your mother."

"That one's a little tired, don't you think?"

He laughed, low and amazed. "You have her mouth, too."

She tried to avoid his eyes. Words were marching through her head as she waved him away with one hand, but what actually came out sounded nasty, even to her own ears. "If you're going camping, you'll probably need an extra canoe just to carry the booze, huh?" Written in black letters just below the bathtub taps were the words *American Standard*, and she was tracing each letter with one of her fingers when he slammed his fist against the door so hard that she jumped back, startled.

"I don't need this shit from you!" Grabbing her by the arm, he pulled her to her feet and threw her against the bathroom wall. The smell of booze on his breath made her stomach lurch and his eyes had the same glassy look they had the last time he'd gotten fired. Refusing to look away, she stared into his face and waited. His fingers finally loosened and he let go, swallowing hard as he staggered back into the hallway and away from her.

"Have a good trip," she said in a flat voice, shutting the door firmly in his face.

IT WAS EARLY SUNDAY MORNING WHEN MAX AND JEAN CAME to the door. Kenly had fallen asleep on the couch the night before, so when the doorbell rang she sat up, blinking in confusion. She pulled the door open and smiled, but neither of them smiled back. They looked uncomfortable, Jean shifting from one hip to the other and Max fingering the top button of his old flannel jacket. Kenly lifted her eyebrows, nervous now as the stirrings of panic took hold somewhere in the back of her mind. Something wasn't right.

Max stepped inside, holding her elbow as he ushered her to the couch. Her pulse quickened and she didn't take her eyes from his face. She wanted to ask what was wrong, but couldn't get the words out.

He took her hand. "Kenly, we have bad news."

She nodded, eyes locked on to his as she braced for what he still hadn't said. Jean sat next to her, sliding an arm around her waist as she murmured that everything would be okay. Kenly nodded reflexively, but she knew now that it probably wouldn't be.

Oh, God, she thought. *Something's really wrong here.*

Jean kept her eyes down and Kenly turned to Max. He shifted forward on the chair as she waited, almost holding her breath. Her arm hairs stood on end and the room went still when he told her that her dad was dead. She heard the words, flinched, and took a quick breath, but all she could think about was how old Max looked, sitting there wringing his hands like that.

". . . and when the police got there he was already dead. I'm sorry, Kenly. There wasn't anything they could do."

She blinked, shaking her head to make room for what he'd just told her, and as the shock set in, she wanted him to say it again, certain that she must have heard him wrong. "I just . . . I don't understand."

Max dropped his eyes. "Your dad committed suicide, Kenly."

It was suddenly quiet.

Kenly dropped her shoulders and stared ahead at nothing. Nodding, she got up and told them she'd be fine, then went down the hallway to her room and curled up on her bed. Weeks later she would remember Jean and Max sitting with her, their backs against the headboard of her bed and their arms wrapped around her as she cried.

For two days, Kenly absorbed what she'd been told in disbelief, but when Grandma Alister arrived from the States, it took only a matter of seconds for her to understand, better than she would have liked to, what her dad's suicide had done to both of them. Grandma was at the table when Kenly came into the kitchen, looking much older than she remembered and with balls of damp Kleenex surrounding her on the floor.

Kenly leaned against the door and fought the urge to cry. The bony ribs on Grandma's back were pressed against a wrinkled blouse that had been tucked into a pair of gray slacks. Gone was the rock-solid, things-will-be-okay confidence that normally rolled off of her in thick waves, and gone was the hair that Kenly loved, replaced now with a badly permed and much shorter version that hung in withered curls against her face.

Grandma turned and lifted both arms. "Ah, my sweet girl," she said and Kenly almost fell into them, fighting an illogical urge to beg her to put things back the way they had been before. "We'll soldier on together now, won't we?" she whispered, and Kenly nodded.

The funeral was arranged and someone asked Kenly if she wanted to choose something for her dad to wear. She did, but an hour later she fell asleep on his bed, curled into a ball and surrounded by clothes that she'd thrown around his room in anger. His favorite tweed jacket lay on the floor in a corner now, next to a pile of crumpled dress shirts. Scattered across his dresser were dozens of ties, and his jeans were in a heap at the foot of his closet.

The morning of the funeral Grandma had to prod Kenly to get dressed more than once. She wanted to stay in bed, where it was warm and safe, and where she didn't have to face what had happened. She moved like a robot until she walked in the front doors of the church, then stopped and swayed as she took in the faces of the people who had gathered to say good-bye to her dad. Her feet wouldn't move and her eyes locked onto the gleaming casket at the front of the church. The lid was open and she could see his fingers laced together peacefully against his chest. Turning, she almost jogged to the back of the church and had to grab hold of a pew to steady herself. She stood there sucking in jarring breaths of air through her mouth and the service had to be delayed while Grandma and Jean talked to her.

No, she wasn't sitting up front, thanks. Sitting right here would be just fine. No, she didn't want anyone to sit with her and could they leave her alone for now?

In the end, a handful of people sat at the front of the church in the first three pews, but Kenly sat alone, in the very last row and as close to the door as she could get, doing her best not to listen to the minister's voice as he told everyone about her dad. How he'd loved teaching and had left his impression on so many lives by doing it well. Or how he'd enjoyed the outdoors and had spent so much time camping and hiking with his wife when he was younger. And how, as a son and a father, he would be sorely missed.

Back at the house that afternoon, her eyes moved slowly around the living room from where she sat in her dad's favorite chair. She watched Max, Jean, and even Tommy as they tried to make everyone feel welcome, and if it weren't such an awful time, she might have seen some humor in how people reacted to Tommy. A few who'd come from out of town jumped back, startled when he held out a hand and introduced himself, while others went pale when he answered the door. He hadn't gone to the service, but had managed to get dressed and come to the house afterward. Kenly's eyes settled on Grandma as she drawled her way through yet another story about "her Steven" when he was in college.

"He was so in love with Lara that he couldn't even see straight," she said, pausing to blow her nose.

"Of course he loved her," Kenly said, raising her voice. "He loved her so much he had none leftover for anyone else, did he? That's why people kill themselves right? Because they're too damned selfish to care about how it will make anyone else feel?"

Standing on shaky legs, she curled her hands into fists and stared into their faces, daring any of them to disagree with her. Everyone lowered their eyes, startled by the outburst and unsure of what to say. It was Tommy who came to her defense, instinctively and with an unflagging confidence that surprised even Kenly.

"This is hard for her," he told them, crossing the room to stand beside her.

Kenly nodded woodenly.

"And it's healthy to say what's on her mind," he explained, taking her by the elbow.

"Healthy," she repeated, her voice a mere whisper now.

He led her to her bedroom, pulled off her sandals, and tucked her in. Then he lingered, in case she needed him. Kenly had turned off the part of herself that wanted to cry and scream. The piece of her that had stood in the kitchen in her pajamas the night before, yelling until she was hoarse. Now she pulled the duvet comforter up and folded her hands on her stomach, listening to the clatter of pots and pans from the kitchen as someone cleaned up. Half an hour later, the steady rise and fall of voices faded as people began to leave.

"You should get some sleep," Tommy said.

She shook her head no, but closed her eyes.

Ten minutes later, he pulled the comforter up around her shoulders, then stood staring at her while she slept. He knew he should leave, but couldn't. Instead, he watched the soft rise and fall of her chest, wanting to reach out and run a finger along her cheek. He couldn't help how he felt about her. If anyone told him it wasn't logical or that he was being unrealistic, he would be the first to agree. From the outside looking in, it made no sense at all, but he also knew they'd see it differently if they felt the way he did. Turning off the light, he closed the door and left, knowing that he'd do anything Kenly asked, even though he was certain she never would.

chapter 9

KENLY DIDN'T WANT TO OPEN HER EYES. IT FELT like her body had been crushed into the mattress and the voices that drifted upstairs from the kitchen made her feel even worse. He may have been a drunk, but he was her dad and at least no one had ever worried about what to do with her when he was around. Max, Jean, and Grandma had explained the realities involving her dad's work visa the night before. How it had been approved for another year just weeks before he'd been fired and, as part of that process, how her paperwork had also been renewed. Which meant that even though she wasn't a Canadian citizen, she could stay in Athabasca to finish twelfth grade, although she couldn't live alone and had to be sponsored by a Canadian family. Max told her he would sign the sponsorship forms; then Jean and Tommy offered to let her move in with them. Overwhelmed, Kenly had thanked them all and slipped off to bed.

When she finally got up and made her way downstairs to the kitchen, Grandma was sitting at the table with Jean. Nervous, Kenly said, "Good morning," and slipped into the chair across from them. "Gran? I was wondering . . . could you . . . could you come live here with me?" It came out like a croak and sounded like a plea, but without an ounce of hesitation Grandma reached over and took her face between both weathered hands. "Of course. I'll stay as long as you need me."

A wave of relief rushed over Kenly, quickly followed by shame. She knew Grandma had just been accepted into a nursing home in Springfield, Illinois, after waiting more than a year to get in. She'd been born and raised in Springfield and had wanted to go back for years. In a phone call a month ago, Kenly had overheard her dad teasing Grandma about turning eighty in her old hometown, with a young male nurse standing beside her to blow out the candles.

"Thank you," Kenly whispered.

Grandma dipped one hand into the pocket of her sweater and withdrew a small envelope, then laid it on the table. Kenly saw her name scrawled across it in her dad's handwriting. Jean and Grandma watched her with protectiveness in their faces, worry pinching their eyes about what he might have written and how Kenly was going to react to it.

Kenly's heart started to pound. "I'll be fine," she said, not fully believing it herself, but feeling the need to say it for their benefit. Then she stood and went to her room where she curled up on her bed before ripping it open, wondering if it would be full of apologies and life-shit-on-me excuses for his past. She unfolded the letter, smoothed out the creases, and read.

Dear Kenly,

I'm sorry. This isn't about you, it's about me, and it wasn't supposed to turn out this way—none of it. Your mom and I were going to grow old together, but my drinking killed her before we had the chance. I told everyone she was driving the night of the accident, and they believed me. It's hard to look yourself in the eye after lying about something like that, especially because she begged me to let her drive, but I wouldn't listen. I laughed it off, took the keys, and told her everything would be fine. But it didn't turn out fine, did it? And it's haunted me every day for almost ten years.

Six drinks killed my wife. Kind of hard to believe. Would four have killed her? Or could I have gotten away with three, driven, and she'd still be here with us? I'll never know, but I can see now that it's starting to kill you too and I can't stand it anymore. Worse yet, I can't stand me anymore. I love you, Kenly, and I'm sorry.

Dad

She was pale and her hands were trembling as she folded the letter and tucked it into her pocket. Snatching her jacket, she slipped out the back door and ran nonstop to the tree house, sliding down the hill into the ravine, and then pushing her way along the trail through the bush after she made it up the other side.

When she finally got there and crawled up inside, she yanked the tin box down off the roof and dropped his letter in next to her mom's red scarf and sculpting tools and all of Tommy's things. Then she slammed the lid shut and placed it back up on the roof. Breathing hard, she sat down, lit a cigarette, and took a long drag, rocking back and forth with her eyes closed and her knees drawn to her chest.

THREE WEEKS TO THE DAY THAT HER DAD COMMITTED SUI-cide, Kenly woke to the sound of Grandma bustling up the stairs and into her bedroom. "Time to get up," she commanded, pulling back the curtains on her bedroom window. Kenly raised herself up on her elbows and frowned, trying to remember if there was some reason she was supposed to get up early today.

Grandma was standing at the end of her bed, hands on her hips and a jaunty little hat balanced on her head. Her hair was curled in waves that framed her face and she was wearing a cotton summer dress covered with gleaming butter-yellow daisies.

"What's going on?" Kenly asked.

Grandma glanced at her watch and tapped her fingers against the footboard of the bed, looking pleased with herself. "You're seventeen today. That's what's going on."

Kenly had a puzzled expression on her face. "And that means I have to get up at eight in the morning?"

"No, it means I can finally give you your present and I can't wait any longer, so get up." Before leaving she pointed at the door and told Kenly to be downstairs in five minutes.

Kenly rolled out of bed and managed to pull on a pair of sweat-pants before heading to the bathroom to wash her face. When she came downstairs and rounded the corner into the kitchen a few minutes later, Grandma was sitting at the table with Jean Naylor.

"Happy birthday, Kenly," Jean said, rising to hug her.

Before Kenly had time to ask what was going on there was a sudden flurry of activity on the back porch. Jean got up and held the door open wide while Tommy and Max maneuvered their way into the kitchen carrying something that was covered with an old bedsheet. Neither of them was moving very fast because they were hampered by the weight of whatever they were carrying. They set it in the middle of the floor and Tommy flopped into a chair. "Happy birthday," he said with a sheepish grin.

Grandma stepped over to the mysterious package, clamping and unclamping her hands. She was having trouble holding herself still and she beckoned for Kenly to join her, then pulled the sheet off. Kenly mouth dropped open and she gestured helplessly at her mother's studio stand, repaired now and in gleaming condition, as was the kickwheel with its flywheel. There was even an old face shield sitting on the seat.

"Happy birthday, sweetheart," Grandma said.

"But . . . h-how did you fix it?"

"I asked Max for some help, and after that, everyone got involved. Tommy found a new seat for the stool, Max repaired the kickwheel, and Walter soldered the flywheel back into place."

Kenly lowered herself into a kitchen chair, shaking her head with undisguised emotion. Her pajama top was wrinkled and her hair was a nest of messy curls, but her face was alive with promise, the way it hadn't been in weeks. "Thank you so much," she whispered, with tears in her eyes. "All of you."

—————

KENLY DREADED GOING BACK TO SCHOOL, KNOWING ALL EYES would be on her after what had happened with her dad, but she buried herself in her classwork and focused on applying to the two universities she'd chosen for their business programs.

"If you want to sculpt, then you should," her dad had said months ago. "But for God's sake, at least get a solid business degree to fall back on first, Kenly. After all, think about how many starving artists are out there who have no other way of making a living."

Kenly had bristled at first, and they'd argued about it for weeks, but now that he was gone, she knew she had to plan for the future. Having the ability to take care of herself was a top priority, so she decided that getting a business degree would be her first goal. She had the rest of her life to chase her dream to sculpt, and one day she would, when the time was right. Until then, never again would she live the way she and her dad had all these years, like nomads with no roots.

By October, Tommy was almost back to normal and had even put on some weight. He and Kenly immersed themselves in the "WIT" column and getting the movie club running and operational. The first movie was promoted and then promptly held over for a second week because of the overwhelming response. By Christmas, the club had offered nine movies and had made a fifteen-hundred-dollar profit. To thank her, the school awarded Kenly with a thousand-dollar scholarship to the university of her choice. Tommy was even more excited than she was.

In January they operated on him again and removed the tumor they'd been monitoring for months. He was home within a week and everyone was pleased with his progress. Then, on Tommy's birthday in February, Max offered him a permanent job with the newspaper writing his weekly column and helping to edit the paper.

Spring came and went uneventfully except for Kenly's acceptance to Northwestern University in Chicago, in its business administration program. She'd applied without telling anyone, certain she wouldn't be accepted, and when an envelope from Northwestern came in the mail, she'd tucked it into her jacket and run to the tree house. Going to Northwestern meant she would only be a few hours away from Grandma in Springfield and wouldn't have to go through the process of applying for a student visa if she stayed in Canada.

Tommy prodded her to open it. "If you don't, I will," he said, pausing from sketching a picture of Lexie into his collage.

Kenly was sitting cross-legged on the floor, her eyes glued to the envelope that she'd tacked on the wall. "What if it says I wasn't accepted?"

He shrugged. "Well, you still haven't heard from the University of Toronto yet, and I'm sure you'll get in there."

Max had talked her into applying to the University of Toronto, but something inside of her wanted to return to Chicago, back to where she'd known her mother and where her parents had first met. Tommy heaved a weary sigh, snatched the envelope off the wall, and handed it to her. "Open it," he commanded, and she did, hands shaking as she unfolded the letter. After she read it, she dropped her face into her hands and started to cry.

Tommy inched closer and gave her a hug. "I'm sorry, Kenly. You probably wouldn't have liked it there anyhow."

"No, Tommy." She laughed, waving the letter in the air between them. "I got in. I made it. I'm going back to Chicago!"

IT WAS THE LAST WEEK OF MAY WHEN KENLY CAME DOWN THE sidewalk from school one afternoon and saw Lexie sitting hunched on the front steps with her arms wrapped around her legs. The last time she'd seen her was at Walter and Florence's wedding nine months ago. Since then, they'd shared a few letters and Lexie had called her twice after her dad died, but for the most part, Kenly had no idea how things were going in Toronto for her.

"Lexie! What are you doing here?" she yelled, waving her arms in the air.

This was the kind of unexpected surprise Kenly needed right now.

She started to run and was in such a hurry that she almost tripped on her way down the hill. When she got to the bottom, she glanced up and saw that Lexie was wearing jeans with a scrubby sweatshirt and had dirty feet pressed into a pair of leather sandals.

"When did you get here?" she called out, crossing the road.

Lexie kept her head down and didn't answer.

Kenly started down the sidewalk, frowning. Something was wrong. At first, she didn't notice anything physically amiss, so she ran up the steps, leaned down, and threw one arm around Lexie, but Lexie flinched and twisted away, murmuring something unintelligible, her face in her hands.

Kenly dropped her books and crouched down in front of her. "Lexie? Hey, what's wrong?"

Lexie lifted her face and started to cry.

"Shh, shh," Kenly whispered, smoothing hair off Lexie's face and lifting her chin so she could see her better. "Are you okay? What is it?" And then her voice trailed off into silence. Lexie stared back, one of her eyes swollen half-shut and the other vacant and unblinking. Her face was pale and covered with straw-colored bruises that looked days old.

Kenly stiffened. "Oh, my God! What happened?" She pulled Lexie close and instinctively rocked her back and forth the way Kenly's mother had when she was a child.

"He . . . he locked the door," Lexie cried against her.

"Who, Lex? Who locked the door?"

"Then he slapped me and r-ripped my shirt off, and when he started t-touching me, h-he was laughing." Lexie's head swayed from side to side while her fingers clawed at Kenly's sweater, pulling on it as the words fell out of her in huge gasps. "He w-was so strong . . . I slapped him and c-clawed at him. I tried to get away. I really did, but he took me by the wrists and p-pushed me to my knees. Then he punched me and . . . I couldn't stop him."

Kenly gently took her arms and held her away. "Who, Lex? Who did this to you?"

Lexie shuddered and wiped at her face with the back of one hand, carrying on in an almost inaudible voice. "I-I screamed when he spread my legs. I screamed s-so loud, Kenly, so loud she had to have heard me in the next room, but the TV just kept getting l-louder and louder and she w-wouldn't come!"

She inched even closer, racked with fresh sobs as she pressed herself against Kenly, shaking and crying because there was nothing else she could do. "Kenly . . . h-he pinched and twisted at my nipples . . . then pinned me with his knees and pulled at my hair, g-grunting like a fucking pig, and *my mom wouldn't help me!*"

Kenly shivered, momentarily frozen by what she now knew had happened but didn't want to believe. Wrapping her arms around Lexie, she made shushing sounds, telling her that everything would be okay.

The front door popped open and Grandma Alister was suddenly there, plucking at Kenly's shoulder and flapping her arms in panic when she saw Lexie's black eye and swollen face. Someone called Lexie's uncle Walter, and then Max and Jean came minutes after he arrived with Florence. Jean bathed Lexie's face with a warm soapy washcloth and Grandma wrapped her gently in fat towels from the dryer.

Kenly paced the kitchen, feeling helpless while the RCMP questioned Lexie, Walter standing stubbornly at her side. Lexie told them that the guy who'd raped her had only been seeing her mom for a few weeks. "I t-told her he scared me," Lexie said in a raspy voice. "That he kept staring at me all the time."

"And she said . . ." The cop let his words trail away.

"That I was imagining things."

She said she didn't know his last name, that her mother had never called him anything other than Bill. He was six foot three, had a mustache and a thick black beard, looked like he was in his late forties, and drove a Harley-Davidson. As she described him, she stared at her hands, shaking uncontrollably. She explained how she'd caught a ride from Toronto to Regina with a friend after it happened, then pawned a ring to buy a bus ticket into Edmonton. Too ashamed to call her uncle Walter, she caught a ride into Athabasca with a friend who was on his way up to Fort McMurray.

When they were finished questioning her, Walter and Florence drove her to the hospital with Kenly sitting next to her in the back-seat. Beyond the obvious injuries on her face and some bruising on one shoulder, they also learned that she had a few cracked ribs.

An hour later, the RCMP were back to tell Lexie that her mother was no longer living at the address she'd given them and that she'd ap-parently quit her job at the diner where she'd been waitressing, too.

Lexie nodded, but didn't say anything. Then she stared out the window, covered her face with her hands, and started to cry.

Walter's eyes widened and he turned to Florence, hands out as he asked for help he didn't know how to give. Kenly stepped past them and squatted in front of her, gently pulling Lexie's hands away. "Take deep breaths," she counseled.

"She's my m-mother, Kenly."

"No, she's not," Kenly said softly, using her thumb to clear away tears from under Lexie's eyes. "You see, I read somewhere that moth-ers lose the right to be mothers when they sit back and allow their daughters to get raped in the next room."

Lexie's eyes filled with fresh tears as she looked at her. "S-sounds like a good rule."

Kenly tried to smile. "Sounds like it should be a law."

And then Lexie was crying all over again and Kenly was trying not to, as Florence's hands fluttered in the air above them and Walter paced in circles, on the verge of tears himself. That day was the only time Lexie ever talked about what had happened, but Kenly never forgot the pain or fear in her eyes as she did—a haunted look that told you she'd survived something she never should've had to face in the first place.

ONE LATE JUNE MORNING WHILE GRANDMA WAS BEGINNING TO pack to leave for Springfield, Kenly toured the house her dad had rented, feeling an overwhelming sense of sadness. She was excited about moving to Chicago and starting at Northwestern University. It was the beginning of her future, the start of a new life she'd been dreaming about for years, but she knew it wouldn't be easy to leave. Athabasca had become home, even though she wasn't a Canadian citizen and knew she couldn't stay forever. She had lived here for two years, longer than she'd lived anywhere since her mom had died.

The night before, Grandma must have sensed what was bothering her because on her way to bed she stopped to give Kenly a hug and said, "When life closes a door, it usually opens a window." Kenly sighed as she slid into her hammock on the back porch and stared at Max's empty fire pit. "Fair enough," she said. "It's just too bad we can't bring the door with us when we go through the window."

Lexie spent the month of June living with her uncle Walter, slowly recuperating, though the emotional scars would never fully fade. Florence and Becky fawned over her, and Kenly and Tommy went out of their way to include her in everything they did, but she was far from the cocky, self-assured young woman they'd known before. She and Kenly were sitting at the fire pit one night after everyone else had left, wrapped in flannel jackets and with a bag of sunflower seeds floating between them.

"Is Chicago nice?" Lexie suddenly asked, tossing a handful of empty shells into the fire.

Kenly perked up. "It's great."

Lexie had been so quiet lately that having her talk at all was a treat. It had been worrying Kenly, watching this introverted, beaten-down version of her friend sitting so quiet and still around the fire each night. So now, she held her breath and waited for Lexie to say whatever was on her mind, knowing that if she pushed her, she might just close up and go silent again.

"You were born there, right?"

Kenly nodded. "We lived in Evanston until my mom died."

"So are you living on campus when you go back?"

"No. Grandma's paying for an apartment for me." Lexie lifted her eyebrows and Kenly flushed. "Only grandchild and all that."

"Have you ever thought about living with a roommate?"

"Not really. Why?"

Lexie suddenly looked shy, keeping her eyes on the fire as she fid-
dled with the buttons on her jacket. "Well, I've been doing a lot of
thinking, and I thought it might be nice to have a fresh start, you
know? Maybe move somewhere new, like Chicago for example, and
take a hair-styling course or something."

A slow smile spread over Kenly's face. "Most people couldn't live with
you."

"But not you," Lexie chimed.

"No," Kenly agreed, stretching out a foot to poke her in the leg. "Not
me."

"You should know that I don't do dishes," Lexie deadpanned.

"That's fine, 'cause we don't have any."

"I can't cook, either."

"Who needs food?"

"And I'm not good at moving."

Kenly leaned over and hugged her. "I'm an expert at it, so we'll do
fine."

THE LAST NIGHT THAT TOMMY AND KENLY SAW EACH OTHER
was filled with hard moments. She got to the tree house half an hour
after he did, noticed her hands shaking, and realized how nervous she
was about saying good-bye. This wouldn't be easy for either of them.
She crawled up the ladder and grinned as she pulled two bottles of
wine from her knapsack.

"White for me and red for you," she said, busying herself with the
corkscrew.

Tommy looked surprised, but grabbed two old coffee mugs down
from the top shelf. "Let me guess. Grandma Alister donated these for
your last night here?"

Kenly popped the first cork and laughed. "Hardly." Dropping her
eyes, she added, "Actually, I found a case in Dad's closet last fall when
I cleaned out some of his things."

They sat in silence while they drank, the sky fading to a dull gray, then to black. Tommy turned on the lantern and poured more wine, then popped Billy Joel into his boom box and leaned back with a satisfied smile.

Kenly rolled her eyes. "We're never going to agree on music, are we?"

"Let's put it this way. I might miss *you*, but I won't miss Bob Seger, Eric Clapton, or Lionel Ritchie when you're gone." He lifted his mug in a mock toast.

She appreciated his attempt at keeping things light. "Well, my plane leaves tomorrow morning at ten, so you don't have long to wait."

"Are you nervous?"

"Very."

"Excited, too?"

"In spurts."

Tommy took a sip of wine. "I'd give anything to be in your shoes right now. Your own apartment, a great university, a city filled with all those blues bands . . ."

Kenly looked at him for a few seconds, then put her wine down, and inched forward. "Why don't you look into it? There's gotta be a way for you to go. Northwestern has a great program for journalism. Maybe you could talk to your mom—"

He lifted a hand in the air to stop her. "Whoa! Slow down. It'll never happen, Kenly. You know it as well as I do. My life just doesn't have those kinds of options."

She dropped her eyes, feeling sick for him, not knowing what to say. Then he moved over and linked an arm through hers. "It's okay. I'll live through you and Lexie. Maybe every six months or so you two can take in a new blues band, then call and tell me all about it."

"About the band or what kind of trouble Lexie got into while we were there?"

Tommy smiled. "Both would be nice."

They took turns operating the boom box, listening to every kind of music imaginable, talking nonstop, then falling into companionable silence as they drank their wine. At one point, Tommy grabbed his sketchbook and started drawing her, tilting his head to the right and then to the left. Kenly stared out the window, past the bird feeders, and into the blackness of the trees cocooning them outside.

"You must miss your dad," he said suddenly, pulling her out of her reverie.

She blinked, fighting back an unexpected lump in her throat. "Yeah, I do. I miss him at the oddest times. Like when Grandma makes roast beef, I find myself cutting up extra onions and setting them off to the side for him. Or when the new phonebook arrived in March, because no matter where we lived, he always checked to see if we were listed when they came out. And I miss him whenever I see a man wearing a tie. I know that sounds nuts, but my dad wasn't a sloppy guy. He always wore a tie when he taught."

"Yes," Tommy said, "he did."

Kenly finished her wine and poured them each another mug full. "I overheard someone at his funeral say that living with him had robbed me of my childhood, and I guess that's true, but living with him also taught me stuff, you know?"

He gave her a sideways glance, but kept sketching. "Like what?"

"Like how to slow down moments most kids either don't notice or else take for granted. He wasn't a big talker, you know, but now and then he'd put his hand on my head as he walked by and when he did, it made me feel little again, and loved. The way I felt when my mom was still alive, when we were a family."

For a second neither of them spoke; then she let out a sigh that floated into the air between them. "I got to him, you know?"

Tommy frowned. "Got to him?"

She lifted her chin and nodded. "I heard him say he didn't want me once, but I knew him better than he knew himself. I knew everything about him. I knew all his hiding spots for booze, how he liked his toast almost burnt, what news channel was his favorite, even how he hated sleeping with a pillow. Everything."

She took a shaky breath and her bottom lip quivered. "And I know he thought having a kid in his life was going to be a headache, but in the end it wasn't as bad as he thought, because he could depend on me. No matter how bad things ever got and no matter who else gave up on him, I was always there." She turned and looked at Tommy with tears in her eyes. "I never left him, you know, not even once."

"No," he said, "you didn't."

"And in the end, he loved me for it," she said, her voice suddenly high and desperate.

He grabbed one of her hands and squeezed. "Of course he did."

Tommy finished his wine and asked if she wanted more. Kenly nodded and he refilled their mugs, watching her from the corner of his eye. "You're going to have to beat guys off with a stick at Northwestern," he said, meaning it, yet knowing she wouldn't take him seriously.

Kenly almost spit her wine up on the rug. Throwing her head back, she laughed and brought her hand up to his face, brushing his cheek with the backs of her fingers. "Oh, Tommy, what am I going to do without you?"

Don't go, he almost said, but instead he leaned in and kissed her before he could change his mind, then quickly put his fingers on her lips to keep her from talking. He climbed up on the wooden crate, pushed the board on the roof to one side, and pulled a package down into the tree house. It was wrapped in blue tissue paper and tied with a bow. He handed it to her and sat down, pressing his back against the wall.

"I wanted to give you this before you left."

Kenly fingered it in surprise. "But I didn't get you anything."

Frustrated, he pointed to the box. "Why do you find it so hard to accept things from other people? This isn't a form of emotional terrorism on my part, so relax. Open it, please. I promise, I don't expect you to run home and wrap up your stereo in return."

She peeled the paper away, careful to keep her head down. Inside was a tin box with a brass lock and key. "I thought you should have your own," Tommy said. And to her surprise, Kenly burst into tears. Even though she was free to chase her dreams now, Tommy wasn't, and she knew once she left here, things would never be the same again.

The lantern lit up her face and Tommy slid an arm around her waist as she cried, pulling her close with one hand resting between her ribs and hips. Kenly wiped at her tears, marveling at how gently he touched her, at how she didn't think of him as disfigured anymore. He was just Tommy, and when she was with him, she felt safe.

When she looked back on it later, everything about their last night together would seem dreamlike to her. Emotions were running high, time was running out, and soon she would have to say good-bye. They lay on the mattress propped on their elbows, drinking in silence as they listened to the Beatles, CCR, and then Carole King. After a few minutes, Kenly rolled onto her side to look out the window, feeling more than a little light-headed from the wine. Billy Joel was singing when Tommy leaned down and kissed her on the neck, the wine giving him courage he hadn't had before.

"Kenly, I need to tell you something," he whispered into her hair. She heard a catch in his voice as he fought with how to say something that obviously wasn't going to be easy to say. "My life . . . my life wasn't half as good before I met you."

She swallowed, conscious of his breathing, then rolled over and slid an arm around him, saying, "Oh, Tommy," embarrassed that he believed she was so much more than she really was. She tried to look into his eyes, but it was too much for her. The tenderness that filled them told her everything he couldn't say. That he didn't want her to go, that he would miss her when she did, that she meant the world to him. All things she knew—things that had been so close to the surface between them for so long, it seemed like he'd said them often.

The wine was getting to her and when Tommy ran a hand over her face, the sensation was so pleasant she felt herself go weak. He bent his head, found her mouth, and kissed her tentatively. This time she kissed back, and within minutes they were fumbling with their clothes. Without speaking, Tommy pulled his shirt off, then gently ran his hands over her breasts and down to her stomach, the sweet magic of skin touching skin bringing them both alive.

Her fingers skimmed his face, caring and uncritical, then traced the cauliflowerlike growth that ran down his right side. He turned away, dropping his eyes. "I'm sorry," she whispered, trying to imagine the pain he lived with every day, hoping she hadn't upset him.

Unlike experienced lovers who knew the intimate secrets of each other's bodies, Kenly and Tommy didn't. They were awkward with each other at first, but the wine helped. When their bodies finally came together, they were trembling with nervous anticipation, and Kenly buried her face in his neck and cried as they lost their virginity together on the floor of the tree house.

As they held each other after, she realized this wasn't like any other experience she'd ever known. Not even close to the three-month love fest she'd had at fourteen with a high-school football player in Boise. A guy so quiet that she couldn't get him to talk, but so gorgeous and confident, so sure of himself, he'd just assumed they'd sleep together— had even expected it. Pushing her down in the backseat of a friend's car and pawing at her, then shattering everything she'd ever thought of him by calling her a tease.

Or the guy she'd dated in Kalispell, a ski instructor of all things. She was fifteen and just starting to find her stride, not believing she was even remotely close to pretty. He was eighteen, already living on his own, saying she was gorgeous every time he turned around and telling her he'd do anything for her. Then all of his interest going out the window when she told him she wasn't ready and wanted to get to know him better first. The way he'd called her the next day and broken it off over the phone, saying she was too naïve for him. And how a wave of sadness had washed over her because what he was really saying was that he didn't give a damn about her. With tears still damp on her cheeks, Kenly took Tommy's hand in hers and fell asleep, proud to know him and glad that her first time had been with him.

Tommy lay propped on one elbow, watching her. He was tired, but he couldn't sleep. Couldn't imagine wasting one minute of their time together like that. Instead, he memorized the shape of her face, knowing that as soon as the sky lightened and the sun rose, she'd have to say good-bye. Knowing that no matter how he felt, it was time for her to leave.

Hours later, when Kenly's eyes fluttered open, she sat up looking uncomfortable. They said good morning and she got dressed, not meeting his eyes, making what happened between them the night before suddenly seem faraway from where they were right now. She looked everywhere but at his face, then slipped into her sandals, and fumbled through her knapsack looking for a hairbrush.

Tommy touched her arm. "Are you okay?"

"I'm fine," she said a little too quickly, "but I have to get going or I'll miss my flight."

Grabbing her knapsack, she stuffed her sweatshirt inside, then sighed as she looked around one last time. Tommy sensed her discomfort and felt the lid closing on the intimacy they'd shared the night before. The wall she put up between them might as well have been visible for how firmly it seemed to take shape.

Glancing at her watch, Kenly thought about everything she had to do before going to the airport. *I need something safe to think about,* she thought, giving him a hug. His eyes followed her as she shouldered her knapsack and pulled on the trapdoor. It was stuck and wouldn't budge, so she slammed a foot down on the floor next to it, then pulled again. Harder this time and with a determination that told him how badly she wanted to leave. It finally yanked free, but a loose screw flew through the air and landed on the rug near Tommy.

"Oh, shit!"

Tommy picked it up. "It can be fixed, Kenly," he said quietly. "Like most things, it can be fixed and it's not the end of the world."

She nodded, turning away. A lump formed in her throat and she didn't trust her voice. Then Tommy whispered, "I love you." So softly she wasn't sure she'd heard him right. So softly she wondered later if he'd even said it at all. And then it was time to leave, and as she climbed down the ladder his words were already fading, twisting back and forth the way words do when you analyze them too closely. At the edge of the bush she turned and waved, and by the time she got home, she'd already pushed his words aside as something she must have imagined, her mind shifting to the long trip ahead of her, determined to leave everything else behind and start looking at her future.

ATHABASCA'S REGIONAL AIRPORT TERMINAL WAS SMALL. THE front of the building was equipped end to end with windows that overlooked a single narrow runway, and the waiting room consisted of eight wooden high-back chairs, an oak coffee table, and a metal desk someone had pushed up against the far wall. Grandma had left the day before, so this morning Kenly had taken Athabasca's only taxi to the airport.

She was sitting with her back to him when Tommy came through the door. He had dark circles under his eyes and a pain in his chest that had nothing to do with his emphysema as he walked across the room. He sat down next to her, leaned forward, and balanced his elbows on his knees, watching a small plane outside on the runway.

"Can I borrow a cigarette?" he asked.

"You don't smoke."

"I'm gonna start."

"It could kill you," she reminded him.

"Can't be any worse than this."

She leaned over and hugged him. "I'm sorry, Tommy . . . I have to go."

"I know," he said, "but I'm going to miss you."

"Me, too."

Two words and his heart skipped a beat, wishing that it meant more than it did. He wanted her to stay, but chose his words carefully, making it as easy as possible for her to leave. "Kenly, there's something I want to tell you."

A soft intake of breath. "What?"

He looked back at the plane outside. "I want you to know that I spend the last few minutes of every day with you."

She looked at him, eyes brimming with tears.

"Every night I swallow four pills, check the air valve on my oxygen tank, and then fall asleep daydreaming about a world that doesn't exist and never will." He stopped for a second, doing his best not to look at her. This was a lot harder than he'd thought it would be. "It's the kind of world where I'm healthy. Where I'm normal and you . . . well, you're that someone special I'll never have the chance to meet. I meant what I said this morning. I do love you, but in a way you might never understand. There isn't a thing about you that's average. You laugh hard, you dream big, and you have this crazy enthusiasm that rolls off of you and wraps itself around everyone."

His voice was softer now, even tinged with pride. "You have the ability to make people believe that anything's possible, and for me, in the last few minutes of every day, it is. And I love you for that."

She dropped her knapsack on the floor and climbed into his lap, crying. When she wrapped her arms around his neck, he closed his eyes and breathed in the smell of her, the ache in his chest worse than anything he'd ever known. "I know you'll have an incredible life," he whispered, "and one day you'll have everything you've always dreamed of."

She didn't say anything, just squeezed his hand and stayed in his lap, alternately wiping away tears and blowing her nose until it was time to leave.

When her plane finally lifted into the air half an hour later, Tommy watched it disappear, then went home, packed a bag, and slowly made his way back to the tree house, where he spent the next few days alone. He didn't take Oscar with him, didn't feel like listening to music, and could've cared less about reading through the letters the "WIT" column had received that week. He felt empty now that she was gone. Max and Jean watched from a distance, giving him space and making sure they didn't stick their noses in.

"I'm worried about him," Jean finally said.

Max nodded. "I know, but his pain comes from being in love, and that's something you always said you hoped he'd have in his life."

Jean nodded, brushing tears off her face. Even though Max was right, she just wished it could've turned out differently than it had.

chapter 10

KENLY AND LEXIE WERE SHARING A TWO-BEDROOM ground-floor apartment just blocks from Northwestern University, and although it was good to see a familiar face at the end of each day, Lexie drove Kenly crazy at first.

"Trust me, you're gonna meet some real jerks on campus. I've heard some of those guys almost stalk you when they find out you're a first-year student."

"I'll be fine, Lex."

"Most of them are just looking for someone to ego-stroke them through the weekends."

"Doesn't matter. I'm not trying to meet anyone, Lex."

"Fine, but you still need to stay on your toes, Kenly. Take my advice. There are some real losers out there. Actually, I was thinking that maybe we could take a self-defense course together or something."

Kenly smiled as she gathered up a load of freshly folded laundry and headed to her bedroom. "I think the pepper spray you gave me will be just fine."

Lexie sighed and sank back into the couch, flipping through a handout from her cosmetology course with Thompson's School of Hair Design in downtown Chicago. Uncle Walter was paying for her tuition and monthly El passes, but she had to pay her own rent, so she'd registered for the fifteen-hundred-hour course, taking most of it through evening classes so she could work part-time at a salon.

THE BUSINESS PROGRAM KENLY HAD BEEN ACCEPTED INTO included a dozen students who were hand-picked for a mentorship add-on sponsored by Chicago's business community. The program started in July for incoming freshmen and carried through with the same mentor for a minimum of two years. To be accepted you needed a 3.5 GPA and three impeccable references; two from the academic field and one from your business community—Max had been hers. When Kenly's acceptance for this specific program came by registered mail in May, she'd had to read it twice to believe it. The mentors involved in the program had a history of success, were sponsored through their employers, and had each received an MBA from Northwestern University. Kenly met hers a week after she moved to Chicago.

"Kenly Alister?"

She was sitting in the reception area at ComTech Training. It was 10:00 A.M. Sunday morning and her appointment was scheduled for 10:15. Security had been given instructions to let her up the elevators. Other than a few fig trees and a stack of business magazines, she'd been alone for the last fifteen minutes.

"Uh, yeah," she managed, getting up and tossing her purse over one shoulder.

He stretched out a hand and smiled. "I'm Ross Lowen. Good to meet you."

Even though she was standing, he towered over her with green eyes that wouldn't quit, a golf shirt accentuating broad shoulders, and jeans that looked too good on him not to notice. Kenly felt awkward and suddenly very aware of herself. Was her skirt too short? Did she look professional enough?

He cleared his throat and waited for her to speak. She flushed, then blurted, "Sorry, I was expecting someone older."

He nodded, amused but not put off. "Well, I'm what you get, so let's get started."

She followed him down the hallway, shaking her head. Great. Even if she did look professional, the airhead comments weren't going to win her any points.

ComTech Training's head office took up the entire twenty-third floor. Kenly had been sent a package on the company earlier that week. They had eighteen locations across the Midwest, three in Europe, had been in business twelve years, and were considered a leader in technology training. The company sponsored two mentors from their management team each year in support of the business program she was in. Their intent was twofold. First, they had a corporate policy to support business students of Northwestern University, and, second, the students they mentored were often groomed and hired after they graduated. At twenty-six, Ross Lowen was already manager of ComTech's business development. *Great*, Kenly thought. *He's gorgeous and a brilliant overachiever. With my luck, he's probably a jerk.*

Ross gave her a tour of the office before they settled into an empty boardroom; then he flipped through a stack of files, distracted and in a hurry.

"All right, we need to schedule two hours a week together and I travel a lot, so are Sundays at noon okay for you?"

Kenly nodded, but didn't answer. Sundays were fine.

Ross glanced back to the paperwork in front of him. "Any other time just isn't as good for me, so if you don't mind . . ."

"Sounds good to me," she said.

He explained that the intent of this add-on to the business entrepreneurship program was to have her create a business plan for a start-up operation. In her case, it had to be a service-driven business, although she could propose the business model. Ross would guide her in its creation, taking her through the pros, cons, market analysis, and so on.

An hour later, after he'd outlined what they'd be working on for the first six months, they said good-bye, and when the elevator doors closed and it began its descent, Kenly leaned her forehead against the wall, smiling. Ross Lowen was gorgeous, and Sundays suddenly looked a lot better than they had yesterday.

THE FOLLOWING WEEK KENLY WAS DEBATING ABOUT WHAT TO wear and had a pile of clothes tossed in a heap on her bed when Lexie wandered in and sat down. "Let me see if I can help," she said, extending wet fingernails in front of her. "You want something casual with just a hint of sexy built in, right?"

Kenly nodded.

"And you want some kind of a reaction from him without necessarily letting him know you're interested, right?"

Kenly smiled. Sounded like a plan to her.

"Then wear what you had on last weekend."

She gave Lexie a blank look.

"Oh, come on! You didn't notice Sara Putnam cranked up to full-tilt pissed-off every time she caught her boyfriend drooling at you in the bar?"

Kenly flushed, embarrassed that she hadn't. Sara worked with Lexie at the hair salon and had invited them out for drinks a few times now.

"You were wearing jeans with a sheer cocoa-colored shirt over a black camisole I'd give anything to look that good in."

Kenly couldn't remember the boyfriend, but she knew the shirt. It was a see-through, button-down copy of a man's that she'd worn a few times. "You think it looks that good?" she asked, feeling skeptical.

Lexie was focused on painting her toes now. "No, but you did. Trust me, wear it with the black camisole underneath, and he won't be thinking about the company's bottom line."

WHEN THE ELEVATOR DOORS OPENED SUNDAY, ROSS WAS AT the reception desk with the phone against one ear, in a conversation that ended as soon as he saw her. Kenly made a mental note to thank Lexie. The cocoa-colored shirt showed off her tanned skin and the black silk camisole, and she was sure she saw a flicker of interest cross Ross's face when he saw her.

"Sorry I'm late," she said.

"No problem. Look . . . I know a park not far from here. Want to eat lunch there?"

"Sounds great."

They had hot dogs on a park bench and what should have been a one-hour lunch ended up being two, half of it spent in a conversation that had nothing to do with business. "So tell me, what do you like to do?" Ross asked at one point. "Bike, bungee jump, Rollerblade, downhill ski?"

Kenly brushed grass off her jeans, laughing. "Let me see. I love biking, but I've never tried bungee jumping and never will, and my downhill skiing needs some work."

"Ah, come on. How bad can you be?"

She grabbed a few files and stuffed them into her bag. "Trust me, just making it from the top of a hill down to the bottom once is enough to send anyone watching to the nearest bar. I've seen it happen."

They started back to the office. "So what you're saying is that when you go on a ski date you don't need skis?"

"Or poles," she shot back.

"Cheap date."

She smiled. "And you're guaranteed a good laugh."

"I'll keep that in mind."

I hope you do, she thought.

Ross was on her mind later that night when a romantic song she'd never paid attention to before came on the radio. Turning up the volume, she sat back and listened to the lyrics, thinking about how attracted she was to him and wondering what it would be like to have him kiss her. "That was Madonna with her hit single, 'Crazy for You,'" the announcer said.

Kenly scrambled to her feet, grabbed her purse, and rifled around for a pen. Scribbling the name of the song on the back of a check, she caught herself and stopped. *What's wrong with me? I hardly even know this guy.* She tossed the crumpled check into the garbage, crawled into bed, and turned off the light, but ten minutes later she was still awake, thinking about Ross. Flipping over, she buried her face in the pillow and groaned. He was her mentor. What was she thinking? Half an hour later, she tossed her pillow on the floor and let her mind wander wherever it wanted to, rationalizing that fantasizing about him wasn't *unhealthy.*

The next afternoon, a salesman at a local department store squinted at the name of the song she'd scribbled on her crumpled check, and minutes later Kenly left with a new Madonna tape in hand. That night she listened to "Crazy for You" over and over again, closing her eyes and swaying to the music until Lexie finally pounded on her bedroom door and begged her to turn it off. *I'm not delusional,* Kenly thought. *I mean, I know this isn't how things are with Ross and me, but there's nothing wrong with wishing it could be, is there?*

WHEN ROSS CALLED THAT SATURDAY AND ASKED IF SHE WANTED TO GO to dinner Sunday night instead of meeting at the office at noon, it caught her off-guard.

"Dinner?"

"You do eat, don't you?" he asked.

And so they went out for dinner. He brought his briefcase. She carried a binder and a handful of file folders. All of it got stacked on the empty chair next to them and forgotten. If you asked Kenly where they ate she'd have to think about it, because being with Ross was the only thing she was focused on. Their conversation moved from serious (the death of her parents and his dad's long battle with cancer) to light (her unshakable passion for art, his for hockey and the Chicago Black-hawks). When they left the restaurant, they dropped their things off in his car, picked up coffee to go, and went for a walk.

He told her he lived in his parents' old house in Barrington Hills, just outside of Chicago. His mom lived in Rockford now and his dad had died from cancer three years ago. He had an older sister who was married with two boys, both budding hockey players. They lived in La Grange and he tried to make it out to as many of their games as he could. Other than spending time with his family and a few friends, he said he was a workaholic. When he dropped her off, it was late, and the air between them filled with awkwardness. She undid her seat belt and thanked him for dinner as she got out.

"No problem," he said. "See you next week."

"Sure. Have fun climbing the corporate ladder."

Ross drove away determined to put her out of his mind, but when a hint of her perfume drifted through the air and he saw her sweater in the backseat, he knew he was in trouble. There was something different about Kenly. The first time he met her, he sensed wisdom beyond her years, but she also had an unusually quick mind, not to mention a breathtaking smile. When they were together he found it impossible to act normal around her and kept telling himself to sit on his hands; not to reach out and run a finger down her neck and definitely not to kiss her.

It wouldn't be a workable relationship, Kenly told herself as she crawled into bed. *He's eight years older than I am and I'd bore him to death.* But as she tossed and turned, trying to get to sleep, she couldn't get him off her mind.

This is insane, she thought the next morning. Snatching a hand towel, she pushed herself away from the sink. *Ross is all I think about. The way he smiles, his voice, his laugh. How his shirt pulls against his chest. God! I'm acting like an idiot.*

Lexie knocked on the bathroom door. "Are you gonna be a while?"

Kenly opened it and mumbled, "Morning," handing her a wet bar of soap as she slipped past her and down the hallway.

Lexie palmed it with distaste. "He's got her so-o-o bad," she muttered with a smile.

WHEN THEY WERE ON THEIR WAY DOWN THE ELEVATOR FOR lunch the following Sunday, as Ross was talking Kenly was imagining what it would be like to be stuck in there alone with him.

He stopped midsentence. "What's the matter?"

"Nothing."

"Then why are you smiling?"

The elevator doors opened and she stepped off, shrugging. "I was just wondering how long it would take for someone to come if the elevator ever got stuck." She wasn't sure, but she thought she saw a smile playing at the corners of his mouth.

"Probably a while, I'd think."

"Where to for lunch?" she asked, glancing at her watch.

They decided on a nearby deli, but then his pager went off and they had to make a quick stop at a pay phone so he could phone his partner. As he talked, Kenly leaned against the phone booth and waited for him. The conversation was short, but what she heard made her heart drop.

"That's great news. If they're in town next week, find out if we can do a presentation for them. Sure, the weekend is fine if we have to, but don't schedule anything for Sunday. I'm planning to spend the day with someone out on my boat so I won't be around."

He said good-bye and hung up, then touched Kenly's elbow and they made their way to the deli two doors down. She opened the door, stepped inside, and felt her appetite slide into a hole. *Damn! He's going to cancel our meeting next Sunday,* she thought. As she grew embarrassed about the subtle teasing she'd done in the elevator, the color rose in her face. *Of course, he's probably seeing someone. And why wouldn't he be?*

A rotund little man from behind the counter said hello to Ross and they shook hands. Kenly stepped away, looking through the glass at a variety of cold cuts and lunch specials, but her mind wasn't on food.

The thought of Ross seeing someone else bothered her more than it should have, more than made any sense. Suddenly he was there beside her, leaning over her shoulder until she felt like she couldn't breathe. She stepped away and surprised him by suggesting they take their sandwiches back to the office.

"You sure you want to do that?"

Even though she had no logical reason to be upset, she had to fight to keep the impatience from her voice. "I have to leave early today, so as long as you don't mind . . ."

On the walk back, she kept her face expressionless as they talked about how her business model was progressing. When she stepped onto the elevator, he followed, pressing the button for the twenty-third floor. Kenly pretended to dig for something in her purse. *Anything to get this damned elevator ride over with,* she thought. Leaning back against the handrail, Ross crossed his arms without taking his eyes off her.

A few seconds later the elevator slammed to a stop and Kenly was thrown off-balance, her arm instinctively flying out to grab the handrail. Eyes wide, she turned, realizing that Ross had just pushed the emergency stop button. She swallowed as he pushed himself to standing. "Let's see how long it *does* take someone to come." He wrapped one hand around hers, his thumb tracing small circles against her wrist as he leaned in closer. "I'm not sure what's going on with us," he whispered against her ear, "but maybe it's time we found out."

She felt the warmth of him against her and her chest rose faster with each breath. When he softly kissed her neck and slid his arms around her, she didn't stop him. Knew she wouldn't because she wanted him to touch her like this.

His lips glossed over her skin as he worked his way up her neck and then to the side of her face. She closed her eyes and bit her bottom lip. It felt so good to be with him like this. His fingers teased the skin on her back, slowly making their way down her arms, thumbs featherlight as they skimmed the sides of her breasts. She trembled as her fingers worked his shirt out from his jeans. Pulling it free, she slid her hands underneath and up to the hair on his chest.

He took a quick breath when she loosened his belt. Pleased, she in-stinctively slid her fingers under the waistband of his boxers, moving them across the skin of his hard stomach. He wrapped a hand around the back of her neck and pulled her to him roughly. She was breathing hard when he undid the zipper on her jeans and the intercom blared.

"This is security," a voice said. "You okay up there?"

Jolted back to reality, they pushed away from each other.

Ross sucked in a breath, running his hands through his hair. Turn-ing, he pressed the call button. "Uh . . . yeah. Everything's fine."

Kenly bit her lip again and buttoned her shirt, her body having a full-blown tantrum that they'd stopped doing what they'd been doing. The elevator rumbled to life, and when the doors opened a few sec-onds later, Ross was smiling, almost laughing, as he reached out and ran a finger down her nose. "Make sure you bring something warm next Sunday. It can get cold out on my boat when the sun goes down."

AFTER KENLY GOT HER THINGS FROM ROSS'S OFFICE, THEY SAID good-bye and a blush worked its way up her neck. On her way back down the elevator, she took a deep breath and rolled her shoulders a few times to pull herself together. She didn't need a man in her life right now and hadn't gone out looking to find one, and yet here she was falling for someone and there didn't seem to be anything she could do about it.

And to top it off he's my business mentor, she thought impatiently, dig-ging an Oh Henry! bar out of her purse. She took a bite and chewed as she worked through the pros and cons of this uncontrollable attrac-tion she seemed to have for Ross.

If this were a movie, I would move to Chicago to start my life over again, meet a Richard Gere look-alike with a villa in the south of France, fall in love beyond any level of logic, and say, "Who needs a business de-gree?" *But this isn't a movie. This is my life. And past experience proves that* nothing *in my life has ever even remotely resembled a movie.* "Which leaves me with one choice," she murmured to herself as she stepped off the elevator, licking chocolate from the corners of her mouth. "To stop this before anything serious gets started."

For the next three days she tried to keep busy, but her mind kept wandering to thoughts of Ross and his boyish, just-out-of-bed look she loved so much. Then, when he called Wednesday night to cancel their boat trip, disappointment slid down her back like an ice cube, even though she told herself it was for the best.

"I'm sorry, Kenly. There's just no way around it and this deal is important. The only day they can fit us in for this presentation is Sunday, so I don't have a choice."

"Don't worry about it."

"If you want to sit in, you're welcome to. It's scheduled for 2:30 and it'll only be half an hour or so."

"I'll pass," she said. "Anyhow, I don't want to distract you."

Ross paused and chuckled. "You *are* a distraction, but nothing can take my mind off business when I'm in that mode."

"Really?"

"Absolutely. Look, why don't you let me take you for dinner Sunday night to make up for it. I know the perfect place."

She hesitated, then decided that one dinner with him wouldn't hurt. "Where?" she asked.

"It's a surprise."

"Think I'll like it?"

"You'll love it."

IT WAS TWO O'CLOCK SUNDAY WHEN THE ELEVATOR DOORS opened on the twenty-third floor and Kenly stepped off. She was wearing a blue silk blouse, cut low enough to be interesting, but still professional, with a long silk skirt that hugged her curves and cut up the front when she walked, flashing some leg, but not enough to be considered out of line. "When you're done, *where* are we going for dinner?" she asked, standing in the doorway to Ross's office.

He looked up in surprise. "I thought you weren't coming."

Kenly smiled, shut the door, and walked to the window to look out at the Chicago skyline. "I changed my mind. Is that okay?"

Turning in his chair, he smiled, obviously glad to see her. "That's fine."

She moved closer. Their eyes met for a second; then she slid into a chair, crossing one leg over the other. Her skirt fell open even more, showing tanned, bare legs and some thigh, but she didn't fix it, just smiled, and said, "I hope your presentation goes well."

Ross's eyes narrowed; then he laughed. "Kenly, you *aren't* going to distract me."

She frowned. "Who said I was trying to?"

He stood and headed to the door. "When I said you couldn't distract me I meant it, but it wasn't a dare."

"Ross?"

He stopped, looked back, and waited.

"I just wanted to wish you luck. That's all."

But when she stood and walked past him, Kenly felt his eyes on her and smiled. "I'll grab coffee and meet you in the boardroom."

Ross shook his head and laughed, part of him sure that he'd read her right, but another wondering if maybe he hadn't. How he felt about her not only surprised him; it confused him. Yesterday he'd caught himself reaching to phone her after they closed a deal he and his partners had been working on for weeks. Lately, he just wanted to hear her voice and kept trying to imagine what it would be like to wake up with her curled up next to him in the morning. To hear her laugh and see her eyes light up with mischief the way they often did. She was intelligent and naturally intuitive about business, but what was even more unusual was how comfortable they were together. He'd dated some incredible women, but until now he'd never met anyone he wanted to spend this much time with.

He watched her leave, admiring the outline of her body until Joel called out down the hallway, "We're all set in the boardroom, Ross."

"I'll be right there," he said, bringing his mind back to where it needed to be.

chapter 11

THERE WERE THREE EXECUTIVES FROM THE COM-
pany Ross was trying to sell services to in the boardroom.
Carl Slater was the president of Shuster Manufacturing, and Ross
and Joel had been working with him for more than a month, analyz-
ing Shuster's business needs and putting together the proposal they
were presenting today. Ross introduced Kenly before they went in, explaining that she was part of ComTech's mentorship program and
there to observe. He was relaxed and the presentation well put together. It quickly became clear to everyone in the room that from a
fixed-cost standpoint Shuster Manufacturing had little flexibility, but
if they decided to outsource their internal training to ComTech their
staff development costs would drop by as much as 20 percent.

"The numbers are impressive," Carl said when Ross was done. "And
from a business standpoint it makes sense. The only issue we need to
work out relates to timing. Outsourcing will mean layoffs across the
Midwest and something like that has to be handled with care."

Carl held the elevator doors and shook Ross's hand.

"Give us a week to tackle the problems at our end and see if there's a fit."

The doors slid shut and Kenly turned to Ross. "Does it matter *who* their staff works for?"

He blinked at her in surprise. "What do you mean?"

"Well, this might not work," she said, feeling the heat rising in her neck, "but if layoffs are a reality behind an outsource like this, couldn't ComTech hire some of their staff? The benefits to both companies outweigh most of the negatives, don't they? Especially if you can use their staff on other projects for ComTech."

Joel looked at Ross, then slapped him on the back and laughed. "She's right. If there's media coverage over the outsource, it then gets a positive spin and their staff already knows how Shuster operates internally, which is a bonus to us."

Ross smiled, never taking his eyes off Kenly. "Okay. We'll call them in the morning and add it as an option to our proposal."

He nodded at Joel, took Kenly's elbow, and moved her down the hallway to his office.

"Your presentation was terrific," she said, watching him from the corner of her eye.

He dropped a file on his desk. "Did I promise you dinner?"

She slid into a chair, trying to gauge his mood. "Yes, but that was before I stuck my nose in on your deal like that in front of Joel, so if you want to cancel . . ."

He came around his desk, smiling. "Cancel? Oh no. Dinner is still on, and as for you sticking your nose in on this deal, I'll pay you back for that later."

Paying her back began on the drive out of downtown Chicago when Ross reached across the seat and handed her a rose, then took the scenic and more leisurely route to Barrington along Lakeshore Drive. They stopped at Lighthouse Beach and he showed her a spot where he and his parents often came when he was a kid. Kenly still had no clue where they were going ten minutes later and when she asked, Ross just smiled and shook his head.

"Remember, it's a surprise."

When he finally pulled into a driveway, he told her the surprise was dinner for two at his place. He opened the door and when they stepped inside Kenly saw that a table was already set outside on the back deck with a hurricane lamp lit and waiting for them. Ross told her the house was twenty years old, had three bedrooms and a small den, but she also saw that the yard backed onto a lake and was full of old oak trees. At almost a third of an acre, it seemed more like she was out in the country instead of a Chicago suburb.

Ross headed for the kitchen, tossing his coat on a chair. "Make yourself at home," he said. "I'll check on dinner, then get us a drink."

Kenly looked around. He'd decorated simply and had a good eye for taste. A few select pieces were placed throughout the room and caught her eye. The floor was hardwood with the exception of a big throw rug in front of the fireplace. The furniture was soft cowhide leather, set in a U shape around the fireplace, almost inviting you to drop down and settle in. She did just that, sliding her shoes off and leaning back, thinking how nice it would be to light the fire when he came into the room carrying a bottle of chilled white wine and two glasses.

"You told me I'd like it," she said. "So far, so good."

"Actually, I said you'd love it," he countered. "And you will."

"You mean there's more?"

"I haven't fed you yet. Where you eat and what you eat go hand in hand," he said, pouring a glass and handing it to her. "Save your judgment until the meal is done."

She smiled. "Fair enough."

Outside, the temperature had dropped, and it looked like a storm was moving in. Ross grabbed some birch firewood from the wood box and squatted to put it in the fireplace. After it was lit, he flipped through a handful of albums and put on some Van Morrison before glancing at his watch. "Dinner should be ready in ten minutes."

"And you cooked it?"

He shook his head, laughing. "Are you kidding? Cooking it myself would have you running for the door. My neighbor is a chef, so I did a little begging until he finally gave in and agreed to give me a hand."

"Are you trying to impress me?"

"Of course, but I'm also making sure I don't poison you."

The meal—lobster bisque soup, grilled salmon with mango, and fresh asparagus—was incredible. Kenly enjoyed sitting outside even when it started to rain partway through the meal. The deck was covered, so other than the few drops that landed on them when the wind picked up, it was wonderful. They learned a lot about each other over dinner, including how they both grew up too fast and became loners because of it.

"With my dad, it was either black or white," Ross confided. "There was never anything in between. He was either in great form or else boiling mad. The worst part was that you never knew what kind of mood he was going to be in or what might set him off."

Kenly gave him a hand clearing the table and they moved back inside. She could sense he didn't want to talk anymore about it and they suddenly became slightly awkward with each other. "My dad was an alcoholic," she offered, stacking the dishes on the counter. "And he couldn't hold down a job so we were always moving from one town to another."

Ross smiled. "I guess we both have our war wounds, huh?"

"With a few common threads, I'm sure. Like how I'm guessing you wouldn't have wanted to have friends over at your house either."

He nodded in agreement.

"Or how hard it was to see your friends' parents sitting in the stands when you were playing basketball and know your dad would never show up."

"Wait," he said, lifting a hand to stop her. "I've got one up on you there. Remember how things were either black or white with my dad? Well, spending time or money joining any kind of sports team was wasteful, so I wasn't even allowed to try out for basketball."

Kenly blinked at him in disbelief. "Oh, you're kidding. How pathetic is that?"

"Very," he said, taking her by the elbow and leading her into the other room.

His deck overlooked the lake and the view was so serene and peaceful that Kenly almost asked if they could sit outside for a while. Instead, Ross threw more wood on the fire and they sat on the rug to finish their wine. It was August, and that usually meant hot and humid in Chicago, but today it was cooler out and nice having the fresh air.

They spent the next few hours talking about anything and everything. Kenly told him all about her dad and how her mom had died years ago; how her grandmother lived in Springfield now; and how she wanted to get her business degree and then eventually an arts degree, too. Ross admitted that he loved his job and hoped to work his way into an executive position and then buy shares in the company. Everything about their evening together couldn't have been more perfect. The meal, the cool evening rain shower, the fire.

"Thanks for dinner," Kenly said finally.

He leaned over and kissed her. "You're welcome."

She pulled back a little, feeling awkward. "You know, I'm not sure about this. I mean, you're my mentor and—"

"Actually," he said, "I'm glad you brought it up, because on Monday I'm going to see if I can get you reassigned to Joel for the mentorship program."

Kenly's shoulders fell.

Ross slid an arm around her and laughed. "Or should we stick to 'strictly professional' and skip all this? Because in the end, it comes down to one or the other, and I don't plan to risk my job trying to hide the way I feel about you."

"You're right," she said, flushing. "It's just that I love working with you, that's all." But she actually didn't care, because she was too busy taking in what he was really saying. That this wasn't just a casual fling for him either, and that they were going to take things a lot further and see where their relationship went.

"We can still work together," he assured her. "Just unofficially."

"Sounds good," she said, trying not to smile as everything she'd been feeling over the last few weeks came bubbling back to the surface.

They sat there for a moment facing each other; then Ross kissed her again and whispered, "Close your eyes," and she did. "Maybe we should finish what we started the other day," he said against her neck as his hands slid across her shoulders. She nodded, already lost in what he was doing to her.

Featherlight, his fingers brushed against her skin as he unbuttoned her blouse and let it slide off her shoulders. Then he kissed her as he tugged at the ties on her skirt and it, too, fell away. He stood and undressed before lying back down next to her. Gently wrapping a hand around her neck, he pulled her to him. They were quivering as they explored each other's bodies. She slid her hands down his back and lifted her head, kissing his neck as she tried hard to pull him closer, but he resisted, holding himself above her with muscled arms as she made soft, whimpering sounds and arched her back toward him.

Lowering himself, he kissed her again, still holding back as her fingers pulled urgently against the skin on his back. He continued tasting her skin with his tongue, the way he felt right now so unexpected and thrilling that nothing mattered more than letting it happen. Then neither of them could stand it anymore, and their bodies finally came together with an urgency that made her cry out, moving against him as she bit his shoulder.

They spent the next hour curled around each other in front of the fire and what didn't come instinctively to Kenly, Ross showed her, gently coaxing as she learned to delight in his body and in hers. And when they were too exhausted to stay awake any longer, Kenly fell asleep with the flames of the fire dancing in the background and her face buried in the curve of his neck.

chapter 12

ROSS CAME INTO THE BEDROOM IN JEANS, TOWEL-
ing off his hair. He stopped and smiled at Kenly like he
knew the effect he had on her, then kissed her good morning, and
pulled back to study her with his eyes. They were both half-dressed and
she was trying hard to look casual, tugging on the T-shirt he'd given her
to wear earlier.

"Stop staring. It makes me nervous."

"You look good nervous."

He leaned over and ruffled her hair, then asked if she was on the
pill. Kenly avoided his eyes, feeling sheepish. "No, but I'll make an appointment and get some right away."

He glanced at his watch and pulled on a shirt. "Great. I'm heading
downstairs to make coffee. Want some?"

"Sounds good."

As soon as he left, Kenly rolled over, grabbed the phone on the
nightstand next to his bed, and called home. Lexie answered on the
first ring.

"Have you got *any* idea how worried I've been?"

Kenly sputtered, trying not to laugh. "I guess . . . I should've called."

"Wouldn't have hurt."

She flipped her pillow over and lay down. "Sorry, Lexie."

There was a pause; then a tap, tap, tapping in the background that told her Lexie really had been worried and was probably sitting at the kitchen table with a cigarette in one hand and her nail file in the other. "If you do it again, I'll have to beat you."

Kenly nodded. "Fair enough."

"Where are you anyway?"

"At Ross's," she whispered.

"Your drop-dead gorgeous mentor guy?"

"The one and only."

Lexie said, "Ahhhh," like it all made sense now.

Ross called upstairs asking her if she wanted toast. Kenly covered the phone and yelled back that she did. "I've gotta go," she whispered. "I'll see you tonight, okay?" She dropped the phone in its cradle with a click and rolled over smiling.

UNTIL NOW KENLY HAD HAD NO REAL UNDERSTANDING OF what it was like to be in love, so how she felt about Ross had her over-the-moon happy. Love songs she used to roll her eyes at now got cranked to full volume on the stereo, leaving Lexie exasperated. Distracted, she daydreamed in class and when the phone rang at home, she lunged for it, almost knocking Lexie over in the process. Now she understood the logic behind esoteric and mystical love poems. The people who wrote them weren't stoned the way Lexie said they were. They were just trying to capture the raw emotions of men and women in love, and that wasn't easy to do.

Over the next month, she and Ross were together as often as possible and they talked every day they weren't, even if he was out of town on business. Hearing his voice always made her day. She didn't feel like she had to be careful about what she said when she was with him, how she said it, or how he might take it. He just listened, never judging her or pushing her to change her point of view.

There wasn't anything Kenly felt she couldn't talk to Ross about, but she also loved the times when they *didn't* talk. Times when they worked side by side—her on case studies and him on business proposals—when she felt a sense of contentment, as if they were on the cusp of something incredible.

KENLY'S DENIAL CAME IN STAGES. IT SHOWED UP FIRST WHEN the alarm went off one morning in early October. Rolling over, she stretched and looked at her wall calendar. Ross wanted to go away for a weekend. "Just the two of us," he'd said. "When's best?" The next two weeks looked crazy. Her mind worked through her class schedule and she decided it would have to wait until the end of the month. Next, she tried to figure out when her period was due. After all, who needed that headache on a romantic weekend away. But the calendar wasn't giving her what she wanted. Nowhere on it did she see the *X* she always scribbled when it started each month.

Sitting up straight, she froze.

Every twenty-eight days. Never late, never a problem.

She touched the sides of her breasts in horror, realizing how tender and sore they'd been the last few weeks. Then her feet hit the floor hard and a tremor of fear went through her. *Oh, God, don't tell me . . .*

She showered in a daze and stood with the water pounding against her back until it went cold. Classes forgotten, she toweled off and ran to the drugstore. Then, after she got home, she sat on the edge of her unmade bed and read the instructions on a home pregnancy kit, unable to stop her hands from shaking. Closing her eyes, she took a few slow breaths, rationalizing that her system was all screwed up from taking the pill and that her cycles had gotten shifted around.

She tucked the box under her panties at the back of a drawer and swatted it shut before leaving the room. *I'm imagining things,* she chided herself. *After all, I'm on the pill, and other than our first time, we used condoms for two weeks until it started to kick in. I'm just late and with everything else that's been going on the last few months, I forgot to mark down when I had my last period, that's all.*

Out of sight, out of mind proved to be the second stage of her denial. She rationalized that when her period did come, she'd pull out the box and have a good laugh when she tossed it in the garbage, unopened. The box stayed there for a week, but her period didn't come.

The third stage involved general panic mixed in with a few full-blown anxiety attacks. Her breasts were getting worse and she was exhausted every morning now. It was getting so bad she was having trouble staying awake in her afternoon classes. When Lexie noticed and suggested that she see a doctor Kenly arranged the appointment two weeks to the day she'd bought the home pregnancy test kit that never did get opened.

The doctor was an older man. Nice, proper, and not outwardly judgmental, even when he confirmed her worst fears and she stared back at him, horrified. He handed her a box of Kleenex and did his best to console her when she dropped her face into her hands, crying uncontrollably. No, there was no one he could call for her and, no, this wasn't a planned pregnancy.

A few minutes later, he gently told her she should go off the pill now that she was pregnant and handed her a sample pack of vitamins. She took them and murmured her thanks, feeling numb. When she finally collected herself and stood to leave, her face was puffy and swollen from crying.

The next week was hell for her. She spent most of her time sleeping and her crying jags got even harder to explain. Knowing she was pregnant terrified her. At first she thought about having an abortion, seriously letting herself go there and consider it as a possibility. But then her mom came to mind, as did the conversation she'd overheard between her dad and Grandma when he said that he'd never wanted her. And in the end, Kenly knew that she'd never be able to have an abortion. The life growing inside of her was her responsibility now, and no matter how she looked at it, her world was about to get flipped upside down very soon.

"ROSS, I NEED TO TALK TO YOU."

They were parked outside a pizza place on Noyes Street near Northwestern University, but eating was the last thing on Kenly's mind.

He shifted sideways to look at her. "What's up?"

She swallowed, picking a spot on the dash to look at. "I'm not sure how to say this. The doctor I saw the other day? Well, he, uh, he told me I'm pregnant."

The words hung there between them and when she looked up he'd gone pale.

"Not the best news, is it?" she asked, biting her bottom lip.

And then she lost it. Just leaned against the door and started to cry. *Here I am, finally on my own and seeing someone I'm crazy about, and I get pregnant. Talk about timing from hell.* Neither of them said anything for a few minutes. Then Ross pulled her against his chest and set his chin on her head, which only made her cry harder.

"Let's get something to eat," he said, "and we'll talk."

Kenly couldn't look at him. She wiped her nose, adjusted her sweater, and got out of the car, silently thanking him for not driving away and leaving her there. After all, she'd had a week to get used to the idea, but he'd just had it tossed in his face like a glass of ice water.

Inside, Ross put his jacket over the back of a chair and sat down. "You okay?"

"Nope."

He nodded like this made sense, then ordered them both something to drink. She flipped through the menu, happy to hold on to anything right now. "Ross, I'm having this baby." It was all she could muster and the last few words squeaked out as she squared her shoulders.

He ran a finger around the rim of his water glass. "What about your degree?"

"I'll be okay. I'll just have to take a lighter course load after the baby's born. My dad's insurance pays for my tuition and Grandma put aside enough money to pay my rent each year so I don't have to work." She flipped her menu shut, lifting her chin. "I'll manage."

He sat back and crossed his arms. "It won't be easy."

"I know. Or at least I think I know, but I'm not quitting school."

Ross took a sip of coffee. "This will change a lot of things," he said simply.

Kenly knew this, but hearing him say it made her realize that she'd already made the decision to keep this baby, even if it meant losing Ross in the process. *Closing a door, opening a window,* she thought, fighting back a fresh wave of tears.

When their pizza came neither of them ate any and Kenly intentionally put some distance between them as the hour slid by, as much in self-defense as it was her way of making sure he didn't feel she was pressuring him for anything. They didn't talk much on the drive home and when Ross pulled up in front of her place, Kenly got out of the car before he could say anything. Leaning back in, she squeezed his hand. "Talk to you later."

"Wait, Kenly—"

"We'll talk later, Ross," she said, cutting him off and closing the car door.

She was inside hanging up her jacket when she heard his car slowly pull away. Not bothering to change, she climbed into bed and pulled her knees against her chest, feeling the colorless gray of the sky outside seeping through to her bones. *How am I going to manage with a baby?* she wondered. Her brain was clogged with thoughts of the future and how a baby was going to change everything.

chapter 13

LEXIE WENT PALE. FISHING IN HER PURSE FOR CIGA-
rettes, she lit one, dragged on it hard, then paced around
their tiny kitchen. "You're having a *baby*?"

"Well, I don't think it's gonna be a puppy."

"Oh, my gawd, Kenly. What are you going to do?"

"At some point, give birth." She took a tea towel and started drying
dishes.

"What does Ross think?" Lexie cut her a look as she continued pacing, then glanced down at her cigarette in horror and stubbed it out,
waving a hand through the air to clear away the smoke.

"What's to say? I'm pregnant and I'm having a baby."

She stopped pacing. "So he doesn't *want* the baby?" Kenly didn't
answer, just went into the living room and sat on the couch. Lexie
trailed behind. "Sorry. It's none of my business."

"I don't think he's passing out cigars right now," Kenly said. "But it
doesn't matter because I'm having this baby."

Lexie nodded, taking this in. "Okay . . . well, it doesn't matter, does it, 'cause we've got lots of room here, so everything's fine just the way it is."

Kenly stretched out a foot and poked her in the leg. "Thanks."

Lexie stood and yanked her T-shirt down over her thighs as if she were trying hard not to let the moment turn soft, but the look in her eyes told Kenly that she was already working on how the two of them would handle this together.

"Lexie? Don't go overboard, okay?"

"Of course not," she scoffed, but when she slid on her jacket and left for her evening class, Kenly saw a new bounce in her step and a gleam of something like excitement in her face.

ROSS HAD LEFT TWO MESSAGES IN THE LAST THREE DAYS, SO as soon as the door closed behind Lexie, Kenly grabbed the phone and dialed his number, almost hoping his answering machine would pick up instead.

He answered on the second ring. "Hello."

"Hey, it's me," she said.

He sounded relieved. "Okay, I forgive you."

"For what?"

"For not returning my calls."

"I . . . I just needed some room to breathe."

"Funny, I don't remember smothering you."

She ran a finger around the phone cord. "You weren't."

"Kenly, this is as much my baby as it is yours."

She sat up straight, nodding.

"So don't shut me out, okay?"

"I agree," she said, standing up and twisting the phone cord around one arm. "But I don't want you to be in this relationship because you feel obligated."

He cut in. "Kenly, I've been thinking about this for days and I've been worried sick about you, so just listen to me, *please*."

She sat on the couch and held herself still. "Okay."

His voice went soft. "No one's ever made me feel like you do and I don't want to throw that away. For the first time in my life, I feel like part of me overlaps into someone else and it takes me somewhere I've never been—somewhere I don't wanna leave. I keep waiting for it to wear off, but it doesn't. I won't see you for a few days and then you walk in, and I'm gone. Nothing else matters but how much I want to be with you."

She had one hand over her mouth, choked with emotion as she held back tears.

"Kenly?"

"Uh-huh."

"I miss you and I really want to see you."

Kenly was half laughing, half crying as she agreed to see him. In less than an hour he was there and it was so good to see him she almost forgot she was pregnant. Lexie was at her evening class, so Kenly saw an opportunity to sit down with Ross and talk about the baby, but no matter how hard she tried to be serious, he wouldn't let her. When she tried to talk to him, he nuzzled her neck, kissed her face, and put his fingers gently over her mouth. She punched his shoulder playfully, held him back with one arm, and told him she wanted to talk.

He shook his head no, said, "It can wait," and scooped her up like she weighed nothing.

"Ross, I mean it," she warned him as he carried her to the bedroom.

But he just tossed her lightly on the bed and shut the door. Stretching out next to her, he propped himself on an elbow, ran a finger down her nose, and grinned. Determined to make him listen, she sat up and crawled on top of him, elbowing his chest and banging her head against the headboard as she did.

He laughed, then flipped her over onto her back. "Are you always this cute when you're being a klutz?"

Lying under his propped elbows, she looked up at him and lost all perspective. She loved him and being with him was exactly where she wanted to be—today, tomorrow, and in the future. Within minutes she was so lost in what he was doing, she didn't care what day it was.

Half an hour later she fluffed her pillow and turned over as he wrapped himself around her in an exhausted heap. "'Night, school-girl," he whispered against her ear. She tweaked his thigh, stretched, and curled back against him, pushing away thoughts of the baby for now. *We'll talk about it tomorrow,* she promised herself.

The next morning, sun was streaming through the window when she woke. Ross was gone, but there was a note on her pillow next to a fresh banana-nut muffin wrapped in cellophane. *Eat healthy and I'll see you in four days. We can talk then. I'm off to Atlanta but I'll call tonight. Love, Ross.* Kenly pulled the blanket over her head, secretly pleased and yet still worried about how a baby was going to affect their rela-tionship.

THE DOOR TO HER APARTMENT POPPED OPEN JUST AS KENLY came trudging up the front sidewalk Saturday afternoon.

"You're home early, aren't you?" Lexie asked with a grin.

"I guess so." Kenly slipped off her sunglasses, then pointed to the Mazda RX-7 parked out front. "Ross is here?"

Lexie bounded down the sidewalk, dangling his car keys. "He cer-tainly is, and I'm out of here." She slid in, waved good-bye, and drove away. Kenly cocked her head, waited a half beat, and went inside.

"Hey, how are you feeling?" Ross asked, coming around the corner from the kitchen.

"Not bad. How was your trip?"

He started to massage her neck. "It was good."

She swiveled to face him. "Ross, I really think we need to talk."

"Relax. We will." He took her by the arm and guided her down the hallway to the bathroom, where a hot bath was waiting for her. "Take your time and when you get out, we'll eat dinner and then we'll talk."

She laughed and said, "You're crazy," but he just smiled and closed the door.

Kenly peeled off her clothes and slid in, feeling the hot water slip over her skin and wash away the achy feeling that she hadn't been able to shake all day. She soaped her legs and then ran a hand over her stomach, noticing a definite swell where there hadn't been one before, surprised that her body was already changing so much. Almost all of her clothes fit differently now. It felt like she was "thickening" from the inside out, and at the same time a calm had come over her she couldn't explain, a sense of belonging and peace whenever she thought of the child growing inside of her. Touching the tips of her fingers to her mouth, she thought of her mother and wondered if this was how she'd felt when she was pregnant.

The water was almost cold when she climbed out and toweled off, then pulled on jeans and a warm sweater. Brushing out her wet hair, she thought of how much her dad hadn't wanted kids and remembered how it had hurt to hear him say that. Setting the palm of one hand against her stomach, she lifted her chin a notch. *I promise your life will be as normal as I can make it,* she thought. *And you'll always feel loved and wanted.*

ROSS LOOKED UP TO SEE HER LEANING AGAINST THE KITCHEN doorway. The table was set, the lights were dim, and there were two candles burning.

"Feel better?" he asked.

She nodded, melting at his thoughtfulness. "You know, this is the second time you've made me dinner."

"Actually, it's takeout, but I'll settle for any credit I can get."

He was in good form. They talked about his trip to Atlanta, what was new at ComTech, and how her exams were going. What they didn't talk about hung in the air between them until he finally brought it up. "I stopped in at Leanne's today," he said.

Kenly got up to plug in the kettle for tea. Leanne was his sister, and Kenly had met her once at his office just the month before. Ross jammed both hands into the front pockets of his jeans and carried on. "We were talking and . . . well, I told her that you were pregnant."

Kenly felt something tug inside. "Really?"

He put his plate in the sink, then slid his arms around her waist from behind. "Kenly? Let's get married."

She had her back to him, her eyes on the kettle and her hands flat on the counter when she said no. "I want us to be sure," she said.

He started to say something, but she held up a hand and cut him off. "Ross, I'm serious. Think about it. We've only known each other a few months, so let's just leave things the way they are for now. Rushing into marriage and raising a child in a relationship that isn't rock-solid terrifies me."

He pulled her to him and rested his chin on her head. "Okay, fair enough."

But she was secretly pleased at the look of disappointment that came over his face, and thrilled when she didn't see any visible signs of relief after she'd turned him down.

TOMMY CALLED A WEEK LATER, AND A TREMOR OF GUILT SHOT through Kenly when she grabbed the phone and heard his voice. Although she'd talked to him a few times since she'd moved, she hadn't phoned him in weeks, mostly because she'd been preoccupied with Ross and finding out she was pregnant.

"Kenly? How are you?"

"Great. How about you?"

"Same dull routine. I just thought I'd check in and make sure you were all right."

She folded one leg over the other. "Actually, my classes are brutal, but I'm enjoying them."

"Great." He paused. "I called last week. Didn't you get the message?"

Nodding, she chewed on an already broken nail. "Yeah, sorry I didn't call back, but it's been nuts here."

"Hey, don't worry." He scoffed like it was no big deal. "I know how it can be."

But he didn't and she knew that as much as he did.

"So . . . how's the new boyfriend?" he asked.

Kenly sat up a little straighter. "Lexie told you?"

"Uh-huh."

She bounced one foot against the coffee table. "You know what? Meeting someone this fast was the last thing I ever thought would happen, but now that I have . . . well, anyhow, I think you'd like him, Tommy."

"No doubt. You have impeccable taste."

She felt him smiling at his end and wanted to thank him for lightening things up.

"How's Oscar?" she asked, changing the subject.

Good. Oscar was good.

"And my buddy, Max?"

Max was having some trouble with his back, but otherwise he was doing fine.

"What about him and your mom? Have they told you yet?"

Tommy chuckled. "No, but I'm having a good time watching and waiting."

"And you, Tommy? How are you?"

There was a pause before he told her that his emphysema was worse and that he was having trouble keeping weight on. "Mom's been running in circles the last few weeks trying to feed me," he said.

Kenly could imagine her standing in front of the stove, stirring a pot of soup, baking high-fat brownies, and cooking a turkey at the same time, just to fatten him up.

He told her the tumor they'd taken out last year had grown back and it had to come out in the next few months. "It's been stirring up a lot of trouble," he said. "Some days it feels like someone's throwing a party inside, but there's not much I can do about it."

Kenly closed her eyes. "God, Tommy, I'm sorry."

She wasn't sure how to tell him she was pregnant, but there was no way around it and in the end the words came rushing out when they both ran out of things to say. "Hey, you won't believe this, but I've got even more shocking news for you," she said.

The line went quiet. She fixed her eyes on the kitchen clock and heard the catch in her voice as clearly as he did. "Ross and I just found out we're having a baby."

There was silence for a few seconds; then his voice returned, only lower than before. "Wow, that's some news."

She stood and paced the room with nervous energy. "It scared the hell out of me at first, but I'm getting used to the idea now."

"Uh-huh . . . well, what about school?"

"I lightened my course load for this year, but I'm not quitting. I'll just get my degree a year later than I thought, that's all."

"And Ross?"

Pause. "What do you mean?"

His voice was impatient when he answered. "What does he think about all this?"

"I think it shocked him as much as it did me, but he's fine now. Even getting a little excited about it." She was doodling on a piece of paper as she talked. Small, tight circles. Her name, Ross's, Tommy's.

"Are you getting married or will you live together?"

He was pushing, and it startled her that he'd even ask. She felt a quaver in her throat, brought a hand up to her face, and brushed back some stray hair. The gesture felt the same and yet she knew nothing would ever really be the same again. She tried to keep her voice from shaking as she spoke. "When we decide what we're doing, we'll let everyone know."

One sentence that clearly said he'd crossed a line he shouldn't have. One sentence that told him, *This isn't something for you and me to share the way we used to.* Tommy cleared his throat and the line went silent for a few seconds. Kenly was sure his expression mirrored hers right now, so she asked him about the "WIT" column, trying to gain some solid ground before they said good-bye. He told her Max had finally agreed to adopt it as a permanent column.

"It's getting such positive feedback from the region that he and Mom are gonna cover for me when I go in for surgery or if I have a bad week and I'm not up to it." Kenly was relieved to hear some enthusiasm edging back into his voice as he talked. "Before I forget, I got you a subscription to the local paper so you can keep up with all the hot advice I'm dishing out."

She grinned. "You did?"

"It'll be mailed to you every week," Tommy said. "I thought it was the best way for you to stay in touch as I grow into a world-famous columnist."

"Sounds perfect."

"Hey, Kenly?"

"Yes?"

Pause. "I think you'll be a great mom."

"Thanks, Tommy," she whispered into the air after he'd hung up.

BALANCING HER PREGNANCY WITH SCHOOL WAS A LOT HARDER than she'd imagined, and getting six hours of sleep each night was almost impossible. Kenly and Ross talked on the phone at least once a day and she spent most weekends at his house, but his job had him traveling a lot that fall, so by the end of November he was frustrated and pushing her to move in with him.

Kenly pushed back. "I'm so busy at school right now that adding a move on top of everything else wouldn't make any sense." She was stretched out on the couch with her head in his lap, the small mound of her belly pressing against the maternity shirt she was wearing. "Let's wait until after the baby comes, okay?"

Her body was changing even more now. The thick waistband of her maternity pants quickly showed through all of her shirts. Her stomach spread, then widened, and finally pinched against anything that blocked it as it stubbornly kept right on going.

At one of her doctor appointments, her obstetrician examined her and then measured her stomach to see where things were. The heartbeat was steady and strong. Kenly didn't have any problems with her blood pressure, and her weight was just over where it should be. But then the doctor frowned, glanced at her chart, and measured Kenly's stomach again.

"I think I'm going to send you for an ultrasound," he said.

Her eyes widened. "Why? Is everything okay?"

He nodded. "I just want to make sure about a few things, that's all."

A week later, a lab technician squeezed a jellylike cream onto her stomach, then ran a probe up and over her belly until a very definite outline of a baby came up on the screen in front of her. Kenly's eyes were locked on to the computer screen with fascination and for the next few minutes she watched her baby stretch a clenched fist up to its mouth, flip over, twist onto its side, and press both feet hard against her tummy. She was overwhelmed with emotion and didn't trust herself to speak, wishing that Ross were here to see this. He'd had to fly to New York on business for a few days and wouldn't be home until the weekend.

Kenly swabbed her stomach clean and got dressed when the technician was done, a seismic happiness taking over her brain. The baby was doing fine, she and Ross were great, and life in general looked good.

An hour later her bubble had popped and she sat staring at the doctor in shock. She licked her lips and stammered, "Y-you're sure? Absolutely sure?"

"Absolutely. I'm estimating that you're twenty-two weeks pregnant, not sixteen, but the good news is that everything looks normal and the baby is doing fine." He smiled and patted Kenly's shoulder reassuringly. "At least this way the pregnancy will be shorter than you thought it would be."

After the door closed behind him, Kenly tried to find a way to accept what this meant. Her hands started to shake and with rising panic she searched her memory for something Tommy had said years ago—that because of all the chemotherapy he'd had, it would be impossible for him to ever get someone pregnant. Yes, they'd slept together once, but when she'd found out she was pregnant she'd automatically assumed it was Ross's child. She walked through the medical arts building in a daze, then made her way outside and down the block to a small park, where she stopped to rest on a bench.

You're twenty-two weeks pregnant, not sixteen—

Not sixteen.

"I don't believe this," she finally whispered, dropping her face into her hands. "Oh, my God. This baby isn't Ross's. It's Tommy's."

IT WAS LATE AFTERNOON WHEN SHE PUSHED HER WAY UP THE front steps and through the door, relieved that Ross was out of town and glad that Lexie had another evening class. She went down the hall to her bedroom, undressed, and got into bed, telling herself everything would be okay. And yet every time she tried to figure out a solution to this "problem" she felt as if she couldn't breathe. She loved Tommy and always would, but if there was a right way—a perfect way—to fall in love, find your match, and sail through life, she knew now that it was how she felt with Ross. That part she was sure about. So, in her mind, the three people involved in this picture were all neatly in their places. It was the fourth one, the tiny catalyst growing inside of her, that could change all of their lives.

"Are you okay?" Lexie asked at breakfast the next day.

Kenly reached for the paper. "I'm fine, just tired."

But it was almost impossible to act normal when, inside, she felt like she was going crazy. She had barely slept the night before and was dizzy getting out of bed this morning. Although the choice should've been simple, she was running from it, looking for any option other than what was painfully obvious. She knew she should tell Ross and Tommy the truth, but had barely managed to absorb the shock herself. *I need time to think about this,* she thought.

Tommy lived with a debilitating disease, dying a slow death, in a tiny room, in a small town, and in a life that she didn't want for her child. Shame washed over her. *What's the matter with you? He's one of your best friends. Good enough to sleep with, but not good enough to be the father of this child?*

No, she thought. *That's not it. I just need time to think about this.*

She made another appointment with her obstetrician and told him about Tommy's Proteus Syndrome. Concerned, he immediately sent her for another round of tests and arranged for a fetal assessment the next day. He explained that if the results were normal, as they had been so far, then she shouldn't be worried.

Kenly was terrified that her baby might have to live like Tommy did, being stared at or belittled because he looked like a monster. She almost made herself sick obsessing over it until the results finally came back a week later and she found out that the baby looked normal in every way. With that worry off her mind, she felt better, and yet she still didn't know how or when she was going to find the courage to tell Ross or Tommy the truth about this baby.

Shame made her toss and turn at night, unable to sleep as she struggled with what to do. She got home from school one afternoon, lay on the couch exhausted, and looked out the window, noticing sun dogs on either side of the sun—little red and yellow pieces of rainbow that Grandma used to say were a sure sign of an oncoming storm.

chapter 14

LEXIE BECAME AN OBSESSED FUTURE GODPARENT without ever being asked to take on the role. Almost weekly Kenly found something new stacked up in their dining room for the baby. There were receiving blankets, bottles, a mobile, a baby jumper, a bassinet, and even a baby monitor.

Kenly was stretched on the couch in their ground-floor apartment one afternoon when she saw a crib go past the window outside, then Lexie behind it, chin up and face beaming. She was dragging it down the street on wheels that desperately needed a shot of WD-40 and when she saw Kenly in the window, she grinned, pointing to the crib.

Kenly opened the door, laughing. "*What* are you doing?"

"I stopped at a garage sale on my way home and I couldn't pass it up," she said. "Look! It's like brand-new and they even included the mattress as part of the deal."

"That's great. How much do I owe you?"

Lexie balked. "Nothing. This is my gift for the baby."

Kenly shook her head and rubbed her growing belly with a smile. *I'm going to have to let her name you just to square things up,* she thought.

THE TWISTED HORMONAL VEIL THAT HAD TAKEN OVER Kenly's body during the first few months of her pregnancy returned full force at the end. Her appetite doubled, she slept like she was hibernating in half-hour spurts, spent most of the night waking up to go to the bathroom, and fantasized constantly about getting her body back to normal. In between, she studied for exams, kept up with the mentorship program requirements, and fell into bed each night exhausted.

Running her fingers over her stomach one morning, she felt the baby kick. Her stomach lurched first to the left, then quickly to the right, and her fingers trailed along behind until they ran into a tiny foot pressed against the palm of her hand. She took a quick breath, held herself still, and felt her throat close.

Time was slipping by and although she saw Ross all the time and talked to Tommy at least once a month, she still hadn't found the courage to tell either of them the truth. "Oh, God," she whispered to her belly. "I wish someone would take this decision out of my hands. I don't know what to do."

LEXIE WAS ON THE PHONE ONE NIGHT WHEN SHE WRINKLED her brow and stopped talking, then leaned into the hallway with a hand over the receiver.

"Kenly? You're due May fourth, right?"

Startled by the question, Kenly shifted to a new position on the couch, then nodded yes without taking her eyes off the TV. Her real due date was March 26, but when it had come and gone, the passage of each new day since had become suffocating. She was edgy and short-tempered, lumbering around the house distracted, or else sitting with both feet on the coffee table and a plate of food balanced on her tummy.

Now, she was lying on the couch with her knees drawn up and a pillow tucked underneath them as she watched the news. *I'm probably the only woman in history who's actually happy to be fifteen days overdue,* she thought.

Lexie bustled into the living room with two bowls of popcorn, exuding the kind of cockeyed optimism Kenly normally admired. The past few days she'd been a hand-wringing wreck, unsure of how to deal with Kenly's constant mood swings.

"I think you'll deliver early," she said, handing Kenly a bowl. "And I mean that only in the nicest possible way."

Kenly popped a handful of popcorn in her mouth and sulked in silence.

"Oh, and Tommy says hi."

"When did you talk to him?" Kenly asked, sitting up straighter.

"Just now." Lexie flicked a hand toward the kitchen, distracted. "He was at Uncle Walter's dropping something off when I called."

"And he didn't ask to talk to me?"

Lexie's hand was poised over her popcorn bowl and the look on her face said she sensed a hormonal pregnancy shift she hadn't seen coming. "Uh . . . no."

Kenly was irritated now. "What do you mean, 'no'?"

Lexie set the popcorn down and crossed her arms. "Let me see. He asked how you were. I told him. Then we talked about what it was like living with you right now and I dished that up pretty straight, too. When I asked if he wanted to talk to you, he passed. Shit, you can't blame him for avoiding a minefield when he sees one coming, Kenly. I mean, you aren't exactly *rolling* in social skills these days."

Kenly burst into tears. "You're right. I don't know how you and Ross can stand being around me right now."

Lexie sat next to her and hugged her. "Hey, it's okay. This will all be over soon. I have a feeling you'll go into labor when I'm away this weekend, that I'll come home on Monday and you'll already be home from the hospital, with Ross sitting here next to you."

Kenly blew her nose. "I sure hope so."

"Trust me, so do I," Lexie muttered. "Now, how about if you sit back, relax, and hand me one of your feet? We got a new nail color at the shop today and I want to see what it looks like on your toes."

ROSS WAS IN MINNEAPOLIS ON A BUSINESS TRIP WHEN KENLY finally went into labor two nights later. The tightening at the bottom of her belly that had woken her an hour earlier had now taken on a definite beginning, middle, and end. She leaned against the wall, braced for another contraction, and pushed Lexie's bedroom door open.

"I think this is it," she said, her voice weak.

Going from deep sleep to wide-eyed panic, Lexie sat up. *"Right now?"*

"As opposed to when it would be convenient for you, yes."

Lexie rubbed her eyes until she saw spots, then leaped out of bed, pulled on a pair of sweatpants, and rummaged around for a bra. "Okay, just stay calm. We can do this!"

"Good. You take the next contraction."

Lexie ignored her. "Did you call Ross?" she asked over her shoulder on her way into the kitchen.

The dull ache in Kenly's lower back was getting worse. "He doesn't get in from Minneapolis until nine this morning."

"Well, maybe we should call now. You know, leave him a message or something."

Kenly's face crunched into a grimace. "Okay. Can you do it?"

Lexie grabbed the phone and dialed, leaving a highly agitated message for Ross when his answering machine kicked in. Kenly was focused on her breathing, but she heard enough of it to make her smile. Something about how freaked out Lexie was, where the hell was he, and could he get his butt to the hospital 'cause no way was she cutting this kid's umbilical cord.

Kenly waved an arm in the air, frantically pointing to the door.

Gathering steam, Lexie helped her down the front steps, then to the curb where she'd parked her newly purchased, seven-hundred-dollar Chevette. Kenly eased herself in, twisting into a position where the least amount of pressure was on her pelvis. The car started on the third try and Lexie rocked it back and forth as she played with the gas and clutch, trying to slam it into first gear.

"I'm gonna kill the jerk who sold me this," she said.

"You're gonna kill me first."

"Sorry."

The next contraction came hard, peaking as they pulled onto Lincoln Avenue. Kenly closed her eyes and started to hum, something she always did when she got scared. *Oh, Jesus, this hurts!*

Lexie's eyes flicked back and forth between Kenly and the road, one hand bouncing off the gearshift, the other on the wheel. When they accelerated past fifty, the car started to shimmy and vibrate until Kenly thought her head would burst.

"This is *unbelievable*," she puffed, pressing her chin hard against her chest.

"Tell me about it." Lexie slapped the steering wheel with the palms of her hands. "Three in the morning on the day I'm supposed to fly to Vegas with Sara and her boyfriend for my first weekend away in a year, and you decide to go into labor early. *Where the hell is Ross?*"

It was then that the car's interior lights started to blink along with everything on the dashboard. Kenly's mouth dropped open. "What's going on, Lex?"

"Oh, calm down! This baby is gonna be born nervous if you don't relax. Remember, we've been over this route a hundred times. I can tell you from experience we've got at least ten minutes before the car craps out and Evanston Hospital isn't even a mile away. *We're fine.*"

Kenly stared at her in disbelief, one hand on the bottom of her stomach. "You mean, it does this all the time?"

"Only when I drive over fifty," Lexie said, lifting her chin a notch. "There's an electrical short somewhere and the motor needs a new fan belt or something."

"Then why the hell did you buy it?"

"Because I rarely drive over fifty and it was cheap."

A sobering contraction hit then, coming on fast and with no warning. Kenly panted through the wave of pain, bracing herself against the dash. When it finally receded, she felt a warm gush of wet between her legs and looked down, pushing her hair back behind her ears.

"Uh, Lex? My water just broke."

"Yeah, sure."

"I'm serious."

Lexie's head bobbed up and down as she took this in. "Okay, and that means what?"

Kenly threw her arms open, sputtering. "What do you *think* it means? I'm having a baby here. That's what it means. It also means we don't have a lot of time, the pain is going to get a lot worse than it already is, and I might be giving birth to this baby in a ditch if this car of yours craps out on us!"

Lexie glared at her, but didn't respond.

Kenly squirmed in her seat as traffic whizzed by and the motor screamed in protest. Two minutes later, Lexie blew through a yellow light, maneuvered the car up a ramp, and slammed it into park. Before Kenly could even unsnap her seat belt Lexie was through the emergency doors, hopping from one foot to the other.

"We're having a baby here! Someone! *Anyone!*"

Kenly trailed behind, a hand at the bottom of her belly. Sitting down wasn't an option, so she waddled to the admitting desk and leaned against it, wiping her sweaty forehead with the back of one wrist and fighting tears. The fear she'd been holding back quickly took over now that they were here. The woman behind the desk took one look at her and said, "We'll fill out the paperwork later. Let's get you into a birthing room."

KENLY HAD JUST GOTTEN SETTLED INTO A BED WHEN THE contractions took on a new level of intensity. She thrashed around through each one, crying out from the pain and clenching Lexie's hand until it turned white. When a heavy nurse with red hair marched in at shift change, Lexie handed her over willingly. Looking up at her ample cleavage, Kenly felt a wave of relief. *Okay, here's someone who knows what to do,* she thought. *Someone who's really been there. I wonder how many kids she has. Two? Maybe three?* She lifted her head off the pillow and gave the nurse a pathetic smile. "Look, I could *really* use something for the pain."

The nurse glanced at her watch, then looked back at Kenly with no expression on her face. "We're going to give it another hour and see how you're doing then."

Kenly's face went slack as panic crawled up her spine. *Shit! This woman has no kids. She's obviously never even gone through labor, and for some sick reason she chose this profession to make her living.* Sitting up as best she could, Kenly craned her neck for Lexie and saw her outside in the hallway, retching into a water fountain with a nurse patting her on the back sympathetically.

There was nothing tranquil about this delivery room. Nurses bustled in and out, checking Kenly's chart, her pulse rate, and her temperature as they monitored the growing chaos. Now and then the doctor would breeze in, check her with clinical disinterest, then disappear again. After one pelvic exam, Kenly bit her bottom lip and asked him how much longer, but he tactfully changed the subject. Then he huddled with the nurses by the door and she heard him say, "The labor is progressing, but she's not. It's been six hours and she's not even two centimeters. The baby's not budging. Wait another hour or so, then we may have to consider a C-section."

Kenly lifted her head off the pillow, waving a hand in the air as she huffed through another contraction. "Let's do a C-section *now.*"

The doctor smiled with more sympathy than the nurses had shown since she arrived. "I'm sorry. We have to give it a few more hours. This is your first baby and your body needs a chance to do this on its own."

Kenly's eyes narrowed. *Asshole.*

Fifteen minutes later, the contractions had turned into waves that lifted her beyond human boundaries and she lost all modesty, willingly accepting comfort from anyone offering it. After a particularly bad contraction, she opened her eyes and Ross was in the doorway. She put out her hand and started to cry, gulping sobs that increased with intensity as he crossed the room. Feeling another contraction coming on, she snatched his arm and held on tight.

Ross's eyes locked onto hers. She pinched hers shut, huffed through the worst part of the contraction, and then screamed. The baby was coming. She could feel it. She propped one foot against the side of the bed and the other against the wall next to her. Then the next contraction took over and she completely gave herself up to the pain, crying out long and hard as everyone else cheered her on.

The nurse with the red hair mopped her face with a wet cloth, leaned over to Ross, and whispered, "Hasn't got a high tolerance for pain, does she?" If Kenly hadn't been groaning her way through another contraction, she would've ripped her head off.

"Buck up, now. It's not that bad," the nurse said.

This thick-necked, wide-assed woman is telling me it's not that bad?

"Bullshit!" Kenly screamed. "It's *unbelievable.*"

An older nurse with gray hair came bustling into the room with a scowl on her face, her eyes clearly saying, *Well, isn't this one a handful.*

Kenly dropped to a squat on the floor, glaring at them all as she wrapped her hands around her IV pole. With her chin tucked against her chest, she tried to find something else to focus on. Anything.

The floor tile was the same color Grandma used to have in her kitchen in Kalispell. *Huff, huff. . . . Ross isn't wearing socks, and the skinny nurse's legs are bug-bitten. Huff. . . The nurse who'd always wanted kids, never had any, and now tormented those who did has thick ankles, and really needs to lose some weight. Pant, pant.*

Kenly's pulse quickened, and the volume of noise in the room seemed to increase tenfold. Bending forward as far as she could, she braced for the next contraction, wanting no one near her right now and yet needing everyone within reach.

"Okay, hold on. *Don't* bear down yet," the big nurse spit into her ear.

Oh, right! Like I have any control over what my body is doing right now. Is this woman insane? Huff, huff.

The arm Ross had been holding yanked free and Kenly swatted at the skinny nurse who was busy rubbing her lower back. "Jesus, will you quit that!"

There were four of them in the room telling her what to do, every machine possible hooked up to her, and yet the pain still came in waves, taking over and tearing her apart. *Why can't they just leave me alone so I can get this baby out? Surely doctors can find an easier way for us to go through this,* she thought. *Give them tons of money—maybe donations from sympathetic women who've actually lived though this—and I'm sure someone could come up with a much better way.*

Her body suddenly took over and she felt more like an animal than a woman. Everyone else in the room faded as a black hole lifted her beyond the edge of reason where nothing else mattered; it was just her and the pain. Then one final push, a rush of release, and it was over. A tiny, embattled cry pierced the air as exhaustion washed over her and the pain disappeared as quickly as it had come.

"You have a boy," a voice said, and someone placed him on her chest.

Kenly's eyes locked onto the baby, her heart racing as she took in a soft swirl of blond hair, a wrinkled brow, ten fingers and toes, and everything else that was exactly where it was supposed to be. She was crying then, sobbing and shaking with relief that her son was normal and that they'd both survived this.

When she craned her neck to look closer, Ross kissed her on the forehead and face, one hand squeezing hers while the other grazed the tiny fingers of their son. His eyes said everything he couldn't as he stood next to the nurse while she weighed the baby (eight pounds, six ounces), measured him (twenty-two inches), and checked his reflexes. Drops were put in his eyes and he was bathed all within the first ten minutes of his life, and through it all, Ross didn't take his eyes off him.

Kenly felt something catch in her throat as she watched them from across the room.

This is how it should be.

Gripped by a sudden chill, she shivered, weak and trembling from the whole ordeal. Then a sudden, involuntary need to push hit her again and she propped up on her elbows, grimacing. "It's your afterbirth," the nurse with red hair explained, mopping Kenly's brow. "Just one more push and you're done."

When she was through, the other nurse brought the baby over and laid him on her chest, all bundled and safely wrapped. Ross leaned down and pushed a few damp strands of hair off her forehead. "He's incredible," he whispered. "Just like his mother."

She brushed her lips against her son's forehead. "Thank God you're healthy."

Ross took her hand. "He's perfect."

One of the nurses came to wash her up then and Kenly carefully handed him over to Ross. Lost in his thoughts, he hummed as he cradled the baby against his chest. *Yes, this is how it should be,* Kenly thought, full of emotion as she watched them, marveling at the tenderness in Ross's face. *How can I take this away from him?*

She closed her eyes and wished for sleep to come so she could clear her head. She felt ruined and rumpled, and her body ached from the physical strain it had been through. A hand touched her shoulder and when she looked up, Ross was beside her again. She half-smiled, but said nothing as he ruffled her hair and leaned down to kiss her.

"You're amazing," he said. "Ten hours of labor and you still look great."

"It's the lights. They complement the hospital gown."

His eyes fixed on her. "No, from where I stand, it's you who complements the gown."

Her bottom lip quivered and she pointed to the door. "We'll get your eyes checked later. Right now I need some sleep."

"Fine. I'll be back in a few hours," he said, handing the baby to a nurse and tucking the blanket around his sleeping form. And then something inside brushed against Kenly's heart when she saw the look on his face, overcome with love and a fierce protectiveness of the son he believed was his.

This is how I've always dreamed it would be.

"He needs a name," she blurted out, and then realized that she'd just committed herself even further to this lie. Ross swiveled to look at her with a grin on his face and it was then that she knew. In that instant, that heartbeat of time between knowing it was wrong and yet wanting it so badly that she made him the father.

"How about Connor?" he asked.

She hesitated a split second, then nodded her agreement. Right then, somewhere deep down inside of her, she knew she'd crossed a line and couldn't turn back.

God forgive me, but this is how it's going to be.

KENLY LEANED BACK, TWISTING HER HEAD TO THE RIGHT, then the left. She was tired and had a cramp in her neck that wouldn't go away. Connor lay swathed in a receiving blanket next to her, sleeping the way she wished she could. They had named him Connor after Ross's father and his middle name was Steven, after hers. He was already a day old, but she still hadn't called Tommy, Jean, or Max with the good news and knew she'd better do it soon because Lexie wouldn't be able to hold back much longer.

She reached for the phone, deciding to get it out of the way. When it rang four times and no one answered, relief came over her, but then Jean picked up on the fifth ring. She was out of breath and Kenly wondered if this had been a bad time to call.

"Jean?"

"Oh, hello, Kenly. How are you?"

She got straight to the point. "I'm great, and I'm calling with good news! I had a little boy yesterday. He made his entrance a few weeks early and surprised us all."

"That's wonderful," Jean said, perking up.

Kenly's head bobbed up and down in agreement. "His name's Connor. He's eight pounds, six ounces, and he's . . . perfect." Her voice cracked, filling with emotion at the sight of him lying there next to her.

"That's great, dear. I couldn't be happier for you." There was a pause at Jean's end. "And your timing is perfect. This is just the kind of news we needed to cheer everyone up."

Kenly sat back and pulled Connor closer. "W-what do you mean?"

"There was a fire here on Tuesday and Max's house burned down. By the time the truck got here it was beyond saving. . . ." Her voice trailed away.

Kenly's heart was pounding. "And Max?"

"Oh, no," Jean cut in quickly. "He's fine. All three of us were at the paper when it happened, but there's not much left of the house. The roof is gone, most of the walls, too. Just the fireplace is still there and a small piece of a kitchen wall." She paused and her voice was filled with emotion when she spoke again. "It was Tommy who found Oscar, curled in a ball and lying there against that wall like he was asleep."

Kenly closed her eyes as Jean carried on.

"He buried him down at the tree house yesterday."

Kenly didn't know what to say. Instead, she cradled Connor against her chest and bit back the urge to cry, knowing how much Oscar had meant to Tommy, finding it hard to think about how upset he would be right now.

Jean sighed at her end of the line. "Anyhow, Tommy's asleep right now, so would you mind if I have him call you back? I could wake him but—"

"Please don't," Kenly cut in.

"He needs rest right now. You see, he's scheduled for surgery in Toronto next week. Max and I are flying out there with him and he'll have to stay at least ten days afterward. They told us this one will be hard on him physically, so I hate to see him run-down."

Kenly twirled one hand around the phone cord. "How are things with Tommy? I mean, long-term, how do things look? He won't talk to me about it."

There was a troubled pause before Jean answered. "Well, he just fights back from one surgery when something else crops up and knocks him flat. If the tumors went into remission and everything stayed as it is now, he could live ten years or more. On the other hand, it could be less than a few years, depending on how much more he can physically take. It's painful to watch him go through this, but the doctors can't do much. He's on more medication all the time and it just never seems to let him be, you know?"

Kenly nodded. "Yes, I know."

Before they hung up, Jean told her that Max would be moving in with them and Kenly sensed a shyness in her voice. "After all, he's much too young to go into a nursing home and he really is like family."

"Of course he is," Kenly agreed, glad to hear some good news in her call to Athabasca. When she hung up, her throat tightened and she closed her eyes, letting the gentle rise and fall of Connor's chest anchor her—not allowing herself to think about anything else, even as the weight of what she'd done settled on her shoulders.

chapter 15

KENLY HAD ARRANGED TO TAKE ONE SEMESTER OFF, but she also had the summer before she had to go back to school in the fall, which gave her almost five months to focus on being a mom. Although she'd taken prenatal classes, she wasn't prepared for the overwhelming feeling of inadequacy that came over her after Connor was born.

"We'll figure this out, won't we?" she whispered to him when she got him home, but it was more to bolster her own lagging confidence than to soothe Connor.

That first week, she tied her mom's red silk scarf to the mobile over his bassinet and did some nervous pacing, then grabbed the phone and called Grandma Alister in Springfield, doing her best to sound casual when she asked, "Gran, did Dad sleep on his back or his stomach when he was a baby?" and, "Do you remember how often you cut his fingernails?"

Of course, she could have called the community nursing line they gave her when she left the hospital, but Kenly worried that if she called too often, they'd question her ability to be a good mother. So at first, she fed him too often and changed his diaper when it didn't need to be changed. There was nail-biting over his first bath, second-guessing about how often to burp him, and the odd panic attack when he cried. Before he was a month old, she'd read at least a dozen books with conflicting advice on every topic from breast-feeding to colicky babies. But for the most part, Kenly adjusted and her aching body began to heal.

If Connor squawked at night, she was out of bed like a shot in front of his bassinet. She soaked up every inch of him as her fingers grazed his eyelashes, ran over his belly, and moved down to his tiny feet. And when he fell back asleep, she turned a flashlight on him every half-hour or so to watch for the steady rise and fall of his chest. Often she was there in the morning when Lexie got up.

"Are you two hard-wired together or what?"

Kenly half-smiled but said nothing. This was the most effortless love she'd ever known, but she couldn't put it into words. Where some women glow when they're pregnant, she lit up after Connor was born. It felt like that natural high one gets when they meet someone incredible, talk all night long, watch the sun rise in the morning, and still manage to function without sleep the next day. Sleep deprivation didn't touch her and the two of them seemed to flourish simply by breathing the same air.

Lexie fell for him just as hard, and quickly lost her long-standing dislike for babies, something she defended when Kenly pointed it out to her. "Yeah, but Connor's different," she explained.

Kenly rolled her eyes and laughed. Connor *was* born happy and he took the term "low-maintenance baby" to new levels. By the time he was three weeks old, he was already sleeping through the night and his disposition was so angelic that whenever he did cry, everyone dropped what they were doing and ran.

Ross was pacing around Kenly's bedroom one night when Connor was nine weeks old. He'd just returned from a two-day business trip to New York and looked exhausted. His eyes settled on Connor, lying in his crib asleep, and his face softened. Kenly was sitting on her bed and he said, "Slide over," and wrapped an arm around her waist.

"Marry me," he said, lifting a finger to her lips so she wouldn't interrupt. "We're a family, and I want to fall asleep with you every night and wake up next to you each morning knowing you're my wife."

Tears filled her eyes.

"If you do, I promise I'll make breakfast every Sunday for the rest of your life."

"You don't cook," she reminded him.

"I'll learn." He leaned back and pulled her down next to him. His eyes roamed over her, taking in the mole on her neck and the almost invisible scar on the bridge of her nose.

"What is it? What are you looking at?" Kenly kept saying.

His expression softened as he leaned over and buried his face in her neck. "It's getting worse all the time," he said.

"What?"

"Everything. How often I think about you during the day. How much I love hearing your laugh."

Her heart started to pound and she hung on to his words.

He chuckled, running a finger down the slope of her nose. "I used to worry about what I'd gotten myself into. Even wondered if maybe this was something I couldn't handle. Now I *know* it isn't, but only in the best way. You do something to me that I don't understand, and I've given up trying. I love you and there's no way around this. We're inevitable, you and I, so marry me." He slid a hand down the curve of her back, tenderly exploring the indentation at the base of her spine as he nuzzled her neck.

Kenly felt breathless, even dizzy as she wrapped her arms around him. "Okay," she said, laughing. "I'll marry you. Anytime, anywhere."

LEXIE WAS ON THE COUCH WATCHING A HOCKEY GAME WHEN Kenly and Ross interrupted to tell her the good news. "Well, it's about time!" She scrambled to her feet, gave Kenly a hug, and then pushed her out to arm's length. "I'm maid of honor, right?"

"Of course," Kenly said, "but it'll be a small wedding, so there's not much to plan for."

"How small?"

"Small."

"No reception? No dance?" Lexie protested, gesturing miserably.

"A dinner with maybe a few dozen people."

Lexie shook her head, then shrugged. "Okay, it's your wedding."

Ross slid his arms around Kenly's waist. "We wanted to ask a favor, though."

"What?"

"Would you take pictures during the ceremony?"

"Absolutely."

Kenly bit her bottom lip. "And there's this other thing . . ."

"Name it."

"Could you watch Connor while we go on our honeymoon?"

Lexie's face softened. "I'd be mad if you left him with anyone else. Consider it done."

Kenly spent the next two nights wrestling with whether or not to invite Max, Jean, and Tommy, but in the end she realized it was unavoidable. There were no excuses she could invent that would make any sense, even though the thought of introducing Tommy to Connor filled her with panic. She pulled out a calendar and looked at her options—a fall wedding, a Christmas wedding, something in the spring? How was she going to do this? Putting her thoughts away, she went into the kitchen to make a cup of tea and had just finished stirring in sugar when Lexie got home.

"Hi," Lexie said, kicking off her shoes at the door. "Is Connor asleep?"

Kenly nodded, tilting her head toward her bedroom. "He's on my bed. I was just going to move him into his crib."

Using her little finger to dip into a plastic pot, Lexie put gloss on her lips. "By the way, Tommy called earlier when you were out."

Kenly put her cup down. "I haven't talked to him in weeks. How are things?"

"Okay. Remember crazy Louie Johnson up at the old folks' home in Athabasca?" Kenly nodded. "Apparently he's started writing a stream of letters to Max pitching his own weekly column, something to do with 'exposing all the mind-numbing horrors of being a senior citizen in the twentieth century.'"

Kenly laughed as Lexie disappeared into her bedroom. "And Tommy?" she called out. "How's he doing? Did he say?"

Lexie came back holding Connor, who was trying to cram a fist into his mouth. "Well, the last few months have been pretty good, as you know. But now that he's stronger, they've scheduled him for another surgery in Toronto this summer. To remove some growth they've been monitoring or something."

Kenly felt a faint pulse of hope. "Did he say when?"

"Yeah, I think it's set for July twenty-second or twenty-third."

Kenly put her cup down.

"What's wrong?" Lexie asked.

"Nothing . . . it's just, well, I was thinking Ross and I would get married in early August," she blurted out. "You know, get it out of the way before fall classes start and everything. But if Tommy's having surgery in late July, that'll make it impossible for him to come."

"Yeah, it would. He's usually in the hospital for at least a week after, isn't he?"

Kenly nodded. "And his recovery often takes months."

They were silent for a bit; then Lexie smiled and gave her a small shrug. "You know what? He'll understand, and he'd hate having you change your plans because of him. Keep in mind, no matter when you get married, there's always a good chance he won't be up to making the trip anyhow, right?"

When Lexie disappeared to put Connor in his crib, tears filled Kenly's eyes and she suddenly realized, as surely as if she could see her entire life laid out before her, that this was only the beginning—she would never be able to stop running from this lie.

KENLY AND ROSS SET THE DATE FOR AUGUST 15, LESS THAN two months away and the week before her birthday. Ross agreed to a small ceremony, just family and a few friends, and they decided on a brief honeymoon before her classes started again at Northwestern in early September.

Tommy did understand, and when Kenly called to tell him, he seemed more relieved that she and Ross were getting married than anything else. "I have to admit, I was getting worried about this guy," he told her. "First of all I haven't met him, and secondly, I couldn't figure out why he wouldn't want to marry you."

Kenly laughed. "I was the one hedging, not Ross. He wanted to get married weeks after I found out I was pregnant."

"Well, I'm happy for both of you. And I'll be there in spirit, you know that, right?"

"I'll watch for a faint aura of light circling around me."

"Good, because it'll be filled with good wishes for you."

"Hey, Tommy?" Kenly said, just before she hung up.

"Uh-huh?"

An unexpected lump worked its way into her throat and she covered her mouth for a second. "Promise me you'll call after your surgery so I know you're okay."

"I will," Tommy said. "You can count on it."

IT WAS EARLY JULY WHEN ROSS ASKED KENLY WHAT WAS wrong. "You've been quiet for days, so something's on your mind. What's up?"

She pushed her plate away and sighed. "I'm worried about Lexie. She's been through hell in the last few years and I feel like I'm deserting her, especially since I know that she can't afford the rent on her own."

Ross shrugged. "So tell her to come live with us."

Kenly blinked at him. "You're kidding."

"No. At least that way she'll be there to help you with Connor when I'm traveling and she can have the basement suite downstairs."

"I don't know," Kenly said with a laugh. "Two women and a baby living under the same roof with someone who's been a confirmed bachelor for years?"

"I think I can handle it," he said, and he seemed pleased with himself now that they'd found a solution to the problem that had been driving her crazy.

It took them just two days to move everything from their apartment out to Ross's house in Barrington, and Lexie didn't stop smiling the entire time. "Are you guys sure about this?" she asked more than once. Ross finally rolled his eyes. "No, of course we're not, but it's a small price to pay for all the free baby-sitting we're gonna get. Now shut up and get packing so we can get this over with."

Lexie glanced from Ross to Kenly, then back again.

"He's joking!" Kenly said, laughing as she taped up a box.

THREE MONTHS AFTER CONNOR WAS BORN, KENLY WAS STILL waiting for the rift he was supposed to create in her life, and as she settled into a new routine living in Barrington, it was Lexie who became paranoid about his safety. A week before the wedding, she ran out and bought three rolls of duct tape and five feet of foam, then sat cross-legged on the floor for an hour, cutting and taping together unique creations of protective padding for every sharp corner in the house. By the time she was done, there wasn't a room that hadn't been hit.

"Lex, he's not even crawling yet," Kenly said with a chuckle.

"I know, but when he does, now we'll be ready for him."

ONE EVENING, CONNOR WAS PLAYING ON THE FLOOR NEXT TO Lexie in the living room as the last period of a hockey game unfolded on TV. "He's going to be a hockey player when he's older," Lexie said.

Kenly frowned and lifted her eyes from her textbook. "What?"

"I'm not kidding. Just look at him, Kenly. Can't you see him as a Chicago Blackhawk when he's twenty? Burning up the ice in the play-offs, then scoring the winning goal in overtime to bring home the Stanley Cup—the oldest trophy ever competed for by professional athletes!"

Kenly bit her bottom lip. "I didn't know that."

Lexie ran a finger down Connor's nose. "Wouldn't that be something?"

"Lex? He's not even crawling yet."

"I know, but he has that *look*. Can't you see it in his eyes? Just watch him following the puck on TV."

She crawled around in front of him on all fours and squinted to get a better look, then stretched out on the rug next to him, twirling her finger around a piece of freshly permed shoulder-length hair. "You guys should register him early, you know? Maybe I could even get him a pair of those bob skates when he starts to walk. Then he'll be ready for skating lessons when he turns three and you can get him playing when he's four."

Kenly laughed and turned back to the case study she was reviewing. "That's a long way off, Lex. Who knows what'll happen in the next few years."

There was a pause as Lexie pulled Connor onto her lap; then her voice went sad. "Yeah. Well, I guess you're right. Who knows what can happen in a few years."

Kenly stopped reading and chewed on her pen. Earlier that night, Lexie had announced that she was going for dinner with some guy she'd met who had been "hounding her" and Kenly almost came out of her chair with excitement.

Maybe this guy will be someone special, Kenly thought.

However, according to Lexie, dinner with Mr. Wonderful was a disaster. "All he did was sit there and stare at me. Shit, Kenly, he kept dropping things and turning red right up to his ears. It made me so nervous I started ordering doubles, then tripped on the carpet and fell flat on my face leaving the restaurant."

Kenly nodded sympathetically. That sort of thing would make anyone nervous, but she thought she saw a flicker of something else, too,
something that said Lexie was intrigued by this guy under that who-
gives-a-shit mask she usually wore so well. Kenly saw why when he
stopped by to pick Lexie up a week later.

His name was Benjy McMillan and Kenly liked him instantly. He
was six foot three, weighed well over two hundred pounds, and
had liquid brown eyes that she swore belonged in a dairy cow. He
moved like a dancer, slow and cautious, like he was afraid he'd knock
something over if he wasn't careful, and he had hands like baseball
mitts. He was almost ten years older than Lexie and he talked in a
steady, calm voice, whereas Lexie usually had to be peeled off the
walls. They were complete opposites, but Lexie pranced around
with more glide in her stride than usual when he was there, trying all
this attention on for size and basking in Benjy's obvious interest
in her.

"What does he do for a living?" Kenly asked the next morning at
breakfast.

Lexie opened the fridge and peered inside. "Uh . . . he's a refuse col-
lector."

"Oh. Well, that's all right."

"Uh-huh." Lexie nodded, glancing at Kenly over her shoulder. "It is
all right, don't you think? For him to collect garbage?"

"Of course. Someone has to do it."

"Absolutely."

They'd met at the hair salon a few months earlier. Benjy worked out
of the same building and often dropped in to get his hair cut. After
Lexie cut it one afternoon, he started to request her and not long after
that, he started asking her out for lunch. Lexie had been turning him
down for weeks when she finally gave in and agreed. Now whenever
he picked her up at the house, he held the car door open for her and
Lexie climbed in with her chin lifted. There was something about him
that had gentle written all over it and Kenly sensed he was going to be
good for Lexie in a rock-solid sort of way.

THE DAY KENLY AND ROSS GOT MARRIED WAS ONE SHE WOULD never forget. She woke up early that morning and went for a run, and even though the forecast was for rain, by three that afternoon the sun was still shining, the heat was manageable due to a gentle breeze, and there wasn't a cloud in sight. The ceremony was held at Lighthouse Beach on the same grassy hill overlooking Lake Michigan where Ross's parents used to take him as a child.

Although Tommy's surgery had gone well, his recovery was slower than before, so Max and Jean decided to stay in Athabasca, although they sent a telegram and a dozen roses. Ross's mother was there, as was his sister, Leanne, and her husband and two boys. Ross's partner, Joel, came and Lexie brought Benjy, who kindly escorted Grandma Alister around on the crook of his arm for the day. They all sat on folding chairs in the grass while Kenly and Ross stood facing each other under a trellis covered with lush vines. She wore a cream-colored slip dress with a single strand of pearls and her mom's red scarf tied around her left wrist. Her hair was pulled away from her face in soft tendrils and Ross didn't take his eyes off her.

Grandma Alister held Connor on her lap during the ceremony. She gave him his favorite blanket while he gummed at the knuckles on her hand and Lexie adjusted her camera and took as many shots of them as she did of the ceremony. Benjy sat next to Lexie, his face hopeful and lit with a tender smile as Kenly and Ross said their vows. When the ceremony was over, Kenly and Ross kissed, and as if on cue, Lexie began to cry. She pried off her shoes and sobbed, chest heaving and mascara streaking down her face. Then Connor started crying, too, wailing even louder than Lexie was.

"Enough crying," Kenly mock-complained, plucking Connor from Grandma's lap. She kissed his forehead and spun him around until he squirmed with delight, and when she stopped, she caught Benjy watching them. He nodded politely, then wrapped an arm around Lexie's waist and gave her a squeeze.

Ross was sure he knew Benjy from somewhere. It had been bothering him for weeks and it was during dinner that night when he finally remembered. "Ever heard of McMillan Waste Management?" he asked Kenly.

She turned to stare at Benjy. "You mean?"

Ross smiled. "Benjy's father is Bill McMillan. He owns McMillan Waste Management, one of the largest companies of its kind in the state of Illinois." Kenly shook her head and laughed. She couldn't wait to see Lexie's reaction when she figured this one out.

Early the next morning, they left Connor and Grandma in Benjy's and Lexie's capable hands while they slipped away to Bermuda for their honeymoon. As their plane lifted into the air, Ross leaned over and kissed her, and when he turned away to ask for wine, Kenly realized that although everything in her life was going well—almost perfectly, in fact—she often felt as if she were holding her breath, waiting for something to go wrong.

It was then that she remembered Grandma arguing with her dad years ago, her face pinched with worry as she said, "Make better choices, Steven! The past always catches up to you." Then yesterday, she'd hugged Kenly after the ceremony, whispering, "You've always looked like your mother, but today you remind me of your father."

Kenly had smiled, even though inside she was thinking, *No, I'm nothing like my father.*

Ross handed her a glass of wine and lifted his in the air. "To our future."

Tears filled her eyes. "Yes," she said. "To our future."

"Are you okay?"

Her voice quavered. "I'm a little emotional, that's all."

He took her hand and squeezed, then slipped his headphones on to watch the news. Kenly looked out the window, into the pillowlike clouds below them, and as she slowly sipped her wine, it occurred to her that she was praying.

chapter 16

GRANDMA ALISTER MARVELED AT THE PICTURES
Kenly sent of Connor and called each week to see how he
was doing. Often she couldn't help herself and gave Kenly bits of advice on how to raise him: "Don't rock him to sleep, that'll spoil him
for sure"; "Make sure you don't give him Pablum too early"; "Are you
using cloth diapers or those awful throwaways?"; "Kenly? Is there anything he needs?" There wasn't, but Kenly always came up with something. "A pair of sleepers would be great, Gran," or, "He could use a
few undershirts."

Ross drove them out to Grandma's nursing home in Springfield
once a month. Her health was getting worse all the time and she was
confined to a wheelchair now, so she couldn't travel anymore. As they
were leaving one afternoon, Grandma put out her arms for Connor
and Ross passed him to her. He was half-asleep and popped a yawn
while she cradled him, murmuring against his face.

"I think he needs a change," she said, handing him back.

Ross grabbed the diaper bag as Kenly went off to use the bathroom.

When she came back, the two of them were leaning over Grandma's bed.

"It's probably nothing," Ross said.

Grandma nodded, but took Ross by the elbow and gave it a squeeze. "Have it checked anyhow."

Kenly shrugged into her jacket. "Have what checked?"

"He has a mark or something on his chest," Ross said.

Kenly stepped past him and looked down at Connor. He was asleep with his shirt unbuttoned and his tiny chest and belly laid bare. Squinting, she leaned closer. There it was, faint and yet suddenly familiar to her. Swallowing hard, she eased one arm underneath him and rubbed at the mark with a thumb as though willing it not to be there.

Distracted, Ross glanced at his watch and stuffed the last of Connor's things into the diaper bag. "It's just a birthmark," he said.

Kenly nodded, buttoning Connor's shirt but keeping her eyes down and away from Ross's. In the back of her mind she could see it clearly again, as though she were right there, back in the tree house on the morning that she left Athabasca. Tommy sitting on the mattress in his jeans with no shirt on and that L-shaped birthmark splashed across his chest. It was larger than Connor's and a deeper burnished brown, but otherwise it was exactly the same as the faint marking she'd just seen on her son. Her arms were shaking and her eyes filled with tears when she handed him back to Grandma Alister for one last hug.

Grandma smiled. "Steven would've loved this little guy."

"Yes, I think he would've."

"Now, you take special care of him, okay?"

"Till my last breath," Kenly whispered.

WHEN KENLY STRIPPED CONNOR NAKED FOR HIS BATH THAT night, she held him up by his armpits for a closer look, and as she cooed, he kicked his pudgy legs and a sick feeling came over her. Gently lowering him into the warm water, she ran a cloth over his chest a couple of times, and the heat from the water made the mark stand out even more definitively than it had before. Staring at it, she bit her bottom lip and closed her eyes, saying a silent prayer.

The next morning Kenly made an appointment with Connor's pediatrician without telling Ross, then made a trip into his office the next day. After explaining everything, she listened as Dr. Browning arranged a round of tests on the phone, and when he hung up she leaned forward expectantly. He jotted an address down on a slip of paper and handed it to her. "If you can be there in an hour, they'll do a workup on him today. It'll take at least a week for the results, but it could be ten days."

Kenly had to look away, out the window, at his desk, or at anything else that would help take her mind off the sick feeling that settled in her stomach. When a long silence took over the room, he frowned at the floor, cleared his throat, and gave her a pat on the hand. "Let me see if I can't put a rush on it for you."

THE NEXT MORNING, KENLY STRUGGLED WITH HER EMOTIONS on her way to the cemetery and even flirted with the idea of turning around, but when she finally parked the car, she knew it was time. A flatbed truck rolled by on the gravel lane leading into the graveyard and two men sitting on the back stared at her with looks of resigned boredom. Next to them were two spades, and painted on the back window of the truck in bold letters was KUBLER FUNERAL CHAPEL. Although she'd never been here before, Kenly knew her mom was buried here next to her grandparents, something her dad had mentioned when she was younger.

She clutched her mom's red scarf in one hand and slowly worked her way through the graveyard. A mental preparation of sorts took hold as she looked at the names and dates on the gravestones she passed—each a loving testament to the celebration of that person's life and the tragedy of their death. When she finally found it, she dropped to her knees on the grass and ran her hands over the gravestone, tracing each letter with her fingers, studying them as though there should be something else to see.

Lara Jurgen Alister
May 28, 1947–August 29, 1977

Next to it were two matching gravestones with her maternal grand-parents' names etched on them along with the year they were born and the year they had each died.

Kenly's chin trembled as she turned her face up to the sky and dropped her hands into her lap. Off to the south, an airplane passed overhead, turned into a tiny silver dot, and disappeared into the clouds. "I barely remember what you look like anymore, but I still miss you," she whispered. "It never goes away, even now—especially now—when I look at my son and wonder if I'm doing the right thing."

KENLY WAS IN DR. BROWNING'S WAITING ROOM FIVE DAYS later with Connor crawling around on the rug at her feet when the nurse called out her name. "Mrs. Lowen?" She grabbed Connor and hoisted him onto her hip, then shouldered his diaper bag, and fol-lowed the nurse down a narrow hallway into Dr. Browning's office. Thankfully, he didn't make her wait long. By the time she sat down and set Connor in her lap, he was through the door. He opened a file on his desk, slapped both palms against his knees, and smiled. "You can relax. It's just a birthmark."

The diaper bag dropped from her shoulder to the floor and Kenly wrapped both arms around Connor and cried, overcome with relief.

Dr. Browning handed her the folder. "I've kept copies on file, but I thought you might want your own. The dermatology report is there; Connor's X rays and ultrasound show nothing abnormal; all of his bones and joints look fine. But because Proteus Syndrome is such a rare genetic disease and so little is known about it, if you like we can always run a few extra tests when you bring him in each year—for peace of mind more than anything else."

Kenly tucked the folder into her purse. "I'd like that, thanks."

When she got off the elevator a few minutes later, she went into the first bathroom she could find and read everything over. She didn't consider herself a good liar and her biggest fear was that Ross would look up one day, catch a brilliant flash of guilt on her face, and know the truth. So as Connor sat in his stroller watching, she ripped each page into shreds and threw them all into the garbage, pushing thoughts of this lie as far away from her as she could get them. She wasn't pretending it hadn't happened, she was simply feeding the coward inside, and her motivation came from not wanting to shatter the lives of everyone she loved, including Tommy.

GRANDMA ALISTER DIED PEACEFULLY IN HER SLEEP JUST DAYS AFTER Connor's first birthday and Kenly couldn't shake the feeling of loss that settled over her. She sat next to Ross in the front row of the full church, listening to a eulogy that filled her with pride. Memories of a friend, woman, mother, and grandmother who had lived a full life. Memories of someone you could count on, someone who believed what went around came around, and George Strait's number one fan. Widowed at the age of twenty-seven, she'd raised her son as a single mother in an era when remarrying would have been the easier choice—an option that was offered to her more than once.

Kenly knew that Grandma's health had been slipping, but the reality of it, the realization that she would never again hear Grandma's voice or see her face, left her feeling like someone had cut her loose from all that had once anchored her.

"You okay?" Ross asked after the funeral.

She answered with tears in her eyes. "She was all the family I had left."

"I know," he whispered, lifting his chin to where Connor was sleeping in his crib, "but you still have us and we're not going anywhere."

Kenly nodded as he slid an arm around her waist and pulled her close, feeling more protective about what they had now than she ever had before.

•

CONNOR FINALLY STARTED TO WALK WHEN HE WAS FOURTEEN months old and when he did, it was Ross who hovered over him protectively.

"Let him breathe," Kenly said.

But he ignored her, grinning like a fool as he orbited around Connor and watched him trundle across the room on legs that quaked like they were made of rubber. Connor's eyes went wide with wonder as he clutched Ross's fingers and every time he stood up, Lexie had her camera in his face. "Look at him, you guys!"

Thumbing through Lexie's pictures one afternoon, Kenly felt something jump inside of her. In one of them, Connor was standing next to the picnic table outside, wearing just a diaper and with his head thrown back as he laughed at something. She ran a finger down the birthmark on his tiny chest. She'd seen it hundreds of times but never like this—never in a picture. It was four inches long now, L-shaped, and a deep toasty brown from the summer sun.

She ripped the picture in half, then in half again before flipping through the rest to see if there were others where the birthmark was visible. Then she stuffed the pictures back into the envelope and buried the torn pieces in the garbage. When she was done, she fished around for Lexie's cigarettes and lit one with shaking fingers. Pulling on it hard, she instantly felt light-headed from the nicotine in her system, but she felt calmer within minutes.

The back door opened and Lexie came in with Connor in her arms. "He's asleep," she whispered, tiptoeing past Kenly.

Kenly crushed out her cigarette and followed, one hand fingering Connor's dangling leg. She could smell him in the air, faintly like baby powder and damp from sweat. It was the smell she loved, the one she drew in when she held him late at night. "How was he?"

Lexie laid him in his crib and blew air out her cheeks with a grin. "Great. And by the way? You quit smoking two years ago, fool. Where's your head?"

chapter 17

KENLY WAS ON THE PHONE ONE NIGHT WHEN ROSS handed her an envelope and mouthed, "Let's talk about this when you're done." She frowned, turned the envelope over, and froze. Written in Ross's handwriting were some notes that jumped out at her.

Air Canada direct from Chicago to Winnipeg
Winnipeg direct to Edmonton
Car rental (confirmed)
Tommy Naylor (780) 555–1014

She flushed, gestured to the phone, and mouthed, "My professor," rolling her eyes. Ross nodded and reached for the newspaper on the kitchen table. "Yes. Well, I'll see you tomorrow and we'll talk about it then, okay?" Kenly dropped the phone into its cradle with a click, trying hard to look casual as she tucked her hair behind her ears. Her heart was racing as Ross kissed her, then pulled back to study her. "I thought

I'd surprise you and book flights for all of us to go to Athabasca."

Her mouth popped open. "Y-you didn't?"

He grinned. "Lexie thought it was a great idea."

Just wonderful, she thought.

"Now I can finally meet everyone," he said, opening the fridge. "Want some wine?"

"Sure," she said, fingering the airline tickets inside the envelope. *A few dozen bottles would be good, thanks.*

He poured her a glass and nudged it across the table. "Everything's taken care of. I got a sale on the seats and Lexie made arrangements for us to stay with her uncle Walter."

Kenly reached for her glass, lifted it with a jerk, and slopped wine onto the floor. Ross looked at her with a puzzled expression and jumped up for a cloth. "You okay?"

"Fine," she said, trying to smile. "Just taking it all in."

But, of course, she wasn't fine. There suddenly didn't seem to be enough air in the room and for the second time in years she wanted a cigarette in the worst way, wishing she hadn't quit when she was pregnant. She rubbed her forehead with the heel of her hand, doing her best to listen to what Ross was saying.

"Oh, and Lexie made arrangements to borrow someone's crib and a stroller for Connor when we're there," Ross said, wiping up the floor.

"That's great," Kenly said. *Connor can have the crib and I'll take the stroller because my legs won't be working real well.*

WHEN A ROAD SIGN FLEW BY ANNOUNCING THEY WERE JUST six miles away from Athabasca, Kenly didn't know where to put her hands. She couldn't stop them from shaking and couldn't get them out of the way. Connor was three now, and it had been four years since she'd been back. Now that they were a few minutes away, panic rose inside of her when she thought about seeing Tommy again. They talked on the phone often, but the thought of him meeting Ross and Connor was overwhelming.

Her heart slammed around her chest as they drove down the hill into town and she crossed one leg over the other, then uncrossed them. "God, I hate this music," she said, flicking off the radio.

Ross sighed. "Okay then. The rental car's too small, we forgot Connor's blanket, and you hate every station on the AM and FM dial. Anything else bugging you I should know about?"

She tried to avoid his eyes as she checked on Connor in the backseat. "Sorry. I'm tired."

"Ah," he said, as if he was relieved everything was out in the open now, but didn't actually believe a word.

It was late September and the hills surrounding the river valley were cloaked in a collage of rust and orange. Kenly looked up and caught her breath, then slowly reached for Ross's hand. A lump worked its way into her throat as she thought of the first time she'd come here. How she'd been so sure she and her dad wouldn't be here long and even more certain that she'd hate it while they were.

Looking out the window, she let memories fall around her that she usually kept tucked away and she suddenly realized how much she'd missed being here. Of course, the reminders were always there. Like how hearing Billy Joel made her think of Tommy or the way the crisp smell of a pine tree brought back the image of flashing northern lights and the memory of the best Christmas she could remember. But right now, she missed Jean's cinnamon buns and visiting around Max's fire pit, listening to conversations that covered everything and yet nothing, voices intertwining until everyone was all talked out and it was time to go home.

Ross squeezed her hand. "Now that you're here, are you glad we came?"

Kenly nodded, unable to speak. She directed him through town to Florence and Walter's, then wriggled out of her seat belt after they parked.

"Did you want to go see Tommy now?"

"No," she said, busying herself with getting Connor out of his car seat. "I'll call him and tell him we'll come by in the morning."

Balancing Connor against her hip, Kenly rang the doorbell,

reassuring herself that everything would be fine. When Florence opened the door, Kenly's mouth popped open. Although she stood there smiling, holding herself with the grace of a lady wearing simple pearl earrings and a gold chain, Florence wasn't wearing any clothes. Instead, she stood tall and regal in a bra that pushed her breasts up higher than they needed to be and a pair of control-top panties that were waging a losing war against the flesh of her stomach.

"Kenly. How good to see you! Come in and let me see this boy of yours." She pulled her inside and hugged her hard, then introduced herself to Ross, babbling nonstop as her rear end jiggled down the hallway and into the kitchen on a pair of stick-thin legs.

Ross raised his eyebrows and whispered, "Lexie's aunt?"

"Only by marriage," Kenly answered, as confused as he was.

Ross nudged her down the hallway and when they stepped into the kitchen, it was hard not to stare. Florence pulled two chairs out from the table, then scurried over to the stove to make a pot of tea. On the table were two plates—one covered with bite-sized dainties and the other filled with pieces of raw beefsteak, swimming in blood.

"Introduce me, Kenly," she clucked over her shoulder as she filled the kettle.

"Uh . . . yes. Okay. This is my husband Ross and this," Kenly said, nuzzling the top of his sleeping head, "is Connor."

Florence glided into a chair across from them and reached for Connor, eyes glistening with tears. "Oh, he's beautiful. You two sit down and have something to eat and I'll hold this little one for a few minutes."

Before Kenly could hand Connor to Florence they heard the front door open and heavy footsteps hurrying down the hallway. Walter came around the corner, eyes bright with anticipation and a wide smile on his face, but when he saw Florence, he flushed red.

"Hello, Kenly," he said, giving her a peck on the cheek. Then he gently took Florence's elbow. "Excuse us, please." As they made their way out of the kitchen and down the hallway, Kenly heard Florence fussing in hushed whispers that he was being rude.

Walter returned a few minutes later, frowning. "Lexie said you wouldn't be here until nine," he said by way of explanation.

"It's okay," Kenly said.

Lowering his eyes, he let out a sigh and started to clear the table. "Six months ago she started to wander around in the middle of the night and couldn't find the bathroom. It took a while before we found out it was Alzheimer's." He shook his head and slumped into a chair. "They tell me it's progressive and there's nothing I can do. Some days are better than others, but when she gets worked up sometimes she forgets to get dressed, and she was pretty excited about having you come for a visit."

Kenly felt sick. "We should've stayed in a hotel."

"Don't be crazy. Becky's in Calgary for a week so her room is free and I'm here to take care of Florence. You two just come and go whenever you like."

"Walter? Why didn't Lexie tell me?"

He lowered his eyes. "Probably because I haven't told her yet."

Kenly passed Connor to Ross, then wrapped her arms around Walter and gave him a hug. "I'm so sorry," she whispered.

He nodded, took her hand, and showed them upstairs to Becky's bedroom. "If there's anything you need, anything at all," he said, "you just yell and I'll get it for you."

Kenly tucked Connor into the crib; then Ross watched her prowl around the bedroom, putting their things away. "Did you want to go see Tommy alone?"

She was brushing her hair and her hairbrush stopped in midair. "No. I want you to meet him. It's just, well, I feel stupid that I haven't been back before now."

Ross slid his arms around her and rested his chin on her head. "I'm sure he understands. You have a husband, a kid, and you're still in college. It's not like you aren't busy."

Kenly bit her lower lip. "Ross?"

"Uh-huh."

"I love you."

He ran a finger down her nose and smiled.

WALTER WAS UP EARLY THE NEXT MORNING MAKING BACON and eggs, but Kenly was so nervous she could barely force down a piece of toast. She and Ross snapped Connor into the stroller and walked to the Naylors' after breakfast. Along the way, she reminisced about what it had been like living here, babbling nonstop to ease the panic that was growing inside of her. She stopped in front of the house she and her dad had rented, pointing out her bedroom window to Ross. Then, when they got to the Naylors', the front door popped open and there was Tommy, face lit up with the same cockeyed grin she remembered from whenever he used to get nervous.

"Where've you been? I thought I was gonna have to sic Max on you."

His hair was shorter than she'd ever seen it and he was much too thin, but otherwise he looked the same. Same bumps, lumps, and everything else. Kenly felt something catch in her throat. "Hey, guy," she said, giving him a kiss. "It's good to see you."

Max and Jean came outside then, almost lifting Kenly off her feet with enthusiastic hugs. When they were done, Kenly stepped back with a knot in her stomach and reached for Ross's hand. "Everyone, this is my husband, Ross."

"Nice to meet you," Ross said, shaking Tommy's hand first, then Max's and Jean's.

"And this is Connor."

Connor stared up at this collection of strangers, tousle-headed and unable to move. Then his eyes locked on to Tommy and he went from being quietly agog and curious to a trembling mass of fear. His bottom lip quivered and he lifted both arms up to Ross as he swiveled in the stroller and turned his face away from everyone.

"He's shy with new people," Kenly explained.

Ross squatted, unsnapped him, and lifted him into his arms. "Hey, buddy, it's okay."

Kenly's face flushed and she reached for him. "Come on, sweetie, let me introduce you."

"Leave him, Kenly," Tommy said as he stepped back up onto the porch. "He's scared so let's just go slow, okay?"

She nodded and lowered her arms. The way Tommy handled the situation was sweet and she wanted to hug him for it. Max came to the rescue, moving toward Ross and Connor with an outstretched hand. "Ross, let's take Connor out back. We have an old sandbox he might enjoy digging in."

Confused, Kenly turned to Tommy. "I don't remember any sandbox."

"Probably because we didn't have one until a week ago," Jean said, laughing as she linked an arm through Kenly's and pulled her up the front steps.

Tommy and Kenly stayed inside making coffee while Max, Jean, and Ross sat in the backyard and watched Connor toss sand all over the grass. Kenly stood at the kitchen window, looking out at all the toys Max had spread across the grass for him. "Oh, great," she said dryly. "He's only three and we're already fighting with him constantly wanting every toy he sees when we go in a store. Coming here for the weekend shouldn't set us back at all."

Tommy was sitting on the table with his feet on a chair. "He's a cute kid, Kenly."

Her heart lurched and she went absolutely still, standing there with her back to him. "Thanks. Sometimes I worry about whether or not I'll know how to raise him right."

"Trust your instincts and you'll do fine. You know what's important and what's not."

Jean came bustling into the kitchen to make sandwiches and they helped her carry them outside. Kenly noticed that Tommy was careful to take a chair as far away from Connor as possible. At first, Connor was oblivious. His eyes were alive with excitement as he squatted in the sandbox and filled pail after pail with sand. Five minutes later, he stood, scratched his cheek, and turned around to show Ross something. Then he noticed Tommy, dropped his pail, and instantly began to cry.

Ross was about to get up when Kenly motioned for him to stay. *No, Connor,* she thought, pushing herself out of her chair. *Please don't do this. Not now. Not after everything else I've done to him.* She squatted and held out her arms. "Come here, it's okay." He hurried over and almost threw himself at her. "Why are you crying?"

"Dat bad man," he cried, pointing to Tommy.

Kenly went pale and pulled him onto her lap. *Please, Connor, I'm not asking for much. Point at Max and ask me why he has no hair, embarrass me by saying you're scared of Jean's sunglasses, just please don't do this to Tommy.* "These are Mommy's friends," she said, setting her chin on his head. "Don't be silly."

But Connor had already made up his mind. "He bad man. Make him go 'way." He clutched her jacket and his thumb crept into his mouth.

Ross got up and held out his hand. "Come on, buddy. Let's go for a walk."

Connor's eyes lit up. "Hold you, Daddy, hold you," he said, clinging to Ross's hand as they made their way across the grass toward the ravine.

Kenly stood and watched them go, too upset and embarrassed to turn around, trying to compose herself before she did. She had imagined the opposite, of course. She thought Connor might go up to Tommy and stare at him, or else try to touch his face, overwhelmed by curiosity. And knowing Tommy, he would've encouraged him, dropping to his knees on the grass where Connor could get a better look—teasing him a little, maybe even playing with him. All hopeful imaginings on her part, and for what? To ease her discomfort? To lessen the guilt she lived with every day? To bring father and son together for one heartbreaking moment she'd remember forever? She turned around and slid back into her chair. "I'm sorry, Tommy. I just—"

He cut her off with a shrug. "It's no big deal, Kenly. Don't forget, I'm used to having kids react that way. You worry too much." But she saw the hurt in his eyes and didn't miss the flash of discomfort on his face.

Nothing anyone did seemed to ease Connor's fear of Tommy. They spent the rest of the day outside, barbecued for dinner, and sat around the fire pit until their breath could be seen in little puffs while Ross, Kenly, Jean, and Max took turns taking Connor for walks, playing with him inside, or putting him down for a nap. It was exhausting, and after dinner Ross took Connor back to Walter and Florence's, insisting that Kenly stay and visit.

After Max and Jean left, Kenly and Tommy stayed at the fire. They were wrapped in flannel jackets, sipping coffee, their empty dessert plates balanced on the chair between them. For a while they didn't talk, just sat breathing in the fresh night air. Tommy finally broke the silence, telling her how old Louie Johnson had called Max the month before, upset with the local radio station for refusing to play any of the Christmas songs he had requested because it was August.

"He wanted to know if Max would do a story to help him expose the station."

Kenly laughed. "For what?"

Tommy arched one eyebrow with comic timing. "For aiding and abetting in breaking both the spirit and individualism of the already oppressed elderly who live in the town of Athabasca."

"That man's crazy," she said, shaking her head.

They talked about a few other things that didn't matter—how Athabasca's nine-hole golf course was being expanded to eighteen, how three rooms at the Hillside Motel had been destroyed by an out-of-town road crew. Then Tommy shot her a nervous look and threw another piece of wood on the fire.

"So, how are you, Kenly? Are you happy?"

The question shouldn't have surprised her but it did. "Yes, I am."

He took a sip of coffee and set his cup down. "Then life's giving you what you want?"

She nodded, keeping her eyes on the fire. "Uh-huh."

"You were happy here, too, weren't you?"

"Of course, but not like this, Tommy."

He propped his feet on the bricks surrounding the fire pit, then reached for her hand and gave it a squeeze. "I think it was Woody Allen who said 'the heart wants what the heart wants'? And who can argue with that, huh?"

She looked at him closely, feeling a sudden pang of guilt. "You know what, Tommy? Our phone calls have been getting farther apart all the time, so let's make a pact right here and now that we'll call each other the first week of every month. We can take turns."

He laughed. "I don't know. I'm a busy guy. I could be in the middle of a 'WIT' column deadline or lying in a hospital somewhere."

"I'll find you," she whispered, "and if you're in a hospital, they can bring you a phone."

"What if I'm sleeping?"

"They can wake you."

"What if I don't feel like talking?"

"Then you can listen."

He looked pleased but she could also see he was emotional. "Sounds like a plan."

They sat there side by side in silence until Kenly was sure she would start to cry if she didn't leave. She looked at her watch and opened her mouth to say something, but Tommy held up a hand and stopped her. He stood, leaned down, and kissed her on the cheek. "Will I see you tomorrow before you go?"

Kenly nodded. She tried to think of something to say. That he was remarkable, that she admired the man he'd become, the boy he would always be—that she was sorry. Her eyes filled with tears and as he turned to go, she said, "Tommy? I love you, you know."

He looked back at her. "I know. Now get going. Your family's waiting." He stuck his hands in his pockets and as he walked across the grass she heard him whistling, and it was the sweetest sound that she had heard in days.

ROSS AND CONNOR WERE UP EARLY THE NEXT MORNING, AND by the time Kenly came downstairs, they were already finished with breakfast and getting ready to go for a walk down to the river with Walter and Florence.

"Want to come?" Ross asked, strapping Connor into the stroller.

"I'll pass," she said, giving him a hug. "I'm going over to the Naylors' to say good-bye to Tommy before we leave."

When she got there Jean and Max were at the kitchen table drinking coffee, but Tommy was nowhere in sight. "He was up an hour ago and had toast," Jean explained, "but then he said he wasn't feeling great so he went back to bed."

Kenly chewed at her bottom lip. "Okay. It's just that we're leaving in half an hour to catch our flight back."

"Then you should go," Max said. "We'll tell him you stopped in."

"I really wanted to say good-bye. Can I go see if he's awake?"

Jean shot a quick look at Max and said, "Of course."

Kenly went upstairs and knocked on his door. When there was no answer, she turned the doorknob and stuck her head in. Tommy was lying in bed with his back to her, the gentle rise and fall of his breathing indicating that he was asleep. Kenly looked around at the oxygen tank next to his bed, the Billy Joel album covers framed in glass on one wall, the stacks of newspapers lined up under the window, at his desk littered with textbooks and Post-it notes—all of it just as she'd remembered from years ago.

Slipping inside, she wrote something on a Post-it note and stuck it to the mirror over his desk. Then she gently pulled the door closed and left, saying good-bye to Max and Jean, moving forward out the front door and down the sidewalk, even though she now suspected that he was awake, that he'd been doing what he had done once before—making it as easy as possible for her to leave.

Upstairs in his bedroom, Tommy stood back from the window and watched her go, the note she'd left clutched in his hand: *You are one of the best gifts life has ever given me.*

chapter 18

KENLY GRADUATED FROM NORTHWESTERN UNIVER-
sity with her business degree two months after Connor
turned four. She'd originally thought it might take five years to finish
when she found out she was pregnant, and in the end all it took was a
tightly managed—although chaotic—schedule. After they got married Ross had installed a blackboard in the kitchen where a monthly
calendar was set up revolving around Connor. Since Lexie worked afternoons and took night classes three times a week, she dropped him
off at day care in the morning. Most mornings Kenly had to be at
school, so she picked him up at five on her way home. And because
Ross traveled every second week, he did one or the other when he was
home to give them each a break. To say their lives were hectic would
be an understatement, and Kenly and Ross recognized how fortunate
they were to have Lexie's help, rent-free or not.

Within weeks of graduating, Kenly took a position with the state of
Illinois working with departments that were downsizing and laying off
workers. She spent most of her time setting up job retraining programs

that would give state employees the option of applying to other departments or finding employment in the private sector. She loved her work and although she found it rewarding, she promised herself that as soon as Connor started school, she was going to chase her dream, take some art classes, and learn to sculpt. Until then, balancing her job and her family life looked like it would be more than enough to fill her days.

One night after work Lexie offered to cut her hair, and Kenly took her up on it as she rarely found the extra time to get it done. She slid into a chair, propped a mirror up against the toaster on the kitchen table, and wrapped a towel around her shoulders.

Lexie examined a lock of hair. "Can I cut it short for a change?"

"Just a trim," Kenly said. "No more than an inch."

"Good thinking."

Lexie grabbed her scissors and set to work, not bothering to argue about it the way she usually did. Kenly watched her in the mirror, waiting for Lexie to crack—sensing she had something on her mind, but knowing that pushing her to talk about it would be a mistake. Five minutes later, Lexie stopped and put her hands on her hips.

"Benjy asked me to marry him."

Kenly smiled. "Again?"

"Yes, again."

This was the fourth time in three years, and although there didn't seem to be a pattern as to *when* he asked, he was persistent about the asking.

"So? What did you say?"

"I told him I need to think about it."

Kenly's shoulders fell. "That's what you said the last time."

"I know."

"But you love him?" Kenly asked.

"Yes, but I want to make sure."

"Make sure about what?"

Lexie scowled at her. "That he means it."

"He wouldn't *ask* if he didn't mean it, Lex."

"Fair enough, but anyone can *ask*. Getting married is serious business.

What if he changes his mind one day and leaves? What would I do if he stops loving me and walks out five years from now?" She cut another lock of hair. "I want to make sure that won't happen, that's all."

Kenly adjusted her towel. "There are no guarantees, Lex, and you know it. You can live with us forever if you want. Ross and I are fine with that, but at some point you have to climb out on a limb and trust Benjy with your heart. He's a great guy, but he won't wait forever and if you keep putting him off, eventually you're gonna lose him."

Lexie stopped cutting.

"Life's not an audition, Lex," Kenly said softly. "This is it and it's the only shot you get. So what are you waiting for? You've got this amazing guy who adores you and he's trying to get you to love him back, and maybe it's time that you just *did*."

Lexie slowly set her scissors on the table. Glancing at the clock, she grabbed her car keys and headed for the door.

"Where are you going?" Kenly asked, patting her hair in alarm.

"To see Benjy."

"Now?"

"Yes, now!"

"Uh, what about my hair?" Kenly asked.

"I'll finish it in the morning," Lexie said, waving her off.

Lexie stabbed some numbers into her cell phone, yanked the door open, and hurried down the sidewalk to her car as Kenly stood in the doorway, speechless. "Benjy? Are you awake? Good, 'cause it's me and I want to get married. Not right now, but pretty quick. Life's not an audition, you know."

THEY WERE MARRIED TWO MONTHS LATER AT THE GRAND Wailea in Maui and at Lexie's insistence it was a tiny ceremony. Other than Benjy's parents, only Kenly, Ross, Connor, Walter, and Florence were invited. "Just the thought of a big wedding with everyone staring at me makes me break out in hives," Lexie confided to Kenly.

Benjy couldn't have cared less where they got married or who

joined them. They were getting married and if Lexie wanted the ceremony on Mount Everest, he was fine with that. Since money wasn't
an issue, he made arrangements to fly everyone to Maui first-class and
then paid for everything when they got there.

Florence's Alzheimer's wasn't any worse than it had been the year
before, but when Lexie told Walter about the wedding, he said he
couldn't see bringing her to Maui for a week. "And no matter how
much I want to be there," he told her as gently as he could, "I don't want
to go without her." Two days later, Benjy hired a full-time nurse to help
with Florence in Hawaii and the problem was solved. "Look, Uncle
Walter," Lexie explained, "I can't get married if I don't have someone to
give me away, and I won't get married unless that person is you."

The ceremony was held in the early evening against the backdrop
of a Maui sunset and Connor was the ring bearer. During the vows,
he got tired and sat down at their feet, pulling off his shoes. And it
was this, the sight of her towheaded son playing in the sand, coupled
with seeing Lexie look so beautiful, that finally brought Kenly to
tears. Walter looked like a proud father and Florence amazed everyone by being more lucid than she had been in months. When it was all
over, Kenly hugged them both and congratulated Benjy. "You're a
lucky guy, you know. We're losing our live-in baby-sitter and you're
gaining experimental haircuts for life."

AFTER LEXIE MOVED OUT, SHE STILL SAW CONNOR AT LEAST
once a week, and thanks to her influence, duct tape resurfaced in their
lives with a vengeance. She introduced Connor to it one day when she
was baby-sitting, and whenever a toy broke after that he'd run and
grab a roll. Nothing was exempt. Superheroes and action figures facing life as amputees were quickly put back together; dump trucks,
tractors, water guns, and plastic power tools all got repaired in a snap.
Then on his fifth birthday (along with an armful of other presents),
Lexie gave him a dozen rolls in a box so he wouldn't run out.

Even Tommy mentioned it during one of their monthly phone

calls. "So I hear that kid of yours is duct tape obsessed. What's that about?" Of course there was laughter in his voice, gentle teasing from someone who knew all about Lexie.

Connor put a strip around the top of his rubber boots so he could tell them apart from everyone else's at school. He covered his lunch box with it, used it to tape up a crack on the seat of his bike, and brought a roll with him to every soccer game. It was easy to find him on the soccer field. Kenly and Ross didn't bother looking for his number on the back of his jersey. Instead, they looked for the blur of silver on his legs when he flew by, since he insisted on wrapping it around his soccer socks.

Looking back later, Kenly would remember that it was at one of Connor's first soccer games that Ross told her he thought it was time they had another baby.

"Now?" she said, setting her coffee down.

He kissed her and straightened to watch Connor run across the field. "Not right here and now." He laughed. "But maybe tonight we could start in the kitchen and make our way through the house until we get the job done."

She slid her arms around his waist. *Why not?* she thought. *Then maybe after I have the baby, I'll look into working part-time and take some art classes.*

But things didn't turn out the way they had planned and they ran into a problem that neither of them had considered—Kenly couldn't seem to get pregnant. Each month her hopes lifted in expectation and then fell again when she got her period. Then, six months after she'd stopped taking the pill, she made an appointment to see her doctor.

"Everything's fine, so I see no reason why you can't get pregnant," he told her, patting her shoulder like a child. "Just relax and give it some time."

She repeated his instructions with a wooden patience, relieved that Ross seemed too preoccupied with work to notice, but worried about it anyhow.

————

KENLY STILL WASN'T PREGNANT WHEN CONNOR TURNED SIX and when she came into the kitchen one morning, Ross was drinking coffee, staring out the window with a faraway look in his eyes.

"Taking the day off?" she asked.

He glanced at the clock. "Not today."

Connor was almost horizontal on the kitchen table, his face inches from the page as he colored a picture of Batman. Kenly ruffled his hair. "Hey, pal, I need a favor."

"Why do I always have to do favors," he groaned.

"Because you love me," she said, pointing to the living room. "Now go clean up your toys because Luke and Jadie will be here in ten minutes."

Mentioning the twins from next door perked Connor up. "Can we have a sleepover?"

"We'll talk about it later. Scat."

After he left, she puttered around the kitchen, rearranging things and waiting for Ross to say something, but he just kept staring out the window. Finally she stepped in front of him and gave him a hug. "Wanna talk?" He hugged her back, but when she looked up there were dark circles under his eyes that hadn't been there before. She stepped back, taking his hands in hers. "What's wrong?"

Ross didn't answer and then he walked over to the window. "I didn't want you to worry so I never mentioned it, but I saw my doctor last week."

Kenly slid into a chair. "Why? What's wrong?"

Ross hesitated for a second. "He ran a few tests and then called me back yesterday . . ."

Her heart started to race and a wave of dread worked its way up her spine. *Please don't let there be anything wrong with him.* Silence filled the room and it felt like she was waiting for the world to cave in. "And what did he say?" she asked.

He stared out at the backyard. "That having another baby might not be possible." If she weren't sitting down, Kenly was sure her legs would've given out on her right then. "My sperm count is low . . . so low that our chances of getting pregnant aren't good."

"Oh, Ross." She didn't know what else to say. She closed her eyes in disbelief, then slowly pushed herself out of her chair and went to him, hands trembling as she reached for his. *This is the moment I've been avoiding for years. I have to tell him the truth about Connor.* A wave of nausea rushed through her and she felt her stomach hitch.

"Of course, he told me it's not *impossible*," Ross said, drawing her close and resting his chin on her head. "Just that our chances are pretty slim."

The feel of his arms around her took over and she suddenly felt paralyzed and incapable of speech. Even though not telling him made her the kind of person she didn't want to know, she just couldn't bring herself to tell Ross he wasn't Connor's father—especially now.

"I guess we'll have to let fate take its course, huh? I mean, let's face it, they can't all be blanks," he said, trying a laugh. "Connor's proof enough of that."

She felt tears behind her eyes but willed them back. "It doesn't matter," she said against his chest. "We'll be fine."

Kenly no longer had a clear memory of the moment when she'd made the choice to lie to Ross about Connor, but she had, and that was something she couldn't change even if she wanted to. She'd often wondered what she would say if he ever broached the subject with her, and it was now—in this moment—that she discovered that her deepest instinct was to protect him from the truth, the same way she wanted to protect Tommy from it; leaving everything as it was, and everyone she loved blissfully unaware of something that could turn their lives upside down.

For months after their talk, she blamed herself, believing this had happened because of her; that what she'd done was coming back to haunt them, playing havoc in their lives by hurting Ross instead of her. After a while, her failure to get pregnant was something they stopped talking about and the faint hope she saw in Ross's eyes began to fade, even though it was always there, an unspoken disappointment they shared, but found too painful to bring up.

———————

THAT FALL AFTER CONNOR STARTED BACK AT SCHOOL, ROSS was promoted to vice president with ComTech Training. The company was doing well, expanding into foreign markets and getting ready to go public. Ross threw himself into his job with renewed energy, traveling again, and spending even more time at work. Although Kenly had originally hoped to go back to school part-time and take some art classes, she decided to wait for a year or so and give Ross all the support he needed.

"Are you sure?" he said when she brought it up one night.

"Absolutely. Let's face it. Working full-time at my job isn't overwhelming, the money is good, and I've got a lot more flexibility than you do when it comes to Connor. Going back to school would change that and I just can't see adding all that extra stress right now." Ross's face lit up with relief and appreciation, and that was all she needed. Sacrificing her dreams for a while seemed the least she could do while he chased his.

Connor's early attachment to tractors and dump trucks moved on to an obsession with superheroes when he turned seven and soon he had every action figure Lexie could buy in the state of Illinois. Kenly and Ross were more than willing to promote the stage that followed, where he sat on the floor quietly building intricate creations with his Legos. Overall, he was a busy kid with an interest in things Kenly was sure only the male gender would find fascinating. One morning he burst through the back door while they were eating breakfast.

"Guess what? There's a dead toad on the sidewalk out front," he informed them. "Wanna see?"

Kenly rolled her eyes and passed, but Ross followed him outside, laughing.

When Ross wasn't working, he and Connor were inseparable. They spent hours playing soccer and hockey, Rollerblading and biking. Connor rarely got sick with anything more than a cold and yet when Kenly took him for his annual physical, she caught herself breathing a sigh of relief when Dr. Browning told her exactly what he had the year before—that Connor was a normal, healthy young boy.

The year he turned eight, he split his forehead open one weekend and Ross had to race him to the emergency room for stitches. When they strolled into the house later that afternoon, Kenly was home from getting groceries, in the middle of making dinner. She turned around, saw him, and felt her insides drop. "What happened?"

Ross gave her a look that said she should leave it alone, but Kenly squinted at Connor from across the room. "Why didn't you call me? What hospital did you go to?" The questions were tossed out too fast for Ross to answer. "Does it hurt?" She squatted in front of Connor, who'd dropped into a kitchen chair.

He rolled his eyes. "I'm fine, Mom."

Ross cleared his throat, trying to get her attention, but she ignored him, running a finger over Connor's forehead. "Well, the stitches on your forehead say you aren't."

He squirmed away from her. "I'm fine, *really.*"

Frustrated, she turned to Ross. "What happened?"

"He fell off the roof and hit his head on the drainpipe."

"He *what?*"

"I told you she'd freak out," Connor said.

Kenly spun around and glared at him. "What were you doing on the roof?"

"Getting a Frisbee," he said matter-of-factly.

She sputtered in disbelief, but Ross must have seen the alarm in her face because he stepped in, taking her by the elbow and guiding her into the living room. "He's being a kid, Kenly," he said, laughing. "Lighten up. You worry too much."

He said it gently and she nodded, murmuring her agreement, even though she strained to look back over his shoulder and make sure Connor was fine, the fear of losing him disguised in the same familiar wave of panic that hit her whenever the *possibility* of something happening to him raised its ugly head. And yet, other than that one minor accident, Connor was a healthy kid. So much so that she was often amazed when she or Ross got the flu but he didn't. There were only two times when he wasn't healthy and in top form: the year he got measles and the summer when he had his tonsils out. And both times, Kenly secretly thought he enjoyed the attention more than was necessary, pushing the envelope of pity a little too far, but Ross just shrugged and laughed at her. "He has a low tolerance for pain, like his mother."

chapter 19

KENLY WASN'T HAVING THE BEST WEEK AND THE last thing she wanted to do was talk on the phone, but she knew Tommy looked forward to their monthly calls and hated to miss them herself now that they'd become such a ritual. He answered on the second ring.

"Hey, Tommy, how are you?"

"Better than you sound. Got a cold?"

"That and a case of chicken pox." She was sitting on the couch with a bag of cotton balls and a bottle of calamine lotion, slowly working her way down each arm, across her neck, behind her ears, and over her face.

"How'd that happen?"

"Connor got them last week and I was next in line. I guess I didn't have them as a kid."

Tommy laughed. "I'll keep our call short then. I have a question for you, though. What's the capital of Tuvalu?"

Kenly groaned. "How should I know? I've never even heard of Tuvalu."

"Then look it up and call me back. How are you supposed to pre-
pare Connor for his future if you don't know these things?"

The line went dead and she stared at it in amazement, then threw
the covers off and went to find an atlas. Over the last few months,
Tommy had become fanatical about geography; a subject she'd always
hated, even when it was pushed on her in high school. When she finally called him back, an atlas was balanced on her knees next to a box
of Kleenex.

"Funafuti," she said.

Tommy sounded pleased. "Well, there you go."

"Okay, what's up? You're applying as a contestant for *Jeopardy*? No,
wait," she said, snapping her fingers. "You're moving to Funafuti because you were offered a job at an almost-defunct newspaper that desperately needs someone to revive it?"

"No, I'm doing tutoring by mail with a girl who lives in Yellowknife."

Kenly's eyebrows lifted in surprise. "How did you meet her?"

"I haven't." There was a pause and when he continued, she heard
something catch in his voice. "My doctor called and asked if I could
give her some help. She wants to finish high school, but she's having
trouble preparing for the equivalency exam. She's got Proteus Syndrome, too, but they don't think she'll live longer than another year."

A sad smile trembled on Kenly's face. "I see."

The atlas she was holding was one that she had used in high school,
and there were miscellaneous notes scratched all over it from when she
used to get bored in class. Glancing down at a few of them, she said,
"I've got a few questions for you, but they have nothing to do with geography."

He sounded surprised. "Ask away."

"How many hours are there in a day?"

"Twenty-four."

"How many minutes?"

After a brief hesitation where she knew he was calculating, he said,
"One thousand, four hundred, and forty."

"And how many seconds?"

A longer pause followed by some shuffling, probably as he grabbed a pen or a calculator. "Uh, eighty-six thousand, four hundred."

She closed the atlas and blew her nose.

"What's your point?" Tommy asked.

"That we all have the same number of seconds, minutes, and hours in a day, and as always you humble me with how you spend yours compared to how I spend mine."

He cleared his throat and rescued them from an awkward silence. "As always, you're too hard on yourself. Look, I'm gonna go, but when you call next month, I'll want to know what system of weights is used by pharmacists so you'd better look it up."

Kenly laughed. "Tommy, *who cares?*"

"I do and you should. Connor may one day decide to become a pharmacist and after our phone call next month you're going to thank me for being able to relate to how he spends his days, even on that one small level."

She said good-bye and hung up, setting the atlas on the coffee table. For five years now they'd been sharing monthly calls back and forth, and today, as always, she was amazed at how much he put himself out there for others and how tenaciously he pushed the envelope in relation to how much he could fit into his life. She enjoyed their calls, but each time she talked to him, smells and sounds and emotions she'd forgotten came back to the surface, reminding her again about the choice she'd made years ago—leaving her weak with fresh shame and regret.

LEXIE'S TENDENCY TO GO OVERBOARD WITH GIFTS FOR CONNOR never completely stopped, even after Kenly spoke to her about it.

"But I don't think I spoil him," she argued.

Kenly rolled her eyes. "Right. Okay, Lex, do you think you could go through one six-month period where you *don't* buy him anything? Can you do that for me?"

"Nothing?"

"Nothing," Kenly repeated, crossing her arms.

Lexie rolled her eyes as if she thought the conversation was ridiculous, then heaved a sigh. "Okay, fine."

Six months later, Kenly and Ross woke up one morning to Lexie's car horn blasting from the driveway. Kenly sat up straight, blinking in confusion, then ran to the window. "What the—?"

Ross pulled a pillow over his head as Connor came skidding around the corner. "Hey, guys, Aunt Lexie's here," he said. "And guess what? She's got this huge box all wrapped up with a bow on it in the middle of the front lawn. Who do you think it's for?"

Kenly rested her forehead against the window. "I can't imagine."

While Connor tore the paper off, Kenly and Ross stood on the front steps rubbing their eyes. Lexie squealed as loudly as Connor did when he opened the box and an eight-week-old golden retriever puppy trundled out at his feet.

"Happy birthday, buddy," she said, clenching her hands together and grinning through tears.

Connor buried his face against the puppy. "But I'm not nine for another month."

"I know, but Uncle Benjy won't let me keep him that long, so you get him a little early."

Benjy gave Connor's shoulder a squeeze on his way across the lawn, his face pink with embarrassment. He half-waved to Ross and Kenly, then frowned like he wasn't any happier about this than they were.

"I tried to stop her," he said. "But you know how she is."

Connor and Lexie were rolling around the grass as the puppy bounded back and forth between them. Kenly sighed and shook her head. "Yes, I do."

During a phone call to Tommy two weeks later, she told him what Lexie had done, hoping he'd sympathize with her. "Just think about it. Do you know *anyone* who'd buy a kid a puppy without asking first?" Without waiting for an answer, she carried on. "And who do you think gets up at night when he has to go outside?" she complained. "Me, of course."

"But the puppy's cute?" Tommy asked, interrupting.

She hesitated. "He's adorable."

"And Connor loves him?"

"What do you think?"

Tommy laughed. "That life's short and he's lucky to have Lexie for an aunt."

"Why are you on her side?" she grumbled.

"This isn't about sides," he said. "It's about how much fuller Connor's life is by having Lexie in it. Think about it, Kenly. That she's head over heels in love with him and has been since the day he was born is the real gift. The puppy's gravy."

Kenly was sitting outside on the deck. An ant was making its way across her foot and her nose was itching, but she sat still, murmuring her agreement as she watched Connor chase his puppy around the yard. It had been an uneventful Saturday. She'd baked a cake and cleaned the house, shopped and done laundry, and now, at four in the afternoon, completely out of the blue, a fresh flash of shame had her trying to put together the image of Connor with Tommy—knowing how much fuller Connor's life would be if she actually could.

chapter 20

THE FIRST TIME KENLY MET JOEY TRAMBINI HE stopped at the house for just ten minutes, and by the time he left, she already knew she didn't like him. He was six inches taller than Connor and he acted superior and sure of himself, never dropping his eyes in that shy way Connor's other friends did and carrying himself with an annoying *been there, done that* swagger that held Connor spellbound and worried Kenly.

"When did Joey move into the neighborhood?" she asked as casually as she could manage over dinner that night.

Connor shrugged. "A few weeks ago."

"Does he have any brothers or sisters?"

"I don't think so."

"Maybe I'll call his parents and introduce myself," she said.

"They're divorced," Connor informed her. "He lives with his dad."

Kenly raised her eyebrows and Ross frowned as if to ask why she felt the need for an interrogation.

"He's sure tall for his age," she commented.

"That's because he's thirteen," Connor said, clearly impressed.

Kenly looked at Ross with an unspoken message that said she saw trouble coming, but he just rolled his eyes like he thought she was overreacting and went back to eating his dinner.

FOUR DAYS LATER, CONNOR CLIMBED INTO THE BACKSEAT OF THEIR car with his head down as Kenly turned on the radio and drummed her fingers against the steering wheel. The shock still hadn't worn off and she was doing a poor job of calming herself down. She took a slow breath, slid her fingers under her sunglasses and rubbed her eyes, then couldn't stand it any longer. As she swiveled around, her eyes burned into him, sitting slumped in the backseat.

"Do you have *any* idea how serious this is?"

"I guess," he mumbled.

When she had gotten the call at work that morning, she hadn't believed it at first, but when she walked into the pharmacy and looked at him, his eyes went down and she knew he was guilty. Now the expression on her face was stuck somewhere between disbelief and disappointment. "What were you thinking?" she asked, the anger in her voice hard to hide. "And what were you doing stealing cigarettes? You're eleven years old."

"They weren't for me," he said, with just enough hesitation that she knew he was lying. "They were for Joey."

"Even if you were telling the truth, *that doesn't make it okay.*" She bit her lip and pulled into traffic, careful to keep her eyes on the road. "As of right now, you're grounded for two weeks and you aren't allowed to spend any more time with Joey, understood?"

She watched his shoulders fall in the rearview mirror. He spent the next few minutes sulking until they pulled into their driveway, then climbed out of the car and made his way into the house looking miserable.

When Ross got home from work that night he came through the kitchen door, kissed Kenly on the nape of her neck, and straightened. "Where's Connor?"

"Last time I checked, lying on his bed staring at the ceiling."

He set his laptop down and frowned. "Everything okay?"

"Actually, no. We had a little *problem* today."

"What happened?"

"The pharmacy called me this morning. They caught him and Joey stealing cigarettes."

Ross blinked in shock. "You're kidding."

"I wish I were."

He ran both hands through his hair. "I can think of better ways to end my day."

Kenly nodded her agreement.

"Okay, I'll go up and talk to him," he muttered, climbing the stairs.

THE NEXT DAY WAS TUESDAY, AUGUST 11, AND IT WAS FILLED with things Kenly would never forget. Like how humid it was that morning or how she knew Connor would argue (as he always did) about taking the garbage out, and how much it annoyed her when Joey showed up.

"Morning, Mrs. Lowen."

Kenly closed the trunk of her car. "Good morning, Joey."

"Connor around?"

She watched with iron self-control as he dropped his bike into one of her flower beds and made his way up the sidewalk, as if it was perfectly logical that he should be here to see Connor and not a problem that they'd been caught shoplifting the day before.

"He's grounded," she said simply.

"Oh, well, can I just talk to him for a couple minutes?"

Kenly crossed her arms. "No, you can't, and I also think you should stay clear of each other for a while."

Hardly a day would go by later when she didn't remember that moment. They looked at each other with open and intense dislike, and it was as though they reached some kind of understanding and, at the same time, an unspoken challenge, too. Joey nodded, but there was a hair-trigger shift in his smile when he jumped on his bike and rode away that bothered her.

On her way out the door ten minutes later, Kenly gave Connor one final warning. "I'm only working until noon today so I should be back by one-thirty, and don't you dare set foot outside this house."

CONNOR WAS LYING ON THE COUCH PLAYING WITH HIS GAME Boy when Joey knocked at the kitchen door an hour later.

"Wanna go for a ride?" he asked with a grin when Connor opened the door.

"Nah, I'm gonna watch a movie."

"We'd only be half an hour. No more than an hour, tops."

Connor looked down at his shoes and hesitated, then glanced outside to where his bike was leaning against the garage. Who was ever gonna know if he went for a quick bike ride?

Joey lifted both hands in the air with his fingers splayed. "Hey, I understand. Scared you'll get caught, right?"

"No," Connor said with fake bravado. "Just gimme a minute and we'll go."

Fifteen minutes later they were biking alongside the railroad tracks. It was a tough ride, but Connor didn't want Joey to see how tired he was. After all, they'd just started out and this had to be worth something if he got into trouble later. They rode side by side in silence until they came to an abandoned gravel road almost overgrown by weeds. It went across the train tracks and then angled up a hill on the other side, disappearing from view a few hundred feet up. When they finally made it to the top, Joey jumped off his bike to tighten his chain and Connor leaned against his handlebars, breathing hard.

"I know she's pissed-off, but it'll pass," Joey said without looking up.

"What?"

"Your mom. She's mad about yesterday, but it'll pass."

Connor bit his lower lip. "Yeah."

"Wanna race me back down?" Joey asked, straightening with a grin.

Connor wanted to wait a few minutes, but he knew Joey's impatience was impossible to stand up to for long so they raced back down the steep slope, bumping recklessly side by side until they broke through the trees at the bottom and pedaled across the tracks. Joey made it across first and declared himself the winner, but Connor just shrugged, happy to be there.

Riding in a lazy circle, Joey came upright and stood on his pedals. "That was wild! Let's do it again."

After they made it back to the top of the hill the second time, Joey got off his bike, dropped it on the ground, and pulled out a pack of cigarettes from his jean jacket. "We've earned it," he said to Connor with a grin, passing one to him.

Connor smiled as he fought to catch his breath. One afternoon a week ago Joey had casually held a cigarette out to him without a word and Connor had taken it. Then, sitting on a bench at the park, they had smoked together, talking about what they wanted to do for the rest of the summer. Ever since then, this had become a special ritual between them.

Connor looked around and noticed a barbed-wire fence running down both sides of the narrow road to the bottom of the hill. Tacked to a tree on one side of the road was a sign that said, DANGER, NO TRES-PASSING. He frowned. "I wonder if we're supposed to be up here?"

"Who cares?" Joey said, lighting his cigarette and handing the match to Connor.

They smoked in silence and then Joey took one last drag off his cig-arette and expertly flicked it into the bush with a snap of his fingers. "Ready to go?" he asked, nodding to the smoke rising up through the trees in the distance. "The train's almost here. We're gonna race it."

Connor swallowed. "I don't know, Joey. I'm pretty tired."

"What's the matter? You *chicken*?"

The dull roar of the train was getting louder now, with a clamoring of metal against metal that lifted the hair on Connor's arms. Joey cupped his hands around his mouth. "Hey, mama's boy? You *chickenshit?*"

Connor knew it was the wrong thing to do, but something made him lift his chin and take Joey's bait. His face reddened and he recklessly decided to show him that he was no chicken. Joey took off on his bike with a surge of fresh speed and Connor pedaled after him with his head low and the handlebars on his bike shaking. He managed to pull ahead for a few seconds, but then Joey eked past him again, shouting, "Faster, *chicken!*" He looked over his shoulder and laughed, giving Connor just enough time to catch up again. They were side by side when Connor's bike hit a pothole and wobbled. Connor almost lost his balance, but instinctively he leaned over and corrected it.

Joey's face suddenly filled with uncertainty as he glanced toward the oncoming train and then back to the tracks at the bottom of the hill. He may have been acting tough before, but now he looked scared shitless. His eyes filled with panic and he braked, sliding sideways and out of control, his back tire glancing against Connor's leg with just enough force to send them both end over end in the process. Connor's foot snagged on something and he felt himself being lifted off his bike through the air. He slammed back down against the ground and then rolled in a vicious tangle with his bike onto the tracks, bouncing like a rag doll and landing pinned underneath it. Fighting not to lose consciousness, he lifted his head and fleetingly caught sight of Joey, rolling around in agony a few feet away.

There was an odd stillness in those few seconds before the train hit him when Connor knew he'd gone too far. He saw it coming like a rocket and lifted one arm in fear, using all of his strength to push out from underneath his bike and scramble to safety. But the front tire had snapped off and the metal rim was embedded into the flesh of his right leg, pinning him down with the weight of the bike. A piercing screech filled the air as the train's brakes were clamped down too late to stop this catastrophe from happening, and the last thing Connor saw was a shower of sparks flying through the air toward him as thousands of tons of steel groaned in protest against the railroad tracks.

chapter 21

KENLY BALANCED A BAG OF GROCERIES AGAINST ONE hip as she fumbled with her keys to open the kitchen door. "Hey, Connor?" she called out, pushing the door open and setting the bag on the table. "I'm home."

She looked at her watch. It was one o'clock and she was early, which was great. Maybe she'd grab Motley and go for a quick run before she and Connor decided what they were going to do this afternoon. As if on cue, Motley came skidding around the corner into the kitchen, spinning in circles at her feet with a stuffed animal in his mouth.

"Hey, boy," she said, stooping to give him a pat. "Have you been outside this morning?" Dropping her purse on the counter, she leaned into the living room and frowned. "I wouldn't mind some help down here," she yelled upstairs.

Just seconds later, she was at the fridge putting groceries away when she heard Joey's voice. "H-help! Mrs. Lowen, help!"

Turning, she saw him stumble up to the screen door with one arm dangling at his side and blood smeared on his shirt and face from what looked like a gash on his forehead.

"*Oh, my God!* Are you okay?"

Never good in emergencies, Kenly yanked the door open and reached gingerly for Joey as she glanced over his shoulder and tried to determine what had happened. The instant she touched him, he slumped against her, sobbing and shaking with rising hysteria.

"It w-was an accident . . . and I c-couldn't stop."

Kenly's heart was pounding and she didn't feel equipped to deal with this. *What the hell was he talking about?* "What happened, Joey? Tell me what's wrong?" She squatted to check his forehead, confused by how much blood there was from what she now saw looked like a relatively small cut.

But Joey didn't seem to hear her. He was pulling at her arm and tugging her toward the door, his eyes wide. "H-hurry; he needs help."

"Who?" Kenly followed him outside. "Wait, Joey. Who needs help?"

It became deadly quiet and he stopped and turned his face away from her, chest heaving from a fresh round of sobs. Then he hung his head and said, "Connor n-needs help."

In those few seconds before the realization hit that he was talking about her son, Kenly instinctively wanted to run back to the house and call the police or anyone else who might be able to take charge and help them. But then his words sank in and her face blackened in anger, then with fear as the sound of distant sirens hit her and her knees almost gave out. Taking Joey by his good arm, she almost dragged him down to the end of the sidewalk.

"*Where is he?*" she screamed, fighting hard not to shake him.

Joey hunched down like she'd struck him, then pointed with fear-stricken eyes. "Up at the t-train tracks . . . on Old Mill Road."

Kenly turned and ran, darting across the road and through a path in the brush she knew would get her there faster. Her heart was racing and she couldn't stop thinking about what she'd heard in Joey's voice, a raw and shaken kind of horror that said far more than his words could. She was already crying when she came through the brush onto

Old Mill Road and saw the first police car, and then an ambulance parked next to it with red lights flashing.

Oh, dear God, please no . . .

She was dizzy and gasping for breath as she pushed her way through the throng of people who'd gathered when they heard the sirens. The first cop she ran into was pigeon-toed, something Kenly noticed as she looked down, gasping for air until she finally managed to tell him Connor was her son. He took her by the arm and helped her over to where a group of police and rescue squad personnel were gathered.

Struggling to see past them, Kenly pushed hard against his chest. "Where is he?" she demanded, brushing away tears in frustration.

And then Joey was there and someone was putting a blanket over his shoulders as a police radio squawked out orders in the background.

"This is the boy's mother," the pigeon-toed cop explained to an older cop with a grim look on his face.

"Which boy?"

He lifted his chin in the direction of the train and Kenly shoved past him, scrambling up a steep hill to where she could see a group of paramedics bent over a stretcher, working.

"Ma'am," the older cop called out. "Please stay back."

Another police car pulled in next to the ambulance with its lights flashing and the place was quickly swarming with even more people, but Kenly ignored them all, watching in horror as one paramedic pressed a mask over Connor's ashen face while another held up a plastic bag of fluid connected by a tube to an IV in his right hand. She was reaching for him when the pigeon-toed cop caught up to her and grabbed her by the arm. It was then that she noticed Connor's bike, lying off to the side, twisted almost beyond recognition and surrounded by what looked like a small oil spill of congealing blood.

"Ma'am? He's still alive but they're going to have to airlift him to Chicago."

Kenly turned and blinked up at him in shock, and it was then that she heard the thunderous pounding of helicopter blades as it dipped into view over the trees and circled, looking for a spot to land.

ROSS'S FACE WAS PALE WHEN HE PUSHED THROUGH THE swinging doors into the hospital's waiting room. Across the room were two sofas, a narrow table overflowing with magazines, and a row of straight-back chairs sitting against a window. Kenly turned at the sound of his footsteps, stood up from the sofa, and put her arms around him, saying nothing.

"How is he?" Ross finally asked.

"They're operating now," she said. "He's been unconscious the whole time and he's lost a lot of blood, but they think he'll be okay."

On the verge of tears, she stepped back and ran both hands through her hair.

"And?" he asked, taking her by the arms. "What else?"

She took a long breath, not able to say it out loud yet, knowing that as soon as she did, it would make all of this even more real and impossible to grasp.

"Kenly, *tell me*."

She hesitated and then whispered, "He . . . he lost a leg."

In the silence that followed, Ross lowered himself into a chair and stared blindly out the window. Kenly sat next to him, aware only of his shallow breathing and the constant metallic tick of the clock on the wall behind them.

"Which leg?"

The question startled her. "The left."

Ross swallowed. "Above the knee or below the knee?"

"Just below the knee," she managed.

"Well, that means he might walk again, right?"

Kenly stood and spread her hands in a gesture of bewilderment. In emergencies, everyone always turned to Ross. He was the calm one where she could be counted on for the hysterics, so she knew this was just his way of coping—gathering the facts, assessing them, and then neatly compartmentalizing until he was ready to face what had happened and do something about it. Turning away, she walked to the window and closed her eyes. "No more, Ross, okay?" she whispered. "Please. Not now."

THREE DAYS PASSED BEFORE CONNOR FINALLY CAME OUT OF his drug-induced sleep, and once he did, no one seemed able to comfort him. Kenly and Ross were there beside him to explain what had happened. How Joey had run to the house for help and had a broken arm, and how the ambulance, the police, and a fire truck were already there when Kenly found Connor. In the end, it took just fifteen minutes to airlift him to the hospital, a decision that may have saved his life because he'd lost so much blood.

Connor blinked and listened intently, but none of it seemed to register until he found out that he'd lost half of his leg. In the end, even though his doctors were in the room with them, it was Ross who told him as Kenly stood with her back to the room, looking out over the parking lot, one hand pressed to her mouth.

Connor's eyes went wide with disbelief; then panic and fear took over his face as he yanked frantically at the blankets. When they fell away and he saw the stump of a half-leg he was left with, the disbelief turned to shock and they had to sedate him to calm him down. For days after that, he was almost catatonic, refusing to eat or talk to anyone.

ONE WEEK LATER, KENLY CAME INTO THE HOSPITAL ROOM TO find Ross demonstrating how easy it was to get around on the crutches the doctors had given Connor until his prosthetic leg arrived. "Look, scout," he said, giving Connor's shoulder a squeeze. "You'll be up and around before you know it." Connor turned his head away on the pillow and Kenly shot Ross an annoyed look.

She found his cheerfulness grating as she fought to keep her own emotions from erupting and making everything worse. She couldn't stop thinking about Tommy—how they talked each month about what was new at his end and what had been going on in her chaotic life—and yet she couldn't bring herself to call and tell him what had happened to Connor.

"Connor's in denial about it," Ross said at dinner that night.

Kenly didn't answer, just continued pushing her food around the plate, thinking.

Ross looked up at the ceiling, studying it as if there were something to see. "The anger will come next," he said, half to himself.

She ignored him, thinking instead about how Connor had looked so pale earlier that day, with his blond hair falling over his forehead as the physical therapist worked on his leg.

Ross speared a potato from his plate. "He could easily slip into depression, so we'll have to watch for that."

"It's here," she whispered.

"Pardon me?"

"It's here, Ross. It showed up with the denial and the anger in one big ball of wax."

He studied her, then slowly set down his fork. "Okay, I guess that's enough of that."

"Enough of what?"

He pushed his chair away from the table. "This conversation. There's obviously no point."

A long, aching silence stretched between them as they surveyed each other and Ross finally shook his head, looking frustrated. "You know what, Kenly? You're living in a world where the glass is half-empty. Maybe it's time you stopped denying what happened here and started looking ahead to the future so Connor can get on with his life."

She stood up and pushed her chair back, lashing out at him for reasons even she didn't understand. "Don't you get it, Ross? We can't make a tidy little list and check off denial and then anger and whatever else it is you think he'll go through on his way back to being whole again, because *he won't.*"

Ross stood, looking so calm it enraged her.

She grabbed the pepper mill off the table and threw it at the window over the kitchen sink, smashing it and sending glass flying everywhere.

"This is a huge fucking black hole for him," she screamed, "and his life is never going to be the way it was before—*ever!*"

He looked calmly at the broken glass, then opened a drawer by the phone, pulled out a measuring tape, and measured the window frame, his jaw tight. Grabbing a piece of paper, he jotted down a few numbers, turned, and was gone.

THE NEXT DAY, KENLY SAT WITH CONNOR FOR MORE THAN AN hour, but he didn't utter a word. His scrawny shoulders were hunched up under the thin hospital gown and his eyes were glued to the TV across the room. When the door swung open and a nurse bustled in with a tray of food, it startled both of them.

"Lunchtime," she said, setting it on the serving stand and wheeling it into position over the bed. But before she even had the chance to remove the lid, Connor pushed the tray onto the floor with an angry swoop of his arm, sending it skidding across the salmon-colored tiles, where it came to rest just inches from Kenly's feet.

"Leave me alone!"

Kenly didn't move even when the nurse jumped, threw Connor a frustrated look, and stormed out with the door swinging shut behind her. Instead she watched in horrified fascination as anger took over his face and he turned to glare at her.

"Why don't you leave, too? Can't you see I don't want you here?" He was yelling at her, outraged by her calm silence, breathing so hard that he was shaking.

She didn't answer, just picked up the remote control sitting next to her and began flipping through channels. She knew he didn't really want her to leave. It was something she couldn't put her finger on, but she felt it, the way a mother instinctively does when she looks into her child's eyes and sees what no one else can.

Reaching over to his nightstand, Connor snatched up the box of hockey cards Lexie had bought him and lofted them across the room at her, missing by at least a foot. His bottom lip was quivering with emotion. "Go, Mom. Please, just go!"

Kenly rose from her chair and began picking up the cards, one by one. When she was done, she picked up his food tray and wiped up the Jell-O smashed underneath it, along with what had once been an egg sandwich. The door swung wide while she was still on her knees and an older man came in carrying a mop and pail.

"I'll get the rest, ma'am," he said.

She straightened, set the tray on the table next to her chair, and turned around to stare out the window. Through it all, Connor's narrow chest moved up and down, his neck muscles standing out as his eyes looked through her as if she weren't even there.

ON HER WAY HOME FROM THE HOSPITAL, KENLY STOPPED AND bought two bottles of wine and one bottle of vodka. She'd taken an indefinite leave of absence from work and had been spending most of her time at the hospital whether Connor wanted her there or not, but right now she felt like she was standing on the edge of a cliff, waiting for the ground to give way underneath her.

She'd almost lost her son, who would never be the same again, and now he was pulling away from her and shutting her out of his life. It wasn't hard to make the leap that he was somehow paying the price for what she'd done years ago, and it took even less for her to find a way to hide from that very possibility.

Filled with self-loathing, she started drinking as a way of deadening her emotions from all that was raw and real and painful about Connor's situation. That first day, she got blindingly drunk, then spent half an hour vomiting into the bathroom sink. When Ross got home from work, she told him she wasn't feeling great, feigning a touch of the flu.

She quickly developed a pattern where she went to the hospital each morning to see Connor (who rarely spoke to her or anyone else when she was there), then came home after lunch and drank until she couldn't stand. Then she would crawl into bed and dream about a time before all of this had happened, long ago before she'd messed everything up.

Ross was away on business for a few days and Kenly had just taken a long sip of wine from the bottle and was lying on the couch with her eyes closed when she heard a car pull into the driveway. She quickly hid the bottle between the chair and the couch, then grabbed two peppermints from the candy dish on the coffee table. Popping them in her mouth, she ran her fingers through her hair (flat on one side and puffy on the other), then hurried into the kitchen straightening her shirt. Lexie was pounding on the door in frustration when she got there.

"What's the matter?" Kenly said, pulling the door open.

Lexie pushed past her. "You haven't been answering the phone. I've been worried."

"It mustn't be working then, 'cause I haven't heard it ring today." In fact she had heard it ring; she just hadn't picked up, worried her speech might sound slurred and that whoever was calling would guess she'd been drinking.

Motley came running into the kitchen to say hello as Lexie marched across the room and picked up the phone. Distracted, she bent to pet him as she listened to the dial tone. "Seems to be working fine," she said, hanging up.

Kenly shrugged, then went to the sink and busied herself with rinsing dishes, keeping her back to Lexie, wishing she would leave.

"Is Ross out of town?"

"Until tomorrow."

"How's Connor doing?"

"About the same."

Their conversation came to an awkward end. Kenly wiped her hands and turned around, leaning against the counter for support. "Lex, I love you for stopping by, but I need to be alone right now, okay?" Her throat tightened and she closed her eyes, suddenly thinking about the half-empty bottle of wine tucked between the couch and the chair in the living room; thinking about her dad years ago, hiding his drinking from her when she knew about it all along. And suddenly she hated where she was going with this.

"Kenly?"

"Uh-huh?"

"You're scaring me. Are you okay?"

She opened her eyes and shook her head. "No, but I will be."

Ten minutes after Lexie left, the phone rang, but Kenly ignored it, staring blankly out the kitchen window at the jumble of weeds growing in rich confusion around what had once been her garden. "You've reached Ross, Kenly, and Connor, but no one's able to take your call. Please leave your name and number and we'll get back to you." *Beep.*

"Uh. Hi, Kenly, it's Tommy. I wasn't sure if you got my message last week so I thought I'd call again." He hesitated and Kenly heard him clear his throat. "I wish there was something, anything, I could do to help. When Lexie called and told us, I couldn't believe it and, well, it took days to sink in." He paused. "I guess . . . anyhow, I'm sure you'll call when you feel like talking about it. I just hope he's doing okay. Talk to you soon."

This was Tommy's second message, but she still couldn't bring herself to call back, knowing that the minute she heard his voice she'd lose every ounce of composure she had left. She would phone him later, when she was feeling stronger—when she was sure she could make the call without falling apart.

She went into the living room, where she took the bottle of wine she'd been drinking, took it to the kitchen, and poured it down the sink. Then she opened the linen closet and pulled out two more, doing the same with them—telling herself that years from now, when she looked back on all of this, at least she'd be able to say that her drinking had stopped almost as quickly as it had started. Her heart just wasn't in it.

chapter 22

IT HAD BEEN SIX WEEKS SINCE THE ACCIDENT AND things weren't getting any better. Uncertain of what to do, Ross phoned and woke Lexie up at 5:00 A.M. one morning in late September. By 5:30, she was standing on the shore of the lake next to him, barefoot, slack-jawed, and with Benjy's jacket wrapped around her pajamas as the morning mist drifted across the water. They stood in silence at first, watching Kenly in a yellow rowboat on the lake as she brought a fishing rod back over her shoulder to cast the line out and then reeled it back in, over and over again.

"Is she coming unhinged?" Lexie asked in a whisper, in case Kenly could hear her.

Ross shook his head. "I don't know."

"Well, has she ever *been* fishing?"

"Not that I know of."

"And you don't fish?"

Ross reddened. "Nope. I love sailing. Hate fishing."

"Whose boat?"

He shrugged, looking defeated.

Lexie's tongue moved over to one side of her mouth and poked her cheek out as she thought about all of this. Connor's withdrawn and sullen behavior was getting to everyone, but over the last few weeks, it was Kenly who had her worried.

"Go make coffee," she said, nudging Ross toward the house. "I'll try to talk to her, okay?"

He nodded, then turned and slowly made his way back up the hill to the house.

Without mentioning it to anyone, Kenly had driven into town the day before to buy a fishing rod, some hooks, a life jacket, and a net. Then she drove home and called the number she'd jotted down from a sign a few days before: BOAT RENTALS, 555-1963. The first time she had seen the sign, she was on her way home from the hospital and she pulled over and stared at it for a few minutes, letting something old and buried bubble up inside of her.

It was a memory of fishing with her dad—one of the few she treasured. She had just turned six and he was on the phone with a friend one night making arrangements to go fishing the next day. As she listened to him plot and plan what sounded like a great adventure, her curiosity got the better of her.

"Can I go, too?" she asked in a small voice when he hung up.

He turned and studied her with a startled expression, then wrinkled his forehead as he considered her request. "How about this? If you're awake, dressed, and ready to go when I leave here at five tomorrow morning, you can go."

Kenly swallowed, never breaking his gaze as she nodded her agreement, recognizing even then that he didn't think she could do it. But her determination to go was unshakable and, with a little help from her mom, she was at the kitchen table, fully dressed and ready to go by five the next morning.

She was on her best behavior that day, staying out of everyone's way and trying to be quiet, but nothing prepared her for the pleasure that surged up inside of her the first time a fish bit her hook and the line began slicing through the water. With a goofy grin on her face, she pulled herself up straight, hyperventilating, eyes wide with excitement. Soon both men had put their rods away to help, taking that first fish off her hook, then a second, and finally giving up altogether as they watched her catch one after another when they couldn't seem to even get a bite.

Her dad's buddy watched her over his horn-rimmed glasses as he drank a beer, chuckling while she reeled in one fish after another with uncontained excitement. "It's not how big the fish is that matters, is it, kiddo?" he said, leaning forward, "It's that they bite at all that makes the heart race."

Kenly had no idea what he meant. All she knew was that every time a fish bit, two or three different expressions took over her dad's face as he craned his neck to watch her from the back of the boat. First, a surge of childlike excitement would light up his eyes, quickly replaced with a cocky smirk as he elbowed his buddy, and then a huge that's-my-kid smile took over like no other she'd ever seen before.

She lost track of how many fish she actually caught that day and in the end, it didn't matter. What did was the short-lived, unflagging camaraderie she felt with her dad. It was something she grew up longing for, even more so after her mom died, but something she never managed to find with him again.

Thinking back on it now, she cast the line out and slowly began reeling it in again. The growing distance between her and Connor was something she didn't know how to fix and her feelings of inadequacy were overwhelming. She finished reeling in her line, changed hooks, and then pulled her nightgown back up over her knees so it wouldn't get wet. Looking down at her bare feet sitting in a puddle of water, she wriggled her toes and cast her line out again. A few hundred yards away on shore she heard Lexie calling out to her just as Ross had earlier, but right now, for a few minutes, she was six again and they were going to have to wait.

"I DIDN'T SAY YOU WERE SUFFERING FROM DEPRESSION," LEXIE argued. "I said that you're *acting depressed* and there's a difference."

They were sitting in the kitchen and Ross had just left for work. Kenly set her coffee cup down. "Think you're telling me something I don't already know?"

"Stop being a bitch."

"I'm not going to a therapist, Lex. My son just lost his leg and I'm a little down. So shoot me, for chrissakes."

Lexie raised her hands. "Sorry! I assumed we had the kind of friendship where I could sit down and talk to you, just like I hope you would if you caught me fishing in the middle of a lake *where there aren't any fish* at five o'clock in the morning."

Kenly reddened. "I told you, I find it relaxing."

Lexie cupped her hands and leaned across the kitchen table. "Hello, Kenly? Are you in there? Because you aren't listening to what I'm saying."

Pushing her chair back, Kenly stood and opened her mouth, but no sound came out. Then her chin trembled and she smiled, a slow sad smile that started at the corners of her eyes and took over her whole face when she was done, even though tears came with it. "So, you think it looks like I'm wigging out?" she asked.

Lexie nodded, her eyes twinkling. "Off the deep end."

KENLY HAD HER PURSE SLUNG OVER ONE SHOULDER AND A BAG in her arms when she came through the door to Connor's hospital room the next morning. "Morning," she said in a forced upbeat tone.

Connor raised his eyebrows to acknowledge her, but continued staring at the TV.

After Ross had gone to bed the night before, Kenly had sat on their front-porch swing until after midnight, rubbing her mom's red silk scarf between her thumb and forefinger, trying to think of a way to get through to Connor, a way to break down the walls he'd built so he would begin to inch forward with his life instead of rotting in self-absorbed pity.

Connor's doctor would be fitting him with his prosthetic leg after lunch today and she'd been bracing for a poor reaction, but now she dropped her purse on the table and set the bag down, feeling confident. "I brought you something," she said.

"Whatever."

Kenly sat down and leaned forward, launching into her setup for what was in the bag. "Remember when you were six and you had that favorite Batman?"

Silence.

"The black one with the blue cape?"

When he still didn't answer she kept talking. "The neighbor's dog chewed one of his legs off and you came home crying, holding him up in the air and *begging* me to make him 'right' again." Her voice caught and she smiled. "Remember that?"

He nodded almost imperceptibly.

"I made him a new leg from a Popsicle stick wrapped in duct tape and even though you looked a little disappointed, he never stopped being your favorite."

Connor turned off the TV and glared at her. "This is stupid."

"Let me finish—"

"Why?" He slapped a hand against his forehead and let his mouth hang open for a second. "I know where you're going with this, Mom. You're gonna yank him out of that bag and hand him to me, right? And somehow you think that's gonna make me feel better about the fake leg they're gonna strap on me today? Hardly . . ."

Kenly counted to ten, stood, and handed him the bag. "No, that's not what I'm trying to do, so maybe you should just listen to me."

Connor took the bag, opened it, and lifted out a tin box. He turned it over and gave it a good shake. Something was rattling around inside, but he tossed it onto the bed next to him with disinterest. "Okay. I'll bite. What's this?"

Kenly pulled her shoulders back and gave him an unflinching stare, determined not to let him get to her. "A friend of mine gave me a tin box years ago and now I want to give you one." She paused, knowing half of her success would be in the timing and the rest in her delivery of this message. "He asked me to write down all the memories from my life that were so wonderful I'd relive them again if I could. Then, when I was finished, he told me there wasn't another list like it on this earth and he asked me to call him when I'd figured out how to fit everything that was on my list into this tin box, because only then would I be ready to appreciate what was *really* important in life."

He gave her a familiar scowl, then snatched up the tin box, and opened it. Inside was his old Batman with the duct-taped leg, a pad of paper, and a pen.

"I thought I'd get you started," she explained.

Connor kept his eyes down, and at first Kenly genuinely believed he understood what she was trying to say. Then he said, "This is stupid," and threw the tin box toward the end of his bed where it rolled off onto the floor, putting a dent in the lid.

Without missing a beat, Kenly walked over and picked the box up, telling herself he wasn't an easy kid to love today because he was working so hard at being unlovable, then telling herself that she'd been too clumsy in her explanation and he just wasn't ready for it. But she was determined not to give up, so she opened the lid, turned the box over on the table beside his bed, and pressed the dent out with her fingertips. Then she closed it and said, "There."

Connor's eyes followed her every move and when she looked at him, they stared silently into each other's eyes, neither of them willing to look away first.

"Please let me hold you," she finally whispered.

"What?"

"Like I used to . . . years ago."

"Don't start, Mom," he said, turning his face away.

"When you were little, you were never afraid to ask me to hold you if you needed me."

"Well, I don't need you anymore," he said, but his cockiness sounded sad and faked.

Kenly went over to him and shoved a bunch of hockey cards out of the way to make room, then slid up on the bed next to him; not touching him or talking, just quietly sitting there. Minutes passed in silence until she finally slid one of her arms around behind him, then carefully, carefully lifted him onto her lap. At first his body was rigid and tense, but after a while he relaxed against her. Kenly took his free arm and pulled it around herself, then leaned forward and rested her chin on his head.

"Oh, what you do to my heart," she whispered in a shaky voice.

She sat there holding him until all the muscles standing out in his neck had relaxed and the stillness of the room felt more soothing than it had in weeks. Eventually, her back started to pinch and one of her arms fell asleep, but she didn't move, relishing the feel of him along with any discomfort that came with it. Finally, he shifted around until his cheek was pressed against hers.

"Mom? What if I never walk again?"

It was the first time that he'd come close to talking about what had happened or what it might mean for him in the future. Kenly's chest constricted and she said, "We'll cross that bridge when we come to it."

chapter 23

FOR THE PAST TWO WEEKS, KENLY HAD WATCHED Connor go through the boring, daily grind of physical therapy with a subtle change. Now, she explained to Lexie, he did his best to smile when he slid off the bed and let the prosthetic leg take his weight, whereas before he would pull on his headphones and mechanically go through the exercises with a scowl on his face.

"That's great," Lexie said, sliding into a kitchen chair next to her, "but how are things with you and Ross?"

Kenly hesitated and said they hadn't been great.

"Well, that's understandable given what you've both been through. I know," she said, snapping her fingers, "why don't you take a week off and slip away somewhere?"

Kenly looked at her sideways and frowned. There was something in Lexie's voice that told her she'd come up with this idea earlier and was just pretending to think of it now. Ignoring her pointed stare, Lexie produced a pamphlet from her purse about a lodge in Minnesota.

"Benjy told me about this place," she said, pointing at photos of four-poster beds, a luxurious dining room, a spa, and a smiling we're-so-glad-we-came couple who probably saved their marriage just by walking through the door. "Of course, you normally have to reserve six months in advance," she said. "But Benjy knows the owners so he could call them. And, of course, I'll watch Connor while you're gone."

Persuading herself to show some interest, Kenly asked, "So can you guarantee this place will turn Ross and me back into a happy couple?"

"I—I didn't say that—" she stammered.

"But," Kenly interrupted, "in theory, that's what you're hoping will happen, right?"

Lexie folded the pamphlet and nodded.

Kenly smiled. "And I'm guessing Ross already knows about this, right?"

She nodded again.

"Let me see. That makes you the delivery person of an idea he thinks I might otherwise shoot down?"

Lexie slumped in her chair and stared at her lap.

"Fine then, I'll go. If John Glenn can go through everything he's going through right now to become the oldest astronaut in the world, I should be willing to invest some time strengthening my marriage."

"MORNING," THE PHYSICAL THERAPIST SAID, COMING INTO Connor's room just minutes after Kenly arrived the next day. She was in her late twenties and walked on the balls of her feet with a look of eternal optimism on her face. Connor rolled his eyes, threw off the covers, and sat up.

"How are we doing?" she asked him, smiling over at Kenly.

Connor shrugged. "Okay."

"Does it hurt?"

"Sometimes, but mostly it just itches like crazy."

Kenly felt awkward listening to their conversation, but she was glad to be here. Although it had been two months since the accident, Connor rarely talked to her or Ross about how he was feeling and, other than the first few times, he hadn't allowed either of them to stay in the room during one of his therapy sessions.

As the physical therapist helped him off the bed, Kenly lowered herself into a chair and watched them go through their daily regime; first with a metal walker, then on crutches, and, finally, a brief go at the prosthetic leg he'd only recently agreed to try.

Frozen to her chair and with Connor's back to her, Kenly forced herself to look at his leg, something she hadn't found the courage to do before. The stitches and dressing were gone now, but the scar that curved up past his knee looked raw and angry.

When they were finished and the physical therapist helped him back onto the bed, Connor's forehead was covered in sweat. "Now you rest and I'll do the work," she said.

Connor shifted down on his pillow as she began massaging his half-leg with a sesame oil mixture she'd been warming in the bathroom sink for ten minutes. Kenly watched as the therapist kneaded and worked at the muscles of his leg, unable to tear her eyes away.

"Connor?" she finally interrupted.

"Uh-huh."

"Dad and I were thinking about going away at the end of the month, but it would mean you'd have to stay with Aunt Lexie." She paused, then rattled on awkwardly. "Of course, we won't go if you don't want us to."

He slid on his Walkman, closed his eyes, and sighed. "I already told Dad I didn't mind."

THE FIRST FEW DAYS AT LEXIE'S HOUSE, CONNOR EXISTED either in a puppetlike state or else with brooding, angry eyes that glowered at everyone. Lexie woke up on the second morning when it was still middle-of-the-night dark and pulled on her bathrobe to find him sitting on his bed, staring at the television. She peeked in at him, all eleven years of him, his narrow shoulders humped up under the

T-shirt he was wearing, and her heart ached.

"He can't keep on like this," she said to Benjy over breakfast.

He nodded his agreement.

"So, I have this idea I wanted to run by you."

Lifting his eyebrows, Benjy pushed back from the table and listened.

Lexie knocked on Connor's bedroom door at noon the next day. When there was no answer she knocked again, then opened it, walked in, and pulled back the curtains. Connor was lying there with the covers halfway up and the TV on. She dropped the duffel bag she was carrying next to him on the bed.

"Time to get up, get dressed, and get packed," she said with a fake brightness as she folded her arms. "We're going on a trip."

Struggling into a sitting position, he frowned. "What?"

She took the remote control, turned off the TV, then caught hold of his chin with her fingers, and turned his face up to hers. "I said we're going on a trip."

"Where?"

"Back."

He looked frustrated. "Back where?"

She handed him an airline ticket. "Back to the best place I know, to where everyone should go when they need a little healing."

His brow furrowed and he opened the ticket to see what she was talking about. Lexie turned to leave, looked back, and pointed to the duffel bag. "I'll be back in half an hour, so get dressed," she said as if it were normal to expect him to do this on his own, even though her stomach was in knots. He looked at her with what she thought was the hint of a smile and gave her an almost-imperceptible nod.

O'Hare Airport was as busy as usual when they arrived that afternoon and Lexie asked the check-in agent if they could get some assistance, a wheelchair or maybe a cart to take them to their gate, but Connor interrupted and told her he didn't need any help.

Lexie raised an eyebrow in surprise and they started off, Lexie carrying his knapsack and Connor slowly working his way through the terminal. Walking with his prosthetic leg was new for him, so she watched carefully from the corner of her eye. He moved with a slow shuffle that involved a lift, drop, and drag of his left leg and then a quick hop of the right one to catch up. It took more effort than he must have thought it would because Lexie could see the discomfort on his face, but he still wouldn't give up.

"You're not making this easy for me," she mock-complained. "Doing it your way, we'll get to the gate with just enough time to board. But if we got a ride, we'd both have time for a quick cappuccino."

"I don't drink coffee," he said, keeping his eyes on the ground.

Lexie laughed. "You also don't hop on airplanes and take spur-of-the-moment trips to Canada, but that's what you're doing right now, isn't it?" He smiled a little and she realized she was getting away with teasing him the way she used to.

"By the way," Connor said, "do Mom and Dad know about this?"

Lexie chewed on her bottom lip. "What they don't know won't hurt them."

For a moment, she saw a flicker of pleasure cross his face and knew she was on the right track. A lump rose in her throat as she watched him painstakingly making his way through the terminal, certain she was doing the right thing by taking him to Athabasca for a visit.

chapter 24

IT RAINED ALL THE WAY HOME FROM THE LODGE IN Minnesota, the kind of rain that often came in the fall, slamming down in angry sheets and carrying with it a feeling of impending doom now that all the leaves were gone and winter was on its way. When they pulled into the circular driveway in front of Lexie's house, Ross was on his cell phone, deep into a call about some catastrophe at his office. "Go ahead," he said, covering the phone with his hand. "I'll be right behind you."

Kenly got out and hurried up the sidewalk. She rang the doorbell and waited, then grinned when Benjy opened the front door. "Hey, we're back!"

"Come in," he said, stepping to the side.

Lexie stuck her head around the corner, looking slightly harried. "Whew! We beat you home by just ten minutes."

Confused, Kenly started to ask what she meant, but then Connor limped into the front hallway with Motley at his heels and she stopped. His eyes were bright and he was wearing jeans that made him look long and gangly, but stronger than he had in weeks. "Hey, Mom," he said, giving her a hug. "How was your trip?"

Lexie laughed a little too enthusiastically. "Connor, come on! Give her time to get in the door first."

Kenly was about to ask what was going on, but Lexie looked past her and smiled as Ross came through the door. He gave Connor a hug; then Benjy asked him if they had liked the lodge. "It was great," Ross said, putting out an arm for Kenly to snuggle into. She did, but she couldn't stand it any longer, so she reached out and squeezed Connor's arm. "What'd you do while we were gone?"

He shrugged and hesitated just long enough for her to know he was being secretive. *What's going on?* she wondered. *Has Lexie gone and spent a ton of money on him?* "Don't tell me," she said, crossing her arms and trying not to laugh. "She took you bungee jumping?"

"No," Lexie said, "but I'd like to before he turns eighteen."

Kenly scowled at her. "So what then? You bought him a car? Taught him how to steal hubcaps?" She turned to Connor in alarm. "God, you didn't get a tattoo, did you?"

"Not even close," Connor said. "Me and Aunt Lexie flew to Canada, rented this hot car, and drove up to Athabasca for a few days."

"Athabasca?" Kenly repeated, like it was the first time she'd ever heard of it.

Connor nodded, smiling.

"Told you she'd be surprised," Lexie murmured.

Kenly's legs turned to rubber. "Y-you took him *where?*"

Sensing she was upset, Ross tried to lighten things up. "You wouldn't remember, Connor, but we took you there years ago. Nice place, isn't it?"

Lexie took Kenly by the arm and led her into the living room. "Please don't get mad," she whispered. "It was great. You should've seen him, Kenly. We stayed at Uncle Walter's and took him to Baptiste Lake for the day. He really came out of his shell."

Kenly glanced back over her shoulder, straining to listen as Connor animatedly described the trip to Ross. "Then on the drive up to

Athabasca from Edmonton we got a flat tire," he said. "And Dad? You won't believe this. Aunt Lexie told me the thumping noise outside was just a helicopter, so she didn't stop the car. She just kept driving, looking up through the windows outside until the whole car started to shake and pieces of rubber started flying everywhere."

As the realization hit home that Connor had been in Athabasca, questions shot through Kenly's mind at lightning speed. *Had he met Tommy? And if he did, how did he react to him this time? What did they talk about?* Panic started to set in and Kenly swallowed, keeping her eyes glued on Connor and Ross.

"Where did you stay?" she asked.

Lexie frowned. "I already told you. Uncle Walter's."

Ross was laughing at something Connor had said, with one hand on Connor's shoulder as Benjy looked on, shaking his head. Kenly lowered herself onto the couch, certain her legs would give out if she didn't sit down.

"We were only there four days," Lexie said, sitting next to her.

"Did . . . did he meet Tommy?" she asked.

"Of course he did."

"And how did that go?" Kenly asked.

"It went great."

"How was Tommy?"

Lexie sighed. "Not good. He said other than his emphysema, things haven't been too bad this year, but Kenly, he's so thin he looks like he's wasting away. He seemed glad we came, though. We were at the fire pit every night and even though he came bundled up, wearing an eiderdown coat, he was always the last one to leave. Connor even stayed with him for an hour after I packed it in early the last night. Tommy walked him to Uncle Walter's later."

Kenly's eyes widened, but Lexie waved her off, misunderstanding. "It's no big deal. Uncle Walter only lives three blocks away and you should see Connor walk with that leg now. He hoofed it through O'Hare Airport like nobody's business. Come on. Forgive me, okay? This trip was great for him."

Kenly hesitated, too stunned to speak. "I'll add it to the list of everything else you need to be forgiven for," she said.

After they got home Connor went upstairs to unpack and Ross looked at his watch. "Not bad. Two hours and six minutes without blowing your lid that she took him to Athabasca without our permission."

"Ross, she took him to *Canada*," Kenly blurted, crossing her arms. *And while he was there, he met Tommy—his real father—who can be so intuitive at times it's amazing. And what if he saw something, a resemblance or some tiny mannerism of Connor's that made him wonder. . . .*

Ross searched her face. "I'm not thrilled, either. But you've got to admit, Kenly, we haven't seen him this upbeat since before the accident."

"No," she agreed, slipping off her shoes. "You're right about that."

Ross took Motley for a walk and when he came back, she was in bed pretending to read the paper, doing everything she could to look preoccupied so she wouldn't have to look him in the eye—so he wouldn't see the guilt and worry that was eating her up inside.

He grabbed a pen, leaned over, and scribbled in the margin of one page, *I love you.* She smiled, took the pen from him, and wrote *Me too* in inch-high letters next to it.

FRIDAY MORNING, KENLY WOKE TO MOTLEY NUDGING HER hand with his nose. She rolled out of bed and padded into the kitchen to let him out, then stood on the deck outside taking in the cool morning air. Connor was going to a friend's after school to stay the night and Ross had left for Boston the day before and wouldn't be home until Monday. Although Kenly had made arrangements to go back to work, she didn't start for another week.

She brewed a cup of tea and curled back under the warm covers of her bed. Bored, she flipped through the channels until she found a TV program she liked, but couldn't keep her mind on it. Something was tugging at her inside, pulling her off-balance, and making her feel restless. She turned off the TV, pushed out of bed, and stepped into the shower.

Half an hour later, she reached up onto the top shelf of her closet and pulled down her tin box. Sitting in the middle of her bed, she opened it and carefully took everything out. Inside was her mom's leather sculpting pouch and her red silk scarf, her dad's letter and his wedding band, three of Connor's baby teeth, his first lock of hair, and a sketch Tommy had done of her before she left Athabasca. She had even kept a handful of cards Ross had written to her over the years.

She untied the sculpting pouch and unrolled it, running her fingers along the metal rasps and picks that were tucked inside. "You'll know when it's right," her mom used to whisper. "You'll feel it deep inside of you and then your hands just . . . take over."

Three hours later, after a quick trip into town, Kenly pulled into the driveway, parked, and dragged three heavy bags from the car into the kitchen. Motley met her at the door, sniffing at them with curiosity. She made a fresh espresso and spent the afternoon cleaning out the spare bedroom until it was empty except for a few prints she'd hung up years ago. It took her a while to set up her mom's old kickwheel, but after she did, she dropped a lump of wet boneware clay on the fly-wheel, feeling like a kid again. Then, for the next hour she tugged and pulled and formed the clay into a piece that resembled nothing in particular, but filled her with a renewed sense of peace and contentment.

The next morning, she rolled out of bed and padded back into the spare bedroom without bothering to shower. She'd gone to sleep after midnight, exhausted from working with the clay and dragging an old armchair into her new sanctuary inch by inch. She was so immersed in what she was doing that she didn't hear Connor come in through the kitchen. She had borrowed his boom box earlier and was hunched over the flywheel with headphones on when he stuck his head inside the room.

"Mom?"

Startled, she swiveled in her seat and pulled off the headphones. "Hey, you're home early!"

"Uh, yeah," he said, shifting his weight onto his right leg.

She stood and wiped her hands on the canvas apron she'd tied over her pajamas. "Did you and Luke rent any good movies last night?"

"A few," he said, staring at the new "home studio" she'd created, bags of clay and paint sitting in various piles on the floor. Kenly followed his gaze around the room, putting a hand on the collar of her pajama top as she shifted from one bare foot to the other. "So? What do you think?"

"About what?" he asked uncertainly.

"Well, all this, of course."

"It's okay, but why'd you set it up like this?"

She took his hand and squeezed. "Because my mom used to sculpt and it's something I've always wanted to do."

"I didn't know that."

Kenly smiled. "Well, now you do."

"Think I could try?" he asked, gesturing to the kickwheel.

She looked at him, more than a little surprised. "Um, sure you can."

For the next hour, she showed him what kind of clay worked best for what, how to center it on the flywheel, when and how to use the various rasps and picks. She lowered the seat and shook out his elbows like her mother used to do, explaining that it was a family ritual and had nothing to do with technique.

Grinning, he set his boom box to a radio station that was a mixture of light rock and easy listening, then got to work. First he made a water bowl for Motley that caved in and quickly got reworked into a lopsided ashtray, which eventually fell apart and morphed into a contorted key holder for his dad. Kenly helped where she could, smiling so hard she had to bite her lip to keep from laughing out loud at times and almost bursting with a pleasant ache from being with him like this. Connor was bent over the flywheel working when Billy Joel came on the radio, singing about an uptown girl.

He swiveled to look at her. "This is the singer your friend Tommy likes!"

Kenly blinked at him. "Yes, it is."

He squinted as he listened to the lyrics and Kenly smoothed back her hair, not knowing where to look. Trying to sound casual, she asked him what he thought of Tommy as he pinched down the corners of the key holder.

"What do you mean?"

"It's just, well, Tommy's a good friend of mine."

"He said you were, like, best friends," Connor interjected.

She smiled. "Yes, that's true."

He went back to working with his clay, his mind on other things, seemingly unaware of her discomfort as Kenly checked to make sure her feet were on the floor since it suddenly felt as if she was losing her balance.

"I liked him," he finally murmured. "He gets talking and after a while you forget there's anything wrong with him, especially when you're looking into the fire and not at his face. Did I tell you Aunt Lexie took me to that fire pit you always talk about?"

Kenly nodded, dizzy and yet equally fascinated with what he had to say.

"The first few nights at the fire, I didn't say much to him. I just sat there and listened to everyone and then I started thinking about how lucky I am, you know? I mean, I lost part of my leg, but I know if I work at it I can still walk and run and maybe even skate, too. Then Tommy and I got talking the last night I was there and you know what, Mom? He told me he thought I was brave."

"You are," Kenly said, tears brimming in her eyes.

Connor looked up. "Not like him. Aunt Lexie told me Tommy doesn't know if he'll live another year or two or three. At least I don't have to deal with that."

No, she thought, *thank God you don't.*

———

WHEN ROSS GOT HOME MONDAY NIGHT, HE PARKED AND trudged across the yard with his laptop. Motley met him at the door and he leaned into the living room looking for Kenly and Connor, then heard them laughing, and made his way upstairs to the spare bedroom.

They had their backs to him when he came into the room. Kenly was sitting at the kickwheel with her arms wrapped around Connor as he worked with a mound of wet clay. Flecks of it were everywhere, and they had clay in their hair and on their arms.

Connor turned and saw him, then threw his arms wide. "Dad! What do you think?"

Ross chuckled. "That you'd both make a great advertisement *against* sculpting without taking formal lessons." But the look on his face said he was thrilled.

"Actually, I told Mom if she could find a weekend class for beginners, I might consider taking it with her."

"Really?" Ross said.

"I think I've got some raw talent," he said, lifting his chin. "Wait till you see some of my work from this weekend."

"Why wait?" Ross said, setting his laptop down. "Show me now."

As Connor struggled to his feet, Ross crossed his arms and winked at Kenly, smiling her favorite smile; the one that started slow and then burst out big and wide, taking over his eyes. The same smile she fell in love with years ago and the smile she hoped to grow old with. Her throat tightened as Connor went past Ross in the doorway, one elbow shooting out to nudge him playfully as he asked how his trip went. Then Ross followed him down the hallway, their voices rising and falling and mixing in with each other, wrapping Kenly in a blanket of contentment.

chapter 25

AS KENLY WATCHED CONNOR OUT ON THE ICE, SHE couldn't believe it had been a year since the accident. With dogged determination, he'd talked his old coach into letting him try out for the hockey team as a backup goalie, a position he never showed interest in until he lost his leg. After he made the team, Ross volunteered as assistant coach and now they spent more time at arenas in the region than they did at home.

Lexie came to as many games as she could and Connor always knew when she was in the stands. Actually, *everyone* knew when she was in the stands. There wasn't a parent or coach who didn't know Lexie and who she was cheering for. Through it all Benjy sat next to her, patiently following the game through the lens of their videocamera, and handing her the air horn whenever Connor's team scored. Today he seemed overly attentive, making sure Lexie was warm enough, wrapping a wool blanket over her legs, running to get her a bottle of water from the concession stand, even though she said she would get one later.

"What's up with him?" Kenly asked after he left.

Lexie reddened—a rarity in itself—then looked down at her hands. "He's being a little protective 'cause I just told him I'm pregnant."

"Pregnant?" Kenly squeaked out.

"Three months," Lexie replied.

Kenly blinked at her in disbelief. Over the years Lexie had always made it clear to anyone willing to listen that she would never have kids of her own. "Me responsible for a baby, can you imagine?" she often said, shuddering dramatically. "I wouldn't have a hot clue how to be a mom." And yet today she looked flushed, even excited about the very thing she'd so often dismissed as unthinkable.

Regaining her composure, Kenly hugged her. "This is great news! But what happened? You've always said you didn't want kids."

Lexie shrugged, looking embarrassed. "I changed my mind."

"When?"

"A few years ago."

Kenly looked offended. "And you didn't tell me?"

Lexie linked an arm through hers and laughed. "I don't tell you *everything*, you know."

"Of course not," Kenly said, lifting her hands and letting them sink back to her lap.

Connor's team scored and she got to her feet with Lexie to cheer them on, suddenly wondering if she'd ever looked that happy when she was pregnant. And then she realized that she probably hadn't, because from the minute she'd learned that Tommy was the father until the day Connor was born, she'd juggled shock, worry, fear, shame, and rising panic that he might not be born healthy. There hadn't been time for the blissful joy she saw on Lexie's face now.

"Benjy must be walking on air," she said, nudging Lexie's arm.

"Ten feet up there," Lexie agreed, grinning.

When Benjy came back, he slid into the seat in front of them and Kenly congratulated him. The back of his neck went pink with embarrassment and she smiled and slid closer to Lexie, pulling half the blanket over her legs. *An aunt*, she thought, feeling a wave of tenderness wash over her. *I'm going to be an aunt.*

———

LEXIE'S PREGNANCY WAS SOMETHING KENLY WOULDN'T HAVE missed for the world. Every possible symptom showed up in full force. She spent the first three months on her knees in front of a toilet vomiting, the second three eating the oddest combinations of food imaginable, and the last few propped in bed with her feet elevated and the phone balanced on her massive belly.

For years Lexie had often repeated such an exaggerated version of the story of Connor's birth that when the five of them were out for dinner one night and she went into labor two weeks early, Kenly pushed back from the table and grinned. "This, I gotta see."

"Better you than me," Benjy murmured, going pale.

In the end, Isabella McMillan was born en route to the hospital on Connor's thirteenth birthday. Lexie swore later that she'd planned it that way, but who in their right mind would have wanted to give birth in the back of an SUV driving down the Dwight Eisenhower Expressway in Chicago?

Connor did his fair share of strutting, touched beyond words when Lexie slipped Bella into his arms just a day after she was born. "Mom, she's incredible," he whispered.

Kenly wiped away a few tears and nodded. "Yes, she is."

JEAN NAYLOR CALLED TWO WEEKS LATER WITH BAD NEWS. "Tommy's surgery didn't go well," she said. "There were complications and when he got home an infection set in."

Kenly nodded, glanced at the calendar on the fridge, and tried to determine how difficult it would be to take a few days off and fly out to Edmonton.

Jean's voice shook as she spoke. "Kenly? They admitted him to intensive care last night."

"I'll fly out tomorrow," she said.

On her way to the airport the next day, she picked up the mail and her weekly copy of *The Athabasca Press* was there as usual. The subscription Tommy had gotten for her years ago still arrived each week without fail, and when she saw it she smiled. Tucking it into her carry-on, she forgot about it until she was in the air, and when she finally read it, tears filled her eyes.

Dear WIT,
I'm a single mother of a fifteen-year-old daughter who's disrespectful and treats my fiancé horribly. We're both ready to give up on her and I don't know what to do. Any suggestions?
                                                    —Mom on the Edge

Dear Mom,
You have your own life on the go (you mentioned a fiancé), so maybe your daughter feels threatened by that. Being fifteen under normal circumstances is tough enough. It sounds like she needs you right now, but may not know how to tell you. You said she's disrespectful, but you didn't say she'd committed murder, robbed a bank, or burned down a building. Remember, she was the baby you rocked at birth so "giving up on her" as a mother isn't an option you should even allow yourself to consider. Kids need the love of their parents most when they're at their worst.
                                                                —WIT

After she landed in Edmonton, Kenly rented a car at the airport and drove to the hospital. When she got there and slipped into his room, his eyes were closed and the fluorescent light over his bed cast a sickly glow against his face. She winced under her face mask as her lungs filled with the antiseptic smell of the room. He had an IV attached to his hand, the tube curling down to the floor, then back up to a half-empty sack of liquid that hung on the pole. There were a few other tubes in his chest and a machine that blinked in the background as it monitored the rhythm of his heart and lungs.

He opened his eyes and his face softened, but she could tell he was still woozy from the drugs. "Kenly?"

She nodded.

"It must be bad if you're here," he managed.

Her eyes fixed on his and she smiled. "I deserved that."

She wanted to tell him she was proud of him, but his eyes drooped a few times, so she just sat beside him and stroked his hair in silence. His chest rattled like something was loose inside and within minutes he nodded and fell back asleep. Almost two hours passed before he woke again, and when he did, she was dozing with her head in her arms at the end of the bed.

"You're still here," he said in a barely audible voice.

She lifted her head. "How are you feeling?"

"Like the poorly constructed human being that I am, but who's complaining?"

"Well, you're still as sharp as ever, so that says something."

There were circles under his eyes and his shoulders were lost somewhere under the thin hospital gown he was wrapped in. He'd lost weight and muscle tone since she'd last seen him, so now the contorted growths on his face and neck stood out even more than they had before. But when he smiled, he was the same Tommy she'd always known.

"I miss you," he whispered.

"What could you possibly miss?" Kenly said. "It's been years."

"How you used to hum when you were nervous, or the way you would close your eyes whenever you ate ice cream."

She sank slowly into a chair.

"Or that," he said, pointing at her. "That quirky habit you have of chewing your lip whenever you're worried about something."

He fought for enough air to say everything he wanted to. She lifted her hand to his face and brushed it against his cheek. Hampered by the tubes and equipment strapped to him, Tommy fumbled to take her other one. "It may have been years ago," he said, "but I still miss you."

He coughed then, pushed himself up on an elbow, and coughed so hard that it scared her. One of his monitors beeped and he waved a hand for her to stay sitting when she jumped up to get help. The door swung open and a nurse rushed in. "You'll have to leave, ma'am," she said, scowling at Kenly.

Tommy was in a full-tilt coughing fit now that shook his entire body, but he kicked the IV pole next to his bed in frustration, startling both of them. "No, not yet," he managed.

The nurse frowned, checking the equipment and skimming his chart for any directions left from the last shift. "Kenly?" he rasped, in a voice just above a whisper. "My body aches all the time now. I'm tired and I want to stop fighting, you know?"

"Lie back, Tommy," she said. "We can talk about it later."

"No, I don't want you to come back."

She was having trouble looking at him. Her lower lip trembled and she suddenly made herself busy straightening the blanket at the end of his bed. "I'm coming back."

"No. I don't want you here."

She focused on his eyelashes as he talked, certain that any second now she would fall apart. "Okay, then I'll call. I'll have them bring you a phone."

"Say good-bye, Kenly," he said, nudging her away, "and go live your life."

The nurse graciously went over to the window as Kenly stared at him and tried to accept what he was saying. She was shaking when she kissed him and the pounding of her heart suddenly seemed louder than the machines as he squeezed her hand and turned his face away. She straightened and stepped back, then made her way across the room and pushed hard on the door. And when the door swung open she was sure she heard him whisper, "I love you, Kenly," before it closed behind her.

DAYS AFTER KENLY RETURNED FROM HER TRIP TO CANADA, she still couldn't shake the somber, heavyhearted feeling that took over. Ross and Connor moved around the house with exaggerated care, uncertain of how to deal with her and polite to the point of driving her crazy. After they both left one morning, she called in sick and curled up on the couch.

Maybe you should've told him, the coward inside taunted.

Oh, sure, she thought. *He's on his deathbed and now I should tell him Connor is his son?*

She nursed her coffee and stared out the window, pushing aside the memories that kept coming back to her. Years ago when she and Tommy used to sit at the fire pit or in his tree house, sharing private stories they never told anyone else, dreaming all their crazy dreams. Dragging a hand through her hair, she finally made her way into the spare bedroom, where she dropped a lump of wet clay onto the flywheel and let her fingers take over.

She had the radio turned up high, hoping it would distract her, but everything that played took her straight back to Tommy. Carole King was singing about having a friend; then Simon and Garfunkel about a bridge over troubled water. And finally Bette Midler's voice filled the house as she sang about someone being the wind beneath her wings.

Kenly rolled her thumbs against the clay, thinking of Tommy, dripping wet as he sloshed around in that creek years ago or with Oscar tucked into his jacket on his way to the tree house. Then his voice came back to her, reaching out like a salve. "Trust your instincts and you'll do fine," he'd said. "You know what's important and what's not."

Her hands took over as she instinctively worked the wet mound of clay until a face began to take shape. It was a face she knew well and when she finished, she sat back shaking, unable to turn away. It was all there. Tommy's right cheek, pushed out like a hardened balloon, the beginning of that cauliflowerlike growth on his neck, extra skin and bone that didn't belong. A face that would turn most people away. A face she loved. Exhausted, she slid to her knees on the floor and cried, knowing that this piece needed nothing else because what was there, every inch of it, was Tommy at his best.

chapter 26

THE MORNING KENLY GOT THE PHONE CALL, CONNOR
came downstairs in his now well-practiced entrance, which
involved a shift of one hip up onto the railing, then a slide down to
where he landed on his right foot with the left one bent at the knee. He
was wearing a City Champs soccer sweatshirt, jeans that were too long,
and a pair of old sneakers Kenly was sure she'd thrown out weeks ago.

"I thought we'd have to drag you out of bed today." She reached out
to swat him, but he arched his body away and dodged her deftly as he
grinned.

"Hey, Dad, can I catch a ride to school?"

"If you're ready," Ross said. "'Cause I'm leaving now."

Kenly nodded to the plate of pancakes on the table. "What about
breakfast?"

Connor ruffled her hair like she was the child, then snatched a banana from the fruit bowl and shouldered his knapsack. "Sorry, Mom.
I'm meeting Luke at the library in twenty minutes."

Ross slid an arm around her on his way by and nuzzled her neck. "He can eat them tomorrow. See you later."

The door slammed behind them, bounced against its frame, and came to rest. Kenly grabbed the plate of pancakes and slid it across the floor to where Motley lay curled in a corner.

"Knock yourself out," she said, tossing the pancake turner into the sink.

She was in the shower when the phone rang five minutes later so she almost let the answering machine get it, but then changed her mind and grabbed a towel.

"Hello?"

"Kenly? It's Jean."

She lowered herself onto the bed. "Uh-huh."

"He's gone," Jean said, voice cracking. "He died last night in the hospital."

Kenly dropped her chin to her chest. "I-I'm so sorry, Jean," she managed.

"The funeral is Wednesday morning."

"I'll be there."

After she hung up, she made her way back into the bathroom in a daze. The shower was still running, steam filling the room. She stepped in, slid down the wall, and let the hot water pound against her as she laid her head in her arms and cried.

An hour later she called Ross at work to tell him, then looked into flights and made another call to Lexie.

"I'm going with you," Lexie said without hesitating.

"Are you sure?" Kenly asked.

"Benjy would love a few days alone with Bella, and I want to go."

IT RAINED THE NIGHT BEFORE TOMMY'S FUNERAL, POURING DOWN hard and strong for hours, and when they drove into Athabasca the next morning, the sky still hadn't cleared. Lexie had fallen asleep half an hour after they left Edmonton and Kenly didn't wake her, enjoying the drive and the time to herself.

The sad orange of Athabasca's Burger Bar was the first thing she saw when she drove into town. All six windows were filled with posters promoting what were probably the same lunch specials they'd had when she'd lived here years ago. The Red Rooster convenience store was gone now, in its place a more user-friendly version of the same thing called Rascal's. There was also a new traffic light halfway down Main Street and Kenly almost drove through it, but slammed on her brakes at the last second, smiling as she thought about the heated discussions this would have created around Max's fire pit.

Lexie bolted upright in her seat. "W-what's going on?"

Kenly pointed to the new traffic light and Lexie rolled her eyes. "I know. I did the same thing the last time I was home. They put it in two years ago." She pulled down the vanity mirror and groaned. "Oh, no, look at me."

"You look fine," Kenly reassured her.

"Right. My hair's a mess. Let's stop at Uncle Walter's and get cleaned up, okay?"

"I'll drop you off and come back in an hour, okay?"

She gave Kenly's arm a squeeze. "Sounds good."

KENLY KNEW HER WAY AROUND TOWN EVEN THOUGH SHE hadn't been back in years. She drove slowly, thinking of her dad and the secret he'd kept from everyone for all of those years. How it had ruined his life and deprived her of a father, and how upset she was when she'd finally learned the truth. *And yet I did the same thing, didn't I?*

Years ago she'd come to Athabasca thinking it would be a pit stop on her way somewhere else, somewhere better, where she would live a richer life than the one she'd been living. Then, when she got here, she spent most of her time planning to leave and now she would give anything to go back. Not to change what had happened between her and

Tommy, just to choose differently in how she had handled it all.

Kenly pulled over to park, thinking of Tommy as a boy again—dancing with gusto as he mowed the lawn; laughing at the fire pit with Oscar buttoned into his jacket; sketching someone into his collage with all the intensity of a world-class artist; or sitting cross-legged in the tree house, going through everything in his old tin box.

Her throat suddenly ached for all that she'd lost and everything she'd so senselessly thrown away. When her mom died, and then her dad and her grandmother, she'd drawn comfort from knowing that she'd enriched their lives. But with Tommy it wasn't like that. He'd died thinking she'd made his life better, when, in reality, she'd taken away one of life's most incredible gifts by robbing him of being a father. For years she'd regretted it and now that he was gone, the guilt and shame were back again, only stronger than before.

People slipped in and out of the pharmacy while two farmers sat parked side by side on Main Street, windows down and deep in conversation. Horns blared in frustration and traffic backed up until they finally moved on. People greeted each other with sharp honks followed by the wave of an arm out a window, and a succession of school buses rolled down the hill on their way to the County Shop now that their load of kids had been safely delivered for the day. Mike's Clothing was still there and so was the Union Hotel, but Kenly saw that they were now building some kind of shopping complex along the riverfront.

Change was slow here, and yet today she drew comfort from everything that had managed to stay the same. Taking a deep breath, she started the car and drove to Uncle Walter's, where Lexie sat waiting outside on the front steps with a cigarette in one hand and a cup of coffee in the other. When Kenly pulled up, she waved her cigarette in the air, laughing. "Can you believe it? I'm thirty-two years old and he *still* won't let me smoke inside."

Walter and Becky had already left for the church; two of the most unlikely roommates now that Florence was in a home, Alzheimer's having claimed most of her faculties. "They said they'll see us at the church," Lexie said, sliding into the front seat.

After they parked, they slipped inside and sat next to someone they didn't know. Kenly saw Jean in the front row, head bowed and hands folded in her lap. Max was sitting next to her, one arm linked through hers in support. The coffin was closed, but sitting on top of it was a picture of Tommy from years ago and as Kenly looked at it she remembered something she'd always loved about him: how she could look straight into his face and know that she'd never be turned away.

After the service was over, she would go back to Jean's and sit on the edge of her sofa, nibbling politely at food she couldn't taste while making small talk with strangers. She owed it to Tommy even though it was the last thing she wanted to do. She knew she would see him everywhere, in each crevice of the house and at the fire pit in Max's backyard, and as she did, she would silently beg his forgiveness for the choice she'd made so long ago.

There were tales of old times in the minister's sermon—Tommy as a boy, physically disabled and socially crippled from a hideous disease no one should ever have to live with. He talked about a young man who had battled the odds, but still managed to contribute to the community, and when he finished, he handed things over to Max, who made his way slowly up to the front of the church.

"Thank you for coming," Max said, clearing his throat. "Tommy would've been pleased."

He paused to gather his thoughts, then carried on. "Sir William Osler was a Canadian physician born in 1849 and he once said, 'It's more important to know what kind of patient has the disease than what kind of disease the patient has.' With that in mind, I have something I'd like to share with you.

"For fifteen years, *The Athabasca Press* ran an advice column many of you have probably read. It was the 'WIT' column and it was geared to give advice to anyone who had the courage to write in and ask for it. It wasn't anything fancy, just the commonsense kind of advice we often can't see unless someone else puts it in front of us. And people did write in, lots of them—old and young. As some of you know, this little column took on a life of its own. A few years ago, the

Edmonton Journal picked it up, and not long after that it won a provincial award for its insightfulness. It was a column that did its fair share of good and for fifteen years I managed to keep the writer's name anonymous at his request.

"That person was Tommy Naylor, but it was important to him that no one ever know. He didn't want people having preconceived opinions about who they were writing to and he worried that his physical deformities might put him in the position where he would be either dismissed or not taken seriously. It bothered him that people might not write in if they thought he was out of touch with the 'real world.'

"Of course, nothing was further from the truth. As many of you know, Tommy was intuitive and wise beyond his years. He had a generous spirit and an unfailing level of common sense that surprised and delighted everyone who knew him. People were drawn to him for reasons they couldn't explain and when they took the time to get to know him, they almost always lost a piece of their heart." Max bowed his head, reached into his jacket, and pulled out a piece of paper with shaking hands. He unfolded it and laid it on the podium in front of him. "There's something I'd like to read now if you'll humor me:

> This is the true joy in life: Being used for a purpose recognized by yourself as a mighty one, being thoroughly worn out before you're thrown on the scrap heap and being a force of nature instead of a feverish clod of ailments and grievances, complaining that the world will not devote itself to making you happy.

He pulled off his glasses and composed himself. "That was written by George Bernard Shaw and it reminds me more of Tommy Naylor than anyone else I've ever known. If ever there was someone who had the right to complain, it was Tommy, but he never did. Instead he spent his time thinking about how he could live his life to the fullest and how he could help others."

Max slipped his glasses back on and squinted at the page in front of him. "A few days before he died, Tommy wrote his final column and he asked me if I'd read it here today. Of course, I told him I'd be honored." He glanced over at Jean with a gentle smile and then began reading what Tommy had written.

This is the last WIT column I'll ever write and it's a tough one. Today you'll find out who I am and tomorrow I won't be here. You see, I'm dying. Actually, I've been dying for a while now, but it's finally coming to an end. My name is Tommy Naylor and I have Proteus Syndrome. If you've ever met me, you'd remember. I'm hard to forget for reasons I won't get into, but otherwise we're more alike than you might imagine.

I grew up with a mother who would've done anything for me and usually did. She shared my life every step of the way, and did whatever she could to make it as rich as possible, usually sacrificing her own happiness along the way. Even now, I draw my strength from her.

I was also fortunate enough to know a man who could've easily been my father, a man who took over the job when the real one didn't step up to the plate. Thank you, Max, for listening when I needed to rant, for pushing me harder than I often thought was necessary, and for loving me like I really was your son. Who I am today has a lot to do with the influence you've had on my life.

Max's voice broke and he stopped reading to flatten the page on the table in front of him and regain his composure. Then he pushed his glasses up the bridge of his nose and carried on.

Like each of you, I had good days and bad. I had friends and family, said hello, good-bye, I love you, and I'm sorry more times than I can count. There were times when I wanted more, but settled for less, days when I wondered what I was here for and then fleeting moments when it all made perfect sense. I was fortunate enough to fall in love once and would do it again, given the chance. It happened years ago, but it changed me. It's hard to measure something like that, but I can tell you the world has never looked the same for me since.

As I write this, I can honestly say I have no regrets. I've made some sacrifices in my life, but then came to know an indescribable joy from having done so for all the right reasons. In the process, I also learned that what we give up in our lives can sometimes brings us more joy in the end than if we'd kept it for ourselves. For this column I've decided to leave a few thoughts behind, life lessons I picked up along the way and came to believe in:

Abraham Lincoln said, 'Whatever you are, be a good one' and I agree. Whether you're a mother, father, son, daughter, friend, or ditchdigger, I think you should fall asleep each night exhausted from giving it your best effort.

Make room in your heart to forgive. We're human, we all make mistakes, and everyone needs to be forgiven for something.

As your children grow, take time to give them the Tooth Fairy, Santa Claus, the Easter bunny, family traditions, and a home where they feel loved and secure. They need these in their lives and will thank you for them when they become men and women.

A few months ago, I read a story about a man who'd been misdiagnosed with terminal cancer. He filed suit against the physicians and hospital involved, then quietly dropped the case months later even though winning the case looked imminent. He later said being misdiagnosed was the best thing that had ever happened to him, because somewhere along the way he'd lost sight of what was important and this had made him see things more clearly. Maybe the next time you hit a rough patch in your life, imagine you've only got six months left to live, and then live like you're dying. Ask yourself how you'll handle what's being thrown at you and you might be surprised at your own answer.

Remember, the most important things in your life are much smaller than you think they are. They are those moments that leave you speechless, a love that won't let go, the hearty laughter of your friends, the traditions we repeat, and the memories we relive over and over, because we can. Do yourself a favor and don't take them for granted.

"Sympathy is something I don't have much time for. Many people have told me over the years that Proteus Syndrome is a devastating and debilitating disease, but it's all I've ever known so I consider myself lucky to have been here at all. The alternative was never that appealing. Tommy Naylor a.k.a. WIT.

Kenly's lower lip trembled and the tears came in a rush. Glancing around the room, she saw that his words had had the same effect on everyone. There wasn't one person in the church who wasn't crying. Max wiped his nose with a handkerchief, then folded the page and tucked it in his front pocket. Kenly was so lost in her thoughts, she didn't realize the service was over until Lexie touched her shoulder and motioned to the aisle. Standing, she shuffled outside into the gray day that awaited them. Walter and Becky called out to Lexie and she slipped away to join them; then Jean and Max were suddenly there in front of Kenly.

Jean gave her hand a squeeze. "He'd be so glad you came, dear."

Kenly nodded, unable to speak. Her voice wasn't working properly, but everything she couldn't say was there in her eyes and Max must have seen it because he smiled, opened his arms wide, and drew her in for a hug. As soon as he did, she crumpled against him.

After a few seconds, he whispered, "He left something for you."

Kenly stiffened and pulled back, searching his face for answers he didn't have. "He did?"

Jean turned to speak to another woman who was telling her how sorry she was. Max took Kenly by the elbow and steered her off to one side, giving her a thoughtful stare. "He said he left it at the old tree house, that you'd know where to find it."

The skin at the back of Kenly's neck prickled. She pulled her jacket tighter, dropping her eyes from Max and chewing at her bottom lip.

"Are you okay?" he asked.

She nodded. "Yes, I'm fine."

He patted her shoulder and left, threading his way through the crowd to find Jean. Kenly managed a dry swallow and crossed her arms as her mind slid back to Tommy's tin box on the roof of his tree house across town.

HER HANDS WERE SHAKING WHEN SHE PARKED THE CAR IN front of the Naylors' half an hour later. Avoiding the crowd inside, she slipped along the back of their garage and down the ravine toward the tree house. She pushed her way along the overgrown path through the bush, hardly noticing the mud on her shoes or the branches that snapped against her legs. Her heart was racing and she suddenly felt like she was sixteen again.

And then she saw it.

Kenly stopped and put a hand to her mouth, sliding to her knees on the muddy ground. Memories of Tommy were everywhere—sitting on the swing with Oscar leaning against him; sloshing in the creek like a madman; untying hundreds of wilted balloons after her birthday; leaving him the note that day. She craned her neck to look up at his tree house, knowing that nothing would ever come close to how this place made her feel.

When she finally climbed up the ladder and slid to her knees inside, her face was swollen and her cheeks smudged black from mascara that hadn't held. The picture window was covered in dust, the yellow paint from the frame peeled and scattered along the floor. Even the electric-blue shelves had faded; now they just looked like someone's attempt at trying to turn a kid's tree house into something more.

Her fingers traced the hinges of the trapdoor until she found one that was missing a screw and she smiled, relieved that he hadn't fixed it and reassured that something had stayed the same. Reaching up, she felt her way along the top shelf until she found the key where they'd always kept it. Rubbing it between her thumb and forefinger, she wondered how often he'd come here after she left, knowing that he had been virtually housebound in the last five or six years. There were still a few posters on one wall, but most of them had broken free now and lay on the floor at her feet, curled into loose tubes and discolored beyond recognition. One by one she slowly picked them up and dropped them into the crate in the corner, knowing that she was putting off why she'd come.

Taking a deep breath, she finally reached above her head, found the loose board, and pushed up, then slid an arm through the hole and moved her hand around outside until it brushed against something hard. Her heart was pounding when she pulled the tin box down into the tree house. A sprinkling of leaves and dirt trailed behind, landing in her hair and on her forearms, but she didn't notice. Her hands were shaking as she laid it in her lap. It didn't look like much anymore, just an old tin box, covered with rust spots. She took a few seconds to brush the dirt off, then fit the key into the lock, and slowly opened the lid.

Inside was a videotape wrapped in plastic. She lifted it out and unwrapped the plastic, then saw a note on it that read, *Kenly, I still spend the last few minutes of every day with you.* Tears sprang to her eyes and her heart pounded with relief. Tommy had found a way to say goodbye!

For days, she'd been trying to come to terms with the fact that he was gone. That she'd never hear his voice or see his smile or listen to him laugh again. *But now I can,* she thought. *Because he left me a message.* Half-laughing and half-crying, she put the tape back into the tin box and set it aside, then stood and brushed herself off before pulling the loose board into place above her head. She would take the tin box with her and keep his tape inside, and she'd pull it out and look at it whenever she missed him, whenever she needed a good dose of Tommy.

Deciding to stay for a few minutes, she sat with her back against one wall, watching a bird circle an empty feeder outside the window. She knew she should go, that Lexie would be looking for her and Max would be worried, but the thought of making obligatory chitchat with a roomful of people was exhausting. Right now she wanted to be with her memories of Tommy. For years she'd been dreading this—him dying and having to let him go, the truth complicating it even more than anyone could realize. She tilted her head back and tried to imagine Connor sitting with him at the fire pit after he'd lost his leg, each of them unaware that they shared something much deeper than their brokenness.

It was then that Tommy's collage caught her eye and she crawled over to wipe away the dust covering it. The dust fell to the floor in clumps from the weight of her hand, and faces from the past were slowly revealed. Tommy as a boy, Max with Sophie, Jean, Florence, Becky, even Walter. She worked her way along the length of the wall until she'd uncovered everyone, including Lexie and one of herself she hadn't seen before. She smiled, remembering when she'd asked Tommy why he hadn't finished it. "It just doesn't feel like it's ready to be finished yet," he'd said.

Frowning, she noticed someone else drawn into the corner next to her and as she brushed away the last of the dust, she uncovered the fingers of a child. *Had Tommy sketched a picture of Bella?* she wondered, moving closer. But no, it wasn't Bella. It was a picture of Connor when he was no more than four or five, laughing at the camera with his head thrown back and both hands wrapped around a hockey stick.

Kenly sucked in huge gulps of air as she pushed back and tried to steady herself against the wall. In the sketch, Connor wasn't wearing a T-shirt and on his narrow chest, as plain as day, was the birthmark that he shared with Tommy. She rocked back on her heels, eyes frozen and unblinking as she stared at the wall.

Then her hand flew to her mouth as nausea twisted her stomach, and she sat down, drawing her knees to her chest. *Oh, my God . . . All these years and he knew. All this time and he never said anything.* Trembling and choked with shame, she looked up at the sketch of Connor again, re-alizing with an overwhelming wave of sadness that it completed Tommy's collage in a way that no other sketch ever could.

It was then that she fumbled for the tin box and flipped it open to grab the videotape, understanding now that he'd left her more than a simple good-bye message—knowing in her heart that it was meant to be so much more than that. Tears streamed down her cheeks as she held the tape against her chest, feeling like the ground had finally given way beneath her after years of teetering on a cliff.

chapter 27

KENLY PUSHED THE LAUNDRY BASKET OVER AND SAT on the couch, squeezing her hands between her knees. It was almost five and Ross would be home any minute. The jelly glass filled with daisies now sat on the coffee table. She'd brought them in after she and Motley went for their run this morning, hoping to revive them after last night's rain. Even though she'd gotten home late last night Ross had been waiting for her on the deck. When she stepped outside, he had hugged her and asked about the funeral, then handed her the daisies, saying, "To cheer you up."

The phone rang and she ran to grab it. "Hello?"

"Hi, Mom," Connor said. "Sorry I missed you this morning. I had to leave early."

"I know. I saw your note," she said, stretching the phone cord out and peering through the living-room window. "How's the tournament?"

"Good, but I'm calling 'cause I need to know what you and Dad can do at this year's wind-up. I brought the form home last week, but you guys didn't fill it out."

"Can't we talk about it Sunday?" she asked.

"Coach needs to know *tonight*."

She rubbed her forehead. "Okay. Tell him I'll volunteer in the kitchen and your dad will donate something for the silent auction."

There was relief in his voice. "Thanks."

"No trouble."

"Hey, Mom?"

"Uh-huh."

"We totally blew 'em away today."

He told her about Luke's winning goal and how the other team couldn't buy a shot, his voice breaking a few times like it did now whenever he got excited. Kenly smiled at a recent memory of him after he'd been named assistant manager for the soccer team. He was in the hallway, posing in front of the mirror in his uniform when he thought he was alone, and she did then what she did now: tilted her head back, closed her eyes, and mouthed a silent prayer of thanks for this kid of hers.

"Look, I gotta go."

"Okay. See you Sunday," she said, hanging up. He had no idea what he did to her heart and she prayed that what she was about to do wouldn't ruin his life. Tommy's tin box was on the coffee table, covered with rust spots that wouldn't come off and dented on one side. She picked it up and the coward inside inched forward again.

Why now? After all these years?

"Because I'm tired of living the way my dad did."

You could lose them both, the voice warned.

"I know," she whispered, and as she held the tin box she thought back to something Max had read from Tommy's final "WIT" column: "Imagine you've only got six months left to live, and then live like you're dying. Ask yourself how you'll handle what's being thrown at you and you might be surprised at your own answer."

———

WHEN ROSS CAME THROUGH THE DOOR, SHE WAS UPSTAIRS,
vomiting in the bathroom sink.

"Kenly? You okay?" he called through the door.

Straightening, she turned on the cold water to wash her face. "Uh,
yeah, I'm fine." She pulled the door open and let him guide her downstairs to the couch in the living room.

He looked worried. "What's wrong?"

She took a breath, fighting to keep her voice steady. "Tommy left
me something."

"What?"

"A videotape."

Ross gave her a puzzled look.

She pushed the palm of one hand against her chest and tried to
avoid his eyes as the words rushed out in a voice just above a whisper.
"There's this thing . . . something I never . . . something I didn't tell
you years ago that I should have."

He frowned and reached for her, but she put up a hand and lapsed
into silence, thinking, *I can't believe I'm doing this to you.* The room
went still and a look of confusion flashed across his face. "Jesus, Kenly,
what's wrong? What is it?"

She grabbed the tin box, her voice sounding small and out of control. "You aren't . . . you aren't Connor's father."

He shook his head like he was clearing away some fog. "Wh-what?"

She tried to appeal for him to listen, with both hands in front of
her. "You see, when I got pregnant and told you, I honestly thought
you were his father. I didn't know you *weren't* until after the ultrasound came back."

He backed away from her like she'd just struck him and Kenly
started to talk faster. "And then when they told me I was six weeks farther along than I thought I was, I didn't know *how* to tell you."

Shock and disbelief collided on his face, and he shook his head from
side to side like he wasn't hearing her right. "Jesus! What are you saying?"

She tugged at the drawstring on her sweatshirt, twisting it around a finger until it throbbed. "It happened before we met," she whispered. "Just the one time."

He held up a hand, gesturing for her to stop, then said in a whisper, "I'm *not* Connor's father."

"You'd already told your family," she said miserably. His face was a sickly ashen color and she felt a quaver in her throat. "Ross, I'm so sorry. I didn't know how to tell you."

She held herself still, waiting for him to say something, anything. Instead he reached for the back of a chair to steady himself, his jawbone jumping as he studied her like he didn't know who she was. "You *didn't know how to tell me?*"

She clenched her teeth to hold in a sob, saw his shoulders sag, and wriggled forward on the couch to reach for his hand, but he moved it away. *Oh, Jesus, how are we going to survive this?* she thought.

He seemed about to say something, then changed his mind. She grabbed a couch cushion and rocked back and forth against it to quell a violent urge to vomit again. Ross looked at the tin box, then back at her, closing his eyes when he realized what she was telling him.

"Oh, God," he whispered. "Tommy is Connor's father?"

The disgust in his voice felt like a punch on an old bruise and she nodded, then flinched when he picked up a chair and threw it across the room, toppling it onto its side with a crash. "I don't even know you!" he yelled, the anger and hatred in his face making her shrink from him. He stood with both hands on his hips, breathing hard as he looked around the room. "So what? Our whole life is a lie. That's it, right? That's what you're trying to tell me?"

She shook her head no, but didn't say anything.

"And all because you didn't have the guts to tell me the truth fourteen years ago?" He turned to leave and smashed his fist against the wall, sending picture frames crashing to the floor, glass breaking all around them.

"You knew I wasn't his father, but you didn't tell me? Who the fuck do you think you are, Kenly? God?"

She stared at her hands, shaking.

"I can't even look at you right now."

He hesitated in the doorway with his back to her, taking in huge gulps of air. "When Connor gets home Sunday, tell him I'm out of town on business."

Where will you really be? she wanted to ask.

"And Kenly? For his sake, make it look good."

She buried her face in the cushion when the door slammed, and she let him go even though she wanted to run after him and beg him to stay. Shivering and useless, she slipped to the floor and crawled along on her knees, gathering up picture frames, holding them against her chest, and salvaging what she could. Snapshots of their life together with Connor. Moments captured from days and months and years when they had seemed invincible. All of them tossed on the floor now like a bad dream. She sat in the middle of the broken frames and rested her back against the wall until the silence closed in on her and she felt like she was going to choke on it.

THE NEXT MORNING SHE WOKE CURLED UP ON THE COUCH AND reached for the phone to call Ross before remembering she didn't have that right anymore. Overwhelmed with emotion, she showered and dressed in a daze, feeling as nauseous as she had the day before. Reminders of him were everywhere. His clothes in the walk-in closet, his shaving cream next to the sink, an article from the *Tribune* on his nightstand, his squash racquet behind the bedroom door. Her heart surged with hope when she realized he had to come back for his things, and it was that thought alone that carried her through the day.

By one that afternoon, she felt like someone had cut off her arms, and even Motley sensed something was wrong as he trailed behind her from room to room. She considered calling Lexie, but knew the minute she did she'd start to cry and all hell would break loose. Lexie would drop everything and be over in a flash, pressing hard for information that Kenly didn't want to share. At four o'clock, Tommy's tin box was still on the coffee table where she'd left it the day before. She made a pot of coffee and dusted around it, and it stayed there while she moved furniture, silently accusing her of being the coward she already knew she was.

Moving furniture had always been a habit of hers when she was worried and now Kenly couldn't stop herself. She tugged and pushed the couch across the living room until it was under the bay window, then pressed her hands into the cushions and found a pair of sunglasses Ross had lost weeks ago. She fingered them and stared at the tin box, managing a dry swallow. She still hadn't found the courage to watch the tape and hear what Tommy had to say. Couldn't bring herself to look into his eyes and see the anger and pain and disappointment she knew would probably be there.

The room was too quiet, so she got up and turned on the stereo, then sat and crossed her legs. Outside the sun was shining, the neighbor's new toy poodle wouldn't stop barking, and Motley was lying on his back on the deck, asleep, like he hadn't a care in the world.

I should watch it now, she thought.

Watch it later, the coward inside argued.

No, I should pour myself a stiff drink and watch it now.

You don't drink, the coward reminded her.

Kenly grabbed the tin box, flipped the lid open, and pulled the tape out. She turned it over, and swallowed as Tommy's voice came to her from years ago when she and Ross had made that trip to Athabasca with Connor. "Trust your instincts."

"My instincts suck," she whispered.

She slid the tape into the VCR and pressed play on the remote, then lowered herself onto the couch and forgot to turn the TV on. "Shit," she muttered, pushing herself back up. The phone rang and she jumped, dropping the remote as she scrambled over Ross's favorite chair to snatch it from its cradle.

"Hello?" she said, dragging a hand through her hair.

More than anything she wanted it to be Ross. Prayed his voice would be at the other end saying that he was on his way home, that he needed to talk, that he didn't think he could live with her anymore, anything.

Instead, it was a nervous young woman telemarketing for a carpet cleaning company that was offering a $49.95 special. Kenly closed her eyes and rubbed her forehead. Yes, she would like to get her rugs cleaned, and when they were done sucking all of the dirt out of her home, could they take away her family's heartache, pain, and grief along with them, too?

"W-what?" the girl asked.

"Nothing," Kenly whispered, hanging up and pressing her back against the doorjamb with tears in her eyes.

SLEEP DIDN'T COME ANY EASIER THE SECOND NIGHT AND WHEN Kenly rolled over on Sunday morning the house was too quiet and she knew she couldn't spend another day inside. Instead, she clipped the portable phone to her jeans and went out to cut the grass and trim their hedges, but still Ross didn't call. She told herself to give him room to breathe, understanding why he reacted the way he did, but still hopeful that he might come back and give her another chance to explain.

Tommy's tape stayed in the VCR all day and she'd almost worked up enough nerve to watch it when the phone rang again.

Her knees almost buckled as she answered it. "Hello?"

Connor's voice came at her as others howled away in the background. "Mom? Hey, we won! Our team took the championship!"

Kenly nodded woodenly, then remembered she should say something. "That's great, sweetheart. Wonderful news."

"Is Dad there?"

Glancing around the kitchen, she shook her head. "No. No, he's not, but I was just leaving to pick you up. The bus is early, though, isn't it?"

"Yeah," he said. "We're early."

When Kenly hung up and looked at her reflection in the mirror in the hallway, she cringed. Her hair was sticking out all over and she was wearing the same sweatshirt and jeans she'd thrown on that morning. On her way through the living room, she stopped and ejected Tommy's tape from the VCR, then put it back in the tin box, and took it upstairs with her. Having Connor stumble across it when he got home wasn't something she needed to deal with right now. Ten minutes later, she grabbed her car keys, turned on the answering machine, checked it twice to make sure she'd done it right, and then closed the kitchen door behind her.

Just in case he decides to call, she thought.

But, of course, he didn't.

chapter 28

THE LAST THING THAT WENT THROUGH KENLY'S mind before the accident was that she had to make sure she told Connor his dad was out of town on business for a few days. It happened just seconds later. It had started to sprinkle an hour ago, but now it was pouring, making her lean forward and squint to see the road. When a child's rain slicker flashed on the road in front of her, she reacted instinctively. Slamming on her brakes, she swerved, missed what was actually an orange garbage bag, and lost control of the car. It skidded sideways across the wet pavement and slammed into a row of garbage cans lined up against the side of a brick apartment building.

The force of the impact simultaneously smashed her head against the side window, sent her steel travel mug flying through the air, and inflated the driver's airbag, which pinned her to the seat. The mug smacked her hard above one eye and Kenly groaned involuntarily, lifting a hand to her face. Touching her fingers to her forehead, she felt something warm and slick, then realized that she was bleeding. *Things have to get better,* she told herself. *How can they possibly get any worse?*

———

THE HOSPITAL SMELLED LIKE DISINFECTANT. KENLY CROSSED her arms, felt her stomach lurch again, and glared at Lexie, who was tucking the blanket around her and fluffing her pillow for the second time. "Will you please stop doing that! I'm fine."

"Okay. You relax and I'll go get Connor. He's at his coach's house right now."

Kenly sat up straight, looking anxious. "Just promise me you won't get him all worked up about this, okay?"

"Could you give me just a *little* credit."

"Well, you do have a way of exaggerating."

"Okay. How about this then? I'll say, 'Don't panic; your mom's fine. Then I'll tell him the rest. Like how you haven't slept in days and shouldn't have been driving in the first place. Or how he shouldn't be upset when he sees you with two black eyes because, really, you're fine even though you've been acting like your life is over, but won't talk to me about it.'"

Kenly pointed to the door. "I don't care what you tell him; just don't exaggerate."

Lexie grabbed her coat, leaned down to give her a hug and left, then stuck her head back through the door. "Uh, were you going to call Ross or should I?"

Kenly's voice flashed with irritation. "I'll call him."

But she didn't, Lexie did, and as a result, Ross came striding into her room an hour later and stopped at the foot of her bed. Kenly blinked in surprise and self-consciously lifted a hand to her face, certain now that she was going to choke Lexie the next time she saw her.

"Are you okay?" he asked.

She gestured to her face. "A little beat-up, but otherwise fine."

His eyes studied her with concern and then he cringed when she lowered her hand. "Looks pretty bad."

She nodded, sensing things were different between them. There was no more than five feet separating them and yet it felt like they were miles apart. The rules had changed and this was new ground for both of them. She tried hard to hide her disappointment, then chided herself for expecting anything more.

"Lexie said they're keeping you overnight?"

"Just for observation," she said, thinking he looked great even though he was pale and had circles under his eyes.

There was a long pause and she was scared he might leave so she told him about the accident, babbling on about it without stopping. He didn't say anything, just leaned against the window and crossed his arms. She told him the damage to the car wasn't bad, then felt something pull at the back of her throat and stopped, fighting the urge to cry.

"At least you're okay," he said, but she sensed a remoteness that hurt.

Folding her hands in her lap, she turned away, knowing she must look ridiculous with two black eyes and a swollen nose. A troubled silence took over the room until she finally cleared her throat and broke it. "What are we going to do, Ross?"

"We'll talk about it later," he said, brushing the question aside. "Connor and Lexie are on their way up."

Kenly didn't care. She wanted to talk about it now, wanted to say, *Tell me how you feel. I can take it.* But he turned his back to her and looked out the window, putting even more distance between them.

Connor appeared at the door with Lexie behind him. Kenly did a double take, struck by the vulnerability on his face. No longer a confident thirteen-year-old, but once again her little boy, begging for reassurance he couldn't bring himself to ask for. She tried to smile. "Okay, bud, here's the deal. You can come in if you promise not to take pictures or make any bad jokes."

His smile was cautious as he limped across the room and leaned down to give her a hug, but it didn't take long before he was giving her a rough time about saving the life of a garbage bag and her new "look." "Very trendy, Mom," he said, rumpling her hair. "I guess I won't be having friends over for a while, huh?"

She crossed her arms and shrugged. "You've gotta do what you've gotta do."

Lexie walked over with a basket from the Body Shop and a guilty smile. "Makeup to cover the bruises, lotion to soothe the skin, and all of my other spoil-me-rotten favorites," she said, setting it on the table and backing away.

Kenly leaned forward to whisper, "It's gonna take more than a basketful of bribes for me to forgive you."

Lexie shrugged. "We've survived worse."

Ross had turned himself in profile to her across the room, his left elbow balanced on the arm of a chair and his face lit up as he listened to Connor animatedly describing something. Kenly's expression softened as she watched them. They were so alike. Always had been. Both of them hooked on hockey, soccer, and each other.

Connor tilted his chair back on two legs, leaning it against the windowsill. "How long you home for?" he asked.

Kenly froze, breathless as she, too, waited for his answer.

"I might have to go out of town next week but I'm not sure yet," he commented evenly.

"You gonna be around for the playoffs?"

"I wouldn't miss them."

Connor grinned. "Thanks, Dad."

Lexie packed up to leave, giving Kenly a quick hug. "I'd better get going. Benjy and Bella will think I'm never coming home."

"Thanks a lot for your help," Ross said, glancing at his watch as he shrugged his shoulders into his jacket. "We'd better go, too, Connor. We both need something to eat and a good night's sleep."

Kenly felt a tremor of guilt rush through her. *I'm sorry, Ross,* she thought. *That you have to go home and spend time with Connor pretending nothing is wrong when your whole world is falling apart.*

"I hope you'll be okay," Connor said, motioning to her face.

"I'll be fine. Go get some pizza and I'll see you tomorrow."

He leaned down and hugged her. "Love you, Mom."

"Love you, too."

Ross stood watching them. He seemed about to say something, then changed his mind and stepped forward to give her a mechanical peck on the cheek. "See you tomorrow."

AFTER THE DOOR SWUNG SHUT BEHIND THEM, THE ROOM went still and quiet and Kenly felt a sudden tightening in her throat. *Enough,* she thought, sniffling. *Crying won't fix anything.* But the tears came anyhow, even as she concentrated on tracing her kneecap with one finger through the blanket, a never-ending circle with no beginning and no end—a frantic way of trying *not* to think about Ross. But of course she thought about him anyhow, which led to thinking about how this whole mess was going to affect Connor, which made her throat tighten all over again.

Over the last week, every time she turned around it seemed like she was a blubbering emotional mess. *Damn it, why can't I be strong and stoic like Grandma?* "If you make a mess, then you clean it up," she used to say. "Ignoring it won't make it go away."

Grandma's logic was simple, and it had applied whether Kenly was six years old and covered in finger paint or caught red-handed at fourteen smoking for the first time with her football player boyfriend. *And that's exactly how Ross and I raised Connor,* she thought. *To accept responsibility for his actions and own up to his mistakes.*

So all of this makes you more like your dad than you realized? the coward inside asked.

"Worse," she murmured. "It makes me a hypocrite."

She turned and stared out the window, thinking about Ross again. It had been raining all day and she suddenly found herself squinting into the colorless gray outside, wishing that somewhere in the middle of it all she might see just a small slice of blue.

WHEN THE SCREECHING WHEELS OF A HOSPITAL CART WOKE her the next morning, Kenly didn't want to open her eyes. Her face felt even more swollen than the day before and her head felt like it was ready to lift off. *This is worse than a hangover,* she thought, rubbing her forehead with the heel of her hand. Ten minutes later, the doctor came in with her chart and she sat up, pushed her hair behind her ears, and waited for his prognosis.

He glanced at her and nodded. "Good morning."

"Morning," Kenly said.

His face reminded her of Abraham Lincoln, long, chiseled, and lined with the kind of wrinkles that were earned from years of deep thinking. Pinching the bridge of her nose as she closed her eyes, she fought back another wave of nausea.

"How are you feeling?"

She opened one eye. "Like a train hit me."

He tapped his pen on her chart and frowned. "And your back? How's your back?"

"Uh, it seems fine."

He set the chart down and asked her to lie flat, then lifted her gown and gently examined her stomach and pelvis. When she was admitted the day before, she'd mentioned to the nurse that she was bleeding slightly.

"Is there any internal bleeding?" she asked.

He shook his head. "Your X rays don't reveal any internal damage so I don't think so, but I've ordered an ultrasound before you leave this morning just to make sure."

Kenly sat up and straightened her gown. "Whatever it takes to get out of here."

He flipped the chart shut. "Just keep in mind, no lifting."

She gave him a puzzled look. *No lifting? What was he talking about?*

"I'm sure the baby will be fine, but based on what you've been through, let's not take any unnecessary chances."

Kenly squinted at him through narrowed eyes, saying nothing.

"Mrs. Lowen?"

I'm sure the baby will be fine . . .

The shock of his words registered and yet Kenly was sure she must have heard him wrong. She nodded slowly, thinking, *It must be the drugs they've got me on, or else that blow to my head loosened something that seriously needs tightening.*

"Are you all right?" the doctor asked.

She waved a hand in the air. "W-what did you just say?"

"That the baby should be fine, but you'll have to take it easy."

She covered her mouth with both hands and her voice was muffled and shaky with tears when she finally said, "Are you *sure?*"

"That the baby will be fine? Well, I can't guarantee anything, of course, but, yes, I think so. You'll have to take it easy for a few more weeks until you're past this first trimester, but then everything should be okay. Just make sure you see your obstetrician."

"My obstetrician?"

The doctor blinked at her, then slowly nodded, looking awkward. "You didn't know you were pregnant?"

She shook her head, unable to speak.

He dropped his gaze. "Is this . . . good news then?"

"Yes!" she said, marveling that he could remain this calm when she was having a baby; stunned that her Abraham Lincoln look-alike doctor wasn't floating around the room bursting with the kind of excitement she felt building inside. "Yes, of course it is."

"All right then," he said, obviously uncomfortable with this sudden display of emotion. "Make sure you get in to see an obstetrician."

When the door swung shut behind him, Kenly sat perfectly still, afraid to move, afraid to even breathe. *I'm sure the baby will be fine . . .* She closed her eyes and smiled, running a hand over her stomach, smoothing down the thin cotton gown. Then, on impulse, she grabbed the phone to call Ross with the news. *We're having a baby! Connor is going to have a brother or a sister. This is what we've wanted for years. Maybe this is exactly what we need. Maybe Ross will rethink what he wants to do.*

"Maybe he'll stay," she whispered.

Her hand froze in midair and she hesitated before slowly hanging up.

She suddenly realized that she couldn't tell him. At least not yet.

Not based on everything else she'd just thrown at him. If he decided to stay and work things out just because she was pregnant, how fair would that be to Connor?

With great care, she slipped out of bed and walked over to the window, wrapping her arms around herself. Outside, the sky was filled with gauzy clouds, the sun was shining, and cars were flying by with their windows open and tops down. And everywhere she looked she saw brilliant slices of blue sky.

FOUR HOURS LATER, SHE FUMBLED INTO HER CLOTHES JUST before Ross and Connor showed up, and when the nurse insisted she had to leave in a wheelchair, Kenly didn't need much convincing.

"Man, that looks like it hurts," Connor said through a mouthful of peanuts as he limped along next to them down the hallway.

Kenly nodded, found her sunglasses, and put them on. Right now all she wanted to do was go home and climb into bed. Both of them slid their arms around her waist on their way to the car and it was then that another wave of nausea came over her. Ross handed Connor the keys and Kenly let him swing her into his arms and carry her the rest of the way. She was having trouble looking at him and when he helped her into the front seat, she mumbled, "Thanks."

He didn't say anything, just nodded and shut the door.

Motley was waiting at the door when they got home and Connor had to hold him back by the collar so he wouldn't jump all over her.

"Looks like he missed you, Mom."

Kenly smiled, but didn't answer, just picked her way across the kitchen, carefully dodging the rawhide dog chews, bones, and toys that were strewn all over the room. She was focused on taking the shortest path possible upstairs, so she didn't bother saying anything about the mess. Normally, she would have given Connor a piece of her mind for dragging Motley's junk in from the garage, but right now she didn't care.

The phone rang and Connor started upstairs, shedding his jacket on the way. "I'll grab it."

Ross took her by the elbow and called out, "If it's for you, tell them you'll call back. You have a mess to clean up down here first."

Muttering something unintelligible, Connor reappeared and limped past them into the kitchen. Ross's and Kenly's eyes met and they half-smiled. She felt a surge of something hopeful, but then he turned away.

"You'll be okay?" he asked, after helping her upstairs to their bedroom.

She nodded, and when he turned to go she said, "Ross? I know you don't want to be here, so if you leave, I'll understand."

He hesitated with one hand on the doorknob, then closed the door behind him.

She chewed on her bottom lip, moving around the bedroom, touching their things, and fighting the urge to cry again. On the dresser was a picture of the three of them, taken last summer when they drove to Vermont. Next to it was one of Connor gumming Ross's knuckles when he was just a year old. She ran her fingers over both of them, then pulled an oversized T-shirt from her drawer and decided to take a hot bath.

She ached everywhere and her head throbbed, but she didn't want to take anything now that she knew she was pregnant. Turning on the water, she lifted her face to the mirror. Staring back was a woman she hardly recognized, one eye swollen half-shut and the other with a deep cut over it. Both were surrounded with angry bruises that continued down one side of her nose. She dropped her shoulders and felt tears sting her eyes as she ran her hands over her face.

I feel like crap and I look even worse.

She sat on the edge of the tub and turned off the water, breathing in the steam around her. When Connor knocked on the door, she jumped.

"Mom?"

"Yeah?"

"Are you okay?"

"Fine, honey. I'm fine," she said in the most reassuring voice she could muster.

"Okay. Well . . . yell if you need anything, all right?"

He sounded concerned, but she thought she heard fear in his voice, too, maybe for what he sensed, but couldn't bring himself to ask either of them.

She shed her clothes and slid down into the water, giving her bones what they'd been screaming for. She closed her eyes and stayed there for half an hour, tired, aching, and heartsick that she couldn't fix what she knew she had broken. The things she didn't want to lose were so intertwined that if you took just one of them away, the whole picture crumbled and fell apart. Like Friday nights when Connor told his friends he couldn't go out and Ross rented a movie on his way home from work. She would order pizza, and then the three of them would settle in together (each in their favorite spot) and watch the movie. It was a ritual they shared at the end of each week and Kenly loved it.

There were other things, of course. Silly things that made her heart swell. Like the way Motley always slept on the floor next to Connor's bed, even when he wasn't home, or those mornings when Connor wandered into their bedroom to chat, even now, at thirteen. How Ross sometimes forgot to shave on Sundays and that soft dusting of stubble that brushed against her face when he kissed her.

And now a baby, she thought, still not able to grasp that it was real. The water went cold and she climbed out, toweled off, and crawled into bed. As tempted as she was to go downstairs, she decided to leave them alone, and within minutes she was asleep.

ROSS WAS HAVING BREAKFAST WITH CONNOR THE NEXT morning when Kenly woke up. She could hear him tapping a spoon against his cereal bowl the way he always did when he was trying to make a tough decision about something. She flipped over and saw his pillow, scrunched up against the headboard, a trademark from when he couldn't sleep. The walk-in closet door was open and there was the faint scent of aftershave in the air. *He slept here,* she thought, and then realized it would've been awkward for him not to with Connor home.

Even so, she allowed herself to feel relieved that he had as she lay there and listened to their voices rise and fall from the kitchen below, Ross's throaty laugh, then Connor's fast-paced chatter.

This is the way it's always been, she thought. *Both of them saying they love each other without ever really saying it at all, with playful punches or by sharing hockey stats instead of using the words themselves.*

Flipping her legs onto the floor, she flexed her back before heading into the bathroom for a shower. When she stepped out five minutes later, the house was quiet and still. She pulled on her robe and made her way downstairs to an empty kitchen. On the table was a note in Ross's handwriting: *I took Connor to school on my way to the office.*

Okay, she thought. *So where do we go from here? I'll hold my breath and you'll either come back tonight or you won't?* She slid into a chair and closed her eyes, knowing whatever he decided was out of her control, but she wasn't kidding herself either. She realized that the sliver of hope she'd been hanging on to was just that, hope in the truest sense of the word, mixed in with a tiny piece of what they had built over the years. A piece she couldn't bring herself to let go of. At least, not yet. Not until someone told her she had to.

chapter 29

IT WAS AN EMOTIONAL MORNING FOR KENLY AND she spent most of it mentally preparing for the worst. Connor wouldn't be home until four that afternoon and if Ross came home at all, he wouldn't show up before five. After she made a cup of soup for lunch, her head was pounding and she ached all over again, so she crawled back into bed and fell asleep.

She woke an hour later, groggy, confused, and sure that she heard something downstairs. Shaking her head to clear away the fog, she tried to remember if she'd left the television on, then slipped down the hallway to the top of the stairs. She blinked in surprise, and her mouth popped open. Ross was home, sitting on the couch in the living room below with his back to her. The TV was turned on low, but he wasn't watching it. Instead, he was hunched over, reading a newspaper with the mail she'd picked up earlier lying next to him on the couch.

Kenly swallowed hard and pressed a hand to her mouth. This week's copy of *The Athabasca Press* had come that morning and she'd flipped it open to read Tommy's final "WIT" column now that it was printed, then had left it open on the coffee table. She was planning to cut it out and tuck it away with the videotape in Tommy's tin box, but she hadn't gotten to it yet.

By the sag of Ross's shoulders, she guessed he was reading it now, too. She knew she should leave, go back to the bedroom and let him read it alone, but she couldn't take her eyes off him. When he was done, he folded the paper in half, ran his hands through his hair, and hesitated for a few seconds before reaching for the tin box sitting on the coffee table.

Kenly sank to her knees on the rug. Her mouth was open, but she didn't say anything. Instead, she stiffened in panic when he opened it, took the tape out, and popped it into the VCR.

Oh, my God . . .

She'd finally found the courage to watch it herself that morning, but she was so emotional when it finished that she'd put it back in the tin box and left it there, never considering that Ross might come home in the middle of the day, never thinking he'd see it and decide to watch it himself. But after everything that had happened, didn't he have that right? Wouldn't she do exactly the same thing if their roles were reversed?

She had to stop herself from going to him and sitting next to him as the tape whirred to life. Pushing forward on her knees, she wrapped her hands around two spindles on the staircase railing and stared down at Tommy's face on the TV below—knowing exactly what was going to follow and unable to stop Ross from watching it.

Ross shook his head from side to side and stared at Tommy as though he was having trouble believing this was real. He leaned forward and pressed his hands against his thighs like he was ready to hit stop on the remote, stand up, and march out the door. *Please don't,* Kenly wanted to say, but as Tommy leaned into the screen below, Ross seemed hypnotized.

Tommy adjusted something on the camera and sat back, clearing his throat. He looked smaller than he had years ago, frail and breakable, the flesh around his mouth more puckered and the swell of his

forehead more pronounced, even though his eyes still promised the
same age-old wisdom they always had. He was wearing a denim shirt,
buttoned up high, but loose enough to hide the growth on the left side
of his chest. His hair was longer than it had ever been before, combed
over on his forehead in an effort to camouflage what he couldn't hide.

He nodded at the camera, suddenly looking nervous and uncomfortable. "Hello, Kenly. You know I've never been much of a letter
writer so I decided to leave you this tape instead. I wanted to say
good-bye while I still could and I also wanted to tell you a few things
I've never told you before.

"Like how it only took a few hours to miss you after you left years
ago, but a lot longer to get used to having you gone. After you went, I
set up your hammock in the tree house so I could stay there for a few
days and then I waited. I'm not sure what I was waiting for. I think I
was hoping you'd change your mind and come back or that you'd call
and say you missed me. When you're in love like that, I think you're allowed to be illogical."

He flushed a little and his face softened. "Anyhow, my world continued on the way it had before and things eventually got better, but as
the years went by, I did come to hate Tuesdays. You see . . . you left on
a Tuesday, Oscar died on a Tuesday, and the day I found out I had a
son, that was a Tuesday, too."

Tears streamed down Kenly's face and her lower lip quivered as
Tommy sat back, dropped his eyes, and seemed to consider what he
wanted to say next. "Then Lexie called to tell us about Connor's accident and did you know that happened on a Tuesday, too?"

Ross pressed his palms against his ears, shaking his head back and
forth like he couldn't believe what he was hearing.

"Of course, I didn't know he was my son when you and Ross came
for that visit with him years ago. I didn't find out until a few years later
when Lexie came home to see Walter and handed me a stack of pictures one afternoon. That's when things finally started to make sense,
like why you didn't come back as often as I thought you might have
when you left. I used to think it was because of that last night in the

tree house, that you regretted it, and were so ashamed of what we'd done that you couldn't face me."

He lowered his head like he was pushing away memories he'd put to rest long ago.

"It was the birthmark that told me everything you hadn't. When I saw it on his chest in one of the pictures, I stared at it so long and hard that I couldn't even blink, and then I started to shake and I asked Lexie if she could get me some water. I was having trouble breathing so she took off for the house and came back dragging Max. They hooked me up to my oxygen tank and I feigned some nausea that wasn't hard to fake before lying down for a few hours. I kept the picture, but you'd probably know that by now since you've been to the tree house. I slid it into my jacket and never told anyone, then put it in that old tin box of mine and spent months pulling it down and staring at him.

"Jesus, Kenly, he was so beautiful it took my breath away. After that, whenever I looked in the mirror and saw this staring back at me"—he gestured to his face—"I was so thankful that he'd dodged what I didn't genetically and came into this world healthy. Eventually, I sketched him into my collage at the tree house and when I did, I didn't need the picture anymore; I did every stroke from memory.

"I wanted to make sure, though, so eventually I called Evanston Hospital in Chicago and said I was doing research on rare blood types for Alzheimer's. I'm still surprised at how easy it was. I got passed around to a few departments until I finally got hold of some woman in medical records and explained that I was doing research with hospitals throughout the state and needed a response to two anonymous questions: How many children were born in their hospital in April and May of 1989 with an AB negative blood type. Then, how many were male and how many female. She called me back two days later and, of course, all I cared about were the results from April. There were only two babies born in Evanston Hospital in April of 1989 with that blood type. One of them died at birth. She was premature by nine weeks. The other was a male and that would've been Connor. Only one percent of the population has an AB negative blood type, Kenly, and I'm one of them.

"At first, I was mad and hurt and it took everything I had not to call you. It almost drove me crazy and then I decided to go see him myself. And I did, Kenly, years ago, after he started school. I begged Max to let me go to a conference in Chicago, then talked our photographer, Andrew, into coming with me. I'd been feeling good for about six months then, so traveling with Andrew wasn't that difficult and it gave me the chance to do what I wanted to without having Max or Mom feel like they should go with me. I'm sure they thought I was looking for a reason to see you, but we never talked about it.

"On the first day of the conference I told Andrew to go without me, that I wasn't feeling great. Then I took a taxi out to Barrington and sat outside Connor's school so I could watch him play. He was only six then, but so confident, so sure of himself, it stunned me. I watched the other kids follow him around and after a while I could even close my eyes and pick out his laughter from the others'. I thought I saw flashes of me here and there; in his mannerisms and maybe even a little in the way he carried himself. Ross picked him up that day and Connor was so excited, he almost threw himself at him. When I saw them together like that, I knew I could never replace Ross as his father."

Kenly's eyes were fixed on Ross now, tears rolling down her face as she watched him drop his head into his hands, back hunched and shaking as he, too, cried.

Tommy paused and then his face softened as he went on. "After Connor's accident, Lexie called here looking for Walter one morning and she mentioned that she was bringing Connor to Athabasca for a few days. Of course, she couldn't have known what a gift his visit would be for me and I'm sure you can imagine that I went out of my way to see him as much as I could when he was here, even though he stayed at Walter's. Lexie must have told him a few things because he handled meeting me without any visible reaction, even though he spent that first night at the fire pit staring at me whenever he thought I wouldn't notice."

Tommy crossed his left leg over his right and shifted in his chair, smiling. "He loved Max, but then who doesn't? And it was great watching Mom flutter around him with tins of her baking while he scarfed it down and poked fun about never getting stuff like that at home. It was so cold at the fire pit on his last night that I should have gone inside, but nothing could've torn me away, so I stayed. Then, when Lexie finally got up to leave, Connor asked her if he could stay a little longer."

His voice was choked with emotion as he carried on. "He stayed for another hour, Kenly, and it was sixty minutes I wouldn't trade for anything. Sixty minutes with my son as he laughed and talked to me about his life, and I sat there aching and cold, but feeling happier than I could ever remember feeling.

"Kenly, I think I know you better than you know yourself and you're probably a mess right now, but don't be. I forgave you a long time ago and you need to do the same thing. I know you didn't intentionally set out to hurt me. Knowing you, I would guess that, at first, you were trying hard not to hurt anyone so you just avoided dealing with it until things got much bigger and more difficult to manage. Of course, it doesn't make what you did right; it just tells me that you made a really stupid mistake—one I eventually persuaded myself was best left alone for Connor's sake."

Ross sniffed and leaned forward with his elbows on his knees, brushing away tears with the back of his hand.

"There's something I want you to know," Tommy said. "In the past seven or eight years, freedom to me meant having the rare opportunity to walk around the block on my own, without anyone else and without dragging an oxygen tank along for the ride. And on the few days that I did, my biggest thrill was meeting someone who didn't cringe when they looked at me. And even on those days, I'd come home and pull out that picture of Connor, thankful that he was living the normal life you'd given him."

He shifted forward on his chair, his breathing more forced now than when he'd begun and his face drawn and pale. "The rest of the tape is for Connor, but I'll let you decide if or when you ever want to show him." He reached for the camera, dropped his eyes, and smiled a slow smile. "And Kenly? I still love you, you know. Always have and always will."

The tape went black and static kicked in where his face had been. A few seconds passed and then he was suddenly there again, dressed in different clothes and looking rested, obviously taped on a different day.

"Hello, Connor. If you're watching this then you probably know by now that I'm your dad." Tommy paused and started to laugh. "Man, I've never been this nervous. That is, unless I don't count the first few times I met your mom, because I had a lot of trouble concentrating whenever she was around. Those eyes of hers used to almost knock me flat . . . anyhow, I wouldn't blame you if you were mad right now. I know most people would cringe if they had to admit one of their parents looked like I do, but even though we've already met, I thought making this videotape was better than leaving pictures behind for you. At least this way you can hear my voice and I can leave a more personal message.

"Maybe seeing me again will prompt you to remember some of the things we talked about around the fire pit when you were here. I want you to know what a gift those four days were for me. Having you here like that allowed me to get to know you a little, but it also gave me an opportunity to show you that I'm not really a monster—I just look like one."

He threw his hands in the air then, loosening up, leaning into the camera, mugging to the left, then craning his neck to the right to give a good shot. "Stunning isn't it? I mean, no matter how many angles you shoot this face from, I *still* look like hell."

He dropped his eyes and gathered his thoughts for a few seconds before continuing. "I was sixteen when I met your mom and we spent a lot of time together during a rough patch in her life. We shared a tree house and a tin box where we kept everything that was important to us, things that might have looked like junk to anyone else. When she graduated from high school and left to go to college in Chicago, neither of us knew how much longer I would even live and that made saying good-bye a lot harder. We spent our last night together up in the tree house and what happened between us was something I've never regretted because if it hadn't, you wouldn't be here."

He hesitated, then looked straight into the camera. "Connor, I'd be lying if I said I didn't envy your dad and I won't lie to you. I only met him once, but it wasn't hard to see how much he loved you and even easier to see how you felt about him. It took time, but I eventually managed to get past how I felt and came to the point where I was thankful that you had him in your life."

Tommy took a deep breath, then chuckled and leaned forward. "Okay, here are a few completely useless things about me you might want to know someday. My favorite movie is *Forrest Gump* and I believe Billy Joel is about the best singer who ever lived. My favorite color is blue, I think Christmas isn't Christmas without the intoxicating scent of a pine tree, and one of my favorite memories of all time is the day your mom knocked herself out with a hammer, right around the time I fell in love with her.

"Here's the lecture part. You know, the part where I give you a lofty piece of advice that you memorize and live by—the part where you get to roll your eyes, even though I actually mean every word. Connor, the greatest thing you'll ever own is your mind; keep it sharp, feed it daily, and remember that it's worth nothing if it's not connected to your heart. As you get older you'll learn that sometimes good people make bad mistakes, things they regret and things they wish they could change. Just keep in mind that we all make mistakes along the way. We all fall. So make sure you leave room in your heart to forgive. Your mom wanted the best life she could give you and no matter what you think of the decision she made, it ultimately took courage to love you the way that she did."

He nodded to the camera, dropped his eyes, and the screen went blank.

Kenly stood and leaned against the railing, shaking.

Ross turned around and saw her, and for a long time he didn't talk—he just looked up at her with tears in his eyes. She wanted to go to him, but stood on legs that felt like rubber and waited while he ejected the tape from the VCR and put it back in the tin box on the table. Then he sat down facing her, elbows on his thighs and head in his hands.

She thought she felt him slipping away so she broke the silence, fighting to keep her voice from shaking as she spoke. "N-not telling you was the biggest mistake of my life."

He looked up and nodded, the dark circles under his eyes hard to miss even from where she stood. She started to say something, but he held up a hand, and in a barely audible voice he said, "Most families would never survive this."

She felt a wave of fear pass through her and she swallowed hard, wanting to say that she didn't know how to be without him, that she wasn't ready to say good-bye, that he was an incredible father.

"And us?" she whispered.

There was another pause, longer this time and more suffocating than any other she had ever known. A wave of nausea came over her and she instinctively touched her stomach, holding her breath until Ross finally stood and lifted a hand, stretching it out into the air between them.